"Ashwood really knows how to tell a story."
—Kelley Armstrong, *New York Times* bestselling author

"A multilayered plot, a fascinating take on the paranormal
creatures living among us, plus a sexy vampire,
a sassy witch, and a mystery for them to solve . . .
Ravenous leaves me hungry for more!"
—Jessica Andersen, author of *Dawnkeepers*

A Moment of Magic

"Holly, are you sure you're all right? Can I take you home?"

She didn't answer. The night had left her a raw wound. It
was only now, when someone offered sympathy, that she fully
allowed the pain.

His hand stroked down the back of her head and neck, traveling strong and gentle over her shoulders. Her clenched muscles trembled, reluctant to release. She'd thought comfort was
what she wanted, but now Holly wanted to weep. His kindness
was making her hurt worse.

He kissed the top of her head.

At that moment, reaching for warmth was the only balm for
her misery. She tilted her face up and took his hard, full mouth
with hers. A quick, tentative pressure. She felt his shiver, the
sudden, erratic beating of his heart. The vibration resonated
through her flesh, heating things deep inside her body. His
mouth was surprisingly warm, almost human-hot. They paused
for a moment, their faces close together.

RAVENOUS

The Dark Forgotten

SHARON ASHWOOD

A SIGNET ECLIPSE BOOK

SIGNET ECLIPSE
Published by New American Library, a division of
Penguin Group (USA) Inc., 375 Hudson Street,
New York, New York 10014, USA
Penguin Group (Canada), 90 Eglinton Avenue East, Suite 700, Toronto,
Ontario M4P 2Y3, Canada (a division of Pearson Penguin Canada Inc.)
Penguin Books Ltd., 80 Strand, London WC2R 0RL, England
Penguin Ireland, 25 St. Stephen's Green, Dublin 2,
Ireland (a division of Penguin Books Ltd.)
Penguin Group (Australia), 250 Camberwell Road, Camberwell, Victoria 3124,
Australia (a division of Pearson Australia Group Pty. Ltd.)
Penguin Books India Pvt. Ltd., 11 Community Centre, Panchsheel Park,
New Delhi - 110 017, India
Penguin Group (NZ), 67 Apollo Drive, Rosedale, North Shore 0632,
New Zealand (a division of Pearson New Zealand Ltd.)
Penguin Books (South Africa) (Pty.) Ltd., 24 Sturdee Avenue,
Rosebank, Johannesburg 2196, South Africa

Penguin Books Ltd., Registered Offices:
80 Strand, London WC2R 0RL, England

First published by Signet Eclipse, an imprint of New American Library,
a division of Penguin Group (USA) Inc.

First Printing, February 2009
10 9 8 7 6 5 4 3 2 1

*For those who kept asking whatever happened
to the story about the vampire, the demon, and the mouse.
Here you go.*

Prologue

Being the evil Undead wasn't fun anymore. For one thing, it was increasingly hard to get a library card.

Even borrowing a book required identification. The same applied to finding an apartment, renting a movie, or leasing a car. Sure, in the old days there was the whole vampire mind-control thing, but now the world was one big bar code. Just try hypnotizing a computer.

In the end, it was easier to give in than to hide an entire subpopulation from the electronic age. The vampires—along with werewolves, gargoyles, and the ever-unpopular ghouls— emerged into the public eye at the turn of the century. While Y2K alarmists had predicted millennial upheaval, they sure hadn't seen this one coming.

In fact, they hadn't seen anything yet.

Chapter 1

"Why didn't you say you were calling about the old Flanders place?" Holly's words were hushed in the street's empty darkness.

Steve Raglan, her client, pulled off his cap and scratched the back of his head, the gesture sheepish yet defiant. "Would it have made a difference?"

"I'd have changed my quote."

"Thought so."

"Uh-huh. I'm not giving a final cost estimate until I see inside." She let a smidgen of rising anxiety color her voice. "Why exactly did you buy this place?"

He didn't answer.

From where they stood at the curb, the streetlights showed enough of the property to work up a good case of dread. Three stories of Victorian elegance had crumbled to Gothic cliché. The house should have fit into the commercial bustle at the edge of the Fairview campus, where century-old homes served as offices, cafés, or studios, but it sat vacant. During business hours, the area had a Bohemian charm. This place . . . not so much. Not in broad daylight, and especially not at night.

Gables and dormers sprouted at odd angles from the roof, black against the moon-hazed clouds. Pillars framed the shadowed maw of the entryway, and plywood covered an upstairs window like an eye patch. A real character place, all right.

"So," said Raglan, sounding a bit nervous himself, "can you kick its haunted butt?"

Holly choked down a wash of irritation. She was a witch, not a SWAT team. "I'll have to go in and take a look around." She loved most of her job, but she hated house work, and that didn't mean dusting. Some old places were smart, and neutralizing them was a dangerous, tricky business. They wanted to make you dinner in all the wrong ways. Lucky for Raglan, she needed tuition money. Badly. Tomorrow was the deadline to pay.

The chill September air was heavy with the tang of the ocean. Wind rustled the chestnut trees that lined the cramped street, sending an early fall of leaves scuttling along the gutters. The sound made Holly twitch, her nerves playing games. If she'd had more time, she would have come back to do the job when it was bright and sunny.

"Just pull its plug. I can't close the sale with it going all Amityville on the buyers," Raglan said. Fortyish, he wore a fretful expression, a plaid flannel shirt, and sweatpants with a rip in one thigh. Crossing his arms, he leaned like limp celery against his white SUV.

She had to ask again. "So why on earth *did* you buy this house?"

Raglan peeled himself off the door of the vehicle, taking a hesitant step toward the property. "It was on the market real cheap. One of those Phi Beta Feta Cheese frats was looking for a place. Thought I could fix it up for next to nothing and flip it to them. They don't care about looks, as long as there's plenty of room for a kegger."

He dug in his pocket and handed her a fold of bills. "Here's your deposit."

Prompt payment—heck, *advance* payment—was unprecedented, un-Raglanish behavior. She usually had to beg. Holly stared at the money, not sure what to say, but she took it. *He's worried. He's never worried.* Then again, this was his first rogue house. Before this he'd only ever called her to bust plain old ghosts.

He looked her up and down. "So, don't you have any, like, gear? Equipment?"

"Don't need much for this kind of job." She saw herself through his eyes—a short woman, mid-twenties, in jeans and sneakers, who drove a rusty old Hyundai. No magic wand, no ray guns, no *Men in Black* couture. Well, house busting—house taming . . . whatever—wasn't like in the movies. Tech toys weren't going to help.

She did have one prop. Holly pulled an elastic from the pocket of her Windbreaker and scraped her long brown hair into a ponytail. The elastic was her uniform. When the hair was back, she was working.

"Surely you knew the Flanders house has a history of incidents," she said. "The real estate companies have to disclose when a property has . . . um . . . issues." Holly eyeballed the place, eerily certain it was eyeballing her back. As far as she knew, Raglan was the first to hire someone to de-spook this house. No one else had stuck around long enough to pony up the cash.

Not a good sign.

Maybe next summer I should try dishwashing for tuition money.

Raglan blew out his cheeks in a sigh, fiddling with a thread on his cuff. "I thought the whole haunted thing wouldn't matter. The kids from the fraternity thought it was cool. Silly bastards. The sale was all but a done deal up until yesterday."

Holly walked up to the fence and put one hand on the carved gatepost. The flaking paint felt rough on her fingers, the wood beneath crumbly with age. The house had a bad attitude, but still the neglect made her sad. The old place had been built from magic by a clan of witches, just like Holly's ancestors had built her home.

Houses like these were part of the family, halfway to sentience. They lived on the free-floating vitality that surrounded any busy witch household— the life, the activity, and especially the magic. It was that energy that kept them conscious. Take it away, and the result was a slow decline until they were nothing more than wood and brick.

Reports of abandoned, half-sentient houses came up every few years. Centuries of persecution, combined with a low birth rate, had taken their toll on the witches. There were only a dozen clans left in all of North America, most with a scant handful of survivors. As their population dwindled, their houses perished, too. Most of these old, dying places were just restless, but a few turned bad, fighting to survive.

Like this one. Only its designation as a historical landmark had saved it from demolition.

Holly's pity mixed with a lick of fear. A gentle tugging was trying to urge her through the gate. Gusts of chittering whispers draped over her body like an invisible shawl. A caress, of sorts. The mad old place was inviting her in, embracing her.

Come in, little girl. So lively, so sweet.

A starved house would drain power from any living person, leaving them tired and achy. A magic user, especially a witch, was much more vulnerable. They had so much more to take.

A flush prickled Holly's skin as her heart sped up, filling her mouth with the coppery taste of fright. The strain of keeping still, resisting the whispers, made her teeth hurt.

Come in, little girl. The path to the front door was just flagstones buried in moss and weeds, but to Holly's sight it glowed. It was the one path, the only important route she would ever take. *Follow it and everything will be better. You'll be coming home at last. Holly, my dear, come to me.*

Holly pulled her hand off the post, putting a few paces between her feet and the property line. Sweat plastered her shirt to her back.

She felt the touch of a hand on her sleeve, but she didn't jump. That particular pressure, the curve of those fingers, was familiar, expected. Instead her heart skittered with a roller-coaster swoop of bad-for-you pleasure.

"I didn't hear you arrive," she said, turning and looking up.

Alessandro Caravelli was about six foot two, most of that long, lean legs. Curling wheat-blond hair fell past his shoul-

ders, framing a long, strong-boned face that made Holly
dream of fallen angels. The leather coat he wore had the
scuffed, squashed look of an old favorite.

"I think the house had you." His voice still held faint
traces of his native Italian, a slight warmth in the vowels. "I
called your name, but you didn't hear me. I was crushed."

"Your ego's hardier than that."

"You make me sound conceited."

"You're a vampire. You're in a league of your own."

"True, and so is my ego." Alessandro gave a close-lipped
smile that both invested meaning and denied it.

Holly pressed his hand where it rested on her sleeve,
keeping the gesture light. Her pulse skipped at the coolness
of his skin. Touching him was like petting a tiger or a wolf,
fascinating but fearsome. Full of deadly secrets.

Some thrills were bad news. Working with a vampire was
chancy enough; anything more would be insane. Besides,
she already had a boyfriend—one who didn't bite. Still, that
didn't stop the occasional soft-focus fantasy about Alessandro, involving satin sheets and whipped cream.

"So, this is the big, bad house on the menu," she said.
There goes the food imagery again.

Dark as it was, Alessandro still wore shades. Now he slid
them off, folding them with a flick of his wrist. The gesture
was smooth as the swipe of a cat's paw, revealing eyes the
same gold-shot brown as Baltic amber. He studied the Flanders property for a long moment, his face somber. Even after
a year's acquaintance, he wasn't easy to read.

"Is this going to be difficult?" he said at last.

"No cakewalk. Raglan actually paid me the deposit already. He's afraid."

The sound of a car door opening made them both turn
around. Raglan was standing by Alessandro's vehicle, peering in through the driver's side. The car was a sixties American dream machine, a red two-door T-Bird with custom
chrome and smoked windows. Holly felt Alessandro coil
like a startled cat. Where the car was concerned, he didn't
share well.

The round headlights blinked on and off in an impertinent

wink as Raglan fiddled with the dash. Alessandro always left the thing unlocked and half the time never removed the keys. To the vampire way of thinking, the car was his. No one would dare touch it. Until now he had been correct.

Raglan backed out of the car and slammed the door. "Sweet ride." Tension rolled off him as he skipped away from the car and gave a sheepish grin. He was acting out like a nervous little kid.

Alessandro made a sound just this side of a snarl.

Holly gripped his arm. "Not now. I need this job."

"Only for you," he said in a voice that whispered of cold, dead places. "But if he touches her again, he's dead."

Raglan cleared his throat. "Is this your partner? Pleased to meet you." He drew near but warily kept Holly between him and the vampire.

Alessandro gave an evil smile, but Holly poked him before he could speak.

Oblivious, Raglan cast a glance at the house, and his expression went from strained to about-to-implode. "So, what now? Can you get started?"

"I'd like to check one thing first. You mentioned that something happened yesterday, something that made you call me," she said. "Can you tell us what, exactly? We need the specifics."

"Yeah, well, like I was saying, yesterday things went wrong." Raglan's voice shook.

Foreboding fondled the nape of Holly's neck.

Raglan hesitated a beat before going on, shutting his eyes. "From what I hear, four frat boys went in late yesterday afternoon for an end-of-vacation party. Not supposed to, because the final papers aren't signed yet, but they forced a window. Wanted to start christening the place, I guess. They never came out."

"Maybe they're still in there, sleeping it off?" Holly said hopefully. She knew denial was pointless, but it was traditional. Someone had to do it.

Raglan shook his head. "There's more to it than that. The police have already been around asking questions."

"The police?" Holly said, startled.

"They went through the house this afternoon, but didn't find a thing. The cops were spooked as hell, but there was no sign of the boys. That's when I called you."

"I can't help you if this is an open police investigation! Not without their permission."

"Please, Ms. Carver." Raglan wiped his mouth with the back of his sleeve, as if he were fighting nausea. "I'll never sell this place. I don't even dare go in it!"

A spike of anger took her breath away. Her voice turned to granite. "You didn't tell me any of this on the phone."

Raglan went on. "Two more went in this morning, some of the professors who were supposed to be, uh, academic sponsors for the fraternity. They never came out either. The department heads called the dean to complain."

"Six people have disappeared inside that house? Since yesterday? *You couldn't have mentioned this on the phone?*" She felt Alessandro's hand on her back, steadying her.

Raglan sucked in air, as though he'd forgotten to breathe for a while. "Ms. Carver, you've got to get those people out of there."

"You're right," said Holly, her voice thick. *The house is hungry.*

"Two questions, Raglan," asked Alessandro, his voice quiet and chill. "How did the department heads know what happened? Who called the police?"

"Witnesses," Raglan replied. "Neighbors saw the kids climbing in through the window. And then there was the screaming."

Chapter 2

S creaming.
Never a good word in her line of work.

Holly sorted through possible plans of attack. She had to get this exactly right. *Six people are trapped inside.*

Raglan was in his SUV, smoking a cigarette and settling himself to wait. Alessandro lounged against the fence, giving her the space to finish thinking. There was no 1-800 Haunted House Help Line she could call. She was it.

Sometimes it sucked to be special.

"Did you ever meet any of the Flanders family?" Alessandro asked, breaking into her gloomy thoughts. Now he was standing close enough that the folds of his coat were softly brushing her fingers. The caress of the leather was sensual, distracting.

"I was in high school when the last Flanders passed away," Holly replied. "Grandma said the family made the House of Usher look like Tiny Tim and the Cratchits. No wonder the old homestead went rogue."

"Oh. Remind me why I agreed to help you with this?"

"I dunno. Because you might get to beat something up?" She gave a wry smile. "You like that part. Plus, I pay you a percentage for it."

"I want more than mere cash."

"What?" Holly gave him a sharp look.

His expression was amused. The fitful light showed all the planes and hollows of his face, the strong nose and the long lines that ran beside his mouth. Fiercely individual. All too handsome.

"Nothing either of us would regret," he said. "Just some assistance with an investigation of my own. I have need of your special talents."

Holly frowned, curious. Alessandro ran his own collections agency, putting his natural vampire aggression to good use, but sometimes he took on less usual jobs. "What do you want me to do?"

His gaze traveled to Raglan's truck, cautious. "What do you know about summoning spells?" He dropped his voice to a whisper. "More specifically, how to track the magic user who is casting them?"

"Why?"

"So that I can rap their knuckles. Someone trashed a client's warehouse. He suspects sabotage. I found the remains of a ritual circle."

Holly folded her arms. "Wait a minute. Property damage? From a summoning spell?"

"Depends on what you summon."

"Oh. Right." Holly considered. "I can do it, as long as no one's tried to cover up the evidence. Shielding spells are something else."

"Too hard to move?"

"I'm all about the small-M, bread-and-butter magic. I banish ghosts and find lost property. Magic with a big, bold capital M—necromancy and the like—is outside my usual sandbox."

He looked hopeful. "Then you'll take a look? As a favor?"

"Absolutely. As you know, magic is always fun until your head blows up," Holly said, only half joking. Her last trip into big-M territory had left her power handicapped, almost like a quarterback who had blown a knee.

"Thank you. I appreciate it."

"You're welcome. Anyway, I'm ready to get started."

Holly wiped her sweating palms on her jeans. As usual, she had preperformance butterflies.

Alessandro pushed the gate open with his foot. The old iron hinges gave a wheezing squeak. They both paused, waiting for a reaction. The house was still and silent.

Vampires didn't need an invitation to enter a derelict property. Alessandro stepped through the gate, his posture poised and alert. She watched him move, pale hair swinging with the glide of his body. She followed, searching with her psychic senses. If Alessandro was ready for corporeal enemies, she could take care of the rest.

Holly felt the presence of the house ahead, curled like an animal waiting to pounce—not exactly patient, but willing to let them make the approach. "This house isn't *almost* sentient," she said in a low voice. "It's fully aware."

Alessandro didn't look back. "I suppose that makes this a fair fight."

"Good to stay positive," Holly replied dryly. "Me, I like my evil entities stupid."

Half-buried paving stones zigzagged to the porch. Fronds of grass brushed her ankles, grit and moss making her soles slide with a wet, crunching noise that did nothing for her nerves. She could smell rotted fruit from beneath the apple and pear trees that filled the corners of the lot. No one had picked up the windfalls.

They were nearly to the porch before the house stirred, a whisper that sounded through the grass and leaves. *Why are you bringing the dead to my doorway? Send the vampire away. I cannot use him.*

"Precisely," Holly replied under her breath. Vampires were the perfect backup. Nothing ever wanted to eat them.

The ground rumbled, a quick, irritated shake.

Alessandro was instantly at her side. "What was that?"

"It knows we're coming." Holly craned her neck, studying the scrollwork framing the porch. There were protective sigils carved into the crumbling wood, but the magic had long since faded away.

Alessandro looked at her expectantly.

"It's safe," she said. "Safe-ish, anyway."

With a rustle of leather, Alessandro mounted the porch, a tall, broad shadow in the darkness. He pulled a slender black flashlight out of his pocket. He didn't really require it, but the extra light helped Holly. "Do you have the key?" he asked.

"We won't need it. It wants me to come in." She joined him on the porch, her footfalls human-loud.

Yes, come in, come in. She felt an impatient tugging, as if someone had her by the front of her jacket. Holly braced against it, but a sudden jerk made her stumble forward.

Alessandro caught her, strong hands pulling her against his side. Her shoulder collided with hard muscle, the cold metal of his coat buttons scraping against her cheek. He held her still for a moment, giving her time to find her feet.

"It thinks I'm literally a pushover." A hot thread of anger wound through her gut.

"It hasn't seen you push back."

Come in, come in, come in. The words came from all sides, from inside her head and out. The voice split into a thousand different pairs of lips, a whispered chaos sipping at Holly's strength of mind. Meaning splintered, all logic crumbling apart.

Holly gripped Alessandro's arm, using the solid feel of him as a focus. Taking a long breath, she clenched her jaw, summoning the anger simmering just below her thoughts. The shards of her will drew together, pushing the invading chorus away.

Back off. I have six people to find. Six souls. Six lost ones. No. They're mine.

Think again, Demolition Sale. You don't get to chow down on your playdates.

Then come in, little one, and stop me. I invite you. I dare you.

The door rattled, the sudden loud sound making Holly's skin crawl. Reluctantly she pulled away from Alessandro as he flicked on his flashlight, shining it on the lock. As she watched, the ornate handle turned, the paneled door sailing open and releasing a stale gust of wood rot and paint thinner. The entryway gaped, empty and dark.

Whispers swirled in the darkness, imitating the motes of dust dancing in the beam of the flashlight. Her stomach cold, Holly stepped over the threshold. The house's energy pressed in on her, a sinister brush of wings over her face and hands.

She thumbed on her own flashlight. The beam caught Alessandro's eyes, and they flared the radiant yellow of a cat's. *Predator.*

At the sight of those eyes, Holly jumped. She couldn't help herself. Instinct made her heart speed. He lifted his chin, nostrils flaring. Could he smell the quickening of her pulse? The sour tang of nerves?

Always interesting when your coworker counts you as a food group, Holly thought to herself. In the time they'd worked together he'd never given her cause to worry, but that faint whiff of doubt never went away either.

"Where do you want to start?" he asked, the question reassuringly mundane. He flipped a light switch on and off, confirming that the power was out. The house was oddly quiet. Whatever magic had cut the electricity also muffled any outside noise.

Holly shone her light to the left. The beam showed a room that would probably have been the parlor. Holly walked forward, playing the light from side to side. The ceiling was high, a threadwork of cracks showing in the vaulted plaster. It was the kind of space that could have comfortably held plush, overstuffed Victorian furniture. Now the room was empty except for a cluster of paint cans and dirty rags, the source of the pervasive chemical smell.

Holly slowed her steps, slotting pieces of her plan together. "By the feel of this place, it's not going down without a fight. Once we find the six victims and get them out of here, I'll try to neutralize the house by breaking the original sentience spells. If that doesn't work, I may be calling the fire department for a more dramatic solution."

Something moved in the consciousness of the house, almost as though it flinched.

Alessandro nodded. "Start with a room-by-room for the missing students?"

"Yeah, visual sweep first." She glanced around, reminding herself to watch for floating or falling objects. The house
could fight with anything, and probably would before the
night was over. With the beam of her flashlight arcing from
side to side, Holly moved through the parlor, Alessandro at
her elbow.

Someone had left a bagel wrapped in a Campus Joe's
napkin and a newspaper. Alessandro picked up the top section of the paper. "It's today's."

"Must have belonged to one of the profs who came in this
morning." Holly skimmed the headlines, irresistibly drawn
by the heavy black type.

Pit Bull Eats Zombie: Murderer or Scavenger?

*Can the Canucks Get Back-to-back Wins with the Oilers
on the Road?*

*New Rooftop Vagrancy Law Makes Gargoyles Homeless
in Richmond.*

She remembered her boyfriend, Ben, going on and on
about the vagrancy law and rent controls over breakfast. He
was sadly both a morning person and a news junkie. He was
already flying on back-to-school excitement, ready to resume teaching his economics students. By the first day of
classes he'd be bouncing off the walls.

Alessandro tilted the paper toward his flashlight, center-
ing the yellow beam on the hockey article before he dropped
the paper back to the floor. "What's in the next room?"

Ahead stood a wide opening that might once have held
pocket doors. Beyond was a long dining room, empty but for
rotting drapes dangling from a thick oak rod. Alessandro
took a step forward, but Holly caught his arm. "Wait. There's
something here."

He set his booted foot down with the care of one crossing
a minefield.

She glimpsed it from the corner of her eye, a glittering
black flow in the darkness. "This is new." If she turned to
look straight on, it disappeared. "It's right in front of us."

"What?" He was looking from side to side, his acute
night vision still missing what her witch's eyes could see.

"I've never seen anything like this. It looks like some-one's pouring down the night sky."

"Pardon?"

The flow broke through the ceiling, coursing down the wall to Holly's left like glittering black syrup. Points of light fell—or perhaps they rose—speeding and slowing, spiraling as the slow drape of thick liquid folded and pooled at the baseboard. From there the ooze snaked across the room inches from their feet, finally running between the cracks by the baseboard. It was impossible to tell which way the river of black progressed—from the basement to the ceiling or vice versa. It somehow looked like it did both at once.

What Holly could tell was that the sparkling blackness radiated a feeling of threat. A prickling sensation ran up her shins, as if an electrical charge surrounded the river, but that was only part of its disturbing presence. It was faintly warm, still fresh from whatever source disgorged it. She didn't know what would happen if they stepped in it, but one way or another, it wouldn't be good.

"Blood. Or something almost like it," said Alessandro, his voice hollow. "I can smell it."

Holly's stomach rolled over, his tone as disturbing as her thoughts. "It's not blood."

"Then what is it?"

"I've heard of this happening in rogue houses, but I've never seen it before. A really bad house doesn't just absorb ambient energy; it goes on the attack. The black ooze is its . . . I dunno . . . its digestive system, I guess. It's hunting. It's draining the six people here. What you smell is . . . um . . . it's their lives." Her voice trailed off to a whisper.

"Where's it coming from?"

"Up there." Holly pointed. "Or beneath us. I can't tell which way it's going. Wherever it begins, that's where we'll find our victims."

At her words, the river of darkness faded from sight. She had seen what the house wanted her to see. It was squeezing its victims dry.

If it was doing that to ordinary humans, what did it mean to do to a witch like her?

The energy level in the air dropped, dragging the temperature down to near freezing. The whispering voices in her head grew fainter, as if the house were drawing away to plan its next move.

This wasn't like any other house-gone-bad she had encountered. Usually they were evil but predictable. Hungry and dumb. This place, on the other hand, had done postgrad work in homicidal malevolence with a minor in seriously creepy, and she sensed it was just warming up.

Things were going to get interesting when it hit full stride.

Chapter 3

The broad oak steps to the upper floor were still covered by a runner tacked down with tiny brass rails, a touch of elegance left over from better times. Holly shone her flashlight up the stairway. There were some boxes and painting equipment left on the steps, but otherwise the coast looked clear.

The voices were all but silent, whispering among themselves. Holly ignored them, concentrating on stepping over a roll of builder's plastic. The beam of her flashlight caught something. A loaded backpack was lying on the small landing where the stairs turned at a right angle. Odd that the police hadn't taken it. Had they been so rattled by the house that they'd missed it?

"At least one of the students came this way," she said, mounting the stairs and kneeling to have a better look. The pack was a common enough style, navy with the Fairview U crest on the pocket. A stainless steel coffee mug was clipped to the strap. She had a similar pack herself, and so did Ben. He had bought them for the first day of classes, one of his sweet gestures. He was so proud of Holly for going back to school. The fact that she had been accepted to the School of Business, his own department, was the cherry on top.

"The pack looks like it was dropped in a hurry," Alessandro observed, scooping something off the landing. "Look. A cell phone fell out."

He flipped it open, but there was no signal. Not unusual in haunted houses. Something in the spooky vibes interfered with reception.

The top of the backpack was unzipped. Holly lifted the flap for a cursory glance. She didn't mean to spend time on a thorough examination. Who the owner was didn't matter, just the fact that they were lost in the terrible, whispering house. Then she saw what was inside, and recognized the sticker on the laptop: *Economists supply it on demand.*

Holly bowed her head, devastation sapping her strength. "Omigod, this is Ben's."

"Merda." Alessandro knelt beside her. "He must have been one of the professors Raglan said came looking for the students."

"He never said anything about sponsoring a frat. Damn it, where is he?" Holly rose and ran up the rest of the stairs. Had Ben said something about coming here this morning, and she'd just tuned out his breakfast monologue? Fear and guilt drove her heart, slamming it against her ribs.

"Holly!" Alessandro surged after, taking the steps two at a time.

The upstairs landing opened onto a large area flanked by two more hallways. A large drop cloth made a ghostly heap beside the banister. Holly looked from one side to the other, searching for some sign of the dark river she had seen in the dining room. Her mind felt suddenly sharp and clear, her thoughts ticking over with digital precision.

Alessandro stopped, lifting his head. He took a short, sharp breath and made a face. "There is death here."

"Where?" Holly said, her voice flat and cold. *Oh, Ben!*

Alessandro pointed straight ahead.

The house's rustling deepened into a throaty female laugh, fading away into a soft chuckle. *The house is a woman.* The fact that it had a gender made things worse. It was more personal. Specific. And the house had Ben, who brought Holly coffee and bagels. Ben, who liked Thai food and classic cartoons and gave great foot massages. Holly's stomach curdled.

Give him back, house. She stalked down the hall, clutching the flashlight like a truncheon. *Ten seconds, or you're plaster dust and kindling.*

The last of the chuckle slipped away, leaving behind empty silence. Holly strode along, her heels loud on the hardwood. She flung open one door, then the next, pausing only long enough to sweep the empty spaces with her flashlight. All she saw were small, plain rooms with slanted ceilings in the far corners. Bedrooms, perhaps.

She thumped the wall in frustration. The center of the house's consciousness was nearby—she could feel it, but the exact location eluded her. "Give it up, Scrap Heap," Holly called out. "Where'd you put your playmates?"

Alessandro glided past her. He opened the last door in the hallway, pushing it open and then recoiling, poised and ready to fight. Holly marched toward him, barely slowing until he raised one hand, palm out. "Wait. This is the source of the black river," he said. "I can see it now, too. There was a look-away spell. That explains why the police didn't see any of this."

Holly stopped next to him in the doorway. He was right. It was there in plain, horrific view, none of the corner-of-the-eye stuff anymore. She swallowed hard, doing her best not to gag. There was the faint trace of heat she had felt before, now joined by a pungent smell, like hamburger left too long out of the fridge.

The blackness flowed along the slope of the old oak floor toward the outer wall, where it ran down into the dining room below. Six bodies lay covered in the sparkling ooze. One victim had tried to make it out the window on the far wall, but now lay slumped beneath it. Holly looked frantically from one to the next, trying to figure out which one was Ben.

He has to be all right. I can't be too late.

The house sighed, low and intimate, as a tingling sensation swarmed up Holly's neck.

"I can't tell if they're alive," Alessandro said softly. "It all smells putrid. What were they doing up here?"

"They probably tried to save one another and got caught like flies in flypaper." Holly's voice was high and choked. She stepped forward carefully, making sure the toes of her shoes did not touch the black ooze. It would have worked, except the ooze edged toward her with a wet, sticky slurp.

"Can you use your power on it?" asked Alessandro.

Holly extended her fingers, giving off a blast of energy. She was gratified to see the blackness retreat from the thin stream of sparks. With hot, tingling bursts of power she chased it back a few feet, approaching the body closest to the door. She flicked off her flashlight, sparing the batteries, and worked by the faint light of her own power.

With a rustle of wind and fabric, Alessandro levitated to the other side of the room, his coat flaring around him. Holly ducked, startled, but was relieved to hear his boots hit dry floor. The ooze hadn't reached the far wall.

She felt the attention of the dark liquid shift to where Alessandro now stood. Black and slick as a seal's head, a pseudopod rose out of the muck, probing the air in the vampire's direction. Alessandro poked it with the end of his flashlight. The slime head lashed out, and Alessandro dodged with the air of a matador.

"Watch out!" Holly exclaimed. "What do you think you're doing?"

Alessandro danced away from the thing, his eyes flaring yellow. "It wants to fight. I'll keep it busy. You look for survivors."

He crouched, his smile giving a flash of fang. Normally that look made her shudder, but Holly was fresh out of fear. Let the vampire play with the slime monster. She had civilians to save.

The dead-meat smell clotted in Holly's throat, as choking as the worry that her strength would fizzle and leave her stranded in the sea of black. Worry became panic when she chased the ooze from the first body and saw what it had left behind.

The figure wore a team jacket, so she knew it wasn't Ben.

The man had been big-boned and dark-haired, but now those bones held up a drapery of flesh sucked dry of life and substance. The face had collapsed like melted wax, flowing and pooling against the oak floor.

Holly made a noise in a voice she didn't recognize as her own and backed away. She stood a moment, panting, trying to pull herself together before she began working toward a second collapsed form that sprawled a few yards away. Was that one Ben? Fear made her thoughts scatter. What if he wasn't here? What then?

A wrench sailed through the air, smacking her on the shoulder. Her arm went numb, the stream of power flowing out her fingers sputtering like water from a pinched hose.

"Ow!" Holly looked around.

"Over there," Alessandro said, pointing.

There was a toolbox in the corner, and now the contents were floating above it, missiles in the house's arsenal. She had seen this before—tawdry poltergeist nonsense, but it could hurt.

A hammer sailed through the air at Alessandro. In a blur of motion he snatched it midflight and used it to smack one of the pseudopods wriggling toward him. He was clearly enjoying himself in a Conan the Barbarian sort of way.

Holly batted an airborne caulking gun with the side of her flashlight and shuffled as fast as she could toward the next body, staying low to avoid the rain of tools. The second body wasn't Ben either. The young man looked pale and blue-lipped, the skin shriveled as if he had been in the bath too long, but he was alive. Holly felt a surge of joy.

"Hey. Hey!" She shook him by the shoulders, but he stayed limp, his mouth half-open.

The young man's breath came in short, shallow rasps. He was fighting for oxygen. She touched his throat and felt a faint pulse. The temperature of his flesh was far too low. He was alive now, but wouldn't survive for long without medical help.

The moisture the goo left behind dried almost instantly, leaving the man's russet hair caked and stiff. It looked like he'd been gelled by a herd of manic hairdressers.

"Don't worry; we'll get you out of here," Holly murmured in his ear. Grabbing his wrists, she dragged him toward the door, farther away from the slime, and then set off toward the figure slumped under the window. It looked like this one had tried to get out, but the window had jammed. The slime grew thicker over the body as Holly approached, ripples of sparkling black flowing toward it like an incoming tide. Apparently the house had figured out what Holly was doing and was rushing to stop her.

Something slammed into her back, hard, and fell with a clatter. The blow knocked Holly to her knees, her eyes filling with tears of pain. She twisted her head around to see the red tool box lying empty on the floor behind her. *Damn it!*

"Holly, are you all right?"

Glancing up at Alessandro, she understood why the house had thrown the box. It had run out of tools. Alessandro had caught them all, stuffing them in the capacious pockets of his coat.

"Yeah." *At least it wasn't a power drill.* She was going to be bruised in the morning.

Holly took a deep breath, forgetting everything but the body under the window. Now it was a shapeless mass, the outline of the limbs lost in ooze. She called her power one more time, digging deep she passed her hand over the blackness between her and the window, letting the energy flow. The goo retreated, allowing her to take two strides forward. She did it again, the heat of the releasing energy making the ends of her fingers burn.

With a rolling, rippling motion the thick mass peeled back from the slumped figure. His flesh was pallid as death but still untouched, still recognizable. It was Ben.

"Sweet Hecate!" Holly lunged forward, clasping his face in her hands. Her heart pounded so hard she could feel the beat in her lips. *Please be okay. I'll do anything; just be okay.* He was shivering and sticky, his brown hair matted against his skull. "Ben!"

His eyes drifted open. They were not the bright green of hers, but the green-brown of brushland in early spring. He couldn't quite seem to focus his gaze. Exhaustion made him look older than a man in his thirties. His jeans and denim jacket were soaked with foul moisture.

"Holly?" he asked, his voice just a rasp. Then he moved, clasping his arms to hold in what body heat he still had left.

She put her lips by his temple, smelling the soap-clean essence of him beneath the sullying muck of the house. She spoke softly, willing the words from her heart to his. "I'm here, Ben. I've come to take you home. I'd never leave you behind."

"Oh, God, thank you," Ben whispered.

"Holly!" Alessandro bellowed, leaping into the air toward her.

A moment of distraction had been all it took. The black river had crept around behind her, a gelatinous ripple drawing the ooze higher. As Holly turned to look, fingers of slime rose out of the mass, reaching for her leg. Freezing cold clamped her ankle. She cried out in shock, jerking away from the numbing clasp, but it held tight.

Alessandro landed behind her, lifting Ben with one hand and swinging him to a safe, dry corner of the floor. He grabbed Holly's arm, but she was caught in the slime. The house had what it wanted and was not about to let her go.

The chill invaded Holly in tendrils, in seeking fingers that delved into her flesh. It ran along her nerves, shooting up her leg and burrowing deep into her viscera.

The house had planned its strategy well. The struggle to save others from the black ooze had depleted her energy. She was a flickering bulb, a battery with only the dregs of life.

Terror blanked Holly's mind, a whiteout of fear. She had to . . . had to . . . *Omigod.* She was going to crack and shatter from sheer panic.

Okay. Okay. Think! The first wave of the cold was already inside her.

Shields! She invoked the image of brick walls. *Hard, solid, strong.* It was too little, too late. The house's energy wiggled through her defenses like the myriad arms of a squid, crumbling her shields to dust.

She was in trouble.

Weightlessness took over as her heart seemed to slow, her blood growing too sluggish to reach her head. She felt her knees buckle, but they felt like someone else's knees. Holly floated away, leaving her body to fall face-first into the killing blackness.

She couldn't breathe. Or move. She was a block of ice, facedown on the floor. Someone pulled at the back of her jacket, trying to haul her up. Dimly she thought she heard Alessandro cursing in Italian. It was hard to tell; she couldn't quite make out the words. He grabbed her arms and tried to pull her free. His fingers brushed the inside of her wrist, flesh to flesh. The touch was a spark on tinder. Her senses sprang open, flooding with his predator's hunger. Fierce. Primitive. The urge to survive.

Holly managed to open her eyes, but could not make a sound. Strong though it was, the spark flickered, wavered. The house was eating her up faster than she could fend it off.

"Damn you, Holly! Fight back!" Alessandro's voice was sharp-edged, nearly frantic.

Like I'm not fighting already?

"Holly! Can you hear me? Fight!"

Vampires. Always needing the big commotion. Such drama queens.

Holly's fear blackened and curled, rage eating her terror in a hot burn. She had to use whatever strength she had in a concentrated burst. Not much could survive a full-on blast of enraged witch rammed right down its throat.

She lunged for her strongest power but smashed against the block of her old injury. It was scar tissue, opaque and impenetrable. There was no way to get past. Not without ripping it—and herself—to pieces.

Fine. The big-M magic was playing hard to get. She could summon it, but it would hurt like hell. Not fun, but her other option was death by goo, and that would just be embarrassing.

How about a little rock 'n' roll, Demolition Sale? I rock and you roll your way to the salvage yard?

You have no power left, the house whispered. *You're drained.*

Cold fingered her vulnerable insides. Was that the house, or just plain fear?

Watch me. In the maelstrom of her mind she began the invocation to call up her big-M magic. The spell coalesced, built, bulged, a pressure cooker charged with psychic steam. Holly felt the power moving inside, a snake sliding against her bones.

Alessandro released her, the hard muscles of his arms slipping away. No doubt his vampire senses told him she had finally made her move.

The power came fast, fire rushing down a tunnel. It felt as if her guts were slowly turning themselves inside out, pain bright as new copper. Heat burrowed up her spine, flaming where the icy cold had frozen, turning her skin white-hot. Arcs of light spiraled along her arms like twin serpents. She was glowing, the delicate bone structure of her hand merely a shadow inside the pink shell of her flesh.

Holly let the energy rip the house's magic apart, burning her nerves in a searing flash of heat. Sudden light flared. A bang. The smell of summer storms.

The black ooze hissed and bubbled where it touched her. It jerked away, scuttling back even as it melted to nothing. Holly pressed her forehead against the hard floorboards, flattening her body to connect with the physical house as much as she could. She had to give the power somewhere to go. Energy rushed through her like a current, far, far too much for the house's magic to handle. She stole a glance, lifting her head just long enough to see that the black river had sizzled down to a fast-vanishing puddle.

The glow was in the walls now, a faint hum washing through the air. Holly could feel the place shudder as the impact of the power blast reached the foundations. It resonated with her body, the sensation oddly intimate. Holly searched with her senses. The voices in the house were dead silent. Still. Gone. Zapped.

Nevertheless, Holly let the energy flow longer, making sure. She'd seen horror flicks. This house wasn't getting any sequels.

A head rush made her glad to be lying down. Tears of relief leaked from her eyes, drying as they touched her hot cheeks. Raising one hand, she stared at the light under her skin, mesmerized. *Great Goddess, I'm still glowing!*

But it wasn't over yet. Drawing on her broken power came at a cost. Holly's flesh tightened, her heart stuttering like a drum tumbling down a hill. She pulled her knees under her, struggling to draw breath, but her lungs were like stone. *No air.*

Thoughts collapsed, puppets hacked away from their strings. *No air, no air!*

Sweat poured down her face. The glow faded. Now she was shaking. Her lungs grabbed a huge gasp, the instinct to live somehow cramming down the power, locking it away again.

And just when she thought the pain might be over, the aftermath hit—anguish so deep, it slashed each vertebra as it passed. Holly screamed a soundless word—she knew not what—and curled into a ball.

I won. I hurt.

Holly sobbed from sheer agony.

This was the reason she never took on more than snippy ghosts.

Chapter 4

Holly had lost track of time since the de-oozing of the hell house. Perhaps an hour had passed. Perhaps two. She couldn't tell.

She slumped on the curb in front of the house and watched as emergency vehicles jammed the street, adding a light show and a wailing chorus of sirens to the commotion. Police stood in a huddle on the lawn, taking possession of what was now considered a crime scene. A few car lengths to the right of where Holly sat, paramedics loaded the last of the unconscious victims into an ambulance.

She was alone. Ben was with the paramedics. The police were interviewing Raglan, who had called 911. She wasn't sure where Alessandro had gone. She needed to talk to all three men—for one thing, she wanted the rest of her fee from Raglan—but everywhere Holly went she was underfoot. It was better just to sit on the curb like an unwanted couch and wait for a break in the action.

Painkillers sang happy songs in her blood, blurring the edges of adrenaline aftermath. The ambulance guys had looked her over, but what could they do for a metaphysical injury? Medical science hadn't caught up to the needs of supernatural patients. The paramedics' solution had been two little green gelcaps—the same kind she used for migraines—

and a bottle of water. At least the bistro down the street had brought hot coffee. When this was all over, she'd come back and put a blessing on the night staff.

Holly tried to run her hand through her hair, but it was stiff with dried slime and sweat. She smelled like ooze. If she were a sock, she'd throw herself out.

"Ms. Carver?"

She started at the touch of a hand on her shoulder. "What? Sorry. Yes?"

"Detective Macmillan." The man thrust a clipboard toward her. "I need you to sign this."

"Paperwork?" she said in a tone that made her sound as if she were dying. The police had already asked her ten thousand questions. Something about being discovered in a house full of dead bodies made them curious.

"Yes, ma'am." He gave a quick, rueful smile. Detective Macmillan was handsome, with dark, wavy hair and a slight scruff of beard probably due more to long hours than a bad-boy fashion statement. "The law moves in triplicate ways."

She gingerly took the clipboard. Staring at the form was useless. Between the pills and fatigue, the words were doing the can-can across the page.

Then the fire brigade arrived, big motors huffing. They maneuvered slowly, the long trucks navigating the narrow, overparked street with the skill of long practice. Bystanders thronging the road were forced to scamper out of the way.

"Where did all these people come from?" Holly wondered aloud.

"Murder brings its own audience. Supernatural murder is a chart topper." Macmillan shrugged. "If you sign the form, you get another cup of coffee. We practice only the finest in behavior modification theory."

He gave a microgrin that came and went in seconds, somehow all the more charming for its brevity. She couldn't help noticing the man knew how to dress, though his suit had the rumpled look of a long, hard day.

Holly sighed at the clipboard. "What am I signing here?"

"A burn order on the house. I understand you were the

certified investigator on the scene. Historical site or not, after this many deaths, we can't let it stand."

Holly nodded. The Corporeal Entity Law stated that only beings adhering to a recognized definition of physical life were entitled to a trial. Sentient houses, along with ghosts, wraiths, and some demon forms, were deemed nonadherent and could be exterminated without a court order. All it took was her signature and the big, bad house would go up in smoke.

After that evening's fun and games, Holly was happy to sign. She scribbled something approximating her name and handed the clipboard back to Macmillan, awarding him a smile of her own.

With a flicker of relief, Holly realized that her job at the Flanders house was officially over. *Burn, baby, burn.*

Alessandro stalked through the house alone. The paramedics had come and gone, leaving only the dead and the Undead. It was a welcome respite from the growing chaos outside.

He had demanded that the ambulance attendants treat Holly first. When he had lifted her from the floor of the bedroom she had fainted. In a moment of panic, Alessandro's heart had begun to beat for the first time in a century.

It was the equivalent of a vampire heart attack. Only the strongest emotions could revive an Undead heart. In this case fear for the woman he held in his arms.

Something was wrong with Holly. After heavy exertion—whether it was running a marathon or wielding magic—exhaustion was normal. The yelps of pain were not. There was a flaw in Holly's powers, an important weakness.

She had never told Alessandro about the condition. Like many others, she was friendly toward him, but that did not make him her friend. Not really.

You would be a fool to expect anything else.

Still, something clenched under his breastbone, a dull, forlorn ache. Alessandro was not prone to brooding over his lost humanity—after six centuries he either staked himself or got over it—but Undeath had its limitations.

It branded him a killer. That led to social disappointments.

Fortunately the paramedics said Holly would be fine. Fortunately the house—one of the worst he had seen—was a distraction from his uncomfortable thoughts.

Instinct drove him through the rooms that he had not yet explored, making him open every closet and cupboard to make sure the house was dead. He would not be satisfied until he walked its boundaries inside and out. Such was the nature of his kind.

But Holly had done her work well. Now the main floor of the house felt empty, like the carapace of a beetle long dead. Even the dust seemed drier, limply coating the walls with streamers of filmy gray. He searched the crawl space and the main floor until all that remained was one last corner of the upstairs.

There was not much to see. He walked down the hall, opening doors. The rooms were empty, mirrors of the ones he had already visited. He thought he was finished.

Until he noticed that one of the paneled bedroom doors hovered behind a haze. *Another look-away spell.* It was a simple piece of magic meant to keep things hidden from the curious, like the police, or a real estate agent, or even Raglan and his workmen. Alessandro had found traces of similar enchantments here and there, including the room where they had fought the ooze. The charm on this door was the only one still active.

Such spells didn't work on vampires, at least not ones as old as Alessandro. Or, if they did, not for long.

The presence of the spell meant that there was more going on than just a house gone rogue. He turned the handle, shattering the magic.

More indeed.

A body sprawled on the bare wooden floor. Alessandro stood frozen, his hand on the doorknob. The figure had collapsed on her stomach, her head turned toward him, eyes open, but unequivocally dead.

Slowly he stepped inside the room. Death did not shock him, but he was surprised. Usually the smell of a corpse was obvious to a vampire. Either the spell had hidden the stench, or it had blended in among all the other death in the house.

He switched on the overhead light. He didn't need it, but felt marginally comforted.

Sprawled just inches from his feet, the still, silent body told its story. She had been a student, judging by the Fairview U hoodie. Blond. Slim. Bare feet in bright white canvas shoes that were laced in a soft pink. She had probably been pretty, but a morbid hue stole her beauty. Alessandro guessed she had been about nineteen.

The police need to know about this. But the visuals held him; he was too affronted to move.

Her feet were lashed with yellow nylon rope, a wad of cloth stuffed in her mouth. Shallow slashes scored her flesh, signs of obvious cruelty. The last—so unnecessary—stiffened Alessandro's shoulders. There was a difference between a hunter and a brute.

Bending closer, he gave an experimental sniff. Cold. Dead a day, at least. No drugs that he could detect, just the sour residue of terror. Alessandro tasted the air again, letting his senses do their work. No more than a lick of blood remained in her veins, but there was only a spatter on the floor and her clothes. She had been sucked dry, her throat chewed open.

A news report, half heard, half forgotten, tugged at Alessandro's memory. Murders on campus. He had assumed it was a human affair. There had been no mention of neck wounds, but perhaps the police had held that information back.

No human did this. Behind the smell of death and fear was the stink of something *other.* A magic user.

But was it a vampire? No one he knew would do this, and Alessandro was the vampire queen's representative in Fairview. A newcomer to town would have paid his respects as soon as he or she arrived. No such overture had been made.

Besides, the injury was wrong. A vampire bite was sharp but neat, the corner fangs large on top, less pronounced on the bottom. The wounds on the girl were obscured, more suggestive of gnawing than a clean bite.

Werewolf? No. A beast wouldn't stop with the neck. They went for the viscera.

A ghoul? There again, it would make more mess. Lots more. It would eat the flesh.

A demon? There were a lot of subspecies, each with its own dining habits, each more appalling than the last.

Alessandro shuddered, his flesh crawling under the wool and leather layers of his clothes. There was no power on earth, above or below, that could induce him to tolerate a demon in his town. It could lay waste to the campus. To Fairview. He'd seen them in action before. The stuff of nightmares, even for a vampire.

Hunt it. Kill it.

Alessandro could feel his heart beating again, a sure sign of stress. The smell in the room was cloying. He cleared his throat.

Stop and think with something besides your fangs.

Time was running out. He could hear the activity outside. Soon the police would be in the house, fouling everything with noise and human odors. He crouched, looking closely for any more clues. There it was again, that scent. He rocked back onto his heels, his head starting to ache with the effort to place that smell. It was vampire with a chaser of . . . what?

Who is it? Who dares to hunt in my domain?

The girl on the floor looked so vulnerable, so lonely under the dirty glare of light. She had not died well. From the position of the body, the girl seemed to have been thrown down. One hand reached up, as if she had tried to protect her face from the fall.

Vampires weren't gentle, but this level of violence was atypical. She might have even died before she was drained. Humans broke so easily.

Alessandro tilted his head, catching sight of something glinting in the girl's upflung hand. He dared not touch her. Vampires left fingerprints just like humans. He pulled out a pen and poked at her fingers, loosening the object in her grasp. Something hit the wooden floor with a clink. Alessandro pinned the object with the tip of the pen, scooting it along the floorboard until he could see what it was.

Cold dread congealed in his gut. The round, flat metal object was familiar. He had one just like it, a gift from his sire centuries ago.

The size of a quarter, the copper disk was old, rubbed thin, the edges slightly ragged. The design was worn away, but Alessandro could still make out the figure of Orpheus, the hero from Greek myth. In one hand he held a lyre; his other rested on the head of a lion.

In legend Orpheus sang so sweetly the wild beasts wept. His song was so powerful that he could walk through the Underworld in safety, for he charmed even the god of the dead.

Vampires left the Orpheus token as a blessing, a gift to ensure that the soul of their prey would travel in peace and safety. It was a ritual of respect that Alessandro hadn't seen practiced for hundreds of years. Tokens were rare. The one in the girl's hand dated from the Middle Ages.

I am searching for someone very old.

Apprehension prickled Alessandro's skin. Apprehension, and a primal need to answer the challenge. He picked up the token and slipped it into his pocket along with his pen.

Alessandro got up and looked out the small, dirty window. The night outside rustled and glittered, a breeze sending the dry leaves and branches flickering across the campus lights. Close up was the university, and a little farther away the community college that shared its grounds. He could see the clock tower and neon signs of the Student Union Building. Through it all streamed the endless glowing pinpoints that signified thousands of human lives.

Why would an old one come to my town and challenge me?

A new noise scattered his thoughts. Heavy men with heavy boots clumped up the stairs. The police had arrived. The look-away spell had been broken.

I'm a vampire standing next to an exsanguinated body. This cannot end well.

Alessandro switched off the room light and closed the door. That would buy him a little time, nothing more. He returned to the window and pulled on the old double-hung frame. It was painted shut. By the sound of the footfalls, Alessandro could tell the first of the policemen had reached the second floor.

A wave of frustration made him reckless. He shoved up the sash with a shuddering crash of splintering wood and paint. A gust of damp, cold air swirled into the room, sweet and clean after the stink of old death.

Predictably, the noise was followed by a yell from one of the cops. The window's opening was narrow, but Alessandro dived through, fragments of broken frame clawing at his clothes and hair.

The night air caught his momentum, floating him through the darkness. Speed made him a fleeting shadow against the bright sea of campus lights, a momentary tingle down the necks of the bystanders. The flight was short, but the thrill drove out the anxiety feasting on his soul.

Landing in the murky blackness of a neighboring lane, Alessandro crouched, listening. Nothing. He was safe. A slow smile tugged at the corners of his lips.

There was a hunt awaiting. A war for territory. A worthy, challenging, dangerous opponent, someone clearly spoiling for a fight.

I'll find you, Old One. The world of cell phones, credit checks, and taxation faded into insignificance. Alessandro was a creature of the rustling night, ready to protect what was his.

Ready for the chase.

He really hoped those emergency vehicles hadn't blocked in his car.

Chapter 5

Macmillan left Holly where she sat on the curb, taking away the signed burn order on the house. Holly shifted, her rump numb from the cold concrete. The happy drugs still had her in a haze, sapping the urge to do anything but sit and drool.

On a good day, if someone had asked her what she wanted in life, she would have said business success, a college degree, and a cute boyfriend with husband potential. At the moment she would have settled for a cushion and a warmer coat.

A few minutes later another flurry of police cruisers arrived, lights flashing. Had something new happened?

"Ms. Carver." One of the paramedics, a thin, balding man, was walking toward her. "Mr. Elliot is asking for you."

"Dr. Elliot," she said automatically. "Ben's a professor." His specialty was in fifth-world macroeconomics, which sounded to Holly like a soy-based breakfast cereal or a grunge band with intellectual pretensions. Nevertheless, Ben was apparently brilliant.

The paramedic looked too harried to be impressed. "Can you follow me, please?"

Holly got up slowly, her legs stiff. The temperature was dropping, an icy, damp wind picking up. There would be rain before morning.

The man turned. "Mr.—Dr.—Elliot is refusing to go to the hospital. We were hoping you could talk him into complying with medical protocol. We'd really like to keep him overnight for observation."

"I'll try. He's kind of stubborn."

Ben was sitting on a gurney, his feet dangling over the side. It was pulled onto the sidewalk beside the ambulance, out of the way of the other attendants, who were still hurrying back and forth. He had one of the thin, gray first-aid blankets over his shoulders and a water bottle clutched in one hand. A tube ran from his arm to an IV bag on a stand. His long face was pale, but his expression was his own. The deer-in-the-slime-monster-headlights look was fading.

Holly stopped in front of him, projecting a hearty energy she didn't feel. "Are you giving the nice ambulance boys a hard time?"

Ben looked up at her, his eyes crinkling with a feeble shadow of a smile. "You look like crap. And you smell." He sniffed his sleeve. "So do I."

A flicker of annoyance let Holly know she was alive after all. "Save a guy from a sticky death, and still he criticizes. What happened to the sensitive New Age Ben? His DVD collection sucked, but he had manners."

"Sorry. The blob monster ate him." Ben passed a hand over his face. "Really. Sorry. That was a bad thing to say."

Holly put her hands on her hips. "Yeah, well, maybe I'll cut you some slack, given the near-death and all. Shouldn't you be going to the hospital?"

"I'm not hurt. Just dehydrated. I don't think the whatever-it-was quite got around to dining on me, thank God." He took her hand. "It sounds woefully inadequate to just say thank you for saving my life—but . . . thank you, Holly. You saved my life tonight. Another hour and the ending might have been different."

Then he shuddered, sinking into the folds of his blanket. The gesture reminded Holly of a turtle. "I just want to go home, turn on loud music, and sleep with the lights on."

Her legs starting to tremble with fatigue, Holly sat down next to Ben. The thin padding on the gurney was barely enough to conceal the hard metal frame. She clutched Ben's hand. It was cold, the skin paper-dry.

"Wouldn't you feel better someplace where there are other people?" she asked.

His fingers spasmed, clutching hers painfully hard. "No. On the surface, y'know, everything seems okay. But underneath . . . it doesn't help me to have to be reasonable. I'm just treading water. I need privacy."

"Treading water has its function. It keeps us afloat until we're ready to swim again. You could compromise. Come home with me, where I can keep an eye on you."

Eyes growing round, he pulled his hand away with a jerk. "Are you kidding? Your house . . . your house is like that one!"

"It is not!" Holly rounded on him, then caught herself, remembering what Ben had just been through. "My house is nice. Friendly. It doesn't talk either."

He buried his face in his hands. "It's creepy."

"It's my family's." She softened her voice still further. "Nothing like the Flanders place."

He looked up, his expression shuttered. "My condo is mine, and it's normal, plain old drywall and concrete. I'm really into normal, nonmagical stuff right now, Holly. If it isn't human or human-made, I don't want it near me."

Even without the words, his tone was like a blow against her breastbone. She flinched.

"I'm sorry," he said. "That was harsh."

"It was honest." She managed a smile, a touch to his shoulder. "You've had enough of the wild side for one night."

"You could say that."

She closed her eyes a moment, but the drug-blurred world shifted sideways. "I wish you would go to the hospital. Just for tonight, to make sure everything's okay."

"What's the big deal? Without medical observation, I'll turn into a slime monster?"

"Don't worry; it doesn't work that way," Holly said quickly, trying to reassure him.

"Oh, God!" Ben raised his hands, shaking his head. "You would know that, wouldn't you?"

Yeah, because I'm one of the spooky people. All through their relationship, her magic had been a delicate subject— sensitive enough that she'd kept most of her witch's tools out of sight. She'd meant to put them out again one by one, to introduce him to them gradually. She wanted Ben to accept that part of her, but somehow she'd never brought out that first goddess figurine.

I'm being a coward. They'd have to confront the whole witch issue soon, but this wasn't the time. Not tonight, anyway.

"Do you want me to stay with you at your place?" she offered, officially giving up on the hospital plan.

"No." He huddled yet further into his blanket. "Like I said, I need to be by myself."

On some secret, selfish level, Holly was relieved to be spared his mood. "Then take care." She kissed his cheek, a quick peck of retreat. "Call me when you get home. Only if you want to. I'll check up on you later."

"Thanks," he muttered, but didn't look up.

Holly slid off the gurney, pausing a moment to find her fatigue-impaired balance, and walked away.

Ben wanted solitude. The only thing she could do was give it to him, but leaving him felt wrong. Everything was off-kilter. Their moment of reunion had gone flat, like biting into a sweet roll to find raw dough in the middle. *Crap.*

The analogy reminded her that dinner had been a long time ago. She drifted down the sidewalk, feeling hungry and emotionally hollow. The crowd around the house seemed to have taken on a new energy, but she was beyond caring what that was all about.

She noticed that Alessandro's car was gone. It had been there before she went to see Ben, so Alessandro must have left sometime since. *He could have touched base.* His omission made her grumpy. After all, checking up on Ben and Alessandro were two of the reasons she was still there. She might as well not have bothered sticking around.

It was time to finish up and go home. She found Raglan and got the rest of her money. Part of her felt bad taking it. Logic said she'd earned her fee twice over, but her guilt-ometer shrieked that she hadn't been able to save half the victims or Raglan's investment in the house.

As she left Raglan he was on his cell, carrying on a vitriolic argument with his insurance agent. From the sound of things, they'd be at it until his battery went dead. She hurried away, his angry, panic-ridden invective clawing at her nerves. The words weren't aimed at Holly, but her sense of failure grabbed them and stabbed at her heart nonetheless. Gulping the cold, damp air, Holly walked a little way to clear her brittle mood.

Then she saw Alessandro leaning against the side of the neighboring house, all but invisible in the shadows. He lifted a hand in silent greeting, the faint haze of the streetlights catching the pale fall of his long, curling hair and giving him an improbable halo.

The sight of him turned the tide on her ebbing energy. As she joined him, he straightened from his slouch against the stucco.

"What are you doing over here?" Holly asked. "I thought you'd left. Where's your car?"

"I moved it," he said. "I'm parked around the corner. I really need to go, but I wanted to make sure you were all right." He stepped toward her, his face intent.

It was the first kind thing anyone had said to her through the whole horrible aftermath of the house. Perversely, it made her want to cry.

"You scared me," he said. Alessandro took her face in his hands.

There was something old-fashioned in the gesture, familiar and courtly at the same time. Her stomach squeezed, warm with a fleeting, half-conscious memory of him picking her up and cradling her body against his chest. Taking her to the ambulance himself.

The feel of his hands on her face was comforting. Vampire skin was soft as silk, cool as satin, and Alessandro had a sensitive, skilled touch. She wanted his hands all over her, wherever there was skin to be caressed, because a little contact wasn't enough. That was the delight and the danger of his species. They always left their victims wanting that tiny bit more.

Holly drew a long breath. "I'm okay." *At the moment I feel more than okay.*

"Good."

"Thank you for getting me out of there."

"Anytime." Unexpectedly he bent, kissing her forehead, his lips cool and smooth. It was chaste. Brotherly. She pulled back, the innocent brush of lips burning her as surely as smoldering desire.

Feeling her start, Alessandro released her, eyes lowered. He recovered, giving her a bland smile. "Blessings on you, Holly. You should go, too. Go home and get some rest. Is there anyone staying with you tonight? Ben, maybe?"

Holly squeezed her eyes shut a moment, really not wanting to think about Ben. "No. I'm alone tonight. I'll be all right," she replied, doing her best to sound casual.

"Then go straight home. Be careful. Don't let anyone in. You've heard about the campus murders?"

"What are you talking about? Oh, never mind. I'm too tired."

"Holly, I need you to listen—"

This was all wrong. Ben had pushed her away, and now Alessandro was telling her to go, and she was cold and exhausted and she didn't want to dwell on death. On top of that, going home sounded incredibly lonely.

At least Alessandro recognized her need for comfort, and that was the best she was getting from anyone tonight. She stepped into his arms again, pressing against the strong wall of his chest. She meant the hug to be sisterly, as he had been brotherly, but heard the soft, surprised intake of his breath.

"Just hold me a moment," she said plaintively. "Just a moment, and then I'll go home."

His fingers curled into her hair, cupping her head as if he held something fragile and rare. "Holly, are you sure you're all right? Can I take you home?"

She didn't answer. The night had left her a raw wound. It was only now, when someone offered sympathy, that she fully allowed the pain.

His hand stroked down the back of her head and neck, traveling strong and gentle over her shoulders. Her clenched muscles trembled, reluctant to release. She'd thought comfort was what she wanted, but now Holly wanted to weep. His kindness was making her hurt worse.

He kissed the top of her head.

At that moment, reaching for warmth was the only balm for her misery. She tilted her face up and took his hard, full mouth with hers. A quick, tentative pressure. She felt his shiver, the sudden erratic beating of his heart. The vibration resonated through her flesh, heating things deep inside her body. His mouth was surprisingly warm, almost human-hot. They paused for a moment, their faces close together.

Holly's blood raced to the pull of his maleness. It drew her like a physical force, as if she could crawl inside his lethal strength and wrap it around her for comfort. A sweet tension began to push against her fatigue, a warm, new curiosity.

She leaned in a little farther, taking his lips again. He pulled back, hesitating, but then returned the soft, subtle kiss with something far more demanding—and delicious.

He tasted of licorice—no, it was fennel seed. Vampires sometimes chewed it as an old-fashioned breath freshener. The cool, sharp flavor made her tongue tingle, and she licked her own lips to get more of the sweetness. She slipped her arms around Alessandro's neck, her hands tangling in the wealth of his hair. He smelled of leather and tobacco and some other unique scent she could not place—the smell of *him*, of what he was. Holly drowned in it.

His hands held her, strong and steady. She kissed him more deeply, tongue glancing off the long, sharp edges of his corner teeth. Her lips quivered at the sensation, and she explored with the fascination of a primitive first seeing fire.

Alessandro's hands were cupping her face, the strong length of his torso tight against her. She could feel the subtle motion of his whole being with each movement of his tongue and lips, his entire body dancing against her as he kissed.

Alessandro slid one hand up her ribs, over her breast, until he found the tab of her jacket zipper. He pulled it down slowly, the grate of metal on metal resonating with an explosive, erotic weight. About halfway down he paused, pulling his hand back as if it had acted without his permission.

He shouldn't have stopped. Holly leaned into him, her breasts aching. He touched her collarbone, the back of his fingers stroking the column of her neck.

"This isn't what I meant for you," he said, his eyes lost in shadow.

Holly's heart thundered, heat roiling in her body. Slowly she drew away, a tremor of yearning down low in her stomach. She wanted this angel of death as she had wanted nothing before. She had totally forgotten all her caution, all the reasons she had to draw a line between them.

Sometimes she really was too stupid to live. *But I want him.*

Holly panted in lungfuls of the cold Pacific air, feeling the wind on her hot cheeks. *I can't have him.*

That kiss had gone far beyond anything she'd planned. She hadn't expected him to respond with such fervor, but there was more than blood-hunger in his eyes. There was all the confused heat and hope of any lover. *Who knew?*

He pushed the hair from her face. "As much as I want this, Holly, I'm not safe. And you have a good life. You don't need me. Not like this."

"I . . ." She trailed off, not sure what to say to the resignation in his voice. It made her angry and pained all at once. She put her hand on his arm, meaning to comfort. "I'm sorry."

"Don't be." He was suddenly restless, shifting from one foot to the other. She looked over her shoulder to see what was the matter, but there was nothing that hadn't been there before. Whatever was making him edgy was coming from inside his head. Doubt? Regret? Embarrassment?

How like a man to get close and then bolt. Apparently basic gender behavior didn't change with immortality. *Now, there's a two-edged sword.*

"I really have to go," he said quickly, looking down. "Honestly. I'm sorry."

"Can I catch a ride home? I'm not sure I should drive."

Something like panic crossed his face, followed by sharp

longing. "I know I offered, but get one of the police to take you. That would be much better."

"Why? Why can't you take me?"

"I have to get out of here. I . . . I'm a vampire, Holly. You shouldn't be catching rides with me. Not after . . . I'll see you later."

The soft leather of his sleeve slipped from under Holly's hand. Her fingers tightened in reflex, but could not hold him as he stepped away, melting into the shadows. Alessandro looked back, a quick glance over his shoulder. His eyes caught the errant light in a flash of amber, but his expression was unreadable.

"Go home," he said. "Now."

"Yeah, okay. Call me," she replied. The words sounded forlorn.

It was way past time for the abysmal evening to wrap up. Holly headed toward the house, planning to double-check with the policeman—what was his name . . . Macmillan?— that she had the all-clear to leave. Floodlights lit up the front porch, making it look even eerier. Yellow tape cordoned off the walkway to the porch. As she approached, three gurneys came down the steps, one after another, sheets drawn over the faces of the victims.

Tears started in Holly's eyes. She'd heard the other professor had been Bill Gamble. He hadn't made it. He was one of Ben's best friends and a really nice guy. Six had gone in. She'd saved only three. Remorse shuddered through her.

Police were everywhere, and they looked anticipatory. Odd. It wasn't as if there were anything to arrest. Now that the ooze was gone, there wasn't even that much to see.

Macmillan had just come out of the house and was walking her way.

"What's going on?" she asked.

He turned and stopped as she spoke, his expression guarded. "It's a crime scene."

Holly folded her arms. "Yeah, but who are you going to arrest? The house?"

Macmillan studied her, clearly making up his mind how much to say. "You're going to need to answer some questions."

"Okay."

His gaze didn't waver, but kept watching, recording her every twitch. "They found another body. She didn't die like the others."

"What?"

"Her death was different. Murder, and not by real estate."

Holly grabbed the sleeve of Macmillan's coat. "How come I didn't see her? Where was she?"

He took a step back, giving her his X-ray look again. "Where's your friend? Alessandro Caravelli? I'll need to speak with him."

"He's gone." Holly felt her stomach plummet to her feet. Alessandro had made an oblique reference to the campus murders. Told her to go home and lock the doors. *He knew about the fourth body!*

Macmillan's look grew cold, heavy with authority. "Do you know where he went?"

Holly gulped back her shock. "No."

Not only did he fail to mention a body, Alessandro had skipped the scene, leaving her to explain his absence to the police. She could kick his butt.

Holly folded her arms, struggling to look Macmillan in the face. "The law doesn't afford the supernatural community the same rights as it does humans. The trials are a joke. Even if I did know where he went, why should I turn him over to you?"

He looked disgusted. "Legal obligation aside, because this latest victim was killed by a vampire."

The words delivered a hard jolt. "What's that supposed to mean?"

His eyes widened, a hint of temper. "Loyalty is great, but how much do you really know about your fanged sidekick? Where—who—does he eat? Where does he go on a night-to-night basis? Who are his other friends? Just because he seems like a stand-up kinda vampire, that doesn't make him safe. Or innocent."

Macmillan stepped closer, his hands on his hips, tie dangling inches away from her chest. The posture lifted the edges of his coat, and Holly could see the straps of his holster. It held the latest police sidearm—some new weapon that shot silver-alloy ammunition with enough power to stop a werewolf in midrampage. Sadly, the new models jammed a lot. Most cops still carried a second, garden-variety gun.

The night was cold enough that she could feel the faint envelope of heat radiating from Macmillan's body. His jaw bunched with temper. "Now—why did Caravelli leave the scene of a vampire murder?"

The happy drugs left Holly's blood on a tide of adrenaline. Alessandro *wasn't* safe. He'd said so himself. *Oh, crap.*

No. She refused to believe the worst of him. "He's a good guy. He pulled me out of that house of horrors tonight."

"That doesn't mean he never gets peckish."

"That doesn't mean he's a slob, leaving food all over the place."

"Where is he?"

Holly barely stopped an eye roll. This was ridiculous. "You should try some basic detective work."

"Really?" The detective's eyebrows lifted.

"It's public record that Alessandro owns a collections agency. Check the yellow pages for an address. Vampires don't live in the sewers these days. They're employed. They have phones."

Macmillan's mouth thinned. Holly braced herself for a snarling comeback, but a uniformed officer waved for Macmillan's attention. The detective shot her a hard glance. "Wait here. I'll be back. We're not done."

He started toward the gaggle of police milling on the porch. Holly folded her arms across her dread-sore stomach. Macmillan had gone straight to the truth: Outside of their working relationship, she knew almost nothing of Alessandro's life.

Fat, icy drops splashed Holly's face. It had started to rain.

Chapter 6

Alessandro turned into the garage at the rear of his down-town apartment, wipers gracefully arcing across the T-Bird's windshield. He had escaped for now, but unless the cops were idiots, they'd put it together that he had been alone in the building with a dead girl. Tedious questions would follow.

In his experience, cops were like cats: The more you tried to avoid them, the more they wanted to get to know you. Unless Alessandro wanted to dump his current life and run—which was not so easy to do these days—he would have to act quickly. The sooner he could point the police in the direction of the real killer, the sooner they would leave him alone.

This new hunter in Fairview was causing a great deal of inconvenience.

He parked the car but sat a moment, unmoving. Holly's scent lingered on his clothes, an intimate ghost of her hair, her skin, her life. The fleeting echo of her presence cut through the maelstrom of his thoughts, and he closed his eyes, dwelling in that instant when she had pressed herself to his lips.

Scent was the one way, the only way he could drink her in and still leave her unharmed. It was barely enough to keep a dream from starving, and yet it was all he could safely enjoy. Memory was sweeter, but more dangerous. Memory made him want more.

Details of the evening played over and over in Alessandro's mind: the curve of her knees, the brisk gestures of her hands. The images fanned the embers of smothered lust. As his blood heated, a savage pang of hunger rent him, twisting his gut and filling his mouth with saliva.

He drained the blood of those he caressed, destroying what he craved. Eroticism and appetite were inexorably linked, like thunder and lightning. Any dream of love was mere delusion. All a vampire had was hunger.

At that Alessandro's yearning fell to ash, leaving him empty. He got out of the car as if there were barely enough spirit left to propel his limbs, but the weather snapped him out of his reverie. The half dozen yards to his apartment block were a gauntlet of pelting rain. He took them at a run.

Once a Victorian-era warehouse, the building had been converted to a modern art gallery and a handful of suites. Alessandro entered at a rear door that led straight into his neglected kitchen.

Halfway over the threshold he stopped, suddenly alert. Nothing was out of place. The door had been locked. The security system was disarmed, but then he rarely set it.

What was wrong?

Rain pattered on the pavement behind him, gurgling down the drainpipes and over the lid of a Dumpster. He could smell the ocean in the heavy, moist breeze, as well as a whiff of restaurants and car exhaust.

That was all distraction. What had caught his attention was a subtle note behind the rest of the sensory noise.

Alessandro pulled the door closed, shutting out what little light came from outside. Water dripped in a steady beat from the hem of his coat to the tiles of the entryway. He shed the coat, throwing it over a chair, and glided noiselessly toward his living room. Tension prickled at the back of his neck, spilling down between his shoulders. He wasn't afraid, but he was wary.

What had been faint was growing stronger, unveiling itself. Now power hung in the air like pungent smoke. Pausing once, he drew a long knife from his boot sheath. From the feel of the energy, Alessandro's visitor was another of his kind.

The living room was pitch-black, the bare brick walls absorbing any ambient light. He didn't need much to see, but he needed some. With his left hand he found the light switch and flipped it, keeping his knife at the ready.

There was a flicker of movement behind him, too fast even for his quick reactions. In a blink, feminine arms squeezed him; tiny hands pressed against the muscles of his chest. Recognition came in a jolt, stilling his blade just before he could strike.

He knew the steely strength in those delicate fingers, and a tiny part of him chilled with terror. This was not, however, a crisis that could be solved with a weapon.

"I have missed you, my Alessandro." Her voice was rich and soft, a brush of fur in the dark.

One hand slid down until it rested on the front of his jeans, making it clear what exactly she had missed. The crawling heat of the Desire rose between them, that call of flesh and power between the vampire kind. It was lust, but also recognition. He was hers, his safety guaranteed by her favor.

He felt the press of her cheek against his back. "Have you been lonely without me?" she asked.

I have been at peace without you, he thought, schooling his face as he turned in her arms. "My queen," he said, sheathing the knife and falling to one knee.

Omara was tiny, dressed in a shift of azure silk, one long black braid over her shoulder. Her eyes reminded Alessandro of dark honey, her skin of pale cinnamon. Ancient beyond memory, she looked no more than one and twenty.

A creature of unfathomable power, she was alone, and in his house. *This cannot be good,* he thought. Random anxieties crowded his mind. He was overdue in sending a report. He had no one to offer as food. He hadn't vacuumed for a week. Then there were the campus murders. *Surely she could not already know one of us is responsible? Why is she here? Why is she here alone?*

The answer came at once as the Desire flared. She bent down and kissed his mouth, caressing with her tongue. Alessandro could taste her power, hot and pungent, as she explored him, licking, pricking her lip on his sharp teeth. Blood blossomed, richer and sweeter than any other. The ichor of a queen.

The twin goads of hunger and lust rose again, drawing him from his knees to his feet. She was his ruler; he was aching to serve her in all things. He knew how to make her forget her royal dignity. Perhaps she could make him forget how badly he wanted Holly.

With a rough shove Omara pushed him back, her eyes amused. "How eager you are." She ran one finger over his lips, wiping away the last of her blood. "And how pleasant that you are entirely mine to enjoy. No clan. No sire still among us. Such exclusive loyalty is surprisingly hard to come by."

Alessandro lowered his eyes, cursing his body's ready response. He feared her, because she knew his weakness. Every day of his immortal life he suffered on the wheel of solitude. One day he would break.

Abandoning him where he stood, Omara crossed to the couch and sat, tucking her feet beside her. She had shown her power over him. The opening pleasantries were over.

"An interesting place you have chosen for yourself." She looked calmly around the room. "Spare, but choice pieces. A suitably Gothic layer of dust. You need a servant."

He stood speechless, mute with strangled need.

She ran a finger over the side table, then inspected it. "Perhaps a French maid?"

Alessandro fought to collect his thoughts. He had been the queen's representative in Fairview for years and her retainer for centuries before that. She had taken him into her household even before she had worn the crown. Long experience had taught him the danger of falling for her games.

But there was tension in her face. What could trouble a creature powerful enough to rule dozens upon dozens of vampire clans? Omara uncurled her legs, sitting up straight. "Please have a seat."

Alessandro sank into an easy chair, looking at his queen across the clutter of library books on his glass coffee table. Resentment roiled inside him, the aftermath of that teasing kiss. "To what do I owe the honor of your visit?" he asked, carefully polite.

She looked down, as if mesmerized by the creases in the leather couch. "My head is filled with problems I cannot solve by fire or sword. I dislike this modern age."

Alessandro took a deep breath, letting it out slowly. The sudden shift in tone was typical of Omara. "Are you disappointed that all the Van Helsings of the world traded in their stakes and holy water for tax audits?"

Omara shrugged. "I have highly paid accountants to deal with those little men."

"Then why dislike this century?"

"Since we came out of the shadows, my role as leader has become more complex. Citizenship. Legal rights. They come at a price. We must obey human rules. If our community makes a mistake, we have so much more to lose."

Alessandro did not reply, keeping his opinions to himself. Most of the supernatural community still existed on the fringe of society, reviled by humans. Laws were fine, but fear and hatred ran deep. Still, he knew Omara would fight like the nightmare she was to further the interests of her people. He would not deny that she was an effective queen.

Omara sighed, as if impatient with his silence. "The human authorities are investigating a string of vampire murders in this area. You know about this?"

Alessandro frowned. "Yes."

"The police contacted me. I came here as a diplomat, to lend the vampire community's support to their inquiries."

"But I only just found out the murders involve one of us. How long ago did the humans call you?"

Omara studied one of her bracelets, twisting it around and around her slender wrist. "They called me two days ago as a courtesy. Every member of our local community is under their scrutiny."

She shook the bracelet back into place and gave him her full attention. "I told them at once you were above reproach."

"They might not believe you."

"There will be others who can corroborate your whereabouts."

"I work alone, and I don't know when the murders took place. There may be no one who can swear to my innocence."

"If you do not have suitable alibis for the dates and times in question, I will see to it they are found." She gave a conspiratorial smile.

Alessandro nodded. "Your confidence is appreciated."

"I need you. You do me no good in a police lockup."

"We may need to work quickly. Tonight I gave the police reason to come knocking on my door." He summarized the night's events.

Omara listened, a small line forming between her brows as the tale ended. "Show me the token you found."

It was in the pocket of the coat he had left in the kitchen. He went and got it.

Omara held the metal disk under the light of the lamp. "It is, as you say, very old." She made a small noise of interest as she turned it over. "Some of these tokens have the image of Eurydice on the reverse. This one does not. That means it dates, oh, from before the Black Death, at least. The metalsmiths included her only after that era."

Alessandro curled his lip. "Is that when those ridiculous fantasies about the Chosen began?"

She looked up and laughed, sudden merriment making her look almost like a living girl. "Ah, if you could only see the derision on your face. The myth of the Chosen sends you to sleep, does it? You do not care how Orpheus risked all to rescue Eurydice from death's embrace?"

Alessandro gave a scornful wave of his fingers. "Fables for fledglings. I am not a romantic."

"Are you sure about that?" Omara smiled, her lips holding a universe of promises. "Come now, the myth of the Chosen is the Grail Quest of our kind."

"Enough. I know the story. True love holds our release

from this vale of living death, just as Orpheus reclaimed his wife from Hades."

"Oh, then how can you resist it? Are you such a sad cynic?"

"I don't care how much a mortal might love a vampire; that vampire must feed."

Omara lifted one perfect shoulder. "Then you miss the point entirely. The vampire Chosen by a living mate can feed on their love, sustained through the lust of the body instead of the lust for blood." Her eyes glinted from under her lashes. "No wonder the legend is so popular. I ask you, what's not to like about that? Except eternal monogamy, of course."

Alessandro caught his breath, snagged despite himself by the promise of the myth. A Chosen could love without destroying. An impossible dream. "Orpheus failed. Eurydice never made it out of Hades."

Omara leaned back against the cushions, clearly enjoying his bleak mood. "A beautiful story, and all you see are the flaws in the metaphor. Orpheus failed because he had insufficient faith. He did not trust the dark gods enough for the magic to work."

"I empathize," Alessandro said dryly. "I have little patience with false hopes and bedtime stories, especially when there are other, more immediate problems to solve—like an unknown vampire leaving his leftovers for the police to find."

"You are a work-obsessed bore." She blew him a kiss.

"I'm a pragmatist."

"And I would rather talk about anything but this killer and his tokens, but our cold, gray new world will not oblige." Standing, she circled the end of the coffee table and knelt before him. Alessandro started to rise, but she caught his hands, keeping him still.

"I did not tell the human police that I know the source of these troubles," she said.

"What is it?" Alessandro asked, surprised.

She squeezed his fingers, reassuring. Once he relaxed,

she rested her hands on his knees, the gesture both pleading and inviting. "I need your sword, my champion."

"Of course." His voice was suddenly rough from the weight of her touch. *What do you really want of me?*

She slid her hands up his thighs, her fingers caressing the worn denim. "I took you in when your clan perished. I gave you my protection when others would have made you their slave."

Her hands slid to his hips, and she leaned forward, her small, perfect body between his knees. His skin craved her, burned for relief from his endless solitude. She could see it in his face; he could tell. Her eyes searched his, seeking and finding his loneliness.

A slow smile showed the tips of her fangs. "You owe me this service."

In a single gesture Alessandro pushed his chair back and stood, putting space between himself and Omara. She looked up at him, amused speculation in her eyes.

"Tell me what you want me to do," he said, his voice carefully void of emotion.

"So obedient," she said, her voice dropping to a husky whisper. She leaned back on the floor, reclining on one hip, exotic as an odalisque from some eastern realm.

"I am your knight. I do my duty."

"Or perhaps you merely want to know the worst. Find out what I want of you. You want to end this moment of suspense."

Alessandro stubbornly held her gaze. He Desired her. He dreaded whatever task she meant to set him, but he would obey because she was his queen. By vampire law, Omara held the slender threads of his existence. He would have given anything to bestow that power on a different, gentler woman.

Omara finally looked away. A small victory for him, but meaningless.

He bowed his head. "What is it you wish, my queen?" he asked, hiding his resignation.

Power assured, Omara gave him a look that smoked with dark satisfaction.

"The first thing I wish is to be taken care of," she said, rising from her knees with liquid grace. She put her hand on his chest. The light touch of her tapered fingers made his skin tingle with anticipation. "Take me somewhere. I have traveled all day, and I want sustenance. I want to walk into the darkest, deadliest places on your arm. We are the royalty of this little city, and I want my homage. Then, when I am rested, we shall talk of murders and enemies."

She kissed his lips lightly. "And after that, we shall see."

Chapter 7

Venue decisions were easy. There were only a handful of places in Fairview fit to entertain a vampire queen, so Alessandro chose the most elegant and discreet, a place named Sinsation.

"Quaint," said Omara, looking through the rafters of the ceiling to the empty loft above.

It was an old building, the interior gutted and left with wood and brick exposed, but the bar was made of granite, glass, and chrome. The light fixtures were something from a futurist's brain fever.

Sinsation was pretentious and expensive, but Alessandro liked the fact that one could carry on a conversation without screaming. A good feature, since he wanted answers. On the way there, Omara had given no hint about exactly what she wanted him to do.

Out of habit, Alessandro scanned the room. The bar was to his left, dwarfed by the shadows of the high ceiling. Toward the back a small, raised stage sat empty, only a man-sized candelabra filling the space with twin branches of flickering light. In front of it, each of the round tables was occupied by two or three patrons, a mix of vampires and humans.

The soft electronic music sounded like New Age gone to

the dark side. It was easy to hear, because the murmur of voices stopped. All eyes, supernatural and human, turned to him and Omara with surprise and a hint of fear.

"Do they always stare this way?" Omara asked Alessandro in an amused whisper. She had her arm slipped through his, her face upturned to give him a sharp-toothed smile.

"They did not expect you, my queen."

As if of a single mind, the vampires rose and then fell to one knee in obeisance, the humans awkwardly following their lead. Alessandro studied each face. One set of eyes lifted and glittered unpleasantly, but looked away when Alessandro met that angry glare with one of his own.

Pierce, Alessandro thought with a flare of annoyance, and then turned deliberately away. The male was as irritating and unwholesome as chewing gum stuck to one's shoe.

Omara nodded to the crowd, bestowing a smile that was somehow both gracious and dismissive. "Greetings, my friends. Please carry on as you were. Enjoy the night."

There was a rustle as patrons resumed their seats. Then a hushed babble of conversation rose, urgent and filled with repressed exclamations. A hostess arrived and quickly cleared the best table. Alessandro and the queen waited politely while she worked.

Omara's hand tightened on his biceps. "John Pierce looks like he wishes to snap your neck."

Alessandro gave a slow smile. "Let him do his worst. I will put him in his place."

Omara laughed. "What an arrogant beast you are."

"I know my worth."

"Does he wish to replace you as my representative here?" The question was taunting. "Or perhaps take over your role as my battle champion?"

"He is nothing but a playboy and a dabbler in spells. More to the point, last year I was obliged to behead his brother."

Her eyes widened with interest. "I had forgotten. Why did that happen?"

"He attacked a human in anger. I merely did my duty."

"As you should, but watch yourself. Pierce will cause you trouble."

"I know. I look forward to his mistake."

The table was ready. Alessandro held the chair for Omara while she sat, an old habit that still lingered. A waitress appeared, clad in black slacks and crisp white blouse that showed soft, warm skin. Omara ordered a complicated martini. He ordered a dark Hungarian red wine, the thick vintage nicknamed Bull's Blood. His usual. The drinks were more props than sustenance, but it was a pleasant ritual. As the waitress left, Alessandro wondered how she might be described on a menu. A young vintage, but with a delicate bouquet?

Omara folded her hands on the glass surface of the table. Her rings sparkled in the dim light, shimmering with every movement of her fine-boned hands.

"To return to the murders, and what I wish you to do . . ." Omara said without preamble.

Alessandro straightened, glad she was finally ready to talk. "Yes?"

She ducked her head, licking her lips. It was a rare show of nerves. "I believe one of my old enemies has returned. I was not surprised when the Fairview police contacted me."

"Why not?"

"My home in Seattle was ransacked. Nothing was taken: not my money nor my business records. Not even my jewelry."

"Your books and implements of magic?" Alessandro asked anxiously. Omara possessed powerful, dangerous rarities any sorcerer would covet for his collection.

Her eyes went wide for a moment, perhaps envisioning that disaster. "No, those are safe."

"A blackmailer, perhaps? Someone looking for information?"

"No demands were made." Omara looked away. "It was odd, disturbing. Then the Fairview police called, wanting my advice, so I came. Perhaps the incidents were unrelated, but I doubt it. I believe the break-in was to put me on notice. Someone desires a fight. They have picked Fairview as their battleground."

"Was it wise to come?"

Her lip curled. "I do not run."

"But why Fairview? Since I've been here it's been a quiet city, at least until these murders."

"That's because you, my champion, are here. I haven't needed to worry about this part of my domain. You keep the law here with a strong and just hand. If something went amiss, you are my natural successor."

Alessandro allowed himself a small, sardonic smile. "You know I have no ambition to be king, and I have never learned the sorcery necessary to hold the throne."

"If you choose, you could learn. You have more than enough ability and natural power."

Alessandro wasn't sure if this was the truth or an attempt to secure his interest. It didn't matter. "If our enemies bring us together in Fairview, they face a double threat."

Omara shook her head. "Still, it puts us both within one killing stroke. There is danger as well as advantage to you and I being in the same city."

"But who is our adversary?"

"If the token you found is a clue, a very old, very powerful enemy. Someone willing to kill to put us in jeopardy with the human police."

Alessandro tried to swallow, but his throat was suddenly devoid of moisture. "You told me once that you foresaw trouble in this place. I began to doubt anything would ever happen here, but you were right."

"I wish that were not so."

He frowned. "There may be more than meets the eye to this adversary. In the last few weeks a magic user has been using summoning spells."

"What?" Omara was all attention.

Perhaps his client hadn't been the target of the spell caster's art, but collateral damage. Such things happened. "And the latest victim was concealed with a look-away spell. Who could work that kind of magic? You say you know the source of this trouble. Who could it be?"

"It must be an old enemy. But which? I could fill a telephone book." Omara raised her eyes to the ceiling, as if to see the names written there. "To begin with, there is every other king or queen who might want my territory, and every other clan leader who covets a crown. The leaders of most other species. Then there are those special few: Morlok. Aloysius. Geneva. Michael. Gervaise. Callandra."

"Demons." He had gone cold. He did not like to admit fear, but there it was.

"Yes, the demons. I've fought one here before."

"But we're searching for a vampire. There was the token."

Alessandro paused. He didn't like the look in Omara's eyes, but he couldn't tell what she was thinking.

She smiled. "Indeed, there was the token. You're right. We must look to our own kind."

The drinks came. Omara brought the bright blue martini to her lips, tasting it with just a dart of her pink tongue. "You'll need the help of that witch friend of yours. The Carver girl. Pretty thing, I'm told."

Alessandro started at her words, his wine sloshing to the lip of the glass. "You know of her?" *Pretty thing.* Yes, all long, walnut-dark hair and emerald eyes. Omara didn't like rivals.

"Of course. She's a Carver witch in my own territory. Rumor has it she can squash a poltergeist in five minutes flat." The queen's eyes asked for confirmation.

"That's true. And she defeated a rogue house tonight. An exceptionally bad one."

"You'll need her magic," Omara said softly. "Get her to raise one of the murdered girls. A little necromancy will go a long way toward identifying my rival. The dead could at least describe the attacker."

Alessandro pushed the wine away, recoiling from the memory of Holly writhing on the floor in pain. Necromancy demanded a huge amount of magic and would be even more excruciating for her. "Is there no one else we can bring in to help? I'm not sure she can do this."

"Of course she can. She's a Carver witch. Their specialty for generations has been calling the dead."

"There is something wrong with her magic. Necromancy would probably kill her."

"Would she survive long enough for the magic to work?"

Alessandro narrowed his eyes, growing even more uneasy. "I don't know."

"I think she might. And still you hesitate. What is a witch's death compared to the defeat of my adversary?" A look passed over Omara's face that he had never seen before: a flicker of . . . terror? "I led the vampires out of the darkness and into this century. I am the one who talks to judges and politicians, lobbying for our rights. I deserve to survive."

He started to interrupt, but her icy gaze froze his words. "If this murderer keeps killing, the terrified citizens of Fairview will turn on the entire supernatural community. They could massacre us without a flicker of remorse. Think of that when you start to feel heroic and protective of some girl with the significance of a gnat."

She leaned across the table, putting her face close to his. They must have looked like a courting couple working up to a kiss. He could feel the slow exhalation of her breath. "Don't disobey me, Alessandro. I don't want to lose you. You're my champion, my questing knight. Harden your heart for my sake. Love *me*, Alessandro."

Without Omara, there was no one, no clan, no kin. Without his queen he was utterly without a foothold among his kind. Eternity was a long time to be alone.

She wrapped her hand around his, squeezing hard. "A rogue vampire—or demon—will feed and feed until all around him are destroyed. I *must* know who is doing this."

"Of course," he said, but his mind was fumbling for alternatives. *I will find another way to solve this. What she asks is unthinkable.* Even if he never touched Holly, never tasted her, she was his partner—she didn't belong to anyone else, not even his queen. Alessandro protected what was his.

Omara took another sip of her drink, a faint tremor in her fingers. "I know you will do the right thing. You always do. It's part of your old-world charm."

He opened his mouth to reply, but any unwise statements were preempted by someone approaching the table. Pierce.

"A moment, my queen." Pierce bowed low, his wavy

blond hair burnished by the candlelight. He still had the grace of an Elizabethan courtier, but a feral streak hid behind those fine manners.

"How may I help you?" Omara asked formally, but there was eager heat in her glance. Suspicion flittered through Alessandro's thoughts. Did they know each other better than either of them let on?

Pierce straightened, a smile lighting his even features. Wearing an open-necked shirt and gray wool jacket, he gave off an air of monied ease. "I come on behalf of Clan Albion to beg the favor of offering refreshment."

Pierce held up his right hand with a graceful flourish, and a human stepped forward from the shadows. The moment was dramatic, just the sort of show Omara liked. The human was also very much to her taste, on the brink of full manhood, a light blue sweater straining across the muscles of his chest.

"It pleases me that you remember the service owed to your queen." Though her words were for Pierce, her eyes were on Alessandro. "My favor shall always go to those who serve me best."

Alessandro returned a false smile, mentally peeling the skin from Pierce's flesh.

Turning to the young human, Omara gestured for him to kneel. She stroked his cheek, caressing the straight fall of his chestnut hair, and then took his right arm, pushing the sleeve of the sweater up past his elbow. The forearm was thick with muscle, but still had the soft skin of youth. The human's face was joyous, his soft lips parted.

"Is this your first time?" she asked gently.

"He is untouched and willing, my queen," said Pierce, as if the human had no voice of his own.

Omara braced the youth's arm on the edge of the table and touched the crook of the inner elbow, looking for veins. She bent her head and bit, her venom sending the young man into shudders of ecstasy. Alessandro knew Omara would not kill the human, she would not mark him as a servant, but she would ruin his appetite for anything an ordinary woman could do. Even a casual bite could shatter a life if the human fell prey to the addictive high.

That brought back the conversation about the token. According to the legend of the Chosen, only a human untouched by a vampire's bite could Choose a mate. The act took free will untouched by the power of the vampire's venom. He watched Omara feeding. The legend was nonsense. Only an addict could love a creature like that. Like him.

Scenting the blood, Alessandro felt his own appetite stir. His skin flushed hot, his groin tightening. The sucking, lapping sounds of the meal made his palms slick with sweat. He rose, making a polite bow Omara did not see.

"Excuse me," he murmured to no one in particular, and headed toward the back of the lounge.

Beside the washrooms there was a back door that led to a dead-end alley. The storm drain was plugged with weeds, leaving a trough of water down the center of the narrow space. Alessandro stood against the wall, breathing in cold, clean air. For all he owed Omara, for all he needed from her, he was glad to escape for even a minute.

To human eyes the alley would be pitch-black, clouds blotting out the moon and stars. He could see a rat scuttling along as if fleeing for its life, burrowing into a crevice in the bricks across the way.

Alessandro frowned. The reasons to solve the vampire murders were mounting. The case threatened his freedom, Omara's safety, and now, indirectly, Holly's—not to mention the lives of the human victims. Yet for all Omara claimed to know it was an old enemy at work, Alessandro felt he still had no solid information. The queen's adversaries were too many to count.

He sniffed the air. Odd. There was something building, a pressure that throbbed in his sinuses. There was a faint sound like tearing cloth. Alessandro wheeled toward it.

The wall at the end of the alley, just before it reached the street, was bathed in a sickly green glow the approximate shade of bile. At first he thought it was a reflection, but the light flared, turning the alleyway a pearly rainbow of pinks and grays that deepened to a bloody orange. The light was coming from *inside* the old brick wall of the radio station next door.

Alessandro pulled his boot knife and began running toward the light, his heels loud on the pavement. He was in a blind alley, and he didn't want to be trapped with whatever that light portended—but he had to know what it was. Now there was a heavy smell of magic in the air, a pungent, charred stink like burning toast.

The bricks of the wall shimmered, putting off a fierce heat. Once, Alessandro had watched a movie screen when film caught and burned in the projector. There was a similar hole melting the wall. Irregular edges flared orange, light pouring from the hole's center. It was small, but appeared to grow with each moment that passed, filling the air with a faint ripping sound. Powdery ash dropped, vanishing before it reached the ground.

He passed the hole, stopping only when he had nearly reached the safety of the street. By then he had figured out what he was seeing: This was a portal; the barrier between the demon realm and earth was burning away.

Shock ran through him, a dismay so sharp he had to fight nausea. A portal meant someone—no doubt his rogue spellcaster and Omara's murderous vampire enemy—was summoning a demon. This was far worse than they'd thought.

The demon had not yet passed through, but it was trying to make a door. The hole had grown to the size of a dinner plate. Alessandro clenched his fists, offended. *This is not your town*, he thought, glaring at the hole in the wall. Frustration leaped through his body. He was no sorcerer. He had no power over this kind of magic. *Who is close enough to help?*

A desperate cry came from the street behind him. He turned to see a cluster of figures pounding through a parking lot a block away. The figure in front was moving fast, but the two creatures pursuing it were gaining ground.

He stared, for a moment feeling nothing but cold refusal to believe. Then horror surged through his flesh, like blood tingling into a sleeping limb.

Bald, hunched, the two in the rear chased their prey with a peculiar, rolling lope. *Changelings.* Squat, gray, misshapen abominations, they were the bastard children of the Undead realm, made from a line that had never Turned properly. They were vampires, and yet they were not. Abhorrent and insane, they were shunned by even the lowest of the vampire clans.

Changelings in Fairview? They're extinct!

But that had been the odd smell clinging to the body of the girl he had found. Vampire, but not. Drinking blood, but unable to bite without mangling the victim.

Then he felt his stomach turn cold all over again. He knew the prey. It was Macmillan, one of the detectives from the Flanders house. Ironically, Alessandro had tried to avoid the cops. Now here was one running virtually into his arms. *And he's not going to make it.*

Alessandro sprinted across the street at an angle that brought him to a point ahead of the running figures. Gripping his knife, he faded into the shadows, willing himself to be one with the darkness. A moment lapsed, thick with anticipation.

Macmillan was track-star fast, but losing ground. Alessandro let him pass, timing his own attack with a predator's instincts. As soon as the man was two steps away, Alessandro lashed a kick at the first of the changelings, sending him flying into the side of a passing Toyota. The metal dented with a resounding thud. The vehicle's owner jumped out with a yell, but Alessandro was already running after the detective and the second pursuer.

The other changeling was easy to catch, but harder to hold. Claws slashed at Alessandro's eyes, forcing him to duck. The movement loosened his grip on the creature's arm. It seized the advantage, landing a hard blow to Alessandro's shoulder. Alessandro got a glimpse of its face, the maw of needle teeth where a nose and mouth should have been.

Macmillan had stopped and turned. As Alessandro drove his elbow into the changeling's chin, the detective pulled his weapon and fired. The silver grips on the sidearm meant it had silver bullets—the standard ammo for stopping a vampire.

The changeling kept coming with the determination of a nightmare, bits of blood and flesh spattering the street. The cop was a good shot, but not fast enough to keep up with the changeling's supernatural speed. He fired again and again, but none of the rounds penetrated the heart or head.

The gun clicked empty.

Alessandro feinted with his knife, drawing the changeling's attention away from the detective. The creature turned, slowed only a little by its gaping wounds. Alessandro circled, looking for a weakness in its guard. He gave an experimental lunge; the creature parried with its claws. Alessandro circled again, testing while Macmillan took cover behind a mailbox and drew his regular weapon—the one meant for mere humans.

"Get out of here!" Alessandro ordered the man.

The changeling edged sideways toward the mailbox, its limbs hunched like a squat spider, its maw gaping wet and red. Then it leaped, using all its limbs to spring. Macmillan emptied his second weapon, the sheer force of the assault knocking the creature sideways. It fell to earth, but got up and lunged again, jaws extended.

The detective vaulted backward, barely avoiding the changeling's grasp. Alessandro tackled it from behind.

"Run!" he bellowed.

Macmillan had no choice. He bolted, disappearing into the shadowy parking lot between his would-be killer and the bright lights of the nearby movie theaters.

Deprived of its prey, the changeling twisted free, howling in frustration. Wounded in a half dozen places, it still had the strength to bound forward in yet another attack. Only Undead reflexes kept Alessandro from its fangs. He swept the knife up, slicing the changeling in midflight. The creature fell to the asphalt, curling in on itself, limbs tucked protectively around its wound.

That was one wound too many. This time it stayed on the ground.

Alessandro looked down at the misshapen thing. The

pink light of a neon sign flickered over its gray skin, picking out the ragged claws where its hands and feet should have been. It gave an eerie, mewling cry of rage. Like all vampires it had once been human, but changelings were different. None of their human personality survived the Turning.

Alessandro was quick, and the knife was sharp. As soon as the spine was severed, the body began to melt into a reeking sludge. He bent to clean his knife on a scraggly patch of grass next to the sidewalk.

Alessandro hadn't seen changelings in at least several centuries. Some claimed they had been hunted to extinction after their last bid to challenge the vampire clans. *Apparently not*, he thought as he ran back to where he had kicked the other changeling into the car. The Toyota, he noted, had left the scene. Just as well.

The first changeling was a puddle of slime. Its neck must have snapped on impact. Alessandro felt a shiver work its way down his spine. Changelings didn't even go to their final death properly. True vampires turned to dust.

Now he just had to deal with a doorway to the demon realm.

He had reached a point across the street from the alley, but stopped in his tracks as soon as he could see the portal. Creatures were worming through the rip between dimensions, emerging from the wall to drop with a splash to the puddles of the alley. They looked like huge dogs, red-eyed and coal black. Their forms seemed indistinct, like beasts made of nightmares.

Hellhounds.

It was one thing to fight a pair of changelings, another to take on a pack of half demons. He stayed utterly still, melting into the shadows. He dared not even take out his cell phone to call for help. Their hearing was even better than a vampire's.

A change in the light caught Alessandro's attention. The brightness was receding, as if something were reeling it back into the portal. Faster than it had burned open, the portal was closing, the edges shimmering and healing. One last hellhound was squeezing through, shaggy black legs pumping as it squirmed through the narrowing gap. It dropped to the ground and raced after its fellows. A drool of ectoplasm coursed down the wall, sticky and faintly phosphorescent.

Then the doorway shrank to a pinpoint and disappeared with a faint pop. The air pressure changed, growing suddenly heavy. Perhaps it was just returning to normal.

No demon in sight. The spellcaster's summoning had failed.

A reprieve.

The hounds faded into the darkness, silent as dreams. Alessandro released his breath. The werewolves could deal with the hounds better than anyone else. He didn't like asking the wolves for help—it never paid to show weakness—but this was a commonsense exception.

Not all hellspawn were so easy to clean up. How many other portals had there been, and what had come through them?

Alessandro walked backward until he leaned on the brick exterior of Sinsation. Too many thoughts crashed through his brain, each one bellowing for attention. He had believed changelings wiped from the earth, but here they were, their scent all over a murdered college student. That raised so many questions. What would they hope to gain by coming to Fairview? What, if any, connection did changelings have to a summoner or his demon? Moreover, what possible connection did they have to Omara?

A rogue vampire would have been a dangerous but far less complex scenario. All these circumstances together reeked of magic and obscure motivations, two of his least favorite things.

Police sirens yowled in the distance. The detective had raised the alarm. Alessandro needed to take the queen and leave.

Chapter 8

How could anyone compare my home with the Flanders place? Holly stood at the front gate, trying to see her house with unbiased eyes. That was hard. She loved it with all her heart.

It was what architecture buffs called a "painted lady." Three stories of gingerbread carving gestured skyward, resplendent in lemon yellow and aubergine. Built in the 1880s, it stood at the crest of a steep rise, looking over a sweep of ocean to the south. Seven generations of Carvers had lived there.

So what if Ben wasn't a Gothic mansion kinda guy? He'd come around. He had to. Their relationship had grown slowly, but their bond was solid. In the last few months things had begun to grow serious. They'd begun leaving spare clothes and other odds and ends at each other's homes. Swapped keys. They'd even begun talking about moving in together.

They really had to have that talk about witchcraft very soon.

And I have to forget that I ever kissed Alessandro. It had been a moment of crisis, but that kiss had still been a mere whisker away from cheating. She couldn't bring herself to regret the moment, but it would never happen again.

Holly pushed open the wrought-iron gate and started up the walk, groping for her keys in her pocket. She wasn't moving too quickly after her adventures the night before. She'd slept until eleven and rose bruised and headachy. Brunch had been soda crackers and tap water. Now it was nearly dinnertime and she was just starting to feel like herself.

Holly's cat, the Kibble-ator, sat on the porch like a fuzzy, twenty-pound doorstop. She'd never intentionally acquired Kibs, but he lived in her home and ate her food anyway. He sniffed at her sneakers, finding all the interesting scents collected during her round of afternoon errands.

"Hey, there," she said, bending down to pet him. He yawned, demonstrating the power of intense fish breath. He pushed his head into her hand and then did a rolling flop, presenting his belly for a scratch. Holly obeyed. With that much cat on her foot, it wasn't easy to move.

Eventually Holly straightened and checked the mailbox. Nothing. Then, turning her key in the heavy brass lock, she caught her breath as the door swung ajar. Someone had left it unlocked. Unperturbed, the cat thumped past on heavy paws, heading straight for his food bowl.

"Hello?" she called out, envisioning burglars loose in her private spaces, rooting through her underwear drawer. There was no response. "Hello?" she called again, gripping her keys like a weapon. She walked through the front parlor, her whole being straining to catch the slightest sound.

There was a noise in the kitchen, a loud, scrabbling rustle like a giant mouse. Creeping up to the doorway, she stopped and stood with her back to the wall. The rustling stopped. She tried to be silent, undetectable, but the rush of her panting breath roared in her ears. Swallowing nervously, she took one step into the kitchen, her footfall loud on the old gray linoleum. The air was damp, smelling of onions and dish soap. The electric clock that hung over the sink hummed softly. She heard another noise, the metallic clunk of shifting pots and pans. She crept forward, ready to pounce.

A nicely sculpted masculine rump projected from the

cupboard beneath the sink. She sighed with relief and exasperation. After last night's experience, he was the last person she expected to find alone in her house.

"Ben," she said, loud enough that he could hear.

Predictably he jerked up, whacking his head on the pipes. Swearing, he scrambled backward and turned, his glasses slightly askew.

"Oh, hi," he replied. "I was looking for drain cleaner."

"I don't have any." The release of tension made her grin wide. Ben was over his fright. Everything was all right. He was not only in her house, but interacting with it as well. A very good sign. *It would be so nice if he would just move in.*

"The house fixes its own plumbing problems," she added.

"I know." He got to his feet, smoothing back his short, thick hair with one hand. "Maybe its self-maintenance schedule fell behind. The sink is plugged. I was going to try a little plain old handyman know-how."

"Good idea."

"I got your message about today being the registration deadline," he said. "I wanted to come over and say congratulations in person. So, congrats for taking the plunge. Happy studenthood. Everything go okay?"

"Yeah." Today was the deadline to pay up and make her registration official. Raglan's job had come in the nick of time. "I skipped the bookstore. It was a mob scene."

"You should wait until I can go with you. I get a discount."

"Thanks." With a contented smile, Holly pulled off her jacket, hanging it on a hook by the back door. Somewhere behind her, Kibs crunched the cat chow in his bowl. The kitchen seemed peaceful, a refuge, the light falling on the old counters exactly as it had when she was too small to reach the cookie jar.

"Did you get any sleep last night?" she asked.

He shrugged. "A bit. I'm really restless. I can't seem to stay still for two minutes. May as well take advantage of all this unfocused energy, so I washed the dishes while I waited for you."

"Thanks for that," she said. He was a much better house-keeper than she was. "I know it wasn't easy to come here."

Moving close to Ben, she kissed him. His lips were soft, his shirt damp with dishwater. Giving a little grunt of surprise, he returned the kiss with one of his own. His warm tongue touched hers swiftly, the merest teasing brush. He had been eating chocolate.

"What's all this?" he asked, his tone far from complaining.

Holly didn't respond. She was concentrating on the chocolate. There were so many things she deeply appreciated about Ben. He did not brood and did not wear black. He liked golf and key lime pie. He was inventive in bed and happy about it afterward. He liked to think he was complex, but he really wasn't. Ben was cheerfully normal.

"I should attend to your plumbing more often," he said, pushing his hands into her back pockets and snugging her hips up against his.

"Uh-huh." she wriggled a little, wanting his hands back in motion.

"Just think if I'd actually found some drain crystals." He grinned. "Then you'd have to reward me for getting the job done."

Holly liked the mental picture of manly wrench action more than chemical warfare, but whatever. "Most people would want a self-fixing house," she teased. "More time to play."

Ben smiled, sort of. It was a rueful expression. "That would be a hotel. I like to handle problems myself. It's a guy thing."

There was nothing to say to that. Guy things were arguments she would lose, because she never quite got the rules. Instead she slipped her hands around his waist and under his sweater, warming them against the heat of his lean back. If he chose guy tactics, she could opt for feminine wiles.

He sucked a quick breath in through his teeth as her fingers skated up his spine. "Ow, you're cold." He broke the embrace.

"Sorry." She crossed her arms, feeling a little lost without his warm body to hold.

"I think you might have to call a real plumber. I'm out of time." He reached for his tweed jacket where it hung over the back of a chair. "I'm tutoring tonight."

The sink suddenly blurped and the water gurgled out. Ben turned and stared, his expression cross. With an abrupt gesture he ran water into the sink, rinsing out the leftover suds and then peering into the cupboard below to frown at the pipes. "Huh," he grunted. "I hate that. That's so creepy. It was completely stuck before."

She shrugged. "The house is like that. Never cleaned the gutters. Never had to unplug the perimeter drains. Never owned a caulking gun. You see, not all these houses are psycho killers."

Ben's face grew serious as he shrugged on his jacket. "I'll see you tomorrow. There're some condos going up by the waterfront we should look at."

Holly frowned in confusion. "What do you mean?"

His expression went tight. "I . . . um. I actually came here to show a Realtor around the place this afternoon."

Holly groped for the back of the chair behind her. "You *what*? Here?"

He looked at the floor. "Just to get an idea what this place might sell for. The location is great. It's got a good view. You could do really well."

"Ben, I'm not interested in selling. I want us to live here."

"She's going to crunch the numbers and fax me a suggested listing price tonight."

"Ben!"

"Holly, I can't be here. I hate sleeping over. It's too effing freaky."

"No, it's not!"

"I can't survive in your world."

"Oh, no," Holly breathed. "Don't do this."

He extended his hands in a placating gesture. "I've already put everything that was mine in the truck. That way it's all clean and simple if you don't want to hear this."

Holly's heart squeezed as if it were stopping. Every detail suddenly seemed too sharp. The soap bubbles in the drain. The folds of a dish towel. The scraped skin on Ben's knuckles. The clear, green hazel of his eyes. It was like sliding off a cliff in slow motion.

"I'm not giving up," he said. "But things have to change. I saw what happened last night. I saw the kind of pain you were in. How can I let you do that? You're dear to me. How can I not try to shelter you?"

"From what? My job?"

"Holly, you were screaming. I nearly died. What kind of a job is that?"

This was it. The difficult stuff the two of them never talked about. They had reached a crisis point if this was coming out of the box. Holly felt her mouth go dry as ash.

"Ben, I understand your concern, but it's no worse than what a fireman does. Policeman. Soldier. There're risky jobs out there. I just happen to have one of them."

"But why you?"

"Because I can."

"But do you *need* to do it?"

"There aren't too many people with my talents. I like to think I have something to offer."

"Is it so important that you risk everything for it?"

Holly felt her good judgment waver, like a glass wobbling on the edge of a table. "I saved your life last night, remember? Was that important?"

Ben looked away. He was biting back some barrage of words he knew she wouldn't like.

She felt a lance of anger so sharp it was almost beyond pain. "I *respect* what I do. It's who I am. It's important to me."

"I get that."

"Then maybe you should support me. Learn some simple spells. There're a few things humans can learn for basic self-protection. Then you might feel better about my world."

"No way. It frightens me," he said quietly. "I didn't think it would, but it does. You can do all this stuff I can't even comprehend."

"Get over it. You're an economist. Nobody understands you guys."

"Don't joke. Not now." He shoved his hands into his

pockets. "You grew up around power. You *have* so much power. I had no idea you people existed until a few years ago."

You people. How many groups through history had heard that phrase turned against them?

One shoulder hitched up, nearly touching his ear. The gesture was oddly boyish. "This new world is hard to get used to. I'm not comfortable being that close to so much magic."

Sleeping with it.

"I just can't compete. It's like suddenly being demoted down the food chain. I don't even understand why you want to be with someone like me, a plain, ordinary guy with no superpowers. It doesn't make sense." He shuffled his feet. "But if I don't see what you can do, I can forget about it. I can relax. That was working for me, but last night changed everything."

Holly hiccupped, a strangled sob dying in her throat. "Then you just noticed that I'm a witch? If that's the case, it can't be so very shocking."

Ben rallied. "That's just what I mean. We can sort this out with a little effort. I'll give notice at my place. You sell yours."

"Oh, no." Holly dropped her hands so they dangled uselessly at her sides. He wasn't hearing anything she said.

"Listen: We can start over together, be normal people someplace new. Someplace equal and fair. You can go to school. I can teach."

"Equal and fair?" Holly shot back. *You mean humans-only.*

He had the education, the money, and the rich relatives. They were nice, good, generous people, but they had so much. All she had was herself and her magic. They were one and the same. If she gave that up, small-M, big-M, or economy sized, nothing would be hers. Even the pain was precious, because it was her own.

Ben raised a hand, palm out. "No. Don't say anything. Just think about it. I'll call you tomorrow. Maybe we can have breakfast and talk it over."

"Sure," Holly replied, forcing her eyes open wide so she could hide the first threat of tears. "Breakfast would be great."

"Good." Ben kissed her one last time, a peck on the part of her hair. "Your hands are shaking."

Holly opened her mouth, closed it, pressed her fingers together. They were cold, but her cheeks burned red-hot. "Last night was hard on me, too."

"Of course it was." He gave her hand a quick squeeze. He smelled like soap and old wool, scents that reminded her of all the afternoons they had spent lying on the lawns of the campus. *I'd bring him lunch. We couldn't wait till the end of the day to see each other.*

He left, the back door clicking shut behind him.

Fear changed people.

Holly was panting, short, ineffective breaths. The house felt empty, all the lazy, lawn-sprawling afternoons, past and future, suddenly gone. *I saved his life. He saw what I could do. He freaked.*

Breakfast would never happen. Breakfast was a metaphor for avoidance. He'd forget to call. Something would come up. Not his fault. Didn't mean to. This was his way of making a graceful retreat.

It wasn't fair.

There was something dead in her chest where her emotions usually lived. In a while the pain would catch up with her.

Then it would hurt like hell.

Holly went upstairs, peeled off her clothes, and ran a hot bath. Her entire future had just been derailed. She deserved some comfort before figuring out her next steps.

Unobtrusive, Kibs followed her upstairs and curled up on the chair by the old claw-foot bathtub, there if she needed company. She added bubble bath to the running water until the foam reached the lip of the tub. Watching the steam condense and trickle down the high, narrow windows beneath the canted ceiling, she soaked.

It would have been pure and absolute bliss if her mind slowed down, but it didn't. One bad thought led to another.

First came the business. What had been a thriving family enterprise had dwindled to just Holly, the last Carver in the biz. Difficult jobs like necromancy made more money, but she was hobbled by pain. As a result, she had to work twice as hard at small, bread-and-butter contracts to make the agency pay. Insurance investigations. Lost pets. Imp exterminations. Over time it was exhausting.

It would have been different if she weren't alone, but her family was scattered. After Holly's parents died in a car accident, Grandma had raised her. Holly's sister had moved away when Holly was a child. Holly's half brother, born from her father's first marriage, had never been part of her life. That left her to carry on the family legacy by herself.

And now Ben had bailed, condemning the very heritage that defined her. Ben was wrong. Damaged or not, her power had come through and beaten the Flanders monstrosity. She had saved lives. *Go, me.*

She wished she felt as brave as that sounded.

The cat sat up, stretching, ears alert. He looked up at the ceiling, his great yellow eyes echoing the fading light. "Mrow," he commented in anxious tones.

She sat up with a slosh, probing the quiet house with her mind. What had alerted Kibs? She couldn't sense anything, but sitting in water mucked up her reception. Feeling paranoid, Holly got out of the tub and dried off. A flannel nightgown hung on the back of the door, left over from her last chick-flick mood. She pulled it over her head.

With her hair wrapped in a towel, they tiptoed down the hall, Kibs for once moving with the silence of a cat. Holly's damp feet left footprints on the hardwood. At the bottom of the stairs to the third floor, Holly hesitated, one hand on the newel post. *What's up there?*

She shouldn't have felt so worried. This was her self-cleaning house, a magical abode, the impervious Carver homestead. Yet her instincts had gone into the red zone.

Why? This is foolish. Nothing should be wrong. Calming

herself, she began to ascend. Kibs stayed close to her heels, his tail a bottle brush of angst.

Holly reached the upstairs landing before she felt it. Something barely tangible—the quality of the dusk, the air pressure—changed as if a door in the ether had opened. Her nerves tingled, the sensation of a zillion ants crawling over her skin and into her nose and mouth. Then the feeling stopped as the door shut again. A breathless moment passed. Kibs inflated to twice his size and hissed like a cappuccino machine.

The third-floor hall ran the length of the house. Mostly empty, the old bedchambers had just a few pieces of antique furniture gestating dust bunnies. The middle room on the left side of the hall was the nursery, and from that doorway spilled a pool of pale light.

There were no lamps in that room.

Crap. Holly took a step forward, Kibs tracking her movement like a furry ankle bracelet. The sodden towel in her hair, warm and wet, listed with the motion until she pulled it off, releasing a mass of long, dark, dripping tendrils down her back. With the towel clutched to her chest like a security blanket, Holly scuttled forward until she could see into the room.

Kibs was down the stairs with a wild scrabbling of claws, his scampering backside flashing white in the dusk. Holly's breath catching in her throat, she turned her head to the nursery door. Her jaw fell open. What she saw was Kibs's worst nightmare.

Mice were cute when they were little. When they were six feet long, hostile, and glowing, they lost their appeal. But, hey, it wasn't slime.

The dirty white creature spotted her and snarled. Its whiskers, thick and sharp like coat hanger wire, quivered and fanned out as it bared fangs as long as her shin. Its rump went up in the air like Kibs's before he pounced. This was going to be short and painful. She took two gulps of air and tried to stop the short, sharp gasps of her breath. *Think!*

After the fight with the hell house, her magic was all but

fried. What she could summon would have to be conserved, used for a single killing blow. She'd try something else first.

Holly beamed happy thoughts with every psychic muscle. "Hi, sweetie," she cooed.

Sweetie hissed, scummy yellow teeth thrust out, mouse spit spewing across the hallway carpet. Something in the slow, snakelike motion of its tail was lascivious, wrong. It snarled again, a ghastly, openmouthed rattle. She was so screwed. In some bizarre homage to Douglas Adams and his *Hitchhiker's Guide*, all she had to work with was a towel.

Holly flung it. *"Terry eleison!"* she cried, making the spell up on the spot.

The towel left her hand, spreading as it flew. Heavy with water from her hair, it landed flat across the mouse's snout with a smack. Holly tried to run. She tripped and fell on the hem of her gown, but hauled herself up, ripping the cotton as she scrambled to her feet. No wonder superheroes wore unitards.

Sweetie was up on its hind legs again, clawing at the magically adhering towel with swipes of its forepaws. Holly backed up and into the hallway. Frustrated and blind, the mouse fell forward, cracking its head loudly on the old oak door frame. It shrieked with rage, a sound like torquing metal.

The tail lashed forward, bullwhip-fast, and caught Holly's ankle. She barely felt its touch until it snapped tight, searing her bare skin in its coils. It burned like acid.

Screaming at the pain, Holly shot whatever energy she could muster. It was enough to smack Sweetie on the nose. The tail released with a slithering noise and Holly scrambled away, smelling her own burned flesh.

The tail came at her again, but she was watching for it. Holly was running out of the hallway. Still blinded, the mouse lunged forward one more time. Holly ran, skidded, and stumbled down the stairs, clinging to the heavy banister.

Sweetie scrambled after.

Halfway down, Holly grabbed the rail and swung her legs over, the same way she had as a kid. A cracking sound snapped the air as her feet left the stair treads, but the old wood held. With a whoop of terror, Holly dropped to the floor on the other side and landed with a gasp, sprawling on her hands and knees.

"Terry eleison!" she spat, her voice barely above a whisper in her fright. With the last of her power she delivered another shock to the towel.

Sweetie, startled, blind, finding no purchase with its claws, tumbled down the stairs and landed in a limp heap. Somewhere on the way down, it broke its neck. The mouse thing lay silent for a moment before shivering and dissolving into nothing, small particles powdering away to thin air.

What the hell?

Jumping to her feet, Holly gaped at the empty space a few seconds, sweat beading over her cold, trembling skin. Her ankle burned, but the heat was fading now. The other pain, the aftershock of magic, throbbed like a full-body bruise.

With glacial slowness, she approached the spot where the mouse had fallen, her bare toes shrinking away from where it had touched the floor. No hint of its presence. No trace. No shred.

A door slammed upstairs. Holly started, but felt a new surge of angry bravado. Racing up the stairs, she froze on the top step. The nursery door had shut. There was a whispering sound—not voices, but something feathery. It was a sound she knew of old, one of the house's familiar noises. The place was healing itself.

The thought that there had been something to heal burned in her brain. What was going on? What had just happened? Hiccuping in fright, Holly ran down the stairs and into the bathroom. She tore through the pile of clothes on the floor, scrabbling for her phone.

The first speed dial on the phone was Ben's. She rejected his number with barely a thought, and not just because he was magi-phobic these days. This wasn't the sort of emergency that could be solved with a pie chart and a tax lawyer. With shaking fingers, she punched a button.

"Caravelli," came the familiar voice at the other end of the line.

"It's Holly."

There was a micropause. "What's wrong?"

His voice held an edge of intent, as if she had his complete attention. She blessed him for it. He was there when it counted.

"Pardon me for asking this," he went on, "but do you have the hiccups?"

Her thoughts suddenly went sideways, like a stack of books tumbling into disarray. "You have to come help me," she said. "I killed a mouse, and it was awful!"

Chapter 9

It took Holly twenty minutes to pull herself together and put on some clothes. She was too rattled to bother with makeup or drying her hair. *So what? In a choice between the fashionistas and Mousezilla, I try to be practical. Low heels every time.*

By then Alessandro was at the door, waiting for his invitation to enter.

Straight from the pages of *Gentleman Goth* magazine, he sported lean black jeans, a black turtleneck, and boots of heavy, silver-studded black leather. A bandolier was slung across his chest, supporting a connoisseur's collection of small weaponry—stakes, knives, and, at his hip, a tightly coiled bullwhip. All he lacked was Fangorella at his feet, fondling his thigh and swooning with terror and desire.

Okay, thought Holly as he strode across the threshold in a swirl of testosterone and leather coat. *He's feeling his inner Prince of Darkness.*

Holly, on the other hand, wore fuzzy pink mule slippers, her wet hair soaking through her sweater. She felt about as sexy as a dust mop.

"Hot date?" she asked, eyeing the whip. "Or do you really hate mice?" *Macmillan is right: I have no idea what he does with his spare time.*

"More like a bad reunion," he said, looking around. It was the first time he had been in her house.

He produced a paper bag from the pocket of his coat. "I was on my way out when you called, but I stopped by the hardware store for you." He extracted a bargain-priced mousetrap from the bag. His expression held nuances of manly exasperation, as if he expected her to shriek and leap onto a table at the first sign of a rodent.

She could have slugged him. Holly closed her eyes and concentrated on breathing for a full ten seconds. "That's very kind, but I think if this mouse's brother turns up, I'll need something a bit larger."

His sensitive-guy face—a stretch for a vampire to begin with—grew a tad condescending. "Was it a rat? How big was it?"

She held a hand over her head. Comprehension dawned, and the smug look faded from Alessandro's eyes. "I see," he said, putting the mousetrap away. "That's different. I apologize."

She decided to let him live. "I felt the doorway this thing used open and close. It came through in the nursery."

Alessandro shook his head, confused. "Say that again?"

"Apparently there's some portal activity going on in town."

"There was a portal *here*?" Panic cracked the last word.

"Yeah," said Holly. "Where else would I get a six-foot mouse?"

He gripped her hand. "And you say it came through? It was not just a portal trying to open—something actually entered?"

"It was solid until I killed it. Real enough to give me this." She pulled up the leg of her jeans to show the burn from the creature's tail.

Alessandro knelt and touched the skin. "Is it fading?"

His cool fingers felt good, bringing back all the sensations from their kiss the night before. Shivers rippled up her skin as he explored the burn, tracing the bones of her ankle with a featherlight touch. As he worked his way around, the shivers became burgeoning warmth. Holly's breath grew uneven.

Now was not the time to remember how good he tasted. In reality, that time would never exist. A regretful sigh caught halfway into Holly's chest, aching. "Yeah, the burn looked a lot worse before."

He sat back on his heels, running a hand through his long blond curls. "You're lucky it didn't get a good grip. That should be healed by morning." He looked around. "Show me the room where it attacked."

Holly led the way upstairs, filling in the details of her encounter with Sweetie. When they got to the third floor her feet froze on the top stair. Suddenly cold and nauseated, she wavered, anxiety rising up like a bad meal. There was no presence there, just memories—but they were bad enough. *That thing came into my home. This isn't like any other job. It's personal.*

One step behind, Alessandro prodded her to move so he could push past to the hallway. Holly felt the brush of his heavy, soft coat and yearned to clutch it like a child with a security blanket.

"That room is the nursery?" Alessandro asked, almost straining like a hound on point. "It's a traditionalist, then. Demons like the symbolism of devouring the innocent almost as much as the feast itself."

"Great. Lovely." Holly mounted the last step. "Are you sure it was a demon?"

"Good odds it was." He laid his hand on her back, comforting, but still intense. He was in hunting mode. "Let's see what your visitor left behind."

All confidence, he pushed the nursery door open with one hand. Holly sidled up behind him. The room was empty, infuriatingly normal. She had a flash of that honest-the-car-sounded-terrible-before-I-brought-it-in feeling. *Really, there was a giant mouse here, sir, tha-a-a-at tall.*

With long, smooth strides, Alessandro drifted in a slow circle around the perimeter of the room, stopping before the old fireplace. "It came in here," he announced, tapping the wall above the mantel. "The smell is strongest where I'm standing."

"It came down the chimney?" Holly asked, incredulous. She giggled. *Okay, I'm getting punchy.*

"As it was a portal, it would be more *through* than *down*, but yes, it came via the chimney."

"That's just . . . absurd!"

Alessandro looked at her, his eyebrows making a perplexed furrow. "I assure you it did."

Holly tried to envision the mouse stuffing itself down the flue. Bad image. Her overstressed imagination added eight tiny reindeer. "Well, yuck. I guess I can't expect Santa to come through there again."

Alessandro gave her a confused look. "What? Santa Claus doesn't exist."

"Does too. He brought me a plush unicorn when I was six."

Alessandro raised a brow. "Do you think if I ask for an Aston Martin Vanquish, he'll bring me one?"

"I doubt you've been quite that good."

He huffed and turned back to the wall, but the absurd exchange had defused some tension. Now Holly came forward to see the site of the offense. With her witch's senses open just a crack, she touched the spot of wall he had identified. It was like plunging her hand into a nest of ants.

"I can feel it. It's all creepy-crawly." She shuddered and pulled back. "The barrier is still weak there. But the seal is healing. In an hour or two it will be sound."

"Amazing." Alessandro looked around the room. "This is a marvelous house, so alive. So full of your family's magic."

"Ben would sell it if he could."

"What?"

"Never mind," she replied in a tone that did not invite discussion. Holly didn't want to talk about Ben at the moment. It was too raw to even think about right then. Or ever. Tears blurred her lashes, and she turned her face away to hide them.

"The Carvers were necromancers, weren't they?" Alessandro asked, something tentative in the question.

"Some were. In her day, my grandma was really good. But you lived here then. You'd know that."

He avoided her look. "Have you ever done a necromancy spell?"

"Know the theory, seen it done, but I've never tried it myself. I just go to the mall if I want to see the brain-dead lurching around. Is there a reason you ask?"

Alessandro didn't reply. Instead he folded his arms and stared into the empty fire grate. It was dim in the room, and his face was only half-lit, but she could make out his features. With his thoughts turned inward, he looked more human.

Holly waited him out, wondering what he wanted.

Finally, when he spoke, the topic was new. "The manifestation here is from the same origin as the disturbance at the Flanders house. That explains why the Flanders place was so strong. It wasn't just a bad house. It had demonic assistance."

Holly's mouth went dry. "How do you know this?"

"It smells the same. The stink clings to the back of the tongue."

"That's the basis of your theory?"

"And logic. The demon—or whoever summoned it—was trying to harness the magic in the Flanders house to open a portal. Vanquishing the house closed it again. Now it tried here. The demon must be getting stronger, or the summoner more proficient, because it worked."

"It was just a big mouse," she said, giving a nervous laugh. "I don't think they got what they ordered."

Alessandro didn't look convinced. "What happened to the mouse, exactly?"

Holly swallowed. "I helped it fall down the stairs. I think it broke its neck."

Alessandro looked bleak. "What did the mouse look like when it died?"

"Kinda still."

His eyebrows contracted in annoyance. "After that?"

"It disintegrated into powder as it disappeared."

Alessandro lifted his chin a fraction, his brows lowering. "Certain kinds of demons will crumble and vanish without necessarily being dead. It's their way of escape. You might have chased it off, but I don't think you killed it. Our demon finally made it through the portal."

"Whoa!" cried Holly, holding up one hand. "Hold it right there! That mouse was an actual demon? Wasn't this just, like, a calling card, a trailer for the main show, but not the demon itself? Wasn't it sort of, um, demon mouse–mail?"

"I don't think so, Holly. Demons often take the form of rodents or serpents because those shapes inspire fear and disgust. It's also easier than assuming their human form. Easier after using all their strength to break through."

Holly turned away, walking to the window. Outside, the streetlights backlit the branches of the oak tree. "Not possible. This house can't be breached."

"Of course it can," he replied quietly, "because it was."

"Why come here? Why attack me?"

"Because you're powerful. Think about it. You beat it last night. To a demon, your soul would look, oh, so good to eat—full of magic it could take for its own."

"Oh, crap." Holly covered her face, dread coming in hot and cold waves, drenching her skin with a prickling sweat. "Sweet Hecate, I need a moment to take this in."

"Let's go downstairs." He touched her shoulder gently and left the nursery.

Holly trailed after him, listening to the echo of her footfalls drift through the empty spaces of the old house. *A demon? Here?*

In the bright kitchen Kibs sat by his food dish, watching the vampire with a judicial air, tail twitching. Holly shuffled up to the kitchen table and sat, hugging herself. The clock in the sitting room chimed nine o'clock. Time flies when you're battling the forces of darkness.

"I know some demon lore, but books don't cover everything. So explain again why I look so good to a demon."

Alessandro took a seat opposite her and folded his arms, a classic posture of unease. "The authors of your books would never have access to a full range of information. We have had more direct contact because often we battle for territory. We are enemies for the most primitive of reasons:

We hunt the same victims. They feed on human life, the soul, the essence, in much the same way a vampire feeds on blood."

Holly mirrored his arm-folded slouch. "Okay."

"Most major demons," he went on, "live in a society that would make any marketing agency proud. Their power structure is a pyramid. The top demon has minions, or servants. Once a demon servant has enough power, it might start to collect minions of its own, and one day those servants will have servants, and on and on."

"And the demon at the top of the pyramid just gets bigger and badder the more servants and subservants and subsubservants it has? Eventually it gets a Cadillac and a timeshare condo in outer Hades?"

"Precisely. And you, being more than usually powerful, would feed your master better than any ordinary servant. Turning you would be quite a coup. It would move our demon right up the corporate ladder."

Holly cleared her throat. "So this is an up-and-coming demon?"

Alessandro shook his head. "More than that. Only a master could cross over. That means it's already powerful and must have some servants helping it." Alessandro's hand drifted toward his bandolier. "Not even a master can come to our world without help."

Holly felt a slither of suspicion. "And you were going to ask those servants out to play tonight, weren't you?"

"Yes, I was going to join some other vampires who are searching Fairview."

"For what?"

"Possible servants. I saw something last night."

"Another dead body you neglected to mention?"

Alessandro looked away, his face creasing with something between guilt and annoyance. "No. A couple of creatures we call changelings. I killed them, but we would like to be sure there are no more. They may well have been the ones murdering young students."

"Okay, wait." Holly held up her hands, palms out. "One, you're telling me a demon popped out of my chimney. Two, it's planning to eat me. Three, it has local servants that you and your vampire pals are going to go hunting tonight. Have I got this straight?"

Alessandro gave a single nod.

She leaned forward, terror grinding deep in her gut. "So how come you know all this and I don't? A heads-up would've been nice!"

His face tightened. "I did not know about the changelings until late last night. There was yet another portal—they might have been connected to it somehow, or not. I'm not sure. Events are moving fast. I was hoping most of this would be just vampire business I could take care of on my own."

Holly's eyes widened with frustration. "Like the extra body at the Flanders house yesterday? Coulda warned me she was there before Detective Macmillan had me trying to rat you out. What the hell was I supposed to say?"

He waved an exasperated hand. "I came back to talk to you, but we got sidetracked, if you recall."

Holly felt herself flush at the memory. "Yeah, right. I'm such a good kisser you forgot you just found a corpse. C'mon, there's a vampire murdering women on campus. I'm starting school on Monday. Any information gratefully accepted."

Dismay pulled at Alessandro's face. He circled the table and crouched next to her chair. "I would never let anything happen to you. I'm your friend, remember? But I'm also . . . what I am. Don't ever kiss me like that and expect me to pass a sobriety test. I really had to leave, for both our sakes."

Uncertainty wrenched her. "You still could have phoned."
Goddess, I sound like a lovelorn teenager.

He looked down. "You're right. I'm sorry. There was a lot going on, but I could have done that much. If it makes you feel any better, I spoke with the police earlier tonight." His expression said how little he had enjoyed the conversation. "They won't bother you again. I told them what they needed to know."

The anger was shrinking to pique. "Yeah, well, you can't

be with me twenty-four seven. I need to be able to look out for myself. I'm a witch. If you give me the facts, I can deal."

Alessandro looked at her sharply, his curiosity a physical force. "Can you? Since we're sharing information, there's something I need to know. Battling that house last night put you flat on your back. Why is—how do you put it?—big-M magic so painful for you?"

Holly turned her face away, suddenly hating the fact that he was so near. She rose from the other side of her chair, got a glass out of the cupboard and started filling it from the tap. "My sister and I, we had an accident."

She said it flatly, as if it didn't matter, but the water jigged in the glass. Alessandro got up and took it from her hand, setting it on the counter. "What were you and your sister doing?"

"You have vampire business. That accident is my business."

He touched her cheek. "If that's the way you want it."

It wasn't. It hurt to argue. Breath caught, jagged, in Holly's throat. "It's not something I like talking about, okay? My ability is what puts food on the table. Something like this could be a career killer."

"I can keep your secret."

Holly nodded, feeling the ache of tears. "My sister and I played around with spells when I was quite young. One blew up in our faces. She never did magic after that. I wasn't hurt as badly, but it seems to have fried something inside me."

"Was there ever a diagnosis of the injury?"

"No, nothing anyone could explain, or so I'm told. I don't really remember that whole year. Huge memory loss. It's like something carved out that little bit of my brain."

"Trauma? An injury?"

"I guess. Grandma had every doctor and psychologist available have a look. They thought it was something to do with the fact that my parents died right around the same time. With the accident on top of all that, it was just too many shocks for a kid to take in all at once."

"Repressed memory?"

"Who knows? Witches never follow the textbook models,

or so they told us a hundred million times." Holly didn't want to talk about it anymore.

As if he read her mind, he crossed to the liquor cabinet, pulling the doors open wide. "Water is inadequate. What do you drink?"

"Scotch, neat," she said automatically.

He smirked. "A warrior woman."

"What do you want? It's been a bad couple of days," she said in a testy voice.

He poured and handed her a glass with a generous measure of amber liquid. "Drink this, and then go to bed. You could do with an early night."

"What, with Demon Mousie on the loose?" She took a sip of the liquid fire, then set the glass down. "Shouldn't I go someplace else? Or would it find me anyway?"

Alessandro leaned forward and took her hand. His fingers were cool and competent. "The demon will be long gone by now. These creatures typically move away from their point of entry and go in search of a fresh hunting ground. Nothing more will happen in the house tonight." He squeezed her fingers and released them. "Nevertheless, I'll make doubly sure we're alone. I'll check every corner and cupboard and watch over you while you rest."

"Weren't you going to go hunting?"

He gave a slow, wry smile, sweet enough to melt any woman. She'd never seen that smile before, and it nearly stalled her heart. "You're more important," he said.

He bent and kissed her brow, as he had before, but did not stop there. His lips caressed her eyelids and slid down to sip, just once, at her mouth. The simple gesture held all the finesse of a skilled lover. Centuries of skill.

Her flesh tingled at his touch, part magic, part pure desire. A need to drown in it roused a soft moan from her throat. She felt his long, supple fingers slide up the side of her neck, resting in the hollow beneath her ear. Her heart seized at the touch, her knees shivering with the need to feel his lips where his fingertips caressed her jaw. Through her lashes she saw the yellow glint in his eyes.

Predator.

Alarm thrilled through her. Holly slid her own hand up, clasping his and pulling it away. "No. Stop, before I can't say no. *Please.*"

"Don't worry," Alessandro said softly, taking one last kiss. "I know what I can't have. I'm on my guard with you now."

He backed away, the space between them empty oceans. Holly's limbs felt heavy, red hot, so she picked up her drink to avoid his eyes. Perhaps Alessandro knew what he couldn't have, but her body wasn't on board with abstinence.

But Holly couldn't push her luck. After all, she had the most to lose if Alessandro fell off the wagon. *Killer houses, vampires, demons. Sweet Hecate, I have so many bad ends in store, I'm going to have to rent a locker.*

That reminded her of something she meant to ask. "You said the demon would want to Turn me. What exactly did you mean by that? Is it different from . . ."

He did not answer immediately, his smile fading like slowly dying light. He understood what she meant. *Than when a vampire Turns you.*

"It is worse. Much worse. They call it the Dark Larceny. Most demons start out human." Alessandro looked away. "They consume your soul and make you one of them. A nothing. A negative."

There was such dread in his voice, she shuddered. "Have you seen it done?"

His face drained of color, suddenly pasty beyond his already pale complexion. "Yes," was all he would say.

Chapter 10

"Hey, Brian." Macmillan sat down at the bar, suddenly ravenous. He hadn't had a decent meal in days.

"Hey, Mac. What's up?" asked the bartender. He was tall and stocky and somewhere in his forties, still fit enough to take care of business if one of the clients got rowdy.

The Bayshore Pub formed one end of the strip mall across from St. Andrew's cemetery. It was Mac's favorite because it was close to the police station and there was always parking. Most days that was all he had the time or energy to consider.

"How are ya?" Brian asked.

"Busy."

"I hear ya."

Macmillan looked glumly at the rows of beer glasses on the bar. Nothing went with the fourth murder in two weeks like draft Guinness. Unfortunately, a sandwich and coffee would have to do. It was back to work after he grabbed something to eat.

"Kitchen closed yet?" he asked.

Brian looked at his watch. "Just under the wire."

Thank you, God. "I'll have the steak sandwich. Medium-rare."

"Fries?"

"Nah." His stomach was a little off. Extra grease was pushing his luck.

Macmillan unbuttoned his raincoat, wondering if that was raindrops or something left over from the latest murder scene along the hem. It was hard to tell. The pub was only slightly better lit than the parking lot.

With weary inevitability, his mind went back to the scene. It had been another college coed. Another blonde. Preliminary estimates on the time of death put it at around four thirty.

Which meant that Caravelli was in the clear, for all that he'd vanished from the Flanders scene. Mac had put surveillance on him and checked his whereabouts for the first murders. His alibis were good. One of his colleagues had even finally managed to question Caravelli right after sunset, arriving on the vamp's doorstep with a pair of uniforms. Apparently Caravelli had been civil but as forthcoming as the grave.

Why was it that all vampires had that jerk-off attitude? Sure, he'd saved Mac from whatever the hell those things were last night, but that didn't make him the bloody Fanged Avenger. Vamps were the same as everyone else. Eternal life didn't make a person anything besides old. The real value lay in what you did with all that time. As far as he could tell, most immortals wasted that opportunity on internal politics and fashion crimes.

"Here ya go." Brian set a mug of coffee in front of Mac. No cream, no sugar. Like all good bartenders, Brian remembered these things.

"Thanks."

"Food won't be long."

"Great." The coffee smelled like nirvana. *That* was what life was. Little things like good coffee, and a place where people knew how you liked it. He sipped gratefully. Vampires might get immortality, but look at their diet. What kind of a bargain was that?

Mac took another sip.

Tonight's body had been found in the wine cellar of the university's Faculty Club. No sunlight ever got down there, so a vampire could have done it despite the early hour. The neck wounds, the bruising, the positioning of the body had been the same. This one had a metal disk in her hand. The only one who hadn't was the one in the Flanders house, which made him think that somehow it got lost. What were those disks, anyway? A religious thing?

He took another swallow of Brian's strong coffee. He could feel his body groping for the caffeine. The only good point to this latest death was that the brass doubled the manpower on the case, which meant Mac finally got to take a break long enough for a hot meal, his first in three—or was it four?—days. He knew he shouldn't be sitting on his backside, stuffing his face, but he needed real food if he was going to pull another all-nighter. Unlike other players in this fiasco, he was only human.

Mac missed his partner, who was on maternity leave. Without her nagging to look after himself, he'd let work grind him down to the survival basics. Food. Clean clothes. He only vaguely remembered the concept of taking time out for himself. *I used to cook for fun. I was really, really good. And when was the last time I talked to a woman about something besides dead bodies?*

Too bad that Holly Carver had a boyfriend. She was everything: smart, pretty, brave, and she had that *something* that let a person know that if she was in their corner, she was there one hundred percent.

"See any of the game?" Brian asked, jerking his head at the silent big screen TV.

Mac looked up. "Not so far. Flyers winning?"

Brian grunted in disgust, rattling glasses.

Mac started in on the bowl of junk food on the bar. He'd never used to be able to eat after a murder scene, but after the first dozen, his body finally took over.

A woman came in and sat down at a corner table. Mac looked because, well, he was busy, not dead. Plus, she looked like the murder victims: blond, pretty, and barely legal. Mac kept an eye on her via the mirror over the bar.

The waitress sauntered over to the girl's table. The girl ordered while the sound system cranked out a hard rock standard. Aerosmith, maybe? Not the pub's usual sound track, but Mac liked it. He needed something kick-ass.

"Hey, there, Suki," he said as the waitress passed by on her way to key the order into the computer.

"Hi, Mac." Suki stopped, thrusting out one hip and tilting her head, which caused the lime green spikes in her hair to list like the rigging of a capsizing schooner. "Chickie over there says if you're gonna watch her all night you may as well join her."

Mac raised his eyebrows. "Oh, yeah?"

"Yeah." Suki gave a cheerful leer. "Your fairy godmother granted you a wish. Don't make me jealous, eh?"

Mac looked down at himself. He liked clothes and tried to dress well, so outside of the possible bloodstains, he was presentable.

"You're gorgeous, Gorgeous." Suki slapped him gently on the side of the head.

"Gotta serve and protect," Mac said with equal cheer, sliding off the bar stool.

The girl was sitting in the darkest corner of the bar—the only light was a candle in a cheap glass dish—but he could tell his first impression had been correct. She was stunning, shapely, and dressed to show it off in a dark, off-the-shoulder sweater. Her face was model beautiful, with high cheekbones and almond-shaped eyes of stormy gray. Her hair was straight, blond, and hung past her elbows. Once, Mac had worked security for a movie set and seen some of the Hollywood lookers. This girl blew them all out of the water.

"Hi," he said, sitting down. That put his back to the door, which he hated, but this once he'd make an exception.

The girl smiled. "I'm Jenny."

"I'm Mac."

Suki was back, setting a fancy coffee—the kind with a mountain of whipped cream—in front of Jenny. Definitely not a model, then, with all that calorie-rich whip.

Then Suki set a pint of Guinness in front of Mac. She leaned close, putting her lips next to his ear. "On the house, hound dog."

Mac laughed as Suki sailed away, green spikes lurid in the pot lights.

Good things like this just don't happen to me. An odd tingling in his stomach—something between hunger and anticipation—made him squirm on the vinyl-padded chair. *Jenny, eh?* An old-fashioned name. Nice. He wanted to devour her with his mouth, with his eyes, with his lovemaking.

"The server seems to think you need congratulating," Jenny said. She sounded almost formal, the way he remembered the supersmart girls in English lit class used to talk.

"I think I do. In the last sixty seconds I've gone from lonely man at the bar to man at a table with a lovely lady. And a beer." Even if he was on duty and couldn't drink it.

"What are you hoping for in the next minute?"

"Dinner. I'm a simple man. How about you?"

"I don't know. Company, I suppose."

"You've got that."

"And you have your food. The star of our fortunes sails to its zenith."

Okay, she's read waaay too much Shakespeare. But Mac was distracted by the arrival of his steak sandwich, still sizzling from the grill. "Aren't you eating?"

"Not yet, but you go ahead."

He did, his mouth watering in anticipation of thc garlic pepper sauce. As he chewed, she snitched a slice of pickle from the edge of his plate and popped it into her mouth. There was a kittenish mischief in the gesture, as if she were bad but knew he would forgive her.

He watched the deliberate naughtiness, idly wondering where it might lead. She grinned, and he was caught by the way the candlelight shone on her perfectly formed teeth. And the perfectly smooth skin in the low neckline of her sweater. That was one fine neckline.

Having finished with the pickle, she took a sip of her cream-topped coffee, then made a face. "Not a good taste combination."

She licked the white cream froth from her lips with the tip of a tiny, pink tongue. A dusting of sugar had fallen from the rim of her cup into the hollow between her breasts, and all Mac could think of was taking his own tongue to that softly sculpted region.

"Hold still." He picked up his napkin and dabbed at a smudge of cream at the corner of her mouth. She tipped up her face, studying him from under lowered lashes.

"You have lovely manners," she said, then dipped her finger into the cream. She licked it off, her tongue swiping around the neatly rounded nail. "Are you proposing to make me presentable with each sip?"

"There are worse ways to spend an evening, honey," Mac replied, "but I'll need something better than a paper napkin for the job."

"Not a good napkin if it can't handle a bit of cream." She took another sip, the rich froth clinging to her lips. She looked like a greedy little girl.

"I am sure you can, uh, encourage it to keep its shape."

She caught his gaze and held it for a long moment.

"You use this pickup routine often?" Mac asked.

One corner of her mouth curled up in a salacious quirk. "Why not? It works."

Every instinct Mac had screamed that Jenny was trouble, but *wow.* He couldn't help wondering whether she had any solicitation arrests. Vice might know.

She did the dip-and-lick routine again, that same circular swipe of her tongue over the nail. His eyes fixed on her lips closing around the dollop of cream. Mac loosened his tie and cleared his throat. What was the matter with him? He'd forgotten about his sandwich, and he had to get back to work. He looked at his watch. Then he looked at Jenny.

Man, I've been a good boy way too long. I so need to have some time off.

"I can see you have to leave," she said sadly. "And we've not even had a chance to talk."

"Duty calls."

"This late at night?"

"I'm a cop," he said, waiting for the inevitable golly-I'll-pay-those-parking-tickets face.

She merely lifted one eyebrow. "What kind of cop?"

"Right now I'm working homicides."

"Fancy that," she said. "Can I call you? You're clearly busy now, but maybe later?"

"Oh, yeah," he said quickly, whipping out his card.

He held it out to her, but she grabbed his tie like a handle and, half rising, leaned across the table to plant a hard kiss on his lips. Her mouth was sweet with sugar and cream, but there was urgency in her tongue, as if he were the meal she had come for. He could feel her teeth crease the tender flesh inside his lower lip, and a sudden trickle of blood.

Mac thought he might have gasped. He wasn't a hearts-and-flowers kinda guy, but even he liked to warm up his engines first.

And then the burn started, somewhere near the backs of his knees. A wave of heat crawled up his body, arousing the flesh as it came, then leaving it exhausted as it passed.

A ripple of life passed from his mouth to hers. It was an orgasm of taking, with nothing of sowing. He shuddered, as if the icy finger of the Reaper had slithered up his spine. Mac fell back in his chair, all but paralyzed. His heart was pounding light and fast, like a bird beating its wings against a window, doing its damnedest to escape.

Jenny stood, and for the first time he really saw her clothes. She wore a skirt and sweater, but they were shabby and didn't quite fit. He knew the look. Stolen. Maybe stolen off the dead.

She dumped a handful of loose change on the table without counting it.

"I'll call you," she said, edging out from behind the table. Her manner was natural, just an old friend saying good-bye till next time.

Next time? No effing way! He couldn't move, either held by some unseen force or else too weak to turn and watch as she pushed open the door and left. He felt the blast of air on his cheek as rain-soaked wind blew in from the parking lot. Then the door clunked shut.

Mac drew in a long, shaking breath, now finding he could drag himself upright in his chair. His head felt too large, inflated to a hyperalert awareness of his surroundings.

How had she done that? What the hell was she?

With horror, he felt the pricking of frightened tears. *Get a grip!*

And then suddenly his appetite was back, and he dove at his sandwich with Cro-Magnon table manners. The bun had gone soggy, but he didn't care. The food filled his universe, the only important act making sure he devoured every last scrap.

He started as Suki appeared at his elbow.

"So," she chirped, "you guys gonna hook up and have some fun?"

"I sure as hell hope not," he said, his mouth full. He took a long swig of the forbidden Guinness.

Suki fingered her nose ring. "Huh. Yeah, I hate dating, too."

Chapter 11

When well-meaning people say romantic train wrecks will look better in the morning, they lie. Ben was gone, and so was the future Holly had planned with him.

She turned off the shower and groped for a towel. Blotting her face dry, Holly looked in the mirror. She looked drawn, her eyes puffy from crying in her sleep. It was bad enough feeling like something scraped from the back of the vegetable crisper; she hated looking the part as well.

There was nothing she could do. Someday she would meet a man who didn't mind a little witch in his woman. Or a lot of witch. With a giant demon mouse stalking her. *So the demon problem is a buzz kill. We all have flaws.* In defiance, she dressed in a skintight scarlet sweater that used to drive Ben wild.

Used to. She repeated it several times, trying to get accustomed to the past tense.

Reality waited outside the bedroom door, but it was kinder than she expected. The smell of fresh coffee, warm and bittersweet, hung in the air. *Coffee? Is Alessandro still here?*

"Hello?" Holly called as she walked into the kitchen.

Curled up by his food dish like a fat, tabby basketball, Kibs meowed a greeting. There were still scraps of food in the bowl, a telltale sign that he had conned breakfast out of Alessandro. She looked around. The coffeemaker hissed as condensing steam dripped onto the hot plate. The sound was as comforting as lambskin slippers, but she was clearly alone.

Of course. It was daylight. Vampires were tucked safely in their beds. She got a mug from the cupboard and poured a hit of caffeine. A note was propped against the toaster. Steam rose from the mug, ghosting before the slanting letters.

> *6:30 a.m. All clear, quiet night.*
> *I will call you at dusk. Stay safe.*

Alessandro had stayed until nearly dawn. As he had promised, he'd watched over her through the night. A twinge grew in Holly's chest, a mixture of gratitude and sadness. He deserved more than she could ever give him. Holly set the note down slowly.

Stay safe. How was she going to swing that?

Picking up the cordless phone, Holly grabbed a coat and took her coffee onto the back deck. She stood a while, leaning on the wide railing and feeling the comforting presence of the house and yard.

Spiderwebs shone like a scatter of silver thread. Still rolling in from the sea, the fog hid the fence, blurring the pine trees with smudges of gray. Marigolds burned like sudden fires. Familiarity didn't make the scene any less beautiful. It was part of her, where she drew her strength. She could never give up her house. *Never, ever.*

Holly propped her chin in her hand. Kibs came out and leaped onto the deck railing, curling up near her elbow. Fuzzy comfort. She sipped the coffee, holding it on her tongue a moment before swallowing. It tasted stale from sitting too long, but Alessandro had made it strong, the way she liked it.

Stay safe. Good advice, if a little short on detail. Ultimately she had to take responsibility for her own safety. Alessandro could do only so much. Besides, Holly had her own weapon—magic. Pain or no pain, it was up to her to take care of business. No excuses.

However, self-reliance did not exclude asking for advice from someone who'd bagged her share of monsters. She thumbed one of the speed dials on the phone.

"Hey, Grandma," she said.

"Holly, is that you?" Grandma's voice was rough with decades of chain smoking, a vice she saw no point in giving up at this late date. After two hip replacements, she wasn't going to be running any marathons, anyway.

"Yeah, it's me. I need your sage advice. Can I bribe you with a treat from the Harvest Sheaf?"

"Maybe. What's the problem?"

"Demons. I need to spruce up the house's defenses. A lot."

"How much is a lot?" Suspicion and alarm crackled out of the receiver.

Holly gripped her cup. "Mega a lot. I need to work some serious protection spells."

"What happened?"

"It's too long to explain over the phone. Can I come over?"

There was a long pause. "Like that, eh? Bring cinnamon rolls." Holly heard the flick of Grandma's lighter and a quick breath as she lit another cigarette. "Double frosting. Wisdom of the ancients doesn't come cheap."

For a supervised care facility, the Golden Swans was nice, and Grandma liked having her own space. She had lived in the Carver house while Holly grew up, and that was long enough for both of them. Grandma deplored Holly's lackadaisical housekeeping, and Holly hated her grandmother's smoking.

Holly took the elevator to the east tower, where the semi-independent-living apartments were grouped around the common rooms. When she got to Grandma's door, she picked up the daily paper where it had been left outside, bundled with an elastic band.

"Grandma?" She opened the door and poked her head in. "Hello?" Her eyes scanned the pin-neat interior.

"Come on in."

Holly entered, blinking a little from the cigarette fog. Grandma was in the kitchen, carefully spooning loose tea into a teapot. Her hair was pulled back in a long gray ponytail, showing off the strong bones of her face. Once plump, she had thinned down to a healthy weight but still gave the impression of solidity. She was dressed in a blue fleece ensemble with a sparkly gargoyle across the front.

Holly kissed her cheek. "Hey, there, Grandma."

"Demon trouble, eh?" she asked, eyeing the cinnamon buns as Holly set them out on plates.

"It followed me home, but I don't want to keep it."

The kettle clicked off. Holly poured boiling water into the teapot and carried it to the table. She filled Grandma in on the events of the last few days, ending with the mouse. "Why is there suddenly so much demon activity in Fairview?"

Grandma sat, hooking her canes, one to each side, on the tabletop. "Why not? Demons are all about manifesting on the earthly plane. For them, Earth is like Vegas, all entertainment, food, and fun. Fortunately, most of the time they can't get here. The demon realm is a prison, after all."

"A prison? I always thought of it as the demon homeworld. Y'know. Hell."

"No, this isn't a place for mortal souls. No fiery pits. Look in the front of Howard's *Realms*, on the top left-hand shelf of the bookcase behind you."

Holly turned, pulling out an oversized red volume that looked about a century old. This wasn't one of the books Holly had read. Of course, she'd never read even half the demon lore in her parents' library—apparently she needed to get right on that. "What am I looking for?"

"Look at the picture facing the title page."

Holly opened the cover, then lifted the thin sheet of onionskin covering the first illustration. It was a black-and-white etching, a snarl of shadows and torchlight and stone walls melting into a maze of tunnels. She could almost feel the cold, damp drafts rising off the page.

"Who knows how accurate that drawing is, but it fits every description given of the place. It's like a prison. A big dungeon. Some people call it the Castle." Grandma shrugged. "Not a very original name, but it was built long ago."

"By whom?"

"Human sorcerers."

Holly carefully turned the page. "Is there a picture of the outside?"

"There is no outside. The entire world is inside those halls."

Holly turned back to the illustration. It was like Escher meets Dracula. "Could use some throw cushions."

Grandma smiled, but her eyes were serious. "Demons come from our world originally. The prison was a means of banishing them. They can't get back here unless someone summons them."

"So every time a demon shows up, there's been a prison break?"

"Yup."

Holly took a large gulp of tea, trying to wrap her head around the idea of an entire prison dimension crammed with demons. A flippant corner of her brain thought of high school.

Grandma went on. "As to why this specific demon was summoned, we can't begin to answer that without a lot more information. There are many different subspecies. What you've described sounds like the kind they call soul eaters."

"Then let's cut to the chase. How do we send it back to the slammer?"

"First of all, we have to find it. A piddly demon would never have made it through the portal, so it has to have power. It will be a master demon, and that means it can shape-shift. It won't look like a mouse anymore."

That has its pros and cons, thought Holly. She never wanted to see that mouse again.

Grandma took a sip of tea. "A very powerful demon appears human. You can't tell the difference just by looking.

You can't even tell the difference sharing magic. Only deep Sight will reveal its true nature."

"Human?" Holly was surprised. "Any demon I ever saw looked like a dark, dirty cloud."

"That's a demon's weakest form. Human form is hardest. In between, they can assume an animal shape. Usually snakes or rats—they like the ick factor." She paused, pursing her lips. "Anyway, nothing less than major spellcraft will work on a master. And you have to work fast, because the first thing it will do is make more servants on this side of the portal."

Holly had eaten a few mouthfuls of cinnamon bun, but now pushed the plate away. "How does the Turn— whatchamacallit—the Dark Larceny work?"

Grandma shook her head. "I don't know exactly." She paused, memory lighting her eyes. "I had an offer for it once. A very handsome man—well, I thought he was a man until I learned otherwise—promised me the moon and stars if I would just let him taste my soul." She smiled wryly as she spooned sugar into her tea. "A bad bargain, but he was extremely nice to look at."

"Oh, Grandma," Holly said in a teasing tone. She never knew how many of her grandmother's war stories to believe. Except . . . her story almost exactly mirrored what Alessandro had said about being Turned.

"Those were good days." Grandma gave a short, dry chuckle. "So, back to the immediate problem. If you're going to protect yourself from a demon, you have to think about where your routine takes you each day."

"Oh, crap." Holly smacked her forehead with the heel of her palm.

"What?"

"Tomorrow's the first day of classes. I can't go to school with a demon on the loose."

Grandma waved a dismissive hand. "Well, on the positive side, you're safer with others around. Demons prefer a sneak attack. A crowded campus is the perfect safety zone."

Holly shook her head. "I don't know. Demon hunting sounds pretty full-time."

"What do you want to do?"

"Well, I *want* to go to classes, of course. Everything's set to go." She felt a wave of unreasoning, frustrated stubbornness. "I want my business degree, for my sake and for the sake of the Three Sisters Agency. I'm tired of not knowing how to work smart. But once again life gets in the way of big plans."

Grandma sat up straighter. "Then go to classes."

"But—"

"We'll manage. You can't let a demon ruin your semester."

Doubt and disbelief vied for top billing. "How can I just show up for class?"

"There're protection spells. I have books of them. If you want school to work out, sweetheart, you have to go for it. Take some risks. Sometimes young people are too cautious."

"But protection spells can't be enough. There has to be something more we can do."

Grandma narrowed her eyes. "Such as?"

"Get rid of the demon for good. How do you kill a master?"

Grandma shook her head. "Witches aren't strong enough to kill them. For a permanent solution, you have to send the demon back where it came from and then seal the portal behind it."

Holly swallowed her tea the wrong way. "That sounds up close and personal."

"Yes." Grandma said the word quietly. It hung in the air in a gust of cigarette smoke. "But Elaine Carver, one of the original members of our Three Sisters Agency, did it back in 1885."

"I've heard about this," said Holly. "There was a war between a master demon and the vampires back then. The demon had gathered all kinds of followers."

"Including the Flanders family, which is interesting all on its own. Anyway, the story goes that Elaine opened a full-blown portal in the customs house right by the inner harbor. She sent the master demon and many of its servants packing."

"How'd she do it?"

"I don't know. I've never seen the spell. Can't be the one you want, though."

"Why not?"

"Killed her. Backwash of power was too much."

"Oh." *That's a big help*. Holly stood up and walked to the window. She had no idea what was outside. She was blinded by a stampede of thoughts and emotions, panic leading the herd.

Grandma cleared her throat. "As I said, protection is the way to go. As for something more than that . . . well, it's hard to find good demon hunters these days, but maybe there's someone we could call in."

Holly turned. "Good demon hunters all have waiting lists. There aren't enough witches left who could do it. The wait could be months, and this thing could have taken over half of Fairview by then."

"Better than you tangling with it. Magic shouldn't hurt you the way it does."

"Listen, that's no reason *not* to fight the demon. We can ward ourselves, but eventually someone's going to get hurt. I'll live with the pain if that means getting rid of the demon for good, and *right now*."

"Are you sure about that?" Grandma said, narrowing her eyes. "It's big-M magic. The biggest. It will be agony for you, and with some of these spells, failing in the middle is worse than never starting at all."

Holly's stomach did a slow roll of anxiety. "Strength isn't the issue. I beat the Flanders house. Besides, motivation is everything. The demon is standing between me and the quiet enjoyment of my calculus classes."

"You're sure you want to start down this road?"

The words came out on a shudder of breath. "*I can do it. I just need to know how.*"

There was a long pause. Holly looked away, afraid she would tear up. Fright? Pride? She wasn't sure what she was feeling. This wasn't a step she wanted to take, but there was no way around it.

"Then we'll work on booting this critter back to jail."

Grandma ground out her cigarette butt, her eyes lowered. "You are your mother's daughter, you know that?"

"Thanks," Holly said, suddenly feeling like a child again.

"There's got to be something in all the books and notes we've gathered up over the generations. If not, I know people to call for information. In the meantime, you can borrow O'Shaughnessy's *Charms and Protections* and beef up the guardian spell on the house. Keep out any more surprise guests. Book's on the bookcase, third row down. Have a look at chapter eight."

Holly pulled the book off the shelf. It was so old, the dark brown leather was flaking off the binding. "Hey, it's got pictures, too. Do you think some of these talismans would work?"

"Not the ultimate answer, but they'll be helpful until we figure out something more permanent. I could whip up a few this afternoon while you look after the house."

Grandma's expression was unexpectedly chipper, as if this were going to be the most fun she'd had in years. By Holly's calculation, it had probably been a decade since her grandmother had seen active service. Perhaps there was only so much canasta an old witch could take before she started jonesing for a dustup with the forces of darkness.

Stiffly, Grandma got to her feet and opened a drawer in the buffet where she stored her magical tools. She began pulling out vials of dried things, balls of twine, and feathers— the makings for charms and wearable spells. With arthritic hands she unwrapped a tiny white-handled sickle, caressing it like an old lover.

"Still sharp," she said, running her thumb against the blade, but she might have been speaking of herself as well.

"Would a talisman work for Alessandro?" Holly asked, laying the book open on the table and resuming her seat. "He's fighting the demon, too."

"Sure. So you're still working with him?"

"Yeah," Holly said, unable to stop heat from rising to her cheeks. Grandma knew very well that Alessandro was still in the picture. She was just fishing for information.

Grandma set the knife down carefully. "I like him, and

I've known him from long before your mother was born, but I'd be careful. Vampires aren't like us."

"He's a good partner."

"Of course he is, but I know what it's like working with the vampires. The rush reminds me of that first whiff when I open a box of dark chocolates. There's so much sweet potential there, but also one helluva stomachache."

"Alessandro is not the bonbon in my life, dark chocolate or otherwise." A horrible idea slithered into Holly's imagination. "Alessandro wasn't *your* bonbon?"

"Heavens, no. I never once took off so much as a corner of the foil wrapping. I was in love with your grandfather, and that was that. I had the rare power to be immortal, but he was human, so I chose to be mortal as well. I gave up using the high magic that kept me young."

"Couldn't have been an easy decision." *There's the understatement of the decade.*

"Choices are easy if you know your own heart. I knew mine." Grandma gave a sly smile.

Holly's cell rang, which gave her an excuse to dodge that look. "Holly Carver."

"It's Conall Macmillan." The dark, strong voice was immediately recognizable.

"Detective. What can I do for you?" *What now? He kept me at the crime scene for hours. What more could he possibly want to know?*

"Something, um . . ." He stalled, sounding uncertain. "I'm wondering if you could answer some questions for me. I need some advice. Nothing related to the Flanders case."

Holly relaxed a little. "How can I help, Detective?"

He cleared his throat. "Call me Mac. Can we meet?"

Anxiety shot back up to the red zone. "Okay. Sure. Where?"

"Uh . . . look." There was another awkward pause. "This is more personal than anything else. I'm home today . . . Uh, can you come over? Coffee? I can cook if you want dinner. But if that doesn't work for you we can meet wherever you want. Soon, I hope."

That rambling didn't sound at all like the Detective

Macmillan she had met. *Personal? Dinner?* What should she make of this?

"Um, I guess so," she replied. "Are policemen allowed to break bread with . . . what would I be—a subject matter expert?"

He gave a short laugh. "Sometimes they even let us go to places with real tablecloths. Listen, if you're okay with it, do you mind coming to my place? I wouldn't normally ask, but what I want to talk about is kind of private."

Uncertainty coagulated in Holly's stomach. "Okay. Where do you live?"

He gave her an address.

"How about eight thirty?" Holly asked. "I've got a few things to do that I can't put off."

"Then let me make you dinner. I'm a really good cook," he said. "You won't regret it."

She caught a note of unguarded enthusiasm. It was reassuring. "Sure. Why not?"

"Look, I appreciate this."

"You're welcome."

"Perfect. Later." He hung up.

Holly frowned at the phone, then set it down on the table. Not twenty-four hours since breaking up with Ben, she had an invite that sounded oddly datelike. A pang she couldn't name sliced through her. Guilt? Sorrow? Apprehension?

While she'd been talking, Grandma had opened the paper to read the headlines. "Another murder. They think it's a vampire doing the killing," she said, scanning the lead story. "How many is that so far this month?"

She passed Holly the newspaper section. She read quickly and then turned the page to scan a related article. A photo made her start. They'd caught Macmillan, all raincoat and wavy hair, in a candid shot outside the Flanders house. "Well, speak of the devil."

"Who's that?" Grandma asked.

"Detective Macmillan."

"You know him?"

"That was him on the phone."

Grandma looked slyly curious. "What's he like?"

Holly hesitated. "He's okay."

"You think he's cute," Grandma answered with an amused air.

"Do not." That was a lie. He *was* good-looking.

"What does Ben think of him?" she prodded.

Holly bit her lip.

"What's wrong?"

Holly sighed. As much as she wanted to avoid the Ben topic, the cat was out of the proverbial bag and already hairballing on the carpet. "Ben and I broke up."

Grandma sat very still for a moment. "Oh. I'm sorry."

"He can't handle the witch thing."

"Idiot." Grandma tapped her ash. "I never liked him anyway. Where does this Detective Macmillan fit in?"

"He's invited me to dinner. Business." Holly set the paper on the table.

Grandma studied the picture and raised an eyebrow. Taking a long drag, she exhaled slowly and eyed Holly through the wreathing smoke. "Uh-huh. Wear something nice."

Chapter 12

The sun's last death gilded the belly of the clouds, darkness rising like water over the downtown streets. Alessandro strode toward Omara's hotel, making plans. It was early for his kind to rise, just dark enough for comfort, but he loved this hour when the night was new and the sidewalks jammed with life. Even after hundreds of years, he needed that sense of a fresh start.

He ran across the four-lane street, dodging cars. The line for the movie theater spilled over the curb, forcing him to swerve. When he regained his path he stopped cold, nearly forcing a skateboarder to run him down. Fixated on a new sight, Alessandro barely noticed.

John Pierce of Clan Albion was parking his silver-gray convertible down the street. All Alessandro's loathing of the vampire surged in, followed by a rush of curiosity. *Why is that worm on the streets at this early hour?* Usually a waster like Pierce would still be in bed.

Alessandro melted into the mouth of an alleyway that ran between two stores. Behind him was all Dumpsters and mildew, before him a panorama of bright lights and hustle. As usual he stood on the threshold, part of neither scene.

Oblivious to surveillance, Pierce checked his hair in the rearview mirror. His suit was pale gray, probably hand-tailored, if one judged by the fit. The vampire was dressed to kill.

At first he thought Pierce might be visiting Omara, but Pierce walked the other way, hands in his pockets, and turned the corner. Alessandro prowled after him.

Am I wasting time? Am I suspicious simply because I despise him? Maybe, but not so long ago Alessandro had been obliged to behead Pierce's brother. The execution had been a sign of the changing times. Stephan Pierce had beaten a local mechanic to death for ruining the engine of his Jaguar. Once, whipping or beating a peasant would have been an acceptable response to poor service, but for better or worse, times had changed.

Clan Albion hadn't. In their arrogance they barely acknowledged their own queen, much less the authority of human police and judges. Nevertheless, human law demanded the execution of Stephan Pierce for the wanton murder of the mechanic. The trial—with mortals only, as no supernatural accused stood before a jury of supernatural peers—had taken no time at all. The sentence was death. The condemned had the option of staking by a human or, as a nod to cultural sensitivity, beheading by one of his own species. Stephan Pierce had chosen the latter. Alessandro and his sword had taken care of business as soon as the paperwork was filed with the courts. As Queen Omara's representative, that was his duty.

He had no illusions that the whole sordid episode had taught Clan Albion a damned thing.

Pierce led Alessandro to a five-star luxury hotel. The lobby was a wonderland of marble and objets d'art. Without glancing to either side, Pierce went into the adjacent lounge.

Perhaps the place was meant to be romantic; it was dark enough to make Alessandro grateful for vampiric night vision. Round tables were encircled by high-backed black leather couches that sheltered the patrons from general view. Fairy lights draped clumps of artificial palms, spangling the gloom with flecks of blue and white. A tasteful jazz track grooved in the background. Alessandro ghosted through the lounge, listening for Pierce's voice. It didn't take long. He was sitting by a window, greeting a human woman. Who was she to get a vampire playboy out of bed before full dark? Alessandro's curiosity doubled.

He sat behind an oasis of palms and ordered his usual red wine. His table was across the aisle from Pierce, but he had to slouch and angle himself to see past the enfolding arms of the tall, curved leather seats. The illusion of privacy worked both ways—it might be hard to see Pierce and his woman, but they had not noticed him. Score one for 007, Undead edition.

The woman was young, with bleached hair falling past her shoulders. She wore a scanty dress of electric blue that sparkled in the dim glow of the fairy lights. Not quite pretty, not quite a coed, but similar enough to the murder victims that he took notice.

Pierce was looking at her with the avarice of a lover.

What exactly is going on here? Vampires courted humans, and vice versa, but only in the vampire clubs, where such behavior was expected. There were two reasons: One, it kept the bald fact that vampires fed on blood out of the public eye. That was one of the unspoken conditions of their truce with human law. Two, Omara wanted to be the first lady in the heart of all her favorites. If this was a romantic encounter, Pierce was running a terrible risk.

"I tell you, it was the strangest old place," the woman was saying. "And the client . . . well, he hated it. I think if he could have, he would have sold it right out from under his girlfriend, but, like, she owns the place, right? All I could do was look around and estimate a listing price."

A stab of shock zinged down Alessandro's spine. He remembered Holly's remark about Ben selling the Carver house if he could. *Is she talking about Ben Elliot?*

"What an unusual situation." Pierce had the woman's hand in his, stroking his thumb over her fingers. His tawny hair and sculpted profile had the same cruel, feline beauty that had won him lovers and enemies since the time of the Tudors. "What did you do next, Miranda?"

She gave a tiny shrug. "I faxed the estimate to him, but I doubt I'll ever hear back."

"No?"

"If the girlfriend's smart, she'll hang onto the property. In a few years that oceanfront area's going to double in price." She gave a derisive laugh. "You never know—she might bite. And, y'know, Ben's a pretty persuasive guy."

That is Holly's house! Is he insane? No witch would ever sell her family home.

"I like the way you think." Pierce lifted her fingers to his lips, dusting the buffed nails with kisses. "A cool business head is one grace that will never fade."

"And I have one tight little portfolio." She preened beneath the warmth of his flattery, sipping a pale green martini with her free hand.

I should kill Elliot. But indulging that aggression was pointless. When she found out about Ben's plans, Holly would want that pleasure for herself. *An amusing thought, except she will be hurt by this piece of stupidity. Then I will kill him, and, unlike Stephan Pierce, I know how to cover my tracks.*

Alessandro impatiently waited for them to get back to the discussion about the house, but now they were making calf's eyes at each other. *Come on, come on, I have things to do.* He pulled out his phone, texting Omara to say where he was, and that he was leaving if Pierce did nothing illegal in the next sixty seconds. He left out any mention of the woman. Another man's bedroom escapades were his own affair.

Then Pierce slipped a ring off his left index finger and depressed a button hidden inside the band. Alessandro nearly dropped the phone. He hadn't seen one of those ring gadgets for years.

From where he sat he could just barely see a sharp, needle-thin barb spring from the top of the carved gold. Miranda held out her hand, the fingers curled in a gesture of languid supplication. Pierce jabbed the tiny blade into her wrist, holding it above his wineglass. Her only response was a short, silent jerk of pain.

Blood dripped and trickled into the wine, but still Miranda made no sound. Her head lolled forward, and then she tossed her hair back, baring her throat. Gradually she began to shudder, gripping the table hard as the venom on the blade took effect. "Oh!"

"Easy, darling." Pierce chuckled.

It was fortunate the high-backed seats hid the pair from almost every angle—none of the human patrons could see what was going on—but Alessandro could see it all. The muscles on Miranda's neck corded as poison raced to her nerve endings on crest after crest of pleasure. The blood ran faster, splashing the sides of the glass with a transfixing scent and sound. The tiny noises she made, the merest catch of breath, nearly pushed Alessandro over the edge.

"Enjoying the show?" Omara slipped onto the couch beside him, leaning over to kiss him full on the mouth. He hadn't seen her coming, but then Omara was a mistress of surprise. Alessandro gripped her tiny waist, feeling the slide of her thigh against his. She had fed, the stolen warmth rising from her cinnamon flesh like perfume.

"Pierce just pulled out a bleeding ring," Alessandro murmured in Omara's ear, strangely unmoved by her touch. Usually she knew how to arouse him, but the queen's lips seemed stale after the kisses he had shared with Holly.

Omara slithered away, straightening the lapels of her elegant pantsuit. Her hair fell in dark sheets around her, diamonds shimmering at her ears and in the notch of her throat. Her attention was fixed on the neighboring table, her eyes growing wide as she took in the tableau.

Her nostrils flared. *Jealousy*, thought Alessandro. *I guessed right. She wants to keep Pierce for herself.*

"And here I thought the best vintage I could get was a perky cab franc. I never dreamed the locals were on tap." Omara glared at Pierce from under her lashes, almost as if willing him to look and see her there—but the object of that scathing stare was oblivious. "Interesting that he should be using one antique artifact, when we pursue a murderer who uses another."

Alessandro studied his queen. Her pupils widened with Desire as she watched the couple, energy gathering around her like a storm. Then she gave an elegant shake, flicking it off like chance rain, but the anger stayed, simmering low. Alessandro sipped his wine, keeping quiet.

"I am fascinated by the possibilities here. Rings, tokens, antique hunting rituals. He plays at sorcery from time to time. Could John Pierce be our murderer?" She said it with relish, as if the novelty of solving a crime were delightful, or perhaps she simply wanted Pierce's head on a platter.

"The murders were the work of the changelings. I'm sure of it," he said. *I can't believe I'm defending the worm.*

"Who is to say that they acted alone? Stealth and planning have been beyond them in the past. It would make sense if there was a proper vampire in the mix to do the heavy thinking."

Would Pierce work with changelings? He wasn't sure. "What do you want to do?"

A bitter look crossed Omara's face. "Bring John to me. And his food."

John, is it? How close are they? Alessandro bowed his head. *Poor bastard.* "As you wish."

Alessandro slid off the black leather of the couch, grateful to be released from its claustrophobic embrace. The noise level in the lounge had risen, but he saw only the waitstaff flitting to and fro. The patrons were all invisible, tucked into their private, high-backed havens.

When he reached Pierce's table, the wineglass was empty, dribbles of red clinging to the insides. The vampire had his mouth to the wound on Miranda's soft white wrist, licking it clean. She was watching, her face flushed from venom and fascination. Slowly she raised her eyes to Alessandro's, the look in them a pitiful blend of terror and adoration. She stood on the road to death, and was high on the view.

An addict. A rich one.

Alessandro had seen that look too many times to count, but once in a while it still staked him where he stood. He slapped the back of Pierce's head, none too lightly. The vampire lifted his mouth from Miranda's wrist, lips curling to show fang. That shot the pretty-boy image all to hell.

"What?" Pierce snarled.

"The queen wants a word with you both." His glance took in Pierce's meal. "Now."

Pierce sat straight, wiping his mouth on the restaurant's damask napkin. It left a scarlet smudge. "Where?" Panic.

Alessandro indicated Omara's table with a facetious sweep of his arm. The queen was peering around the edge of the couch, a come-hither smile flickering on her lips. Pierce swallowed hard. The lines in his face spoke of dread, but he would be dignified about it.

Pierce waited while Miranda rose and steadied herself. She seemed light-headed from venom and the loss of blood, but the wound on her wrist had closed. Vampire saliva had healing properties, all the better to keep a food source from wasting precious fluids.

When he returned to his seat, Alessandro saw that Omara had ordered a bottle of cabernet and fresh glasses. The server, nervous in the company of vampires, fumbled the corkscrew and barely managed to draw the cork without opening a vein.

Impatient, Alessandro took the bottle away from him. "I will pour. You may go."

The man fled, leaving Alessandro in the role of waiter. He filled the glasses while they waited for Omara to speak. The queen regarded Pierce as if he were an incontinent dog.

"So, John," Omara began, "you have chosen a very elegant hunting ground. Very public. Very full of prominent city leaders."

Pierce did his best to look coy. "No laws have been broken, my queen. It was not a hunt, but a meeting. Fully consensual, I might add. Ms. Anderson and I are already *well* acquainted."

The queen was unimpressed. If she had a tail, it would have been lashing. "My rules are simple, Pierce. Humans are easily upset. If you're going to feed in their territory, get a room."

Miranda leaned forward. "But I'm not upset. John knows what I like. The thrill is doing it where we might be seen."

Omara looked almost shocked; then her face hardened to fury. Awkward silence grew rancid. Omara lunged across the table, grabbed Pierce's wrist, and yanked the bleeding ring from his finger. He gasped in pain, but the queen paid no heed. She thrust the ring under his nose. "These old ways are gone! How dare you flaunt your bloodlust? Would you bring this peace we have forged with the humans crashing down upon our heads?"

Pierce flushed pink, his cheeks hot with stolen blood. "I broke no laws. She asks for it."

"You broke the spirit of our pact. We can feed, but no one wants to see the thing done. To them we are nothing but foul leeches."

"And yet you accepted my offering the other night."

Omara's eyes widened with irritation. "That was our own ground, where we rule. This is the human realm, where I come to flatter and amuse the day-dwelling potentates. This is where I cozen and beg for every scrap of legal protection for our kind. You *will not* shatter my efforts with your idiot games!"

And you will not betray me. The words were unspoken, but Alessandro heard them all the same.

Pierce fumed, muscles bunching beneath his elegant gray suit. "Those 'idiot games' are our traditions, my queen. Would you so easily discount our honored past?"

Omara jerked as if slapped.

That's enough. Alessandro lashed out a hand, snatching the collar of Pierce's jacket. "When the queen speaks, you do not question."

Pierce moved to strike, but Alessandro caught his wrist. Miranda covered her face, her breath coming in frightened sobs.

Calmer now, Omara picked up her glass and took a sip of wine. "Easy, my champion. Let him go."

Reluctantly Alessandro uncurled his fingers. Pierce slid back into place.

"You do not like this new world, John?" Omara asked softly. "You miss the old ways of terror and mystery?"

The anger was still there, but with a degree of pain as well. Pierce had wounded Omara, and that surprised Alessandro. *Interesting.* She was vulnerable to the worm.

Pierce ducked his head. "I do miss the past. It is so much harder to survive now."

"You could always get a job," Alessandro said helpfully.

"But he has," Omara said, her voice dark. "Dare I guess what you are about tonight, John? You were charming this pretty businesswoman. She has what you need: blood and money. In other words, you've gone for the oldest profession of all."

The last words were steeped in disgust. In reply Pierce gave her a look charged with sexual heat and defiance. "So what if I have? Women like Miranda appreciate my skills."

Alessandro snorted. "You're a gigolo."

He saw the word sting. Pierce lolled back in his seat, putting his hand on Miranda's bare knee. His leer showed fang.

Omara leered right back, but made it terrifying. "Does she taste good, John? She smells of diet pills and carbonation."

Pierce grimaced with embarrassment as Omara grabbed the girl's arm and sniffed the inside of her wrist, lingering above the freshly-closed wound. "I grant you her skin is beautiful to look at, like alabaster touched with rivulets of lapis. Sadly, you can't judge a vintage by its label."

"Hey, I don't swing your way!" Miranda protested, trying to twist her arm away. She whimpered beneath Omara's crushing grip, anxiety banishing the haze of the venom.

The queen's honey-gold eyes turned as hard as agate, her lip lifting to show the tips of her teeth. "You dare to tempt us with your snow-white flesh. Now you will do what you're told, meat."

She dragged her tongue along Miranda's inner arm, sucking a little where the veins rose beneath the skin. A human heartbeat passed. In that moment Alessandro saw the naked hunger in Omara's face, the veil lifted from a millennia of carnage. He knew that appetite of old, had seen it in the queen's face time and again. He felt it in his own flood of arousal. His saliva began to run.

Alessandro heard the low, almost inaudible growl of Pierce's territorial protest. The air grew heavy with threat.

Miranda shot Pierce a look of wild panic, the truth

slamming her with the force of a train. She finally wrested her arm free. "Omigod, let me out of here."

Surprise! We're monsters! Alessandro thought dryly.

Pierce touched her shoulder. "Miranda, please don't go."

The mere command was enough. Miranda froze, cradling her arm. "What do you want me to do?" Her voice was small and hushed. The sound of a venom-slave. No will of her own. No future beyond the next bite.

Pierce shot a glance at Omara. The queen nodded. Pierce turned back to his human. "Go upstairs now. Go on. Get up."

Miranda rose. Pierce stood as well, handing Miranda her purse and kissing her lightly on the cheek. "Go upstairs to the room. I'll meet you there as soon as I can."

Alessandro watched the woman retreat, the sway of her hips in the electric blue dress almost, but not quite, worth a moment's distraction. *Junk food.*

"Well, John, I wonder what other secrets you've kept from me?" Omara asked icily. "There have been some curious incidents in Fairview of late."

Pierce gave her a bewildered look.

Stupid? Alessandro wondered. *Or just a very, very good actor?*

Omara was impassive. "We need to speak in private."

Alessandro saw Pierce turn sheet-white. He glanced at the queen. She was studying Pierce with a wistful expression. Normally a private audience with Omara meant punishment. Here Alessandro wasn't sure what would happen, and he didn't like mysteries where the queen was involved. She was unpredictable enough.

As if to illustrate his thoughts, she made one of her mercurial shifts. "Alessandro, come."

She rose. He followed her. Pierce stayed behind, tossing back one glass of wine, refilling it, and then drinking that, too.

Omara stopped close to the entrance to the lounge.

"Are you sure you want to see him alone?" asked Alessandro.

Omara gave him a veiled look. "That is what I wish."

He stifled a curse. "Do you truly think he's mixed up with our enemies?"

"Or perhaps a vapid, self-involved twit. Or both. Leave it to me." Omara's tone brooked no further argument. "Despite what I said earlier, the bleeding ring is not evidence of anything but poor judgment. However, it is a good excuse to frighten him into confessions."

"What about the woman?"

Omara gave a slow smile. "John must learn to share. Do you have any idea who she is?"

"A Realtor. I overheard their conversation. Holly Carver's lover is trying to sell her house. Idiot bastard."

"A fool indeed. A witch never parts with her home." Omara's brow contracted. "Wait a moment. Did you say your little witch has a boyfriend?" Playfully Omara wound her finger in one of Alessandro's curls. "You are in her life, you admire her, and yet she loves another? How does that happen?"

Dangerous territory. Alessandro shrugged. "You are my queen."

Omara gave a rueful, lopsided smile. The expression was unusual for her. "You fear my jealousy, so you aim to please. Not a bad plan, except you're a pathetic liar. I may be your queen, but I do not rule your heart."

Alessandro opened his mouth, desperately trying to think of something to divert her thoughts from Holly. But Omara caught his chin in her fingers, and shut it. "I see the look in your eyes when you speak of your witch. You try to hide it, both for her sake and for mine. Your loyalty does you credit."

This was a softer side of Omara than he had ever seen. He didn't trust it.

She went on. "Your witch should be falling at your feet, and not those of another. You are my sword arm and defender of my honor. My champion should be adored."

Dangerous territory. "But the lady has some say, does she not?"

Omara rolled her eyes. "You're hopeless. Put some effort into winning her over. Try wearing something besides black.

Women like a bit of color." She patted his cheek. "And see to it that you get her assistance. Soon. She should be raising the dead for me by now." She looked at her watch. "I have to go."

"Be careful of Pierce."

"He is the one who should have a care." She pursed her lips. "I'll call you later."

Alessandro bowed as she left. *Get her assistance.* If Alessandro's favors bought that aid, so be it. He was for sale, even at the cost of Omara's monumental jealousy.

Emptiness yawned inside him. One day his disappointment in Omara would swallow his loyalty. She was an excellent queen, but there was little in her that was human enough to love.

He had to check on Holly. He rang her home, then her cell, but got no answer. Not a big surprise. She often turned off the phones if she was working magic. But, just to be sure, he called her grandmother.

She gave Alessandro a full report. He was stunned.

Ben had left Holly? *Idiot.* Up until the business with the house, Alessandro had always tolerated Ben. On some basic level he just didn't present much of a challenge. But she was having dinner with Detective Macmillan. Why Macmillan? She'd met him only once. Why the sudden interest?

And why was Macmillan making advances now, when he should be paying attention to his job?

This new development was worrisome on many levels. The detective was different from Ben Elliot. Macmillan was a man of action and authority. He counted.

Alessandro started toward the door. He couldn't just let this slide. *Rival*, he thought, every instinct alert. Maybe he couldn't be with Holly the way he wanted to, but he was damned if he was giving her up to Macmillan. Not until he was convinced that Macmillan was the better man.

That would be never.

Holly is mine.

Halfway out the door, he paused to survey the spacious lobby and the upscale boutiques that lined its perimeter. He remembered the queen's words. *Try wearing something besides black.*

Alessandro strode to the adjoining mall with grim purpose.

Chapter 13

A ll too soon Holly faced the ultimate test of feminine protocol: what to wear when one was not sure whether business, pleasure, or both were on the dinner menu. As a rule, no lingerie decisions could be made until one decided how the evening should end. For instance, if one were reaching for the three-for-one panty hose in basic taupe, the night would be over before it began.

Better in that case to stay at home with the remote.

She'd barely met Macmillan but, cop mode aside, he seemed like a nice guy—maybe even worthy of fishnet stockings. But right now? There was a vampire she couldn't have and a demon mouse she wished would go away. Not to mention Ben. *Maybe footed sleepers with a plunging neckline would send the right message.*

Then again, it was just a dinner invitation. A business thing. Maybe she could save the angst until after he offered to coat her in chocolate sauce and lick it off to the strains of the 1812 Overture. That would give hosiery choices some meaning.

Ugh! She glowered at the closet. *This is why I had a steady guy. After a while they don't notice what you're wearing anyway.*

Up till then it had been a good afternoon. Holly had spent

time with O'Shaughnessy's *Charms and Protections*. Reinforcing the protection spell over every door, window, chimney, and light plug—basically wherever there was an opening in the wall—was tedious, but not difficult. Her powers grudgingly rose to the occasion with no more than a few sharp twinges. By late afternoon she was exhausted but thoroughly satisfied. She wanted to keep that glow.

Not so easy, once the wardrobing debate began. Why did Mac need her help with something *personal*? That one word held so many possible scenarios, some of them alarming. *Better go with the little black dress.*

But then she wore the metallic teal spike heels. They looked like castoffs from *Hookers from Outer Space*, but there was no need to strike all the fun off the menu.

Holly arrived a few minutes late. Macmillan lived in a nice but slightly older downtown condo block. As Fairview's housing prices caught up with the rest of the country, it was the kind of place working folk would soon find too expensive to afford. The woodwork in the lobby was faux mahogany; the fittings in the elevator were finger-smudged brass. Soft carpet in the hallway nearly mired her heels as she teetered her way to the corner suite, and her calves were aching by the time she knocked on Macmillan's door.

Alessandro answered. Holly frowned in confusion. *Did I get the right address?*

"Good evening," he said, just this side of Bela Lugosi. "Come in. May I take your wrap?"

"What are you doing here?" she asked, handing over her mohair stole and the bottle of merlot she had brought.

Fleeting irritation crossed Alessandro's face. "Detective Macmillan cannot abandon his culinary creation, so at the moment I am his butler."

"Well, the uniform looks good on you. Nice, um, shirt."

Alessandro shifted his weight to one hip, settling into his insouciant slouch. Hot-pink silk framed an expanse of pale, muscular chest. His long curls of pale blond hair slid with languid ease over the fabric, the sound a faint, suggestive whisper.

"I came looking for you," he said. "Your grandmother mentioned where you were going, and that you would be coming alone."

His eyes caught hers for a moment, but gave away nothing. She wondered how much exactly Grandma had said—but Holly couldn't reply, her mouth too dry for words. Her gaze lowered to the perfect pale chest in front of her. And the shirt. It was so . . . pink. Hot. Very hot.

Finally he shrugged. "The detective and I agreed that we three could discuss what we know about recent events. He has been interviewing me as he chopped parsley."

Holly felt a flicker of irritation. She felt confused, torn between Alessandro's bare chest and Macmillan's microgrins. She hadn't wanted a steamy date with the detective, but now she felt unaccountably cheated that it wasn't even a possibility. *Damn.*

"Why do you care about sharing information with the police?" she asked.

Alessandro shrugged. "I need to know what he knows. He has forensics, databases, and all the rest of the modern world's monstrous wealth of information. I'm willing to dangle a few tidbits to get access to that."

"Did you learn anything?"

"Only that there was a fourth murder. Same as before. Apparently it was on the news tonight. The detective and I could make quite a team if he would simply get past the not commenting on an active investigation.

"Besides all that," he said, leaning closer, "aren't you glad I'm here? What do you really know of this man? Why did he suddenly call you?"

Holly raised an eyebrow. "I think I can look after myself."

"No doubt, but I prefer to examine him before abandoning you to his clutches. I always wonder when people do something unexpected."

"A man asking me to dinner is unexpected?"

"You met over a pile of dead bodies mere days ago. Now he's carving little radish garnishes and humming to himself. It's creepy." Alessandro turned, nodding to his left. "The living room is through there. Make yourself comfortable while I open the wine."

Just what I need. A chaperon. Piqued, she went to take a seat but then stopped cold as she entered the room. The sight made her breath catch in her throat. The room was small, but tall windows stretched across most of two walls, showing the glittering sweep of the harbor beneath a waxing moon. The city lights were so bright she could almost taste the colors like berries on her tongue.

"Hi. Come on in." Macmillan walked into the room, casual in an oversized, V-necked red sweater. It showed off the strong muscles in his neck and shoulders.

"Nice view," she said, doing her best to mean the skyline and not the man. *This place is full of good scenery.*

Macmillan smiled. "Down there is your neighborhood." He pointed, and she leaned into him to follow the line of his finger. "And just along the horizon—yes, there—you can see the lights of Port Angeles."

His hand moved to her shoulder and he turned her to see the blur of tiny sparkles wavering on the Strait of Juan de Fuca. Holly could feel the line of heat where his body nearly brushed hers. Her eyes traveled from the window to Macmillan.

"Thank you for cooking dinner," she said. "I'm surprised, with the investigation, that you get a day off."

Her words were light, but she'd been wondering a lot about that point. She'd have guessed Macmillan to be the workaholic type, and weren't homicide detectives supposed to be slaves to their jobs at times like this?

His face tensed. "Actually, I was sick today. Nothing catching, I'm sure."

She watched as the tips of his ears turned red. There was something he wasn't saying. "Are you okay?"

He shrugged. "Yeah, I was starting to feel better by the time I called you. I'll live. In fact, right now I feel great. Maybe the rest did me good."

He was so close, Holly could feel the heat of his breath on her cheek, driving away all other thoughts. "Well, I hope I can help you with whatever it is you need."

He gave her a melting smile. "I hope you can, too."

Okay, he said he wanted to talk for personal reasons, but just how personal did he mean?

Alessandro clattered pots in the kitchen, breaking the moment. Holly took the opportunity to glance around the rest of the room. It was lived-in but tidy for a bachelor's place, old and new furniture blending in a comfortable sprawl. A litter of books and magazines showed a wide variety of interests, from mountain climbing to UFOs. There was a big, manly TV supporting framed photos of family, friends, and a grinning black Lab. One shot showed Macmillan receiving a police award. He looked good in uniform.

Alessandro entered with a tray of wineglasses, a cloud of delicious cooking smells wafting around him. Holly's mouth started to water. Alessandro, on the other hand, looked vaguely green. Vampires hated strong food odors.

Macmillan waved toward the couch and chairs. "Dinner'll be another few minutes. Shall we sit?"

The detective clearly meant to sit next to Holly, but he was thwarted. With lazy grace Alessandro sprawled right where Macmillan was headed, taking up enough room with his long legs for three. He flung one arm along the back of the couch, the full sleeve of his pink shirt draped to advantage. As he looked up at the detective, eyes wide with innocence, a taunting smile played along his lips.

Macmillan and Holly politely took the side chairs, effectively separated. More amused now than anything, she crossed her legs, dangling one hooker shoe. "Well, you two started the party without me. Where are we in the great information exchange?"

Alessandro laced his fingers over his stomach. "I was about to begin discussing the mouse. It is, believe it or not, relevant to the murders. At least, that is my theory."

Macmillan narrowed his eyes. "All right, I'll bite. Mouse?"

Holly tilted her head, watching the two men. Macmillan didn't blink. The detective had guts. Few men dared to stand their ground with a vampire, much less Alessandro.

Alessandro gave a lazy wave with one hand, but he regarded the detective intently. "What do you know about doorways to hell?"

She saw Macmillan's jaw clench with tension. "I think there's one that leads to my desk at work."

"We do not jest."

"Hell, huh?" Macmillan gave a short laugh. "What, I'm going to be arresting the devil next?"

"No, no, it's not really hell in the usual sense," said Holly. "Not fire and brimstone per se. It's called the Castle. It's a prison built for demons."

"Then it's a jail. You're not talking literal hell?"

Holly opened her mouth to reply, but Alessandro broke in. "Eternity imprisoned without hope or future. Do you have a better name?"

Mac shrugged. "Okay, fine. What's hell—or prison, or the Castle, or whatever—got to do with a mouse?"

Holly and Alessandro looked at each other, then took turns describing the portal in Holly's house. After that, Alessandro filled in more details about the portal that had opened up behind Sinsation. It was the first time Holly had heard the whole account of that night.

"Y'know," Mac said incredulously, "I've worked in this town for years. Sure, there's some supernatural crime, but this stuff is outside the box."

When he spoke, his strong-boned face was mobile and young. When he was still it fell into the lines of a mature man, tired and a bit hard. His eyes reminded Holly of a surgeon she knew, that same look of someone who had seen the insides of too many people.

As a cop, perhaps he had.

"So how do portals work?" he asked. "How do the prisoners break out?"

Holly replied, because, between spellcasting and figuring out what to wear, she'd been thumbing through a couple of books Grandma had loaned her. "Demons might have the strength, but they can't find their way on their own. Someone has to summon one, usually by name. Set up a beacon to show it the path, if you like. At least, that's the theory. I don't have direct experience."

"So the summoner sets the beacon and the demon opens the portal?"

"If the summoner is powerful, he or she can send power to help the demon, but yeah, that's the basic idea. Sometimes the demon makes it through on the first try, or else it just keeps poking holes until it manages to crawl through. Until it makes it to our side, it can't stray far from the point of summoning. If it does, it'll lose the connection that allows it to cross over."

As they talked, Macmillan's color rose. He looked fascinated and appalled. "So this is going to happen again?"

"It already has," said Alessandro. "Several times."

Holly picked up her wineglass and had a sip. "But the demon has come through now. I don't know if there'll be any more portals."

Macmillan got up and then came back with his notebook. He flipped it open and started scribbling. The intensity in his movements and expression reassured Holly. She hadn't yet figured out why Macmillan was playing the host with the most tonight, but this was normal cop behavior she could understand.

"So," he said, "there has to be a summoner out there somewhere."

"There is," said Alessandro. "Holly, remember I asked you about tracking that spell when we first got to the Flanders place?"

"Yeah, we never got back to that. You said your client was having problems with someone calling up a destructive entity in his warehouse."

"When was that?" Macmillan asked sharply.

Alessandro gave a wry smile. "A few weeks ago. About the same time as the first murders. Violent death, or the blood from it, contains power of its own. It might be a necessary ingredient for opening a portal."

Holly nodded. "I've seen that in some of the nastier spell books."

"Then that's our connection. The summoner and the murderer—or whoever is directing the murders—might be working together. They might be one and the same." The detective thought for a moment, flipping notebook pages back and forth. "The murder of the girl in the Flanders house probably relates to the portal there. The murder in the wine cellar did happen right before your mouse. I don't know about the first two deaths. Maybe those are your warehouse incidents."

"Would that be around the same time the changelings arrived in Fairview?" Holly asked.

Alessandro refilled Macmillan's glass, then Holly's. His own was still full. "I don't know. I only saw them once. I thought those two were the killers, but now there has been another murder."

"Unless there're more . . . whaddya call 'em . . . changelings somewhere," Macmillan added. "Though I have to say we—the police—never found any others."

Alessandro folded his arms. "Neither did the vampires."

"But why would they be involved at all?" Holly wondered.

"Vampire politics." Alessandro shrugged. "In the past they fought for territory. They lost badly. That is why there are so few of them now. I thought they were extinct."

"Are they servants of the demon?" Holly mused. "Are they looking for revenge?"

"I don't know," said Alessandro.

They fell silent. The only sound was the ticking of the kitchen timer.

Alessandro sat back. "Those pieces fit together well enough to explain at least some of what's happened. That still doesn't tell us who's behind this, but last night they succeeded. They got their demon."

"What are they—whoever they are—going to do with it?" Macmillan asked. "More important, what are we going to do about it?"

"I was reading one of Grandma's books," said Holly. "It suggests finding the name of the demon. It won't get rid of it, but if you know its name, you're one step closer to controlling it."

"Like finding its rap sheet? What it's capable of?" said Macmillan.

"More than that. Names have magical significance,"

Alessandro replied. "Holly, is there a way witch magic can find the demon's identity? Or the killer's?"

Holly squirmed, pulling her skirt down over her knees. Catching her breath, she held it a long moment, then released it slowly to still the butterflies in her stomach. She had an idea she really hated.

"You mentioned necromancy. I could raise the dead," Holly said in a dull voice. It was easy to be brave and determined just talking to Grandma, but now that she was committing herself for real, her head was starting to throb. "We just need to identify the grave of someone who walks between the worlds. A restless ghost. Then I can bring that spirit forth for questioning."

Alessandro shook his head, a somber look on his face. "That is an excellent idea. I would have liked to have made the suggestion myself, but I've been afraid that if you use the power required for necromancy, you will be hurt."

Holly shrugged. As miserable as she was, she wasn't going to backpedal now. Holly tossed back her wine in a gulp and set the glass down on an end table with an audible click. "I don't want to do this, but this demon was in my house and threatening my life. It has to go. I'll do whatever it takes."

The men looked at each other, clearly conflicted. "I don't know what the problem here is," said Macmillan, "but I'll help however you need me to."

Alessandro just frowned.

"All right then," Holly said softly, tension knotting her cold, cold stomach. A timer in the kitchen began to ding. The high-pitched bell felt like a spike in Holly's skull. The detective headed to the kitchen to check on dinner.

Alessandro leaned forward and fixed her with his amber gaze. "I don't like this, however useful necromancy may be. I'm not undermining your decision, but if you change your mind at any point, just say the word."

"I can't. So much is at stake. Including me."

"What are the risks?"

"It's big-M magic."

"And so I am right to believe that it will hurt?"

"Yeah." Holly sighed. "And sometimes necromancy's just disgusting."

She poured herself another glass of wine, her innards wobbling at the prospect of raising the dead. That was big-league stuff, the majors. *What am I doing?*

Alessandro's cell rang—a tinny rendition of Beethoven's Fifth Symphony. He made a face, then got up and dropped a kiss on the top of her head. "As the detective said, whatever you need. *Anything.*"

He flipped open the phone. "Caravelli." He listened. "Excellent. I had a thought for you to follow up. Ask him where he was yesterday afternoon, about four thirty. I'm serious. Certainly."

He walked into the next room, which looked like a study. She watched him go. *Where was who yesterday afternoon?* The last murder had been yesterday afternoon at about four thirty. *What's going on?*

She could hear Alessandro, even though he was keeping his voice down. Curiosity won out. She rose and crept forward, her steps silent on the carpet, and paused just outside the door. It sounded as if he were having an argument.

Alessandro was speaking. "Impossible." He shifted impatiently, listening to the reply. "Let me get my hands on the creature. Hold off for an hour or so, and I'll be there."

There was no ambiguity in Alessandro's tone. There was an implied threat in the words that made Holly suddenly cold.

"I'm old enough to know better than to say too much," Alessandro growled. "And I'm here protecting my interests."

Protecting his interests?

"All right, if that's the case, I'd better come." He snapped the phone shut and turned.

Startled, Holly backtracked to the living room at a trot. His hand caught her arm before she quite made it. "Ow!" Holly protested, fighting the rough strength in his fingers.

"I could hear you breathing outside the door," he said into her ear. His breath, cooler than a mortal's, raised the hair on her nape. He released her. "Be careful of eavesdropping. Be cautious of everything you do right now."

His size and strength were just too *there* all of a sudden. Even as a mortal he would have been formidable. As a vampire he had at least ten times a man's brute power. She swallowed hard, frightened and intrigued by the expression in his eyes. It was demanding and hungry and it made him handsome as sin.

Holly's heart began to speed. "I just heard you say you know better than to say too much. What aren't you telling me?"

He glared, his irritation sparking off of Holly's. Attraction and frustration hummed between them. "Am I that untrustworthy?" she whispered.

Frowning, he picked up his car keys from the coffee table. "Don't put words in my mouth. Enjoy your dinner." His voice held a world of disapproval.

" 'But don't enjoy it too much'?" she quipped, lifting her eyebrows in mock innocence.

He wavered, looking at the keys in his hand as if they would unlock more than the car door. "Precisely. I would rather stay here with you, keep an eye on things."

"Why? Am I in danger of being poisoned?"

He drew close, his silky sleeve brushing against her bare arm. That was all it took to send her thoughts scattering like seeds in the wind. His nearness made blood rush under her skin, as if he had called it. Perhaps he had. Half the vampires' power lay in their magnetism, that innate ability to fascinate their prey.

Sweet Hecate! Past kisses hovered like ghosts, nearly tangible but just a hairsbreadth out of reach. Anticipation ached in her body, making her want to crush herself against his chest. *I want him too much.* She had tasted him. She knew how good those lips could be. *Deadly good.*

He dropped his lips to her ear, his fingers tracing the curve of her waist. "Do you think I want to leave you here with that man? I don't like his smell. He's hiding something."

Whoa! Holly's pulse tripped in her throat, fueled by the urge to be near Alessandro and a desperate need to back away. "Who made you my watchdog?"

Alessandro's eyes glittered, but he left her challenge

alone. He put one hand on her hair, his fingers combing through its length. Holly shivered. He was beyond crossing the boundary they had carefully kept between them. He was five miles down the road.

His hand drifted to her hip. "I would stay, but I'm needed elsewhere. Come with me. Let me take you home, where it's safe."

Safe? Being alone with Alessandro was definitely not safe. Holly felt the brush of his fingers low on her spine, making her hot and weak with longing. Dangerously needy. It was taking a supreme effort to think. "Why don't you trust him?"

Alessandro blinked slowly. "You would not understand."

Yeah, I do. It's one of those guy things. Two tomcats in one backyard.

She took a deep breath, doing her best to resist the electricity that seemed to flicker between them, skin to skin. "Big bad witch here. If I can handle the Flanders house, I can handle dinner with the detective." *More than I could handle being alone with you.*

He nodded, his expression guarded. A burst of sound came from the kitchen, probably a blender. They both relaxed, welcoming the cover of noise.

She blew out a sigh. "So what was that phone call?"

The corners of his mouth pulled down. "The smallest possibility of a lead."

"Aren't you going to tell Macmillan?"

Alessandro shrugged, lifting his eyebrows. "I don't think so. The suspect we have would literally eat him alive."

Chapter 14

Without meeting Holly's startled gaze, Alessandro turned and left. Frustrated lust climbed up her frame, heating every muscle along the ladder of her bones. Holly pressed her palm to her forehead. Her skin felt prickly, her cheeks burning.

Men.

Vampires.

I suppose it would seem strange if I asked for a cold shower before dinner. Fortunately Macmillan seemed too absorbed in his culinary extravaganza to notice her distraction.

The dining room was more formal than the rest of the place, as if he put more importance on that room. The carpet had a dark gray and plum Afghani pattern, the chandelier a sleek, modern design in pewter. The table and chairs were black. By contrast, the green salad looked positively startling.

They began with a light seafood bisque, then medallions of lamb in rosemary sauce, accompanied by peas and couscous. Halfway through her plate Holly was full, but it was too good to stop stuffing herself. If Macmillan quit the force, he had a future as a cook.

They ate with such gusto they barely spoke at first. "I don't get vampires," Holly finally said.

"Who does?" Macmillan replied with a shrug. Now that they were alone he was much more relaxed. "Your friend showed up on my doorstep and refused to budge. This after dodging my calls for two days. He gives me absolutely golden information on the case and then takes off without a word. It makes it hard not to wonder what the hell he's up to."

Protecting his interests. "I think he was called away."

"Probably that queen of theirs. From what I hear he's her local go-to guy."

"He never talks about her."

"No surprise there. Omara's a piece of work. About as big as a saltshaker and rules the vampires in a third of the continent. I saw her when she came by to see the brass at the police station downtown. If nothing else she knows public relations, how to schmooze the suits. But if you catch her off guard, her eyes say you're nothing but a bug."

"A vampire's existence is about hunting and territory. Probably the right analogy is livestock."

Macmillan laughed, the light catching the dark waves of his hair. "Y'know, I get that. After working a few cases that involve the supernatural, I think I've stopped taking growing old for granted."

Holly savored another bite of lamb. "Speaking of winding up as someone's dinner—and I know this sounds very clichéd—it is unusual to meet a man who cooks so well."

"I like food. I really love cooking, but I don't have time to do it much."

"Where'd you learn?"

"My mother was a terrible cook. I learned out of self-defense." He gave his fleeting smile, but it lingered in his eyes. "She worked in a land developer's office. She used to own this place."

"Any siblings?"

"Nah, my dad died not long after I was born, but I have plenty of aunts and uncles and cousins. I think I'm related to half the city. The Scottish half, anyway."

He set his fork down, a slight tensing of his body signaling a change in mood. "I'm glad you came, because I really need to talk to you. Going over the case was great—it was actually really helpful—but there's this other thing I needed to ask you about."

"The personal thing." Holly felt her senses go on high alert.

"Yeah." He sat back, turning his face to the window. "Something really weird happened to me last night. Given what's been going on, that's saying something."

Holly put down her fork. "So, Detective, what could be stranger than killer slime?" *Did I just say that?*

"Call me Mac." Rising, he took the plates into the kitchen, as if he needed a break before he continued. He returned a moment later with parfait glasses filled with chocolate mousse. He set one in front of her with the air of Michelangelo unveiling his *David*.

"Omigosh," was all she could say.

It had layers of dark, light, and medium chocolate topped with melted fudge and mint leaves. He set a long-handled silver spoon beside it. "This is my party piece. Enjoy."

"It looks amazing." Holly thought about how stuffed she was, but knew she would eat every bite. "How come you're not either married or four hundred pounds?"

"I don't eat like this often," he replied. "And I do have serious character flaws."

She took a spoonful, speechless as the chocolate melted on her tongue. He watched her reaction with obvious pleasure.

"How serious are those flaws?"

He looked down at his dessert, showing long, dark lashes. "I like handcuffs."

"Oh, yeah?" Holly took another spoonful of parfait. She remembered *parfait* meant *perfect* in French. "Fur lined or regular?"

"Negotiable." This time he smiled enough to show strong, slightly crooked teeth.

"Sorry," she said, mentally backpedaling. "Chocolate

brings out the flirt. You were going to tell me about the weird thing."

He sat back, all the humor gone. "I've been home today. Some sudden bug."

Holly set the spoon down. She hadn't actually believed his sick-day story. "Yeah?"

Macmillan's gaze drifted away. "Maybe it was food poisoning. I dunno. I went back to work after dinner last night. I got into a completely stupid argument with my supervisor. Then I got deathly ill."

"Any ideas why?"

"I went for dinner and met this hot girl. Her name was Jenny."

Holly's eyebrows went up. "And this is a problem?"

"She kissed me."

"Woo-hoo," she said flatly. *Definitely not dinner-date conversation.*

Macmillan gave her a level stare. "I think she did something to me. It felt weird. She felt weird. I felt weird after."

"Can you elaborate on the weird part?"

"Angry. Hollow. Sick to my stomach. Sort of like I'd lost my life savings and been pumped full of toxins at the same time. I don't think it was ordinary, y'know, science-based stuff. It was worse. Bad magic."

"But you're okay now?"

"Yeah, by the afternoon I was starting to come around." He lifted one shoulder in a shrug. "The only aftereffect is that I'm hungry all the time. Starving. Probably why I went on this cooking binge."

"Could be worse, I suppose."

"Yeah, but now I'm nervous about what happened. It doesn't feel totally gone, and I can't afford a relapse in the middle of a multiple-murder case. I won't have my leads handed over to archrivals and bumbling goofs."

Holly nodded. Now everything was making more sense. "So basically you want me to find out what sort of whammy, if any, this girl put on you, and whether it's over and done with."

"In a nutshell. I remember thinking I wanted a day off, but hey, not like that."

"Right." Holly pondered a moment. "It's true I might be able to detect something if you've got some sort of psychic flu."

"How?"

"Um, different ways. The easiest is really pretty primitive. If she gave you something by kissing you, I could sense it the same way. By kissing you, I mean." Holly couldn't hold his gaze. "All in the interest of medical science, of course. Witches are generally immune, so there's no chance of passing it on."

Macmillan looked both startled and pleased. "Hey, this is like playing doctor the way it should be done."

"Yeah, well, um, witch doctor, maybe." Holly fought to look cool and professional, as if this were all in an average day's work. "Let's just do it, okay?"

They both got up, as if pulled by the same string, and moved to the end of the table. Macmillan took her hand. "No need to rush."

Holly stopped, looking down where he clasped her palm in his. His fingers were strong and square-tipped, a practical man's hand. Slowly her gaze traveled up the expanse of his soft red sweater to his face. *He is awfully good-looking.*

At his touch Holly's body fell still, though her heart began to race with anticipation. Macmillan's fingers slid up her arm, the slow brush of flesh against flesh. It fanned the embers of her moment with Alessandro, rousing an appetite not yet sated. She turned in to his chest, wanting to feel more of him on more of her. His hand traveled over her shoulder and up her throat, coming to rest in the thick fall of her hair.

Yup, this is more than a diagnostic kiss. More than I bargained for.

But it was just one kiss, and maybe it would serve as an antidote to forbidden desires of the vampire kind. An amiable lust danced in her blood. Macmillan—Mac—was warm and friendly, and his obvious interest made her feel desirable. It was liberating. No expectations, no future. No unrequited longing. He was just a good, plain, sexy man, easy on the heart.

Holly's fingers scrunched the thick knit of his sweater, the springy fabric full of the aromas of cooking and the clove aftershave he wore. She caught his earlobe in her teeth, thinking he was the most delicious, edible man she had ever met. His food obsession was taking over her thoughts.

Mac kissed her eyelids, his lashes flickering against tender skin. Holly raised her hand to his cheek, fingertips tracing the first shadow of roughness. Then her mouth found his, their lips hot and sweet with sugar.

Down to work. She opened her senses, searching for traces left by his mysterious Jenny. There was a whisper of something, subtle as a falling feather. She pursued it, considered it, but found no cause for alarm. Probably just the passing shadow of Jenny's presence. No hints of anything more. In fact, every double X chromosome in her said there was *nothing* wrong with Detective Macmillan.

Distraction shattered her thoughts. Strong and competent, Macmillan's hand quested downward, cupping her backside. Enough heat rose between them to threaten the synthetics in her little black dress. *Oh, yeah.* Cooking was not his only skill set, and she writhed against him, taking an animal pleasure in being stroked in all the right places. She felt warm, and fed, and wanted.

She pressed against Mac's weight, enjoying the sheer physicality of their bodies in space. Whether or not the encounter had a future, its present was damn fine. Delicious languor radiated from her belly, making her lean in even as she broke the kiss. Their lips parted with a faint electric tingle.

"Wow," she said, feeling suddenly shy.

If possible, Macmillan's eyes seemed even darker than before. There was a sheen of perspiration at his temples. He was feeling the heat as much as Holly was. *Goody.*

"What's the verdict?" he asked in a whisper.

Holly felt a sloppy grin cover her face. "Oh, I think you're healthy. You shouldn't have any more problems."

Relief widened his eyes. "Hallelujah. Then go make yourself comfortable and I'll bring our coffee." He gave her a sly grin. "Maybe we can discuss a program of preventive health care."

Holly gave a bemused smile, all logical thought having swooned away. She wandered into the living room, the air around her chill after the heat of their embrace. Her skin felt alive to the texture of the couch, the brush of her skirt against her thighs. Mac's embrace had held unexpected depths. It buzzed with the prospect of more. Holly felt like a skydiver at the brink of her jump.

But did she want to jump? Or did she want simply to walk away?

The sound of running water came from the kitchen, coffee on its way. What sort of a conversation would follow a kiss like that? What was Mac expecting? Holly leaned her head against the back of the couch, not sure what she wanted to happen. Even with all the spells she had at her disposal, she didn't have the gift of reading minds, especially her own.

The water sounds stopped. Coffee was getting closer and, with it, the need for decisions. Holly grabbed her handbag from where she'd left it by a chair, reapplied her lipstick, and waited.

And waited. Then she took off her shoes and picked up a magazine. Holly flicked the pages impatiently while she waited some more. *How long does it take to make coffee?*

She got up and went to the kitchen, expecting to hear more running water, maybe the clatter of silverware, but it was quiet. And empty. Dishes were piled in the sink; the dishwasher door was ajar. The coffeemaker carafe sat on the counter, full of water. It looked like Mac had set it down, interrupted in the middle of making coffee, and never come back.

Holly put her hands on her hips. Perhaps he had passed out somewhere, overwhelmed by her womanly charms. She checked the bathroom. It was white and chrome and empty of sprawled bodies.

Next Holly tried the study. It was a small, spare room

with a desk, computer, and filing cabinet. On the wafer-thin monitor, a string-art screen saver did slow cartwheels in the darkness. She wiggled the mouse, but no *Help, I've been abducted by aliens* message flashed onto the screen. She was getting irritated and a bit scared.

Onward to the bedroom. Images of furry handcuffs and stethoscopes danced in her mind, giving life to all the bad-date urban legends that lurked in her imagination. By now in no mood to find Macmillan reclining on a fur rug, she flipped on the overhead light.

Mac was sprawled facedown on the bed, one arm dangling off the side. Then she smelled sickness—psychic sickness, a faint, desiccated, dusty smell, as if death had been dried and ground into a powder.

Omigod, how did I miss this? Alessandro said Mac didn't smell right!

Holly ran to the bed, grabbing his shoulder. The sweater was soaked through with perspiration, his hair trailing in sodden waves. "Mac?"

His only reply was a gurgling haul of breath.

Panic lanced through her. *Sweet Hecate, this happened so fast!* There must have been something there, festering, but something so foreign she didn't recognize it. Something hiding.

She dug her fingers into Mac's shoulder muscle, hoping for a flutter of consciousness that didn't come. She bent close. "Mac, can you hear me?"

The foul energy rolling off him nearly made her gag. As she recoiled, he made a noise between a grunt and a moan. At least it was something. Holly grabbed the phone from the bedside table, dialing 911.

"Ambulance, please!" Holly pleaded.

The plastic receiver slipped from her sweating palm, forcing her to give it a white-knuckled grip. The dispatcher was saying something. Holly stared at Mac's prone form, chewing her lip.

"What is your address, please?" the voice on the phone repeated, the woman's tone sharp.

Holly gave directions, stammering when she tried to

recall the apartment number. No, she didn't know what was wrong. Yes, she would be there to answer the door.

She was panicking. It was the horrible, cloying energy, black like tar, thick in her throat. Rot. Decay. Despair. Not a smell so much as an aura of horror. A gray tide sloshed across her vision.

She dropped the phone. *I'm going to be sick.*

Window. Hard to open. Lock sliding through her fingers.

The dispatcher's voice came in tinny mumbles from the dropped handset.

A blast of cold air rushed into the room. Holly braced herself against the wall, her mouth nearly touching the wire mesh of the screen. The wind seemed impossibly sweet, the room unspeakably foul.

"Oh, God."

She turned at the sound of the wet, rasping voice. The fresh air must have revived Macmillan, too. He was trying to sit up, but every limb shook until the bed itself rattled. He angled his face to her, the whites of his eyes wide with terror. "What's happening to me?"

Holly shook her head. "I don't know." The confession brought a sting to her eyes. *I failed him. I should be able to help, but how?* Tears slipped out, hot with guilt.

"You said I was okay." The words came out like a cry from the heart.

"I couldn't find anything. Honestly. I've never seen this before."

"No." He was on his side now, his legs curling into his chest. His breath was coming in jerks, as if each would gag him with the effort. "No, it can't be. *Oh, God, it hurts.*"

He stopped speaking, his eyes squeezed tight. His mouth opened in a soundless scream as fresh rivulets of sweat ran down his cheeks, soaking the pillowcase. Warped power rolled off him in waves, as if his very soul were vibrating out of phase.

Holly's gorge rose, but she fought it back, steeling herself for his sake. She fell to her knees beside the bed. "The ambulance is coming. They'll help. They'll make it right." *They won't have a clue what to do, but they may keep him alive long enough for me to find an answer.*

"Don't leave me," he said, gripping her hand so hard that it cramped.

"I won't," she said.

"Holly, I'm losing myself."

Chapter 15

"**D**amn you, Pierce, you killed it!" Alessandro folded his arms and looked down at the changeling, disgust welling. Disgust at Pierce's clumsy job of questioning. Disgust at the sight of the grease spot where the creature's body had melted into the carpet.

"It was an accident," Pierce protested.

Omara stood a few feet away, her expression that of an irritated schoolteacher. She was still dressed in the pantsuit she had worn earlier, reminding Alessandro of a carnivorous Emma Peel. They were in one of the hotel's plush conference rooms, the mahogany furniture pushed against the wall. Two of Omara's security vamps stood either side of the double doors, arms folded.

"You could have waited for me," Alessandro growled at Pierce. "Interrogation is my job. I know how to do it properly."

"You always get to question the prisoners."

"Apparently I'm better at it."

Omara cut in. "Boys, I'm glad you're both in touch with your respective inner children, but skip the tantrums."

Her jibe did nothing to improve the atmosphere. *Why did she let Pierce screw this up? When I left, she was angry with him for feeding from the human woman in public. Now she is letting him serve her? Letting him do* my *job?*

Alessandro rounded on Pierce. "The changeling was the best lead we had, and now it's gone. Did you kill it to cover your tracks?"

"What?" Pierce gave him a what-the-hell look. "You think I'm in league with changelings? Why?"

Omara inspected her rings, tilting her hand so the gems glittered in the light from the overhead chandeliers. Their divisive squabble seemed to please her. It certainly gave her the position of power. "Alessandro is determined to think the worst of you. It's the sad effect of centuries of bad behavior, darling. People start to judge." Omara snapped her fingers, bringing the security vamps to attention. "We're done here. Tell the concierge to clean up."

Alessandro swore in lusty, antique Italian. He had left Holly for nothing. Right now she was enjoying a meal with Macmillan, having a pleasurable bonding experience he could never offer her. In so many ways the detective outmatched him.

He wrenched his thoughts back to the mess in front of him.

"Where did you find the changeling?" he asked.

Pierce replied. "University Laundromat. One of the local werewolves phoned in the sighting as a courtesy."

Alessandro furrowed his brow. "The changeling was doing laundry?"

"No, but it was eating someone who was. The werewolves pulled it off the student and held it until we got there. The changeling was pretty, um, subdued by then. I think the wolves were enjoying themselves a bit too much."

Lovely. "Did you manage to get any good information before you turned him to sludge?"

Pierce shrugged. "He was too afraid to talk."

It was all Alessandro could do not to bang his head—or Pierce's—on the wall. "We. Are. Vampires. *We* make the prisoners afraid. Us."

Pierce's eyes narrowed. "Whatever master it served was worse."

The demon. Demons were the only creatures more feared than vampires. Despite losing a suspect, Alessandro felt a flutter of satisfaction. His emerging theories were holding up.

Omara cut in. "The changeling's name was Arnault, and there are others of his kind in Fairview. That was all we learned."

Alessandro frowned. "What about these others? The police looked for more changelings. We looked as well. None were found."

The queen shrugged. "Obviously there are hiding places we missed."

I should have gone with them on the search, Alessandro thought, but he had been watching over Holly. There had been the demon mouse. He couldn't be everywhere at once.

Then he looked at the splotch on the floor where the changeling had melted. *I should have done the questioning.*

Frustration chewed at his gut. He had to work harder. Faster.

Just then the double doors to the conference room opened, and the janitor with his cleaning cart entered, followed by Omara's security men. One vampire carried a Shop-Vac.

"I'm done for the evening, gentlemen," Omara said to her security. "Finish up here, and then you're free for the night." She turned to Pierce. "You can go, too. I think you've done enough damage for one evening."

The last remark was icy cold. Pierce's eyes flared, anger and shame in competition.

Omara touched Alessandro's sleeve. "Let's go upstairs."

She led the way out of the room, crossing the lobby to the elevators. Pierce was left standing alone next to the stain on the carpet.

"Did the changeling say how many others there are?" Alessandro asked. *Surely they got something useful out of the discussion. Omara did not get to be queen without knowledge of how these interviews are done.*

"No, though it sounded like quite a few." The elevator doors opened and they got in. Omara pushed the button

for the top floor, where she was staying. The doors slid
closed.

"So what now?" asked Alessandro. "Another search?
Find another changeling to question?"

"What's the point?" asked Omara softly. "The wolves
captured the changeling, and so it made sense to see what
we could learn. But to chase down another? They are barely
articulate. Their tolerance for pain is legendary. A waste of
time. We need to find their master."

The elevator doors slid open and they got out. Omara
started down the hall to her room, Alessandro at her side.

"I don't understand what happened tonight," he said.
"When I left you earlier, you were going to question Pierce."

Omara waved a dismissive hand. "The affair with the
changeling was more urgent."

"You let Pierce interrogate the changeling."

"Pierce was here and you were not."

"So, just like that, you let him deal with the prisoner?"

"I wasn't about to touch the changeling myself. Besides,
I knew I could count on John's cruelty. He needed a chance
to redeem himself after tonight's little performance with the
human."

She sounded almost—he searched for the right word—
indulgent. Not like Omara at all.

Alessandro tried again, frustration making him push.
"But what if he is in league with them? Wasn't that what we
were wondering? The tokens, the bleeding ring? Murders?"

Without answering, Omara stopped in front of her door
and handed Alessandro the passkey. He swiped it and
pushed open the heavy door, holding it for his queen. The
balcony doors were open, and the sitting room was cold but
fresh. Omara switched on a table lamp, showing expensive,
spacious, and utterly anonymous decor. Alessandro entered
after her, locking the door.

"Consider this," he said. "Pierce's clan is well versed in
magic. Someone has been casting summoning spells. If Clan
Albion wanted to stage a coup, what better way than to raise
an army of changelings and summon a demon to perform
their bidding?"

Omara turned, throwing her arms in the air. "But why? *Why* would there be an alliance between Albion and a race of hideous mutants?"

Thrown on the defensive, Alessandro raised his voice. "I can remember when they were your rivals. Albion was bitterly ambitious. Only your superior sorcery stood between them and the crown, and they would have taken your place as ruler had you faltered for one instant. Do you think they have changed so much since those days? Besides, changelings would never challenge you on their own. They are too few. They *have* to be working with somebody else."

"But John Pierce is not capable of any of this. He is pretty, vain, and foolish. A man with a child's need for reassurance. He behaves badly because he wants my love."

"Earlier tonight you thought he might be the murderer."

"Earlier tonight I was angry with him."

"But the Albion clan has always been a problem. I beheaded Pierce's brother for breaking your laws."

"John would never hurt me. Nor my throne. He adores me."

There was real anger in her voice. Alessandro stopped, not sure he believed what he had heard. Possessiveness. Protectiveness. *She is defending Pierce against me!*

A thrum of alarm traveled through him. Pierce was a wastrel, his family a pack of villains. Omara knew that. *What is going on here?* "Does he know about the portals?"

"I have not discussed the subject with him. Just the murders." Omara fell into one of the beige tub chairs that faced the balcony. The position turned her face from Alessandro. "I do not know how many ways I can say this. John is selfish. He is not, however, a mastermind of evil."

The vulnerability in her voice shocked him. He stared at her profile, and she stared out at the dark, sparkling night. *She loves him, but treats him like a dog. He abases himself in order to wound her, but still seeks her favor. They are engaged in some bizarre, destructive affair. A queen cannot behave this way. Not with the throne in the balance.*

His voice grew soft, but cutting. "Is it possible that one who has walked the gardens of ancient Babylon and has seen the sun rise and set on the pharaohs could stoop so low as John Pierce? The notion is breathtaking, and not in a good way."

Her tone was glacial. "Don't criticize me, Caravelli. I've slept with *you*, after all."

"But you would still tear my eyeballs out in a human heartbeat if you thought I'd crossed you. You forgive Pierce everything."

Omara gave him a scathing glare.

After all that the queen had put him through, Alessandro felt a petty thrill of satisfaction. He had found her out. "You like him. You *love* him. He challenges you."

Omara looked away.

Alessandro went on. "Ancient evil though you may be, you still fell for the bad boy. Perhaps that is why you've promised to share Desire the last times we've met, but never kept that pledge. I am not Pierce. I no longer please you."

Her profile was marble, yielding nothing. His triumph melted to pity. For all her power and ferocity, Omara had surrendered to a charming smile. That wouldn't be so bad, but Pierce was Pierce. "You can't afford to lose your judgment. Not now, with your throne under attack. You know it."

"I know it." Her voice was small. "In all these centuries I've made only this one blunder of the heart. I know I am in the wrong. A queen's mistakes are the errors of a whole people."

Alessandro sat in the tub chair next to hers, stretching out his long legs. They sat, sharing the view of the skyline. The moment was oddly companionable. The power balance between them had shifted, if only for that tiny slice of time.

"Is he involved?"

She sounded weary. "He showed no mercy to the changeling, as you saw."

Alessandro pondered that. "Where do you think the changelings are coming from?"

"Maybe the portals," Omara answered. "The changelings disappeared from the earth, and then here they are again. It is one possible answer."

He sat up straight. "I thought only demons dwelled on the

other side. Demons and the damned souls sent to keep them prisoner in their hell. In the Castle."

"There is more to the Castle than that. It is a danger to all the supernatural species."

Alessandro's shoulders tightened. "How so?"

"It was meant as a prison for us all."

"What?" Alessandro held his breath, shocked.

She sank further into the chair. "The only nightmares I ever have are about getting trapped there."

She stopped talking. A TV went on in the room next door, loud at first; then someone turned it down. After a minute or so Omara went on.

"When I was young, magic was commonplace. Demons and dragons prowled freely in the dark places. Humans were not the all-powerful species they are now."

She stopped again and toed off her shoes.

"And?" prompted Alessandro.

"The human sorcerers banded together." She sounded far away, her voice rising and falling in the rhythm of the old storytellers. "They believed, in the beginning, that they would weave a great spell to help protect their people. In the end they built a monument to their own absolute power."

"A prison for nonhumans?" He had never known where the Castle came from.

"Yes. They gathered together and raised a powerful force, the most fearsome since the birthing of the sky and the seas. They created their prison for the demons and the dragons, the hellhounds and the werebeasts, the vampires and the fey. They gave it existence outside the laws of time and place, and there they locked away any creature that possessed the merest whiff of magic."

Alessandro saw the irony at once. "Any creature excepting themselves, of course."

"Indeed."

"But they failed," he put in. He didn't want to believe what she was telling him. "The supernatural never left this world."

"Not entirely, but it was close. What followed was geno-cide. A few, like me, managed to escape their armies. It took centuries before our numbers came back to even a fraction of what they once were. And only in these last few years have the supernatural races walked as we once walked, openly and in freedom."

"So is that why you spearheaded the move to let the humans know we were here?"

She gave a small smile. "That was part of it. I remembered what it was like not to hide. Some called me a visionary. Really, I was just bringing back a way of being that I had once taken for granted."

A beat passed in silence. "But if so many members of the supernatural races were hunted down and taken prisoner," he said slowly, "what happened to them all?"

Omara went very still. "Those that were taken never returned. The sorcerers stole human men from their families, gave them unnatural powers, and forced them to guard the Castle for all eternity."

"But . . . no one summons a vampire or a werewolf. Only demons. If those original prisoners survived, they're still trapped."

Omara watched his face, her own carefully blank. "No one who goes into the Castle ever comes out. Ever. And if the guardsmen come to our world to hunt, they capture any supernatural creature they find and drag it back to their hell."

Alessandro felt a cold nausea. *All those unfortunates are still trapped there, forgotten.* In the next room the television murmured on.

She continued as if she had never paused. "There are tales in the wind that the Castle is crumbling and disorder rules its halls. They say the guardsmen are dwindling and those who remain have gone mad with despair. They say the inmates have run amok. Perhaps, after all this time, the Castle's magic is fading. Even I don't remember the names of the self-proclaimed sorcerer kings who built it."

Alessandro stared out the window, nursing a slow, welling anger. "Why has there never been a rescue mission?" he asked. "Why have I never heard that there were more than demons being held?"

Omara brushed the air, flicking away his outrage. "It is

kept a secret because there can be no rescue attempts. All the nonhuman leaders agree."

"Why not?"

"Would you really want to share our world with powerful beings who have been locked up in the silent dark for thousands of years? They would be mad, warped things by now. Once you opened the floodgates, there would be no telling what horrors would come vomiting out of the breach."

"So you let them all rot." His voice was a razor.

Omara raised her hands in surrender. "Tell me who has the resources to provide social services to an entire hell dimension! For centuries, those of us who had escaped capture had all we could do to survive."

"But now?"

"Trust me when I say the rest of the vampire council is even less sympathetic than I am. No one wants a refugee problem. Not when we're still trying to earn rights for our own people."

"How enormously practical."

"What would the humans think if they found out? What if they learned there was a prison full of demons and deadly lunatics just beyond their back door? It would be disastrous." She paused, breathing hard. "And don't forget the guardsmen. They follow where portals have opened and look for escapees. That is one more reason we must return the demon to the hell it came from. They may not notice that a pack of hellhounds got loose, but they certainly won't let a master demon roam free. If they find our community in Fairview, we'll have to battle them, too. Some of us might be dragged into that hell."

Alessandro clenched his teeth, sitting hard on his instinct to fight Omara's pragmatism, to ride to the rescue. As little as he liked it, she had valid points. Still, he wasn't letting this go.

"Is that how the changelings became imprisoned in the Castle?" he asked. "They were captured by the guardsmen?"

"That's not the only possibility. A few modern sorcerers know how use the place as a cosmic garbage can for their troublesome enemies. Your witch's ancestor, Elaine Carver, used a portal to rid Fairview of a demon over a hundred years ago."

A puzzle piece fell into place with a cynical snap. He finally saw Omara's plan. *You bitch.*

Alessandro turned in his chair. "Of course. Witches do their magic by manipulating energy. You need Holly for more than necromancy. You need her help to control the portals!"

Omara smiled.

He felt his heart give a single, desperate thud. "That portal killed Elaine Carver."

All the vulnerability in Omara's expression was gone. Her eyes mocked him, because she knew she had struck his tender place. Dread—or perhaps it was a premonition—rolled over Alessandro. Hot fury rushed in behind it. He was starting to understand a great deal, or at least to make some good, ugly guesses.

"So you remember your history," Omara said quietly.

No! There was no way he was going to let Holly start down a fatal path. His thoughts scrambled, seizing on one horrible realization, then another. He made one last leap of logic.

"You've had me watching Fairview for over a hundred years, monitoring what you said was strong, unstable coastal magic. Was that the whole reason you wanted me here, rather than at your side, where a champion ought to be?"

She looked amused, as if waiting to see what trick he might perform. "Whatever do you mean?"

He felt his lip curling back, revealing fang. The old loyalty that bound him to his queen was hanging by an unraveling thread. "A mere surveillance job could be handled by any reliable hireling. You didn't need a warrior here, unless there was something big that might need fighting."

Omara's chin jerked just a fraction. He'd hit the target. "Do you have a point?"

Alessandro hesitated, but ultimately let the words go. "You worked with Elaine Carver when she banished the demon before. You expected that demon to find its way back out of the portal. You just didn't know when, or how it would manage it, but *you knew it was coming.* You've had me watching for it."

"And if I did?" Her eyes were bright and hard. "What does that matter now?"

"Why the secrecy? Why pretend you have no idea what is going on?"

"Up till now, I did not want to admit that, despite my magic and the Carver witch's sacrifice, the portal might reopen. To say such a thing would be to invite accusations of weakness."

"But now the demon is here, and yet still you say nothing. Why not?"

A long beat passed, and Omara's expression crumpled into a rictus of agony. She buried her face in her hands, her body collapsing into itself.

What now? What more could she possibly be hiding? Alessandro scrambled to his feet, automatically offering comfort, but she waved him away, hugging herself.

She lifted her face. Her eyes were dry, but her expression was raw. "I pretend ignorance for a good reason. I cannot say I know about the demon and then do nothing to stop it. I've been waiting to see what your witch can do. I must be sure of my resources."

"What do you mean?"

"I don't have the power to stop the demon anymore." She stood up, her arms folded across her body. "When my Seattle apartment was ransacked, the thief took my grimoires, all my magical tools."

"What?" Omara had lied to him in Sinsation. An utter lie. His stomach was a lump of granite. "You said none of those things had been taken!"

"They were all taken. Every tool I need to perform the smallest shred of sorcery. Every magical instrument that I took decades to attune to my power. It will take me a century to replace a tenth part of it all."

The queen angled her back to him, staring out the window at the nightscape. She dropped her arms to her sides, her breathing heavy and slow. He could see she was deliberately, brutally forcing her emotions under control. "No one knows I am powerless. I've been pretending for weeks. Stalling. Bluffing."

Alessandro's mouth went dry with shock. *"The Book of Lies?"* He named the tome of demon magic that had won Omara her throne.

"Gone." The word came out like a curse.

It was Omara's best weapon. Indescribably deadly. Full of violent secrets. And it wasn't as though she could order another from Evil4U.com. She had stolen it from a demon herself, a bold stroke that had nearly cost her everything.

Omara looked nowhere near so victorious now. Her fires banked, she seemed small and frail. "I have enemies that would tear me to pieces if they knew I've lost the book. You're right about Clan Albion's ambitions, and they are just one name on a long list. I cannot be exposed. That's why I need your witch's help so badly. *She must work the magic that I cannot.*"

He touched her shoulder with his fingertips. She flinched as if they were red-hot, but did not shake him off.

"Why didn't you tell me?" he asked, fear for her pushing aside his earlier anger. "You took me in when I had no clan. You are my queen. You know I will always protect you."

"Because I can't even defend my throne from other vampires, to say nothing of demons. Your loyalty, brilliant flame though it is, cannot protect me from everything. It was information I could not afford to share. Not with all the work I have done. I've made too many gains with the human lawmakers to lose my seat halfway through the game."

She spread her hands in a gesture of despair. "I've been trying to hold on, to find a solution before my weakness is made public. There is no one with my skill and patience willing to negotiate with the humans."

"I know. We have everything to lose. Who took the book?"

"More important is where it is now, and how I can get it back." Omara lifted her head, pride warring with a look of numb misery. "I'm afraid."

Alessandro felt his body go cold and still. There was

something else, something neither of them wanted to say. There were no ex-monarchs among the vampire clans. Crowns were always taken by a combat to the death. It was the one fight where champions weren't allowed.

Without her power, Omara was as good as dead.

Chapter 16

Holly experienced an acute sense of déjà vu. Here she was again, following a medical emergency crew, her male companion of the moment felled by a mysterious evil. Even one of the ambulance attendants was a repeat from the Flanders house.

Maybe dating immortals has its merits, she thought, fighting off a wave of grim hysteria. *At least the Undead are hardy.*

She tailed the ambulance in her Hyundai, trying to steer while hitting a speed dial on her cell. She had no idea what she was dealing with and wanted backup. So far tonight she was batting zero. First she'd failed to identify Mac's malady. Then she hadn't been able to tell the ambulance attendants what they needed to know about his medical history or even his emergency contact numbers. The hospital would have to call the police station for his personnel file. Now Holly had to figure out what—and how much—to tell the doctors. Supernatural illnesses were a matter of hot debate in the medical community. Some doctors refused to treat such cases altogether.

Alessandro's phone went to voice mail. Whoever had called him away had him fully occupied. *Damn.* She closed the phone without leaving a message. She was going to have to handle this one on her own.

It was nearly midnight when she skidded through the doors of Emergency, her high heels sliding on the bare tile. She blinked and squinted, the bright light surreal after the darkness of the streets.

"I'm looking for Conall Macmillan," she said to the nurse behind the admitting desk. "He came in by ambulance a few minutes ago. How is he doing?"

"You a relative?"

"Sally Macmillan. I'm his sister." *Goddess forgive me a white lie.*

The nurse typed something, glancing at the computer screen as it refreshed. Her expression never flickered. "Can't tell you anything one way or the other. There's nothing here. The doctor admitted him, but that's it."

"Why not?"

"It's busy tonight."

Holly bit back a protest. "Can I wait with him? Where is he?"

The nurse pointed down a hallway to the left, her attention already on somebody else. Holly headed past the cluster of chairs filled with walk-ins waiting their turn for attention. She stripped off her wrap, feeling grossly overdressed. The air was hot and antiseptic, a dying ballast flickering the fluorescent lights overhead.

There was little to see anyway. The hallway was painted a muddy yellow, but little bare wall was visible. Filing cabinets, metal storage lockers, and even desks crowded the corridor, making impromptu offices. Narrow rolling beds filled any spare hall space, the occupants waiting for the doctors. Not enough staff, not enough room. Fairview was growing faster than its hospital funding.

The chaos made it harder to find Mac. He had been rolled headfirst into a narrow linen closet, his feet still poking into the hall. Holly grasped the metal rail at the foot of the bed, feeling as if she had found the prize in a treasure hunt. He was unconscious, pale but otherwise normal—probably the result of a sedative. At least he wasn't in pain.

"You with him?"

Holly looked over her shoulder. A young nurse in pink scrubs was making the rounds, checking on the overflow patients.

"I just got here," said Holly. "Can you tell me how he is?"

The nurse stopped and wedged herself in beside the bed long enough to check Mac's pulse and write a note on the chart hanging at the end of the metal bed frame. "You'll have to speak to the doctor."

"When will that be?"

"Hard to say. Three people from an MVA came in." The nurse paused, looking at Holly's shoes with a mix of envy and amusement. "You might want to go get a coffee and try again later." With that, she moved on.

Holly edged her way into the closet beside Mac's bed. Out in the hall a phone rang and rang, none of the staff hustling by taking the time to answer it. Holly put her hand over Mac's. The skin was cool and dry, almost normal. The strange waves of energy that had rolled off him earlier had stopped. Now he had barely any aura to detect.

Guilt bowed her head. *Why didn't I see this coming?* She wove her fingers through Mac's, studying his face. His breathing was light, lips slightly parted as if to speak. He had a handsome face, dark-lashed and strong-boned. A lot of women would be grateful to wake up to a man like Mac.

He had come to her for help, and she had totally screwed up.

Queasiness rolled through her, half emotion, half a reaction to the hot, stuffy, disinfectant stink of the ward. Holly released Mac's hand and leaned against an open shelf stacked with towels. Her movement must have penetrated his sleep. Mac turned his head, brow contracted. Holly trailed her fingers over his forehead, smoothing out the tension. She hadn't been able to help him so far, but that didn't mean she wouldn't keep trying.

Okay, what do you know? she asked herself.

Alessandro had picked up on something, but all he said was that Mac didn't smell right. She'd put that down to male rivalry. Could have been more. She knew that Mac's case and the whole vampire-changeling-demon connection could be significant.

The diagnostic kiss had been deceptive. For one thing, she'd hoped Mac could distract her from wanting Alessandro. That had kind of skewed her concentration. Sure, that was her fault, but maybe it wasn't the whole story. Grandma had said that demons could conceal their true natures, even while sharing magic. Could the same be true of their spells? Maybe she'd missed whatever magical germ Mac had picked up for the simple reason that it knew how to hide, waiting for the right conditions.

Is that even possible? Am I jumping to conclusions?

The only firm clue she had was the girl Mac called Jenny. That encounter seemed to be ground zero. *What kind of supernatural cooties get passed on in a kiss?* How long would they hide in a person's system? Had Holly's kissing Mac, pushing her own magic into the mix, somehow kicked the bugs into action?

Her range of diagnostic tests was limited to one. Holly unzipped her purse and rummaged for the antidemon charms she'd picked up from Grandma earlier that day. Physically, they were tiny silk bags of herbs and feathers, hung on a string so they could be worn around the neck. The construction was basic, but the magic packed inside was powerful.

Should have thought of this sooner. She should have already been wearing one, but had thought Mac's dinner would be safe. *That says so much about my social life.*

Following the natural law of handbags, the wad of charms had sunk to the bottom of Holly's purse. She pulled them out, untangling the pendants until she could work two free. She slipped the fine leather thong of one over her head, tucking the small bag down the front of her neckline.

The charms worked only if there was a demon on the scene. If the area was clean, nothing would happen. Holding her breath, Holly slipped the second charm over Mac's head. Rippling energy raised the hair on her nape. Holly fell back as Mac sat bolt upright with the smooth motion of a puppet pulled by a string. His eyes opened, shocked and sightless.

"Mac?"

Clawing at the bag, he began to scream.

"Stop! Don't!"

"What do you think you're doing?" came a new voice.

Holly wheeled around, expecting to see the young nurse. Instead there was a blond woman in jeans. This time Holly's witch senses hit a home run. *She's the demon!*

And not bothering to hide her power now.

A brilliant flash smashed Holly against the wall.

Mac was incredibly cold. He was dreaming of Jenny. She was kissing him again. He was hollow, empty as a bowl, and she filled him up with hot, greedy wanting. A burning sensation made Mac shudder, as if he trembled from a fever. It was beyond fleshly desire, beyond mere friction and release. This hunger was piercing and its satisfaction far beyond flesh.

He was dissolving into a black mist. That part was weird.

And then it was over. There was nothing but a fleeting moment of completeness, and then a wrench as she pulled away. Flooded again with pain, he tried to scream, but could only float, disconnected, his cry a wisp of thought inside his head.

Then the pain impaled his chest like a stake through the heart. His scream became a solid thing, a stream of red-hot fire leaving his throat with the force of a spear. Suddenly he was sitting up, his eyes open. *Where the hell am I?*

The dream dissolved, but the pain still flamed in his chest. Gasping, he scrabbled at his flesh, his fingers stiff claws.

"Stop! Don't!"

Someone. Female. *Holly.* White-hot pain subsumed every thought, and she was the cause.

He screamed out his agony in gouts of inhuman rage. A dozen hands held him down. A prick in his arm was followed by a soft cloud of euphoria. His mind rolled sideways, capsizing into seas as warm as blood.

Someone ripped the burning thing from his chest, and he surrendered to velvet oblivion.

* * *

When Mac woke, something fundamental had changed. He had no idea what it was, just a bad, bad feeling.

The logical part of his brain still stood, like the steel ribs of a burned-out building. He was in a different place now. White walls with white curtains around the bed. The room had the all-time, no-time light of hospitals. He wondered how long he had been there. He couldn't tell whether he was hungry or just sick to his stomach.

Then he saw she was there. Not Holly, but Jenny.

Jenny? Instinct made him want to hide, but he couldn't take his eyes off her. Uneasiness stalked him, circling like a hungry cat. He wasn't sure how he knew, but his future depended on what Jenny chose to do now. Right now.

He was afraid. She was evil, and not human. *Don't need superpowers to figure that one out.* So he watched, barely daring to breathe, belly-up and flat-out like a goddamned sacrifice. She was waffling about what to do with him. There would be pleasure for both of them, but part of *her* pleasure meant *his* destruction. Her will was bleeding into him, killing him drop by drop.

He had no idea how he knew that. He just knew.

Mac tried to move his arm. Restraints. That surprised him. *What the hell happened? Did I hurt somebody?*

"You put on quite a show, Detective," Jenny said, as if she had heard his thoughts. Probably had.

She shifted her position on the visitor's chair, uncrossing her long legs, crossing them the other way. Dark jeans. High-heeled boots. Scarlet hoodie. New clothes all around. *The evil-entity business must be improving.*

"What did you do to me?" Mac barely recognized his own voice. Every syllable vibrated in a raw, parched throat. Vaguely he remembered shouting. Hurting. Both that memory and the present were surreal, as if he were floating along in a theme-park ride and events were just murals on the wall.

Jenny heaved a bored sigh and wound a lock of long blond hair around her forefinger. "Hard to explain what I did. What I am. What you're going to be. A bit like telling a baby how to walk. It'll all make sense soon enough."

"Spare me the supervillain crap."

"Don't knock it till you've tried it." Rising, she crossed to the bed and rested one hip by his knees. The mattress dipped, and he felt the warmth of her body through the covers.

Bending forward, Jenny began unbuckling the strap that held his right wrist. Her hoodie was only half-zipped, showing a skimp of black tank top beneath. He got an eyeful of warm, white, round flesh that looked as soft as goose down. *Oh, yeah.*

She seemed to be taking a long time with the strap. The blanket over his belly stirred, his mind backpedaling but his body stupidly game.

"In case you're wondering," Jenny said, "I sent your friend on her way."

Holly. He had a fleeting image of Holly's face looking down at him. That snippet was followed by other, harsher sensations. Sickness. An ambulance. Pain. Mac blinked, the recollections quashing his body's reaction. "Is she all right?"

Jenny kept working at the stubborn buckle. "Of course. The charm she wore limited what I could do in the few seconds before hospital security came running in answer to your screams. She won't remember being here, though. Nothing, in fact, after finishing the dinner you made. She has great memories of that meal, by the way. Your culinary skills made quite an impression."

"How did you—"

"As a point of fact, I did not have to do much at all." She glanced up, eyes glinting with mischief. "She had to leave. The hospital staff thought she'd been torturing you with a voodoo curse and tossed her out on her ear. Nasty things, those homemade charms."

"Wait. Wait. What charms?"

"That's what burned you. That's what kept me from really getting a grip on your friend."

Foreboding suffocated Mac. "Then how did you wipe her memory? Did you kiss her?"

"Not yet." Jenny gave a sly smile. "Don't worry; she'll wake up safe and sound in her own bed, believing you're just fine. I put the rest of her memories back where I found them. There just wasn't time to do more."

The strap came loose, and Mac flexed his arm, feeling a rush of blood to his fingers. *If Holly doesn't remember anything after the meal, she won't know where I am or what happened to me. No one will. Oh, God, what do I do?*

Jenny reached across his body to work on the other arm, her breasts close and ripe. "It wasn't time for me to take her yet, anyway."

"Huh?" The other strap released, giving him blessed freedom.

"I tried to take her before, but she was too strong. When I'm ready"—Jenny smiled, tapping one finger on Mac's chin—"and I've made her weak, you're going to bring her to me."

A lock of her hair brushed Mac's arm, too intimate, too close. The strange fascination Jenny held for him snapped like old string. He lunged, his hands wrapping around her slim throat, bearing her down onto the bed.

"Let me go," he growled. "Whatever you've done, take it back."

Jenny gasped, then chuckled, daring him with her eyes. A thrill of revulsion curled his innards. Mac squeezed harder, desperate to silence that mocking laugh, sure the delicate architecture of her spine must snap.

She scrabbled for his hands, prying them apart with horrifying strength. Quick as a cat, she grabbed Mac's shoulders and pressed her mouth to his, thrusting deep with her tongue.

He suddenly knew he wasn't getting out of there alive.

This kiss was nothing like the first time. Her lips were cold, sweet as chilled melon, smooth as moonlight—and she was feeding him something. It was the stuff of life itself clinging to her tongue, slipping over his teeth and into his soul like a pearl of iced honey. He shuddered with an echo of release, as if on some other plane they were having mind-blowing sex.

Here, the orgasm was all about drinking life.

Within a moment all sickness vanished. His body surged

with tingling energy. He was reborn, both the spirit and the warm, hard-bodied man. Reborn wholly and bestially ravenous.

She was feeding him her sweet evil.

Demon, he thought. He'd read about them, but now the word meant new things.

Powerful things.

Jenny kissed him again, and his entire being surged toward her with bloodthirsty greed, squandering itself for a taste of that cold elixir. As he begged with his body, with his lips, Jenny licked and sucked, consuming, teasing, devouring Mac's life force and poisoning him with her own, one delicious drop at a time.

That poison was his sole relief. He drank it down even as a dark vacuum blossomed inside him, leaving a damnation of hunger in place of his soul.

Demon!

Chapter 17

Holly woke from a bizarre dream about her big sister, Ashe, driving around in a tiny blue toy car. The car was about six inches long, but in the logic of dreams, her adult sibling fit in it just fine. If the image had significance, it was expertly disguised.

Odd, because Holly seldom dreamed about her family. She and Ashe rarely even spoke.

Rising from her bed, Holly stopped in surprise, her foot halfway into her mule slipper. She never went to bed without getting undressed, and yet she still wore the little black dress from last night. With morning-after-the-night-before paranoia, she began checking herself over, stomach knotting at what she might discover.

The charm bag had wound its way around so it was hanging down her back. *When did I put that on?* It looked a little deflated, but she had been lying on it.

Holly gazed into the mirror, contemplating the Dalíesque ruin of her makeup. She had raccoon eyes from not-quite-waterproof mascara. Her hair was doing the bed-head thing. Otherwise she was fine. *Weird.*

Was I drunk? No, if she'd had that much to drink she'd feel sick. Had Mac slipped something into her drink? That didn't seem likely, but everything after dinner was a blank.

This had happened once before, after that big-M spell went bad when she was a kid. The spell that she and Ashe had done. *Maybe that's why I was dreaming about her. Something similar happened.* Except then a whole year had disappeared. This time she was missing only a few hours. And it tasted different in her mind, a mustiness she couldn't quite place. *Not the same, then.*

She looked out the window. Her car was in the driveway, paint intact, everything normal. *Double weird.*

Wheeling away, she went to take a shower. *I have to shake this mood.* It was the first day of school. *Remember? The cute boyfriend, the college degree, the successful business? Time to go for your goals.*

Yeah, right. Goals seemed laughably out of reach. She'd settle for twenty-four hours of something approaching a normal life.

When she was dressed, she phoned Grandma.

"I had a blackout," Holly began.

"So either your detective is a real keeper or a complete bore. Wake up with anybody you didn't recognize?"

Great. The bad-old-lady routine. "No. I woke up in my own bed, fully dressed, alone."

"Where's the fun in that?" She heard Grandma exhale smoke. "Get a life, girl."

"I'm serious. I don't remember leaving Mac's place, or driving home, or anything after we finished eating."

Grandma's voice dropped, becoming serious. "How do you feel?"

"Fine. Tired, but injury-free and unmolested." *And blue*, she added silently.

Kibs jumped up on the table, pushing his head under her hand. She petted him absently, scratching under the white bib of his chin.

"Were you wearing one of the charms I gave you?" Grandma asked.

"Yup. I was wearing it when I woke up."

She heard Grandma's breath release. "Then I wouldn't worry. You warded the whole house yesterday, more work than you're used to doing. Stretching your magic has resulted in memory loss before. You probably just pulled a muscle in your interior spell factory."

"You think so? That's a pretty poor performance."

"Well, you're not used to doing that sort of thing, are you? It takes practice."

The hearty note in Grandma's voice didn't fool her. A blackout of any kind was serious, but they'd been down this road before. The holes in Holly's memory had always been a mystery. No medicine or magic had ever helped. Now that she felt fine, it seemed almost pointless to bring it up.

"What should I do?" Holly asked, more because she wanted comfort than anything else.

She wasn't going to get any. "Stop worrying and go do something useful. I'm busy hunting down demon prophylactics."

Demon prophylactics? "Antidemon spell" sounds so much better. "Is there any way of getting back my memory of last night?"

"Probably not, and playing with memory is dangerous. Is it that important?"

Frustration nipped at her. "I keep feeling like there's something I should be taking care of. Something urgent."

"Like what?"

"I haven't a clue."

"Does it have to do with your first day at the university?"

"Could be. I'm not sure."

"Wouldn't surprise me. You've got a lot to think about, especially right now," Grandma said grimly. "Adult students have more on their plates, you know. There's stress even without the demons."

Holly sighed. "I just wish I could *do* something about the demon."

"Like what?"

"Anything. I'm still not a hundred percent about going to school with this thing on the loose. If you want, I could pick up the reading lists and then come over and give you a hand."

Grandma made an exasperated noise. "Go. Be educated. There's nothing you can really do to help me today. I can research faster without you hovering, and I'll feel better knowing you're in a public place. Most demons prefer the old classic dark alleys."

At first, Macmillan wasn't sure where he was. Nothing made sense until he felt the sheet drag across his skin, and then the soft brush of a female knee over his thigh. *She* was with him in his bed, in his home.

Daylight filtering through the curtains gave the place a soft-focus glow. Jenny's hair scattered like corn silk across his chest, the long strands stirring as her fingers traced the arch of his ribs. He only vaguely remembered the night. At some point they had returned from the hospital. At some point friends from the police station had come, checking in. Jenny had sent them away, bespelled and trading jokes about Mac finally getting some. Jenny had come and gone after that, sliding into his bed as dawn warmed into day.

And then he had slid into her, over and over. It had been a revelation of hungers.

So many irrelevancies had fallen away, including concepts like "him" and "his." The borders of his self were breaking down, and he was becoming one of Jenny's limbs. Everything was Jenny, and she was all. Mac was merely a half-forgotten state of mind.

At the moment the universe was all female and pushing a breast into his eager hand, the nipple hard and ready for communion. Mac obliged, rubbing its tip with his palm, tweaking its crest. Whatever pleasure he gave, he was rewarded a thousandfold with the taste of her.

Jenny had gone out hunting, drinking souls, feeding on wandering humans with her kiss. She brought the silver energy home, giving him that sustenance one sip at a time. She did so now, leaving him shivering with pleasure, hard and ravenous for more.

"I want you to do something for me," she said.

"Anything." He suckled at her breast, making her close her eyes with a little gasp.

"The vampire who is always with the witch, Omara's man—what is his name?"

"Caravelli."

"I want you to phone him." She took Mac's face in her hands, forcing him to look up.

"And say what?"

"I'll tell you what I need you to say. I have a plan. I have a dream." Her finger traced the curve of his lips. "And you're part of it. You, my love, gave me the power of your formidable strength and will. It called to me like a strong and savory scent. What a gift." She kissed him lightly. "And I have been growing stronger since."

Mac felt a welling happiness. He had pleased her. Then he felt sad. "I am not enough. You need others."

"You have been the best"—she kissed her fingers and pressed them to his mouth—"but I want the Carver witch. She has real power."

Mac smoothed the tumble of her hair. "Yeah, she'd be good." He had kissed Holly. Now that he had changed, he understood the strength of what he had tasted.

"She's been too strong for me up until now, but she trusts her friend the detective. You, my love, can take her by surprise."

Mac imagined Holly's power, imagined how it would caress his tongue. *Holly has more power than she knows how to use. But in many ways she is weak, while I am growing stronger.* "Can I be there at the end?"

Jenny reached up a hand, stroking his forehead, his cheek. "You want a taste of her. We can arrange that, yes. You are precocious, my love."

He grabbed her hand, kissing the palm, tasting the echo of her magic in the salt of her skin. She gave a low laugh, other hand searching under the covers until she found the prize she sought. "You will need to learn to hunt for yourself soon."

"Please," he whispered, begging. "Teach me." He had already tired of mere scraps. He could feel the need building inside like a slow, rolling thunder. A taste here and there was not nearly enough.

He'd never been one to pick at his food.

*   *   *

Once Holly was on the campus, back-to-school excitement finally kicked in. She endured the gauntlet of the bookstore, emerging one of an overburdened and penniless herd. Tonight was a late class, and the soft blue-gray of the early evening wrapped the walkways and buildings in a watercolor shroud. A needling rain dampened the air, making the smells of coffee and cedar sharply extravagant. Her backpack was heavy with clean new textbooks and pristine highlighters. A rare fresh start was ahead. She treasured the mood, imprinting it into her memory.

Holly's route took her between some of the oldest brick-and-ivy buildings on the campus. Except for the denim and fleece wardrobes of the students, there were parts of this old area that looked as they had during the Edwardian age.

The path looped within view of the Flanders house. Holly reluctantly looked in that direction. The ornamented black gables still rose above the other roofs like the top tier of a macabre cake. Mac had mentioned that the police were still conducting their on-site investigation, delaying the execution of the burn order.

Even though the house was a block away, its presence chilled Holly. It was all memory—there was no whisper of power there—but she did a good job of spooking herself. Holly stopped, oblivious to the other students passing by her, bumping her with clumsy packs and bags. *I beat that house. I should feel victorious when I look at it, but I'm uneasy. Why can't I just pat myself on the back and move on? Where's the unfinished business?*

The clock tower chimed the hour. She'd have to navel-gaze later, or be late.

The Business Studies Building was one of a cluster of modern structures that sprawled on the far side of a vast parking lot. The entrance was hidden among a welter of flower beds and stairways that seemed to go nowhere, and Holly walked all the way around the building before she saw the welcoming glow from the glass double doors. By then she was hot and out of breath.

"Holly!"

She stopped. It was Alessandro. "What are you doing here?" she asked.

"I need to talk to you." He leaned against the concrete wall, nearly hidden by the shadows of the entryway, a cigarette in one hand. He smoked, she knew, to mask the scent of a crowd of humans. Apparently it was a bit like walking into a restaurant—the smell of so much food whetted the appetite. Given that excuse, she'd never asked him to butt out.

The end of his cigarette flared red as he stepped into the light. *Wow*, she thought, forgetting everything else for a moment. *Not subtle, but wow.*

Tonight his legs were encased in black leather with rows of fringed decoration that spiraled around his thighs. His hip-length coat was festooned with matching fringe. The long streamers of leather swished and slinked with feline grace, making her want to stroke them, braid them, run them through her fingers.

"What can I do for you?" Holly asked, imagination supplying some graphic suggestions. "How did you find me, anyway?"

"It's the first day of classes. I knew you'd be here. With slight encouragement, the administration office was most willing to assist with your schedule and room assignments." Alessandro took another drag on his cigarette, exhaling dragonlike through his nose. She watched the white smoke, transfixed. "I wouldn't bother you, but I need your help."

"With what?"

"Let's go someplace to talk."

Holly nodded, her mind still tangled in the fringe. "I have a class starting, and I'm nearly late. Is this something that can wait an hour?"

"An hour," he said, clearly tamping down impatience. "Yes, I suppose."

"I don't want to miss my very first class. It's important."

Alessandro seemed to come to a decision and shrugged. "Then I'll come with you. We can talk afterward. The instructor is a friend."

"A friend?" Alessandro never mentioned friends.

"Yes, he set up my laptop."

Holly smiled. "You, Alessandro, have a computer?"

He tilted his head to one side, half-coquettish, half-reproachful. "You think that is so ridiculous? That I am perhaps too old or too blond to keep up?" He rolled the cigarette between his fingers, studying its glowing tip.

Holly shrugged, her mind slowly refocusing from his outfit to the class ahead. "I just didn't think you'd be interested in techie stuff."

He mimicked her shrug. "Who does not want to surf the Web?" He raised one eyebrow, daring her to respond. When she was silent he grinned, showing just the tips of his pointed teeth.

"What on earth would you surf for?" she asked, her imagination supplying several yucky suggestions.

"One has to keep up with the times." He crushed the cigarette and held the door open for her, fringe swinging as he moved. "There are so many interesting chat rooms, and so many daylight hours to kill."

"What, you can get high-speed Internet direct to your coffin?" Holly looked around her for room numbers. She turned right.

Alessandro made a rude noise. They had gone about three steps when he asked, "How was your dinner last night?"

"The food was good," she said lightly, thinking about the phone call that had taken him away. When would he get around to telling her what had happened?

"If all you remember is the food, next time I should plan the evening." Alessandro thrust his fingertips into his pants pockets. The pants were so tight, that was all that would fit.

"I doubt you could cook like Mac."

"Mac, is it?"

"We had a very nice conversation. Very relaxed. You're just being a pain."

"I have six centuries of experience wooing women." He gave another slow, fang-tipped smile. "I have a surprising depth of knowledge when it comes to interpersonal relations. When I have a woman in my arms, I do not aim for 'nice conversation.' "

Holly rolled her eyes and walked into the classroom, heading to the back of the room, where the last two empty desks sat with their humming computers.

Yes, it was a night class, and she should have known it would be a mixed population. All those folks who couldn't come in the daytime were there. A few students dressed in ultra-Goth looked like they had goblin or perhaps Unseelie heritage. A young-looking vamp read a Howlywood fan mag, filled with gossip on supernatural screen idols. One nerdish ghoul hungrily gnawed his pen and eyed the other students as though they might be his next chew toy.

Holly dropped her backpack with a thud. A spiral-bound course manual marked, *Computer Concepts: From E-mail to E-business Platforms,* lay neatly on the desk. She wiggled the mouse to kill the screen saver and brought up the start screen.

At the front of the room a man was standing next to the digital projector. He looked about the same age as the students, but was apparently the instructor. For a moment Holly felt ancient. He smiled diffidently at the class and nodded to Alessandro. With wavy brown hair and a narrow, sensitive face, he was cute in a youngish way. When he filled out in a few years he would have hunk potential. She felt ancient for another moment.

"Hello, and thank you so much for coming," he said, all charm. "My name is Perry Baker."

A loud crunching came from the right side of the room. All heads turned curiously, and the crunching stopped as suddenly as it began. Holly stretched, trying to see over the heads between her and the source of the noise.

Perry pushed his glasses up the bridge of his nose. "Um, please don't eat the mouse."

Baldly curious, she stood up to get a better look at the show. The ghoul sat perfectly still, a belligerent expression on his face. The cable that normally ran to the mouse ran into his mouth, dangling like a tail. His cheek bulged, evidence of guilt.

This should be interesting.

The ghoul chewed once and a plasticky crunch resounded, like a very loud potato chip. Holly never thought a peripheral could sound so tasty.

A nervous giggle rippled through the room.

Tugging authoritatively on his oversized black T-shirt, Perry Baker marched up to the ghoul's desk. He held out one long-fingered hand. "Spit it out."

The ghoul glowered as only ghouls could, with mean little eyes and a wrinkly nose.

Beside Holly, Alessandro stood up as well, his eyebrows drawn together. She guessed he was deciding whether or not to intervene. Ghouls could be nasty customers when riled, and vampires were one of the few species able to beat them in a brawl.

But Perry was as yet unfazed. "Spit," he repeated slowly and firmly. "It. Out!"

The ghoul growled, a disgusting sound like something rotten just come to the boil. That made Perry take a step back, but it was more a regrouping than a retreat. He drew himself up as much as his youthful dignity would allow and pulled off his glasses.

Without warning his lip curled up, his lower jaw dropping almost to his chest. Fangs sprouted from his gums in a painful-looking wash of blood and saliva. His mouth grew huge, pushing forward to accommodate more and yet more of those sharp white teeth. A long, lolling red tongue surged wetly past his jaws, questing toward the ghoul.

The growl that emerged from Perry rumbled like low thunder, rattling the pen on her desk and rising to a crescendo that vibrated Holly's breastbone. Hair stood up along her neck, her instinct to flee at war with the instinct to be small and invisible. After a long moment the growl finally stopped, but it echoed in the air, cowing the room into silence.

Holly blinked. Perry looked completely normal. He pushed his glasses back on and extended his hand once more. Without moving the ghoul spit out the mouse. It fell to the desk in a clatter of gummy, crushed plastic, the workings spewing like entrails to the floor. Perry looked at the mouse, his brow wrinkled in consternation.

"Consider yourself expelled," he said, and walked back to the head of the class.

Holly sat. Alessandro sat. There was nothing like a werewolf for maintaining classroom discipline.

Chapter 18

Like a good teacher, Perry made the rounds of the work-stations, making sure he had happy little students. When he leaned forward to see Holly's screen, she caught the musky scent that clung to weres, a smell that reminded her of oiled leather. It wasn't bad, just not human.

"Good," he said, straightening. "You're at the head of the class." He looked at her curiously, his eyes a dark blue behind his glasses. "I just wanted to ask: Are you the Holly Carver that, uh, knows Ben Elliot?"

"Yes," she said, trying to read his tone. Was the fact that he knew her good or bad?

Alessandro looked up from pondering an online auction of lingerie, obviously eavesdropping.

Perry pulled off his glasses, polishing the lenses with the hem of his oversized shirt. "I heard about . . . Well, he's an idiot. If you need anything, you let me know. Anytime. I'm almost always here or in my office."

After class Alessandro and Holly walked across the parking lot back to the main campus. It had started to drizzle, a thin, persistent wetness more mist than rain.

"Why would a ghoul take a computer class?" Alessandro said unexpectedly.

"Is this like a chicken joke?"

"No, I'm serious."

Holly shrugged. "I guess ghouls have aspirations, too."

"Equal rights for all," Alessandro mused. "Interesting how that plays out."

They walked along, moisture gleaming on the sidewalks. As the trees at the edge of the parking lot swayed in the wind, shadows brushed the glistening pavement. Holly turned up the collar of her coat. Alessandro didn't seem to notice the cold.

"What was that comment about Perry being there for me?" Holly asked. "That was awkward. Has our young professor got a grudge against Ben?"

Holly looked up at Alessandro. Beneath the streetlights he looked almost human, the pallor of his skin tempered by the shifting shadows. Her fingers longed to trace the angles of his face. *I shouldn't be alone with him, and yet every time I turn, he is there.*

"Perry is much like your Ben," he said. "A cherished son, brilliant, young, and always able to have whatever advantages money could buy. Perry's pack owns a large gravel company west of town."

"Are you saying they're too much alike?"

"They would be very alike, except Perry isn't human, and Ben is one of those spearheading a petition to keep nonhumans out of the faculty. Support for his movement is gaining ground, and if the nonhuman teachers go, it won't be long before the open-admissions policy will disappear. It's all part of the prohuman backlash."

"You've got to be joking!"

"Believe it. Already Perry has to post a notice on his door warning students they are entering the office of a monster. Ben probably doesn't even know Perry is a competent sorcerer, and will only make matters worse if he finds out."

Holly swore. *This is ridiculous.* The werebeasts' ability to shape-shift was hereditary, not contagious. They kept to themselves and, unlike humans, worked hard on maintaining civilized behavior. Ben had never mentioned any prohuman activities to her. *Was he a bigot all along, and I didn't see it?*

Maybe love really was blind, or else Ben was a better actor than she thought. "So how did Perry know about me and Ben?"

"I don't know. Ben must have said something. Staff room gossip. They're in the same department."

Holly felt sick. "Great. Did Perry tell you Ben and I broke up?"

Alessandro tilted his head, studying her for a long moment. His expression was hard to read. "Your grandmother told me. And I try to know everything about you."

Holly swallowed, feeling her heart skitter. "You know that's possessive and creepy, right? Like showing up at Mac's? Showing up here? Why do you keep doing this?"

"There is a demon on the loose, and it knows you."

"Right. Yeah. I noticed. That mouse was hard to miss."

He thrust his hands into his pockets. "It's not that I don't have confidence in your ability to protect yourself. . . ."

"And yet everywhere I go, you're always showing up. It's called stalking."

He gave a single, short laugh. "You don't want to see me? You want me to go away?"

Oh, great. "It's not that. It's . . . It makes me feel helpless. I don't need that."

He stopped walking and turned to face her. "Are you sure you're not sending me away because I frighten you?"

How I feel about you frightens me. Holly ducked her head. "Alessandro, we're standing in a movie cliché. Female student on campus at night, alone with the predator. I wouldn't be here if I didn't trust you with my life. I'm not stupid, and I'm not unprepared. If you or anything else jumps me, I will fry your ass with every scrap of magic I can summon. Got it?"

He gave a lopsided smile. "And you are worried about feeling helpless? What is there left for me to do? Sometimes . . . sometimes I don't know how to approach you. Where I fit."

His lost expression made her want to bang her head on a wall. *Alpha males.* "I'm so not good at this."

She felt the pull of his magnetism and the corresponding

push to be free of his seductive influence. If it were only the vampire part of him, it would have been easy, but the man was every bit as compelling. "I'm not trying to get rid of you, but you're my friend, not my private thug. I can't have you doing everything for me. I don't *want* a bodyguard twenty-four-seven."

At that he nodded, his expression closing down. Despite her best efforts he'd taken her words as a rebuff. Irritated, Holly looked away. *He just doesn't get it.*

He pressed his lips together, a quick gesture of decision. "Well, then let's even the account. As I said before, I need you to do something for me. Tonight."

"Okay." She almost sighed in relief. At least it was a change of subject.

"Let's go somewhere warm, where we can talk and you can stop shivering."

Barnaby's Café and Tearoom wasn't technically on campus, but it was close enough. Dripping with faux Victorian atmosphere, the cafeteria-style eatery had etched-glass windows and an elaborate rolled-tin ceiling.

It also had the best bakery in town. Holly bought a brownie—not because she was hungry, but because it pleaded with her through the glass case. She sat facing the tall windows, enjoying the thrum of energy that pulsed through a city when night fell and the neon came to life.

Not interested in food, Alessandro had dropped her off so that she could go through the line while he parked. Now he glided toward her, his tall, black-clad figure alien amidst the human patrons. Pulling up one of the flimsy metal chairs, he sat, knees bumping the underside of the tiny table. With an irritated mutter he shifted back, unzipping his fringed jacket to reveal a mesh T-shirt beneath the leather. He tugged the jacket collar into place, crossed one lace-up boot over the other, and shook his pale hair free until the longest of the curls brushed the arm of the chair.

It was quite a performance. Holly wanted to applaud. Alessandro, the perfect picture of rock royalty, had *arrived*.

He tilted his head, looking at her intently.

"So, you need me to do something for you," Holly prompted, plowing her fork through the thick fudge of the brownie.

"I do," he said.

With one finger he began making roads through the crumbs on the tabletop. His jacket swung open to reveal a metal shape under his arm. A gun? Holly felt her eyebrows lift in surprise. She hadn't noticed it before. He must have had it in the car. He noticed her looking and shifted to better hide it.

"Expecting something unusual?" Holly asked, her voice tight. Her gaze roamed the café. There were three other occupied tables, but they were a little way off.

"Yes. That is what I wished to speak to you about." He looked at the remnants of her brownie as if it were swamp ooze. "Are you done with that yet?"

"No." Holly sipped her coffee. "But you can start talking."

"You recall the conversation we had with Macmillan about questioning a spirit."

"Yes, the one where I heroically volunteered to perform necromancy, and you got a mysterious phone call that prompted you to leave, muttering about bad smells."

"That would be the one." Frowning, he flicked a crumb onto the floor.

"What about it?" The reminder brought back the irritation she had felt the night before.

"Macmillan called this afternoon," he said. "He has a lead on a grave at St. Andrew's. There've been reports of spirit activity. He wants to meet us there in about, oh, an hour."

Holly sat back, the flimsy café chair giving a plaintive creak.

"Tonight?" Her voice had the same tone as the chair. She didn't want to do this. She hated necromancy. She hated herself for volunteering. *So much for Ms. I-can-look-after-myself.*

"Yes. Are you still sure you want to do this? You are free to say no."

She wasn't sure how she looked, but Holly felt pale. Still, she nodded yes.

Alessandro noticed her hesitation. "The spell doesn't take much time to prepare, right?"

"Not if we're just raising a ghost rather than a body, but . . ."

"Ah." He took out his fancy gold lighter and began toying with it, turning it over and over in his hand. It was a classic smoker's fidget. "You need more time to prepare yourself?"

Now Holly's stomach wasn't happy about the brownie, at least not after a chaser of panic. "No, no, I'll be all right."

"You sound like you're trying to convince yourself."

"I'm putting positivity into the universe in hopes that it will manifest."

That earned her a slight smile. "There is one change that might make this easier. Or not. I am not sure." He leaned forward, putting his lips inches from her ear. "My queen believes she can identify the demon. All we need our spirit to do is confirm her suspicions."

Holly went cold, as if her blood had suddenly stopped pumping. "How long has she known this?"

A look of bitter frustration passed over his face. He was obviously biting back something he couldn't say. Holly sipped her coffee, but it suddenly tasted off, as if the conversation had tainted it.

"What's going on, Alessandro?"

He looked cautiously around the café. "The information just came to light."

"Do I really need to raise the dead just to check her answers?"

"There's more. We need the spirit's assistance in finding a lost article. It's my understanding that magical artifacts can be traced through the ether."

"Yeah, it's all part of being stuck between worlds."

Holly noticed that the patrons at one table were leaving, scraping chairs over the floor and chatting at top volume. She looked at the clock over the door. It was nearly ten. The place would be closing up soon.

"So, what is it we're after?" Holly asked. "Ruby shoes? A spray can of Demon-B-Gone?"

"I can't tell you."

"That's ridiculous. I can't work like this."

Faster than her eye could follow, his hand was on hers, his long hair swinging from the sudden motion. His voice was so quiet she could barely hear him. "Listen to me. There was a theft. Many books and objects were taken, but we seek one book in particular. It holds the secrets to weaken a demon's powers so that it can be banished. We have to find that book."

Mollified, Holly hitched her chair forward. "Okay."

His eyes shifted sideways. "You must say nothing of this. This is not information we can share with anyone, not even the detective."

"So you're finally trusting me with one of your secrets. Hurray. I need more. Was this book stolen from a sorcerer? A vampire? What's the history of this theft?"

He narrowed his eyes. "Just remember that not all secrets are safe to know. Your job is to raise the dead. Let me question the spirit."

"Because you know the specifics, and I don't." She glared at him, waiting for a response. "Such as, let me see, what book this is, or who lost it, and why this one in particular was stolen."

"Precisely."

"Keeping me in the dark like this doesn't help. Do you realize how it makes me feel?"

He raised an eyebrow. "Understand this: I'm keeping your skin whole. In time we may not be the only ones looking for these items. Not all vampires play well with others, and the less you know the safer we all can sleep."

Holly looked away, furious. She could understand his point, but she liked hers better. "We're supposed to be partners."

"You get the car keys when we're beating up on a possessed house. Right now I get to drive."

She made no reply, trying to calm down enough to find a new argument. *This is absurd. How am I supposed to convince a ghost to help us find a book when I don't even know the title?*

"Trust me, Holly; I know what I'm talking about."

"Can I?" She shrugged, letting her annoyance show. This was the crux of the matter. "I can't trust somebody who won't trust me."

Alessandro's expression turned cold. "Don't try blackmail."

Riding a bubble of frustration, Holly nearly lunged across the table. "You keep hiding things from me. It hurts."

Alessandro put his hand on her cheek. The touch was nearly human-warm. He had fed that night. "I'm sorry, but I can't give you everything you want. There are secrets here that aren't mine to tell. I can't betray them. Honor is one of the few things I have left."

There was no arguing with his expression. In fact, she wanted to wipe that look off his face before it broke her heart.

Holly pushed his hand away and flopped back in her chair. "Fine. If it gets us a step closer to a demon-free existence, let's just go do the deed. Where's Mac?"

With a stormy look Alessandro stood, jacket fringe swinging. "He said he'd meet us there."

"You boys come up with all the fun activities, don't you?"

Chapter 19

They took his T-Bird, the rumble of the big engine in competition with the guitars ululating from six overpowered speakers. Apparently they were through with casual conversation. Holly was quiet, wrapped in a sulk like a cozy blanket.

The guitars died midshriek as he killed the engine. St. Andrew's spread out before them, draped in a mantilla of sea fog. Holly got out and buttoned her coat against the clammy wind.

"I can't see a damned thing," she complained.

"Then stay close to me." Alessandro pulled out the gun, the holster making a whispery rasp of metal on leather.

The sound made Holly's skin crawl, but then her eyes adjusted enough to see the gun properly. It was one like Mac had, made for silver bullets. He fitted a suppressor onto it.

Cold sweat slithered down her back like an inquisitive snake. "What are you afraid of?"

He turned, his features lost in the darkness. "Not much. But I am cautious."

Walking around the long nose of the car, she put herself on his left side, away from the gun. He gripped her hand.

"Follow me," he said, and he led Holly between the graves.

Short iron fences enclosed many of the plots, just the right height to trip over. Holly strained all her senses, trying to keep from stumbling. Water dripped from leaf to leaf. She could smell the sea, the cold mist salting her lips and turning her cheeks to ice. Above, the clouds thinned and rolled, the moonlight fading in and out, making gossamer trails in the fog.

Alessandro stopped, and she bumped into him. With a brush of his arm he swept her behind one of the small mausoleums that dotted the cemetery. Gun poised, he crouched. She ducked down behind him, bracing herself on the gritty stone of the building.

"What is it?" Holly whispered.

He pointed. To their left shadows moved in and out of the fog. Shifting backward, he put his lips close to her ear. "Ghouls, and not the college crowd."

Her next breath shook. A pack of ghouls was something to fear. Never needing an excuse to snack, they would shred and eat a lone human in a matter of minutes. She blessed Alessandro for bringing the gun.

Twin notes of a foghorn moaned. She put her hand on Alessandro's shoulder, leaning in close. "What do we do?"

He shook his head, the brush of his hair soft against her skin. "We wait and watch. They don't normally come to St. Andrew's. It's too far into the city. If they're sniffing around here, somebody sent them."

"If they're being good little soldiers, then who's the general?"

He held up a hand for silence. The creatures were crossing in front of the mausoleum, drawing close enough that Holly could see their outlines against the moon-whitened fog. She felt the glide of muscle and bone beneath Alessandro's jacket as he took aim. The physical contact was comforting, but she drew back to give him more room to move.

There were a half dozen ghouls moving in a close-packed clump. Each about the size of a twelve-year-old human, they looked gangly and skinny, walking with a boneless, slumped posture. Many had ball caps and baggy pants, but ghouls never wore shoes. Their fingers and toes had long, curving claws that would shred through any canvas or leather in seconds. Holly shuddered, pressing against the rough, mossy rock of the mausoleum, wishing she could dissolve into it.

Then she felt Alessandro tense. Pointing again, he indicated a figure that was pushing forward to assume the lead position in the pack. It was not a ghoul. Holly stared, squinting as if that would somehow make what she saw prettier.

If it could have straightened up, it might have been as tall as a man, but the creature's spine curled over until the head seemed to thrust forward. Barrel-chested, hairless, and nearly naked, it half ran, half waddled in a rolling gait more animal than human.

It stopped, turning to the ghouls. It hissed something at them, gesturing toward the ocean side of the graveyard. The ghouls milled in confusion until it cuffed one on the ear, knocking it to the grass. Then it waved a long, malformed arm again and turned to lead its charges away. As the pale light caught the thing's face, she could see enough of its features to make her stomach roll. It had no nose or mouth, just a slitlike opening full of needle-sharp teeth. Holly cringed back, sweating with petrified revulsion.

A long minute passed before Alessandro spoke. "They're gone."

"What was that thing?" she asked, feeling cold beads of perspiration run down her ribs.

He turned, his eyes flashing gold in the moonlight. "That was a changeling."

"A vampire?" she said, aghast.

He rose to his feet, looking around. "We do not acknowledge them as vampires."

"Where do they come from? How did *that* happen to them?" Holly rose from her crouch, feeling the blood return to her toes.

Alessandro peered around the corner of the mausoleum before answering. "We do not speak of it, so do not repeat what I say."

"Okay." Was this confidence her consolation prize, to make up for all the things he couldn't tell her?

"We do not gratuitously make vampires. We control our numbers. There can be only so many, or . . ." He shrugged.

"Too many wolves for the number of sheep?"

He shifted his feet as if embarrassed. "Precisely. But it is also a complex process. It can easily go wrong, and if it does, the results are abominations."

"The changelings."

"Yes. Things happen during the Turning. Centuries ago there were blunders. The mistakes were allowed to perpetuate. Those were the changelings." He turned and looked around the corner of the building again. "I think it is safe to go on." He glided out of sight.

Holly crept after him, her tennis shoes quiet in the long grass. She threw her senses open for a moment, testing the immediate area. She could feel Alessandro, a dark, still presence. His vampire mind was closed to her, but palpable. All around the spirits of the dead whispered to themselves, a low level of consciousness punctuated by the occasional restless mind. It was like any other graveyard. She could sense nothing else. Where, then, were the ghouls and their changeling leader? She should have been able to sense them if they were still on the grounds.

Alessandro stopped and whirled, gun rising and braced in both hands. "Holly, get behind me!"

Four changelings emerged from behind the tombstones, two on either side of the path. "Ssssandro!" one of them hissed. It might have been laughing, but its batlike face made it hard to tell.

"Giuseppi," Alessandro replied. "How lovely to see you. It's been so long."

He aimed his gun at the creature's forehead and pulled the trigger. Even with a suppressor, the noise seemed huge in the still, fog-laden night. Holly flinched away, but she still saw the back of the changeling's skull explode all over a stone angel. The silver bullet was pretty much gravy. A shot like that would kill anything, supernatural or not.

There was a microsecond of suspense, the aftershock of violence shushing through the cedar trees. Then ghouls exploded out of the greenery, loping on all fours, gibbering and yipping like monkeys.

Already Holly was behind Alessandro, moving as he moved, backing into the trees. He fired again and again, dropping a host of ghouls and one more changeling.

Holly had no gun. She was her only weapon. With her senses open she felt the space around her, seeking a source of energy to use. The air of the graveyard was thick with ambient force, the magic of death and departing souls—no shortage of raw material. She just had to figure out how to use it.

Power swam under her feet, viscous and sweet as syrup, a vein waiting to be tapped. She reached for it, but wavered. *How bad is this going to hurt?*

The gun clicked empty. "Holly!" Alessandro shouted. "Quickly!"

Agony. Learn to love it. She grabbed at the graveyard's ambient power and threw a blast at three ghouls charging from her right. She thrust blindly at the danger, relying on pure reflex. Sheet lightning flickered and the ghouls flew backward, end over end, their clothes aflame. Holly reeled, staggered by the recoil, nauseated by the pain and vertigo swirling in her head. Her aim was sloppy, but she'd gotten the job done.

Alessandro faced the last two changelings. Pulling a knife from somewhere, he growled, fangs bared, pure menace in the sound. Holly backed away a few steps, her blood zinging with terror.

With a roar he grabbed one changeling and threw it hard on the ground while the other jumped him from behind. The knife fell to the grass. The force of the attack knocked them all sideways, but Alessandro threw the second creature off, never letting go of his first opponent. The changeling on the ground beneath him snapped and writhed as Alessandro crushed its throat with bare hands.

The second changeling rolled, snatching the knife as he got to his feet. Holly grabbed the empty gun from where Alessandro had dropped it and charged in, too wild with adrenaline to think clearly. The second changeling thrust at

Alessandro, ripping the leather in strips from his jacket. She swung the gun like a club, catching the creature behind one pointed ear. It howled, a shattering, feral racket, but it dropped the knife.

Wheeling, it lunged at Holly. Claws whipped out, swiping at her face. Holly blocked the blow with her forearms. Heat lanced down her right wrist as one claw caught her skin.

She ducked away, cradling her arm, and saw the full horror of its face, what features it had now mashed and distorted beyond even B-movie imagination. *That was once human?* Worst were the eyes, shriveled and yellow, but they blanked as Alessandro crushed its neck.

Knees wobbling, Holly stumbled to the ground. The other changeling, the one Alessandro had thrown down and choked, was already dead.

"We were ambushed! How come I was blind to them?" She gasped, trying to catch her breath. "I felt around earlier, but they weren't there!"

Alessandro picked up the empty gun and holstered it. Then he retrieved the knife. His hands were steady, but he was grim. "My money is on a demon shield. The demon is helping the changelings fight us."

Her jaw dropped. "A shield?"

Alessandro grabbed her hand, pulling her up. "Demons can sometimes hide behind a psychic screen, rather like supernatural stealth technology. It's rare that they can screen more than themselves, but I've heard of it."

"Sweet Hecate! If it's a shielding spell, it's huge! And so subtle you don't even know it's there." This was not good news. That meant the demon had enormous power.

He tugged her toward the path. "Let me take you home. I don't want to find out if there're more ghouls where those came from."

Holly didn't argue. They ran toward the car, the moon a fitful searchlight sweeping the fog. As soon as the T-Bird was in view, he stopped, sniffing the air. "Are you all right?"

"I think so. You?"

"I'm unhurt." He ripped a dangling piece of leather from

his ruined jacket. His eyes still glowed in the darkness, the aftermath of his fighting rage.

They slowed to a walk, then stopped beside the car. Holly leaned against the familiar planes of its hood, panting hard. Alessandro stood before her, crackling with tension. He was close enough that his toes brushed hers, the fringe from his pants brushing against the soft denim of her worn jeans. He held out his hands, offering to pull her upright.

She wavered. A moment ago those hands had been wrapped around a changeling's throat. The memory spooked her, but also made her feel safe. He had saved her life. Her vampire, the one on her side, had been the most deadly. The comfort of that was primal, gut-level, and as fierce as the power that had sung through her moments ago.

Holly took his hands, letting him pull her to her feet. She leaned on him as he held her arm, his fingers resting on the sensitive point just above her elbow. The night hummed around them, the electric darkness alive with expectation. Holly drank it in, letting it intoxicate her.

They had battled an immediate, flesh-and-bone enemy. They had won.

He protected me. I protected him back.

His mouth brushed hers once, twice, and then took possession with ferocious appetite. The moment was as primitive as the deadly fight, the kiss merciless. Holly savored him, tasting and tugging, making demands of her own. At last she had the fringe within her grasp.

Adrenaline thundered in her blood, driving it hard in her ears. Her fingers scraped against the ruins of his leather jacket, her nails finding patches of his mesh shirt and skin beneath. She worked her fingertips through the tears, caressing the hard planes of his chest beneath. Breathing harder, more raggedly, he pulled her hips against his.

This was not all vampire magnetism. It was there, but only like an interesting garnish on world-class cuisine. Holly tore her mouth away, her gaze seeking his. His eyes were dark amber fire, a delicious alchemy of danger and need.

I'm not supposed to be doing this. I'm supposed to be the strong one.

The moment broke, or perhaps it only spun into something new.

"You're hurt," he said, the words breathed more than spoken. He pulled her left hand from where it had burrowed beneath his jacket. He stretched out her arm, turning it palm up. Blood stained the torn sleeve of her coat.

"I didn't even remember that," she said. "The changeling scratched me."

But now that the wound had her attention, it hurt like hell. Alessandro tore back her sleeve, exposing a long shallow gash that wept blood in a slow ooze. He bent to the wound and inhaled, a faint rush of air that was oddly erotic.

"The injury is clean." He gave her a sidelong look, carefully veiled. "But I can stop it from bleeding, if you'll let me."

"Uh, no, I—"

He bent his head, his long golden hair falling like buoyant silk across the inside of her elbow. Then his tongue slowly slid along the bottom of the cut, rounding it with delicate precision.

Oh! Holly shuddered, transfixed and strangely aroused. Surprised, more than anything else. It felt . . . seductive.

He raised his head, eyes wide and wild. "Is that all right?"

Holly gave a mute nod. The moment stretched out, swollen with significance.

Hot and wet, his tongue traveled up the length of her forearm, gentle and firm. Holly felt gooseflesh covering her from nape to toe, bringing her breasts to hard, aching peaks. There was the touch of teeth, nothing more than the glance of a hard edge in passing—but whenever she felt it, a jolt like honeyed fire speared her through.

He took the blood with the humility of a supplicant, but with a sensuality distilled from centuries of unslaked lust. So much invested in a single act. She shivered, her body hot and cold, restless and yet hypnotized into a heavy stillness.

When he reached the sensitive, ticklish crook of her

elbow, ready to start down the other side, Holly made a tiny sound. Alessandro pressed his lips to her flesh where he worked, leaving a kiss. She put her other hand on the back of his head, losing her fingers in the thick, springy hair, cradling him against her.

"I am yours," he whispered, his cheek brushing her skin.

The truth of it trembled in her like the voice of a bell.

The slow ritual of his tongue was rhythmic, patient, and tender. As Alessandro promised, the bleeding stopped, her life sealed safely back inside. When he was finished, he bound her arm in his large white handkerchief. Holly had always wondered why a vampire would carry one. Now she could guess.

There were no words to speak. Holly leaned into his chest and he held her, the night whispering to itself all around them. How long they stood, she could not say. She felt cherished, at home.

He is mine.

Now what do I do?

Unexpectedly, Alessandro caught his breath. "Macmillan."

Holly stepped out of his arms. "Oh, Goddess, we were supposed to meet him!" And if the ghouls had found him first . . . Holly could not even bear to complete the thought.

Alessandro already had a cell phone out, but Holly didn't recognize it.

"Whose is that?"

"It belonged to one of the changelings."

"Why are you using it?"

"To see who is expecting a call from this phone."

Holly heard the ring at the other end, but she was distracted by the gathering frown on Alessandro's face. She heard the click of the phone being answered.

"Giuseppi?"

It was Mac's voice. Holly sagged against the car.

Alessandro shut the phone. "We were set up."

Chapter 20

Macmillan is going to pay for this stunt.

Alessandro signaled to turn. He was going to see Holly safely home, report to Omara, and then tear Macmillan's head off. He might reverse the last two items. Options were important.

"But *why* would he do something like that?" Holly smacked the dashboard.

Alessandro flinched, protective of the car. Who knew what an angry witch could do to vintage leather? "I don't know. Somehow our enemies got to Macmillan."

Holly looked perplexed. "Last night he seemed fine."

"What did you talk about after I left?"

She sighed. "I don't remember. I kind of blanked out. I was doing a lot of magic, warding the house against more demon invasions. Grandma thinks I might have popped a psychic gasket. Like I was telling you before, I seem prone to memory loss."

Alessandro frowned. *This isn't good.* "You lost all memory of last night? I thought you said you had dinner and conversation."

"Yeah, well . . ." Holly twisted her ponytail, as if pulling at her hair might stimulate brain cells. "I remember dinner.

Good food, but pretty much everything else after you left is just . . . gone."

"Are you sure it was simply stress?"

"What else would it be? That's what Grandma thinks, anyway."

Holly's grandmother was seldom wrong. He relaxed a little. "It wouldn't be the monotony of the detective's company? Perhaps there was nothing worth remembering?"

"Yeah, right." Once more Holly thumped the dash with her fist. "What happened to him? He seemed like a nice, normal guy."

He hated seeing her so upset. *How can I fix this?* "Leave Macmillan to me. I'll find out what's wrong. If he can be helped, I will see that it is done."

Holly turned to face him, her features fading from light to dark as they passed under streetlights. "Thanks. I'd hate to think he ended up collateral damage."

"You like him."

"He's a decent guy. I'm sure he was pleasant company, even if I don't remember."

"A night with me would be unforgettable." Alessandro let all the unspoken heat between them leak into his tone, let it wash away the fear and uncertainty he could hear in her voice. "You would not forget *me*."

Holly's eyes glittered in the darkness. The look was pure feminine fire. Whatever else was happening that night, there was still unfinished business between them. *Is it business we can risk finishing?*

Alessandro pulled into her driveway. Streetlights shone through the lacy branches of the hawthorn trees. He turned off the motor, a stampede of sensations raging through him. The taste of her was still in his mouth, everything she was, the salt and the sweet.

The blood he'd tasted had been the merest tease, but it was all he'd dared take without causing harm. It had been her perfect trust that had saved her. If she had struggled just once, the instinct to hunt might have won.

She trusted me. He loved her for that. All of him, the

vampire and the man. He would go to his final death, walk into hell itself, if that meant she would live her life in safety.

The solemnity of his thoughts brought on a moment of panic. Not even Omara had that kind of power over his soul. *I think I am in trouble. How can I lose a heart that barely beats?*

Holly shifted, leaning over the seat to get her backpack. The air stirred with her scent, reeling him closer still. "Are you coming in?" she asked, getting out of the T-Bird.

Alessandro sat for a moment, his hands clutching the wheel, before he could move. He was frozen, caught in a brief wave of terror and need. He was a monster. She was vulnerable.

I love her. I will make sure everything is safe inside her house; then I will leave. "Of course. I know you warded the house, but I still want to check it over. Just in case."

"Yeah, I'd hate to have to send you out for more mouse-traps." Holly ran up the steps to unlock the door. There was a flirting invitation in her tone that was impossible to miss. He followed, using vampire speed to catch up.

He allowed himself to dream for the split second it took to reach her. *What if I could be the man, and not the monster, for the smallest slice of time? Surely that is not asking the moon and the stars?*

He shouldn't. There was too much to do. He had responsibilities. There were risks.

She switched on the entry light. "Come on in."

"Thank you," Alessandro said, wavering for the merest second before stepping inside her doorway.

Holly watched as he stood for a moment, every line of his body uneasy. Then, after a quick look down at himself, he peeled off the shredded remnants of his jacket, dropping the ruin on a chair. She would miss that fringed leather, or at least the fantasies it inspired.

"Make yourself at home," she said, leading the way into the living room. She grabbed for a note of normalcy. "Can I get you some tea?"

"Yes, thank you." There was a shred of uncertainty in his

voice. Things had changed between them, but neither yet knew what that meant.

"I won't be a moment."

As she turned to head for the kitchen, he directed his attention to her shelf of CDs, methodically flipping through the jewel cases.

I let a vampire taste my blood. That should have terrified her, but it didn't. The experience hadn't been frightening at all. Instead her stomach felt curiously light, buoyed by nervous anticipation. Maybe all her assumptions were wrong, and there was some way that she and Alessandro could be more than partners. Or maybe she was just believing what she wanted to think. *How can I know?*

The kettle quieted to a rolling boil, rattling gently on the crooked old burner. She spooned Lady Grey, lemony and comforting, into the pot and filled it. Steam curled out of the spout, reminding her of a miniature ghost.

She let the moment linger, full of possibilities. Around her the house felt serene, its consciousness turning inward like a cat drowsing by the hearth.

It was a moment of peace. *I'm so tired.*

Holly took the tea tray into the living room and set it on the old walnut library table that sat under the window. With deliberate care she poured the tea and passed Alessandro his cup. He sniffed the steaming liquid, holding the raku vessel in both hands.

"Do you think we will be safe here tonight? No more changeling armies on the agenda?" she asked.

"Between us, I think we can handle any nuisance callers." He shrugged, smiling a little. The mesh T-shirt he wore showed off his chest and arms. He had hard, practical muscles, the physique of the pre–industrial age. It made the shrug a fine thing to watch.

She sat down. The crisis was over and with it the need to act. *I'm so tired.* She sipped her tea, feeling its warmth sliding down her throat like an elixir.

The moment of ease was treacherous. Just like after the battle with the Flanders house, the backwash of fear and magic took an emotional toll. Tears started to slip down her face before she even noticed them. Hastily she put her cup on the coffee table and wiped her eyes with the back of her hand.

This is ridiculous. There had to be a box of tissues nearby.

"Holly?" Alessandro rose. She could hear the confusion in his voice.

"Sorry." She jumped up, but he grasped her hand. For a moment she could not bring herself to raise her eyes, but stared at the holes in his mesh shirt instead. His flesh looked ivory white where it peeked through the threads. Twisting away slowly, she tried to turn her back without making the gesture seem angry.

Instead he put his hands on her shoulders, holding her still with a grip gentle but unyielding as rebar. When a vampire wanted a person to stay, they stayed.

"What is it?"

"It's been a long day," she said, blinking the wetness from her eyes. The storm of tears slowed but left her queasy. "It's no one thing. It's everything. Mac. The demon. School. Everything."

"How can I make it right?" Alessandro asked, his hands sliding from her shoulders to her arms.

"It's nothing you can fix. I'm just tired." She leaned into him, feeling the honeycomb of his shirt on her cheek. All those long, lean muscles were beneath her fingertips.

"Holly," he whispered, putting his hand on her hair, stroking it. "I am sorry. I wish everything were easier."

Resting there for a long moment, she drank in the feel of him. A single heartbeat thumped under her ear, just audible over the quiet music he had put on the stereo. She raised one hand, playing her fingers over his biceps. The knot in her chest was easing as courage flowed from the mere act of touching skin to skin.

"What are we going to do?" she asked.

"About what?" He traced the curve of her ear with one finger.

"What about Mac? And the changelings? What you said about their history was incredible." She raised her head to look at him. "You know, you've never said a word about *your* history."

His mouth twitched. "Never ask a vampire who they were."

"Why not?"

Alessandro closed his eyes. His lashes were a light brown, long and thick enough to make a cover model jealous. "They do not always wish to remember."

Holly froze for a long moment. Having no answer, she kissed him. His eyes were still closed. She could feel his body respond to the touch of her lips, the inhalation at the unexpected contact, a flinch that was at once self-protection and unabashed need.

"You know I am a bad bargain," he said.

"Why?" Her voice was a whisper.

Alessandro put his hand on her arm, squeezing lightly. "You already know the answer. Vampirism is not just a matter of peculiar eating habits."

Holly pulled away, feeling inhuman strength even in the gentleness of his grip. "But that is only half of you. . . ."

His eyes drifted open. "Don't make that mistake. There is no separation of the two. I lost myself when Kalil took me. I left your world."

"Kalil?" she asked.

Alessandro stared into her eyes, and for a moment she saw nothing more than another soul. "Kalil," he repeated, as though the name held countless associations. "You want to know who I was? I was a gift to him. He made me what I am. He was my sire."

"A gift?"

He hesitated, then nodded once, slowly. "It may sound strange to you, but absolute control over another person was natural enough in my time. You and I are separated not just by our species, but by centuries of custom and culture. The world I was born into was very different."

Holly remained silent, digesting what he had just said.

He frowned, as if unsure where to begin. "In my time as a human the Medici were a rising family of bankers, ambitious to achieve political power in Florence. They had money beyond imagining. I worked for them as a household servant, one of their many musicians. In every way that mattered I was theirs to give."

Holly squinted, struggling to envision people who would give a man away like a case of beer. "Did they know Kalil was a vampire?" *Did they know he would eat you?*

"Yes. He was an honored guest at their home." Alessandro paused. "That was why their gift had to be special. They wanted to impress him, for he had great influence with the merchant traders from the eastern lands."

"So they gave him you?"

"They gave him many gifts. I was but one. I was a curiosity, like an exotic pet. The people from my village were descended from the northern hordes—the great warriors from Germania who had brought Rome to its knees hundreds of years before. We were physically impressive, fair-haired and tall, a novelty. Besides that, I played many instruments. I sang in seven languages. I was an exquisite token, the way a fine horse is a prized gift."

Okay, not man as case of beer, but man as entertainment unit. The situation still mystified her. She groped for something, anything she could relate to. "I met you at a musical concert."

"Yes. I still enjoy listening to it, and I still play. That, at least, Kalil did not take."

"He decided you were a gift that ought to keep on giving? Forever?"

Alessandro smiled, but it was sour. "Perhaps he wanted to preserve my ornamental value the same way one might preserve a flower by dipping it in wax."

"Ornamental?"

He shrugged. "I was pretty and made nice sounds. I didn't learn to fight as a warrior until after I was Turned. I had no real taste for battle before that. Kalil's curse brought a hunger for the sword."

"What happened to him?"

His face grew shadowed. "Human hunters. They came in the day, while my clan slept, and killed them all. I survived by pure chance. I was away on a trip to buy horses."

"Thank the Goddess," Holly murmured.

"Thank an argumentative and hard-dealing trader. Now you know all there is to know about me," he said, touching her cheek with the back of his fingers. "Nothing more happened that was good or kind until the night you and I met."

"I think you're editing history to suit the moment."

He gave a smile that answered nothing, his eyes searching her face. "I remember that coffeehouse concert. You walked over and handed me a listing of who was playing there that month."

"You looked like you were enjoying the music."

"Still, it's rare for someone to make such a gesture, a casual kindness, to one of my species. And for good reason."

Holly blinked, trying to follow what he was saying and not making it. She was falling into his gold-shot gaze.

His voice dropped to a whisper. "You looked at me and responded to what was there, just as I was at that moment. Everyone else in the room saw a hunter, a danger, but you saw me."

She waited as he kept stroking her face, and all she wanted was that touch. The words were incidental.

"Holly, you deserve as much from your lovers. You deserve someone who will look at you, your house, your work, and adore all of it. Ben could never have seen you, or he would be here laying his heart at your feet."

Oh. Her own heart drifted in her breast, a giddy, sideways ache of sweet pain. Holly could feel the blood creeping under her skin, rising under his touch. *Oh.* "Alessandro . . ."

"Yes?"

"Can we be together without it going all wrong? Just once?"

Holly was not sure what she expected him to do or say. He sat still and silent, as motionless as only the Undead could be. Then he drew her close, his body hard against hers.

"Once." He said it like a prayer, as if he bargained with his soul for that single chance.

His lips touched hers, the sensation melting all the way down the back of her legs. Holly's fingers slid down to caress the tight leather encasing his thighs, winding the fringe around her fists. She used it as leverage to pull closer to him, arching her torso against his chest.

Holly took his mouth greedily, his teeth sharp against her tongue. She shivered, imagining their pressure against her skin. She was testing their self-control in dangerous ways, but she had run out of the stamina it took to resist. "I've wanted to do this since I first saw you," she breathed.

"Where is your bed?" It came out as a demand, rough and deep.

He picked her up and she grabbed his shoulders, the electricity that ran between them humming in her belly, up her spine, tingling in her fingers' ends. A faint sheen touched Alessandro's cheekbones. He was feeling it as much as she was.

"Upstairs," she replied, not sure how she convinced her mouth to form the word.

Sure-footed, he found his way up the dark staircase. As he shouldered through the half-open door to her bedchamber, she used her magic to light the candle on her bedside table. She needed to see the look of wild tenderness on his face, to savor it in her memory.

He set her down on the bedcovers like a jeweler laying out his finest piece. He sat on the bed beside her, fanning out the long, dark tendrils of her hair, smoothing them from her forehead.

"I love you," he said. "Never forget that."

The words liberated her, giving her a certainty she had been afraid to want. Holly touched his lips, her own mouth gone dry with need. "My memory isn't that faulty."

He pulled off the mesh shirt, the long, lean muscles of his chest and stomach exposed to view.

"And I'll certainly remember that," she added.

That surprised a laugh from him. She held up her arms, and Alessandro came to her at last, sinking to her side. His skin was cool, smooth as silk.

"I need to feel you," he said, running his hands under the hem of her sweater.

He was growing warmer as they touched, his heart thudding slowly, erratically. *It's like bringing him to life by making love. Like being a goddess.*

The sweater came off, followed by the rest of their clothes. She buried her hands in the wealth of his hair, wrapping herself around his lean, long body. He was all sinew, muscles working in ivory perfection. He was also impressively male, long and thick enough to make her insides coil with need and hesitation. No wonder Kalil and his clan had wanted Alessandro preserved forever.

Hard kisses left her lips feeling flushed and raw, the force of his demands a rush all on their own. His hands shook, and he plunged them into the bedclothes, twisting the blankets into his fists. The muscles of his neck and forearms strained taut as ropes. *He's controlling himself.*

That was wrong. She didn't want that. She wanted him to be as free as she felt. Holly began to stroke him harder, seeking out the places where he felt the most pleasure, but he caught her hands. "No, I don't dare. Let me take care of you. It's much safer that way."

"But—"

His face was tight. "Trust me. Let me. I know where I can lead this dance."

Holly allowed him to pin her arms and take control, but she felt cheated.

He didn't let her feel that way long. Alessandro tasted her skin from earlobes to collarbone, circling over her nipples, leaving only the faintest rake of fangs in his wake. It was a tease, a dangerous game, but, oh, so thrilling.

Holly squirmed and twisted under his touch. Now he was raising the temperature degree by degree. By the time his lips reached her stomach, she ached for more direct satisfaction. The silky hardness of his shaft was ready to be put to good use, but he had other ideas. Immortals had forever to explore the possibilities of delayed gratification.

Or perhaps he was just clinging to sanity. He looked up, his eyes bright with a smoldering hunger. Holly caught her breath, half fear, half anticipation. The hunter was dancing just beneath the surface of his gaze, roused by feral lust.

That look alone nearly pushed her over the edge, but Alessandro held her in his relentless control.

With featherlight brushes of hair and lips, he continued his way over her flesh with deliberate precision. His path crept ever downward, but bypassed the most sensitive areas. That was fine—he found erogenous zones where none had previously existed. Her ribs. Her hip. The inside of her wrist. He stopped only when he reached the inside of her thigh, the soft stretch where blood and nerves lay under translucent skin.

He was sweating, trembling under her touch.

"Are you all right?" Holly asked.

His eyes were mere slits. "Don't talk now," he said. "If you love me at all, don't distract me."

With inhuman strength, he held her down with one hand splayed across her ribs and closed his mouth over that hot, fine flesh of the thigh where the artery coursed downward from the heart. She thrilled, cold and hot and electric with arousal. She could feel his teeth against her skin, intimate and deadly. Her body yearned to writhe in craving, and yet she dared not breathe. She could feel the strength in his jaws, her pulse straining against the hard, sharp fangs.

Her skin pinched with every throb of her heart.

He was going to bite her.

He was aching, shaking, fighting not to.

The sensation, so near her sex, was erotic and terrifying. Every pulse grew in intensity, pushing, filling her with the rush of her own blood.

Alessandro slid one hand up her thigh, pressing himself closer against her flesh. Her life dangled by the thread of his control, an unraveling weave of reason and appetite. Her fear made the moment exquisite. The universe was nothing but her heartbeat and the moment he would take that rush of life for his own.

Holly came in sharp, helpless, excruciating need.

Alessandro released her with a gasp like a swimmer breaching the surface. He kissed the swollen, tender flesh between her legs, releasing her from the frozen trance. She grabbed his hair, pulling his mouth to hers. She was shredded by the sheer intensity, her own control ripped up by the roots.

He groaned, surrendering to her. Then he plunged inside, giving himself with hard, urgent thrusts. Holly was slick and wet, more than ready.

When he climaxed, his hands tore into the sheets as if they were paper.

Chapter 21

Alessandro had split in two. He felt as though he had been standing in the desert sun. Parched. Drained. Bewildered. Denied.

At the same moment his soul unfolded like a shriveled plant finally given rain. He felt the touch of living warmth, a pure and generous pleasure he had been denied for over half a millennium.

His perception splintered. His body and soul felt the languor of satisfaction, and yet his guts raged, unslaked, unfed, empty. Primitive terror vibrated below the smoothness of his skin, an animal's panic that food was nowhere to be found.

He knew why. The vampire in him had never before been denied. Over the centuries, he had tried to make love without feeding, but he had never been strong enough to tear himself apart like this, to divide emotion from hunger.

About halfway through lovemaking, sheer panic had fueled his control. The parts of his brain that governed thought had gone down under a tidal wave of lust. All that had been left was need and appetite. The *need* to protect Holly had won.

Just.

Now she lay beside him, her breath rushing softly across

the landscape of rumpled and torn bedclothes. He was going to have to buy her some new sheets.

Holly was on her back, fast asleep, her face turned toward him. The tangle of her straight dark hair webbed her features from view, spilling like the hatch marks of an illustrator's pen over the white contour of her shoulders. One hand reached up, fingers loosely curled around Alessandro's. She had fallen asleep holding his hand.

His scent was on her, and hers on him. *I am hers. She is mine.* Shifting slightly, he raised himself on one elbow, letting his lips linger against the warmth of her flesh. *Like the spun-sugar sweetness of pears.* Or what he thought pears were like. Memories of that kind had faded.

Hunger filled his mouth like acid, throbbing in the bones of his jaw. He parted his teeth slightly, relieving the pressure on fangs aching for the hunt. He *needed* to hunt.

She is mine to take.

Alessandro was on his feet beside the bed before he could even reject the thought. He had moved so fast, Holly hadn't even stirred. Naked, he watched her breath, hearing her heart beat in the quiet room. Appetite slunk through his body, hardening his flesh, reviving fires he had conscientiously banked. He was full and ready to take her, *desperate* to take her blood.

No.

And yet he did not move. He did not dare. She was everything—had given him, against all odds, everything— and yet his instinct was to destroy her. One lapse of concentration and he would be back on the bed, plundering life from the heart that had surrendered to him not even an hour ago.

I am worse than I even imagined. Did I really think some better angel would rise from these slavering, venomous hungers? That because I loved I would be anything other than myself?

Disgust gave him the strength to step back, and step back again. He bent and picked up his clothes from the floor, his limbs heavy with grief. He had to get the hell out of there before he made another near-fatal mistake.

The only thing he could give her was his absence.

He went home, cleaned up, and went to Sinsation. His arrival caused a stir, as it always did, among the venom seekers. When it was whispered that Caravelli wanted a companion, the humans flocked to him like plump and foolish birds. Alessandro was beautiful and his venom was strong. The pleasure he gave was legendary.

He switched off what he could of his conscious mind, letting names and images slide by without sticking, slick as rainwater over glass. He didn't want to be aware of what he did. Not so soon after brushing so close to bliss.

The honeycomb of small rooms at the back of Sinsation was neat and utilitarian. Alessandro was shown to a room with a couch and a lamp of cheap stained glass. His meal of the night reclined on the couch, her face slack with the anticipation of ecstasy.

I am a monster.

But even with hunger raging in every cell, with his meal spread languorously before him, he balked. It was too soon. Too intimate. The image of Holly lying beside him was sacred. He would not sully that image with the shadow of another.

I would sooner lie down like a dog on his master's grave and die.

He'd never felt like this before. Never refused to feed. Still, the decision was abrupt and final. He got up and left the room, ignoring his meal's cry of confusion. Sooner or later he would have to give in, but not yet.

Standing at the back of the lounge, he surveyed the tables occupying the space before the door. The patrons were an irrelevant blur, but their energy sharpened his focus. It was a place filled with predators and prey. Even if he was not willing to look for food tonight, he was still on the hunt.

Action was good. His spirit was too sore to dwell on Holly. *So don't think about her. Think about what needs to be done. Macmillan. The book. Anything but Holly.*

Alessandro eased from the back into the main room, skirting along the shadowy periphery of the tables en route to the door.

"Hey."

He felt a hand on his cuff and looked down, tensing, but it was only Perry Baker, drinking a beer alone in the corner with his laptop for company. Reluctantly he sat down across from the young werewolf. He didn't want to take the time, but the look on Perry's face made him stop.

"What's up?" asked Alessandro. "You look ragged."

"Everything." It came out almost like a grunt. "I hate my life."

The complaint was oddly comforting, as if Perry's misery put his own in perspective. "At least you have life," Alessandro countered. "Try being Undead for six centuries."

"You don't get fleas and you don't teach three sections of first-year Comp Sci geeks who can't wait for you to turn into Fido and pee on the mainframe." Perry gave the hem of his oversized T-shirt an irritated tug.

Alessandro sat back in his chair. "No, I managed to dodge those particular bullets."

One of the waiters dropped off another beer and a glass of Alessandro's usual red wine. There were things to be said for being a regular, even if he didn't really feel like drinking.

The waiter paused. "Was there something amiss with your meal, sir?" He was addressing Alessandro. Perry's eyebrows rose with interest.

"The meal was fine. I simply found I didn't have an appetite after all."

"Very good, sir. Let us know if there is anything else we can provide." The waiter left.

Perry's face was full of questions, but Alessandro quashed them with a look.

"So." The werewolf snapped the lid of the laptop shut. "Um, Dad said the queen called him. Something about portals to the hell dimensions?"

"You think I know something."

"You have on an apocalypse kind of face. Plus, we found that changeling in the Laundromat. There's something up."

Alessandro drained half his glass in one slug. Maybe he did want the wine after all. "There's no point in spreading panic quite yet. The queen is calling the leaders of the supernatural community, giving them time to talk to their councils. They need to be on the lookout for trouble, because it could come anytime."

"What kind of trouble?"

"Demon."

"No wonder you look tense."

"It's been a bad week."

"More than just a demon? My wolfy senses are tingling."

Oddly, Alessandro didn't mind Perry's prying all that much. Perhaps it was because his interest was genuine. Wolves were your friends or they weren't. For some reason Perry had taken to Alessandro.

"I had one of those nights when I understand what I am. We look human. We do many of the things humans do. Sometimes I forget that I am a monster."

Perry signaled for more alcohol. "Yeah, I know what you mean."

"You? You're the poster child for integration. Young, good-looking, brilliant. If you can't fit in, none of us has a prayer."

Perry looked into his beer. "Ah. Well, for what it's worth, I went on a date after class. Nothing much, just a movie."

"And?"

"The girl turned out to be more than just a drop-dead gorgeous roller-derby babe. I *hate* those vigilante freaks."

"Roller girls?"

"No, effing self-proclaimed hunters. She tried to behead me. Had this bloody great katana in the car. Now, that's a buzz kill. Like, I mean, what did she think I was going to do? Shed on her upholstery? The chick was way over the top."

It wasn't really funny, but Alessandro couldn't help a smile. "Isn't that what you get for finding fun outside the pack?"

Perry hitched a shoulder. "I fell to the lure of the exotic, I guess. It's not like I'd ever marry a human. I mean, I want a family someday. Our genes won't mix."

Werewolves were all about their cubs. Family was something Alessandro would never have. But Holly might. Holly should. There was so much he couldn't give her.

But she gave me one shining gift: She wanted me. At least I know what it is to be loved—neither because nor in spite of being a vampire. Just for me.

Perry, who had experienced no such epiphany, emptied his beer. "I don't get it, though. What's with human women? Why try to lure me to my death? Why not just tell me to go away and date someone else? I didn't deserve that. It makes me feel . . . like a B-movie hairy guy eating virgins. Y'know, a cliché. Life sucks."

"I prefer: Suck life. The best antidote for depression is a bad attitude."

Perry chuckled. "I can see how hanging around with you is going to help me grow as a person." He leaned forward, curling one hand around his beer. "Speaking of monsters, don't look now, but the boy wonder just walked in."

Alessandro looked around, not sure who Perry meant. His mouth dropped open. Ben Elliot stood in the bar full of vampires and werebeasts, looking around like a tourist fresh off the cruise ship. He watched with morbid fascination as Ben wandered up to the bar and ordered a drink.

"What's he doing here?" Alessandro marveled.

"And look who's coming to join him. Son of a bitch."

It was Pierce. Alessandro hadn't noticed him sitting with a handful of other Clan Albion vamps. Pierce was wearing a soft linen suit, more appropriate to Miami than the rainy Fairview autumn. With slight stubble and a turquoise silk shirt, he looked every inch the rent-a-rake.

Alessandro narrowed his eyes. Pierce was leaning on the bar, perching one tailored butt cheek on the bar stool adjacent to Ben's. He ordered a drink, casual and unhurried, and turned to give Ben an incandescent smile.

Ben's answering nod was less casual, more businesslike, as if he had been expecting to see him. *Do they know each other?*

"So, does Elliot swing both ways?" the werewolf asked speculatively. "I wouldn't have thought so, but from that eye contact, it looks like a pickup."

Ben handed something to Pierce. The gesture was too fast, too sneaky for Alessandro to see what it was. Pierce slipped it into his pants pocket.

Alessandro and Perry exchanged astonished glances. *What business would a prohuman economics professor have with a vampire gigolo?*

"Excuse me." Alessandro stood. Evidently he had one more task before he could leave.

"What're you going to do?"

"Either rescue a kitten or eat it. I'm not sure which." Alessandro strode across the wooden floor, feeling the weight of his long leather coat swinging as he moved.

Pierce saw him coming and slipped from the bar before Alessandro reached them. That left the stool next to Holly's ex-lover vacant. Alessandro took it. Ben gave him a look of all-purpose dislike. Apparently he'd forgotten Alessandro's part in his rescue at the Flanders house.

"What are you doing here?" Alessandro asked, not bothering to hide his distaste.

"What's it to you?"

"Curiosity." *Perhaps you'll give me an excuse to snap your neck.*

Ben took a sip of what smelled like rum and Coke, putting it carefully back on its coaster. From the glazed look in his eyes, he'd started drinking long before he got there. "I wanted to see the wild side in its natural environment. Thought maybe I'd figure out why Holly picked this over me."

"So, have you found an answer?"

"No. There's nothing special." Ben glared around him. "I don't get it."

You wouldn't. "What do you want with Pierce?"

Ben's head jerked down as he averted his gaze. "He says he'll show me the sights."

A feeling of sick, impatient pity washed through Alessandro. "You think a tour of our cozy slice of hell will make you understand why Holly chose to be herself instead of turning into a female clone of you? Did you think perhaps you should love her for who she is?"

Ben didn't reply, but took another pull at his drink.

"Go home, Elliot. You won't like what Pierce has to show you, and I don't want Holly reading your obituary. In fact, I'd rather she never thought about you again."

He peeled the rum and Coke out of Ben's hand and hauled him off the bar stool. He could afford to be generous with Ben Elliot. Ben was of no account.

With Perry's help, he got the professor into a cab. The young werewolf left at the same time, catching the last bus in a drizzling rain.

Alessandro stood outside Sinsation, searching for the threads of his thoughts. It was two in the morning. About an hour ago he had been planning to go in search of Mac. There was still time to get something done.

"Where did Elliot go?"

Alessandro recognized Pierce's voice. Irritated, he turned. "He was drunk and obviously didn't know what he was doing. But then, you were quite aware of that."

"You think I was going to show him a good time?"

"That's what he thought."

"Huh. Okay."

"Am I wrong?"

"What else would I be doing?"

Good question. But maybe he was reading too much into the remark. *Pierce is drunk, too.* Alessandro was faintly impressed. It took a helluva lot of alcohol to get a vampire intoxicated. Pierce's condition showed years of dedication and practice.

"I didn't offer the professor a refund," Alessandro said, guessing it was cash he had seen change hands.

"His money's already spent." Pierce gave an acid smile. "Texas Hold 'Em can be damned slippery. There were some arrears."

"Elliot deserves a fine for his stupidity." And so did Pierce, who was well-known for his gaming debts.

"Why do you care what happens to the professor? He's an ass."

True. Alessandro lit a cigarette. "Why do you care so little?"

"Because I'm despicable. It keeps things simple."

"And you like to degrade yourself."

"It's my business. Not yours. Not the queen's. I'm just selling what she doesn't want. Who knew it had cash value?"

"It hurts her to watch, you know."

"That's the point."

Alessandro laughed.

"Is that funny?"

"I was really depressed tonight. Then I started talking to other people."

"Whatever. I need a drink." Pierce wandered back inside, his stride unsteady.

Alessandro looked out at the night, marveling. *Everything looks impossible between Holly and me, but maybe there's hope yet. At least we're not insane. That's got to count for something.*

Finally left to get on with his night, Alessandro pulled out his cell and turned it on. He'd switched it off before going into St. Andrew's cemetery.

His stomach turned cold.

He had five messages from Omara, all thirty minutes apart.

What now?

Chapter 22

On Tuesdays Holly had two midmorning classes: Marketing and Financial Accounting. She went because she had no idea what else to do, but it was a waste of time. Lectures on income statements and product distribution faded to a drone of white noise. She squirmed in the hard wooden seat, uncomfortable and overheated

Memories of the night before crashed like a surf, over and over, filling her mind's eye and thrumming in her blood. Images of Alessandro touching her—she could still feel the imprint of his fingers on her flesh—were infinitely more stirring than any fantasy. He was right: She would not forget her night with him. Ever.

And that was without his biting her. *How is it possible that he didn't? Holy Goddess, what would it be like if he had?*

Holly drifted from one building to the next, climbing stairs and fumbling textbooks, wrapped in her private drama. The faces of the other students bobbed by, irrelevant as pigeons. *I'm useless. Maybe he skipped the blood and took my brain instead.*

Holly gave herself a mental head slap. She needed to take control, focus on things that nccdcd hcr cncrgy. For one thing, the attack by changelings meant they hadn't raised so much as a wisp of a ghost. As a result, they knew nothing more about the demon or the stolen book.

Just before they went into the Flanders house, Alessandro had asked her to use a tracking spell to find out who was casting summoning spells in his client's warehouse. That gave her an idea.

After classes she took a walk to St. Andrew's cemetery. Although it had been crawling with ghouls and changelings the night before, at midday they would be tucked up in their beds. Even demons slowed down a bit in daytime, so she gambled that a solo trip would be safe in sunlit hours.

Not that there was much sun to speak of. That afternoon it poured in fine Pacific Northwest fashion, an uninhibited downpour that brought arks and pairs of animals to mind.

Her aim was to find the area where they were supposed to meet Macmillan, in the oldest part of the graveyard. She was betting the location was significant. Doggedly she trudged up to the iron fence and away from the path, gum boots miring in the soft earth as she worked her way between the graves. The sunken plots were filled with a skim of rainwater, just enough to splash as more drops came down. Holly read the headstones, thinking how cold and dank the earth would feel around her bones. She sneezed, inhaling rain.

Time to get busy before she caught pneumonia. Holly turned in a semicircle, her senses open to energetic disturbances—restless ghosts or the cosmic thumbprint of a possible portal. Holly's boots, long coat, and umbrella made the movement clumsy, their bulk forcing her to move as one unbendable unit. Sinking into the waterlogged turf, her feet moved with a sound like the Swamp Thing taking an ooze bath. Good thing psychic investigation didn't demand fashion points.

Then she stopped thinking about anything but the coppery taste of fear.

The demon was here.

She could feel the echo of its presence, but diffused, the same way one could tell a smoker had passed through a room. What she was looking for was more specific—the actual cigarette. That was harder. There was a spell fogging the energy, much the same as the cloaking spell that had hidden the ghouls and changelings from psychic view.

The energy seemed to settle on a grave to her left—old, unkempt, and spacious. The headstone had been smashed, probably by kids. With umbrella in one hand, she held the other above the grave, feeling for any unusual energy signatures. The technique involved just scanning the surface, looking for the memory of who and what had passed that way. It was easy, painless work that took more subtlety than force, but the slow process worked better without spectators. Alone, Holly could take all the time required to do a good job.

Necromancy—or rather, the dead it raised—might give specific answers, but that was useful only if you knew the right questions. This would give Holly a snapshot. If she was lucky, maybe she'd get some background as to what the hell was going on.

At first there was nothing, just the mute knowledge of the earth and grass. Beneath that there was the shadow of the buried woman, a young mother taken a century ago by the weakness in her lungs. She was nothing but a wisp of memory, her soul long moved on to a new life. She was one of the good dead, the peaceful dead. No demons there. The cloaking spell had pointed Holly the wrong way, but she'd caught it in the act.

Gotcha.

Holly searched outward, her mind probing, ranging in larger and larger circles that spiraled out from the woman's grave. There was no feeling of disturbance. How much was the spell hiding from her sight?

Then she felt *something*, like a cold finger down the back of her neck. Clumsy in her rain gear, she turned. In her mind's eye she saw a memory shadow, a residual imprint of a night not long ago. In the memory changelings were passing by, hurrying to join a group of others who were bowing down, cowering, terrified. Changelings and someone else— a man or a vampire—backlit by torches, reading from a book. Strange gear—sickle knives, torches, bottles made of colored glass—littered the ground around them. The smell of blood and ichor.

The trappings of ritual, Holly thought. *Not a nice ritual.*

The summoning ritual? Was that book the one Alessandro was after?

Then the image flickered to nothing. Holly dropped her hand, now soaked from the cuff down.

The ritual in the vision had taken place a dozen feet away, right in front of a tall stone angel with upstretched wings. Holly shifted uneasily, and a flood of water sheeted from the edge of her umbrella. A shiver coursed over her limbs, half cold and half creepiness.

The angel was just a grave marker, but it made a perfect focus for the ritual. The changelings had made it represent whatever it was that they desired. *The angel became a demon.*

Holly took a few steps forward, still searching the ground with her mind. Her senses were filled with the tang of damp cedar and wet earth, the drumroll of the rain on her umbrella, but she could find nothing more. As she approached the angel, nothing became less than nothing. The edges of the area's shield were detectable by only the subtlest probing.

Holly sought more carefully now, teasing out one fact, then another, like silver tinsel lost in the grass. Thoughts, ideas, things that the participants of the ritual had known.

Yes, this was where the summonings had taken place. They started in the warehouse of Alessandro's client, but the last, most elaborate, and ultimately successful rituals had happened where she stood. No wonder Mac—or whoever was giving him orders—had tricked her and Alessandro into coming here. This was a place of evil power.

A scattering of junk covered the feet of the angel, telling the tale. *Offerings.* Holly bent, poking in the mud with one cold finger. Candle stubs. Half-burned tablets of incense. Miniature liquor bottles—either libations or party favors. There were a few round metal disks about the size of coins. Holly picked one up, holding the disk to catch the rainy daylight. The metal was stamped with the figure of a man with a lyre.

She didn't know what it was, but it must have significance. She slipped it into her pocket, eyeing the stained, chipped features of the angel as she did so. *Creepy.* The blank stone gaze gave away nothing, but she could feel malevolence coming off it in waves.

The consciousness of the place knew she was there. Magic stirred beneath her, an attack dog getting to its feet. The cloaking spell wanted her gone.

Crap. Holly backed away from the grave as fast as the mud allowed, turning only when she had made it a few yards away. Her feet managed a slurping trot until she was well out of the graveyard.

Well, that was interesting. She had assumed the demon was calling the shots. Maybe it was now but, in her vision, it was the hideous quasi-vampires who had desired the spell. The man with the book was no more than a technician. The changelings had opened the portals to call others of their kind. They had raised the army of ghouls. Only then did they summon the big demon guns.

What did the changelings want? Were they planning another revolt against the vampires?

Holly could imagine it all now: She pictured the dreadful creatures, uncool social outcasts hanging out in somebody's basement, sucking back the vampire equivalent of cheese puffs and beer and dreaming of vengeance. Now they had a demon, a supernatural bully to kick sand in the face of the queen who sneered at them. No doubt they'd bitten off far more than— No, she thought. No biting analogies where vamps were concerned.

But who was the guy with the book?

Someone was working with them. The summoner, surely, but it definitely didn't feel as though he were in charge. The energy he gave off in the vision was much more subdued.

She had to tell Alessandro. She hitched up her sleeve to look at her watch. It was just past one. There were still hours to go before any vampire would be up. The only thing she could do right now was get home, where it was safe.

As her feet splashed through the puddles, her right boot started to leak.

"Holly!"

She turned, just in the process of opening the front door. Mac was hurrying up the walk, the collar of his raincoat turned up. "Where have you been?" he asked. "It's long past lunchtime."

What's he doing here? "Did we have a date?"

"I think we should." His hair was damp, rain glistening in the dark waves, his eyes alight with warmth.

Her hackles rose as he climbed the porch steps. *He lured us to the attack in the cemetery last night—but he doesn't know I know that. Or does he? Did he see us fighting the ghouls? Did he watch while we kissed?*

Mac was carrying two paper grocery bags, one with each arm.

"What have you got there?" she asked, forcing a friendly tone into her voice. *Is he the one the changelings worked with to open the portals?* The silhouette she had seen in her vision looked different, but she couldn't be certain. How could she find out?

By luring him in. Gaining his confidence.

"I brought food." Following at Holly's heels, he set his two bags on the floor of the entryway and bent to take off his wet shoes. "We had such a good time the other night that I thought we could do it again."

The night I can't remember. Did he have something to do with that? Holly's skin crawled. "How could we possibly top that?"

He winked. "You ain't seen nothin' yet. Lunch is my specialty. Have you eaten?"

And Alessandro can't crash brunch. Holly pulled off one boot, losing a sock in the process. "No, I haven't had anything to eat today. Aren't you back at work yet?"

"No. Bureaucratic crap."

His irritation sounded real, but disbelief fingered its way down her spine. Holly summoned a smile. "Do you mind getting started while I change? I'm soaked through."

She was taking a huge risk, possibly a stupid one. *But I'm on my guard now.*

When she got upstairs Holly turned on the shower, stepping under the hot spray only long enough to get warm. Then she left it running, using the noise as an alibi to buy time.

If she was going to confront the man who had tried to hand her over to the changelings, there was no way she was doing it unprepared. Holly dressed, but layered charms in every pocket and fold, tucking them into her bra, beneath her T-shirt, even inside her socks. Kibs sat on her bed, watching her, his yellow eyes following every motion.

She got down on her hands and knees, groping under the bed for the long, flat box where she had stored many of her witch's tools out of Ben's sight. When she lifted the lid, it was as though she were being released from the confines of the box, too. She unpacked her silver knife, an incense burner of hammered brass, the square of Chinese silk she used as an altar cloth, and quickly arranged them on her dresser. She could set up a proper altar later.

Why did I hide all this? How could I let myself do it? Was I that desperate for a boyfriend? It seemed ridiculous now, but at the time she had been so anxious not to frighten Ben off. *I'd like to think I was just being considerate, but I wasn't considering myself.*

As if commenting on her thoughts, Kibs yawned, showing every tooth in his head. Holly gave a small, silent laugh. Ben and his squeamishness were in the past, and she had a bigger worry making a late lunch in her kitchen.

She prepared four candles, rubbing spell-saturated oils along their length and carving protective symbols into the wax. She went up to the third floor and placed one candle in a window on each side of the house. Standing at the top of the staircase, she invoked the fiery energy of the candles, reinforcing the protective wards that guarded her home. Mac was already inside, but the magic would help give her the upper hand. He was on her turf.

Holly felt the heat of the spell course through her bones, sinking down to the house's foundations to draw energy from the earth beneath, then up to draw the power from the rainy skies above. She let it flow into the house, giving it strength. The house seemed to inhale, as if its natural vibration went up a notch. The evidence of success was heartening. The magic had come easily and with only a little pain, as if she had found a better groove. She had stretched herself these last few days. Maybe the exercise was paying off.

Kibs bumped her ankle. She knelt, stroking the cat's thick, warm fur. *I'm ready, but I don't want to face Mac. This isn't going to be pleasant.*

Kibs gave her wrist a hot, rough lick, then began cleaning his paw.

The message was clear: *Get going. Get it over with.*

By the time Holly joined Mac in the kitchen, he was pulling a pan out of the oven. It held an omelet, puffed and browned. The kitchen was heavy with the aroma of onions and cheese.

Mac set the pan down on the stove. "So, can I ask what's between you and Caravelli? I get the idea he's a little more than a partner."

Holly felt her face grow hot, wondering again what Mac might have seen in the cemetery. "Why? What does it look like to you?" She eyeballed a bottle of wine he had opened, but decided she needed a clear head.

"From the sharp little edges on your words, I'd say you aren't comfortable with the subject."

"I'm not."

Mac picked up a whisk, examining it as if it were the most interesting invention. "I just want to know if I'm wasting my time here."

"Are you asking if I'm available?" *This is too strange.*

"Yeah. If you're not, just say so and I'll back off." He put the tool down and met her eyes. They were dark and serious. "Caravelli does seem like a nice guy, for a dead man."

Holly's face flamed. "He is."

"You're together?"

"Yeah."

He lowered his eyes. "Okay."

Holly suddenly felt horrible. *Maybe we were wrong. Maybe he is innocent, and all he wants is a girlfriend.* "I'm sorry," she said.

Mac gave his fleeting microsmile. "Nah, we still have lunch. No one can take that away from us." He cut the omelet and slid sections onto plates. Steaming cheese oozed out the edges.

Holly set the table and they sat. Mac dug in right away, stopping only to pour the wine. Holly followed suit more slowly, her stomach clenched with tension.

She took a bite. The omelet was airy, melting on her tongue in a kiss of butter and fresh tarragon. *Oh, Goddess!*

"Hold still," he said, leaning across the table. He dabbed a bit of cheese from her mouth with a corner of his napkin.

"Thank you." Holly self-consciously licked her lips.

They ate in silence, but she wished she could relax. The food was amazing. Everything seemed normal. *There has to have been some mistake. Why would he arrange for an attack one night and feed me like this the next afternoon?*

Still, her instincts were sending off flares like an exploding ammunitions dump.

He tilted his head to one side, a flirtatious gesture. "Do you have room for dessert?"

"You are obsessed with food and eating!" she protested, pointing her fork at their half-finished lunch.

Mac blushed, as if she had truly embarrassed him. "Yeah, I seem to have a real appetite lately."

"This is delicious, but—"

"No, no," he said, hopping up to remove their plates. "I made too-large portions. We have to save room."

Holly jumped up to wrest her plate away. It was still full of steamy, delicious eggs, and she wasn't ready to relinquish it. "Give that back!"

He set the plates on the counter and put himself between Holly and her lunch, his face full of mischief. "Too tasty to waste, eh?"

He grabbed her, holding her loosely, playfully. The feel of his hands sent a thrill up her spine, a mix of alarm and involuntary pleasure. Mac was solid and warm, his breath spicy with the scents of wine and tarragon. Holly put her hands on his shoulders, remembering the hot pressure of his lips the night he had cooked her dinner.

"I'm taken," she reminded him, her voice firm.

"So you said, but you're such a good kisser, I was hoping I'd get one for the road."

His hands slid behind Holly's back, pulling her tight. "Hey!" she protested, trying to wrench away.

He kissed her lightly, not on the mouth but everywhere else—eyes, cheeks, throat. The contact was firm but soft, a savoring more than a taking. He pressed into her as if the sheer act of touching were the most important thing in the world.

What's going on here? Holly opened her senses. The flood of his need hit her, filled with uncertainly, loneliness, desperate hunger for human touch.

Holly reeled. "Whoa! Slow down!"

In their squirming, they had turned until her back was against the counter. She could feel the metal rim pressing into her spine, putting an edge of discomfort into the moment. She braced her hands against his shoulders and started to push.

It had no effect. Alarm squeezed her breath, threatening to snowball into panic. As little as she wanted to, she would have to use real force. Holly started to gather her magic, but then his lips met hers. A tingling flowed from her toes up through her belly, making her a lightning rod for ecstatic energy. A feeling of life surged through her, blossoming in her chest and throat and coming to a pinpoint of rapture in their lips.

Delight prickled along her nerves. This was not merely an effusion of lust, though that was an important part of the sensation. There was something more going on.

Oh, Goddess. The charms she had tucked into her clothes were starting to heat up, burning where they touched her flesh.

Demon? That's not possible!

There had to be a mistake. She still didn't want to risk

hurting Mac. Holly used her magic gently, just enough to push him away. "What kind of a kiss was that?"

Mac fell back a step. His eyes, already dark and liquid, seemed to be all pupil. They were both breathing hard. He wiped his mouth with the back of his hand. "That was incredible."

"What were you doing?"

"It feels wonderful!" he panted. "You have so much power, and it tastes just like I imagined it would."

Holly braced herself against the counter. "What the hell?"

A slow smile lit Mac's face, reaching his eyes with a mix of pleasure and craftiness. "That was just a sample of what I can do. Say yes and I'll do it all again."

He took her hand, running his fingers down the length of her palm in a slow, erotic glide.

"Omigod," she breathed, trying to banish the sensation of his touch, but failing. His hands felt hot, full of sensuous fever. If he could accomplish this much with hand-holding . . .

"Yes is good," he murmured. "Yes is everything I can do for you."

For one moment his pull was stronger than the protective magic of the charms. She stepped into his arms, giving an upward slide along his hip as she moved. As he moaned, she felt a surge of that exquisite energy pass between them, turning her belly into a liquid, molten ache.

The moment wavered, poised like a drop of water about to fall. Holly yearned to fall, biblically speaking, right along with it. But even as she unraveled in Mac's expert hands, the power of the house beat against her own, knocking, waking her up. The charms hidden in her clothes burned hot.

Holly shook her head, unscrambling her thoughts. "Stop!"

It came out as much a moan as a command. Mac took a deep breath, his power crawling like static all over her flesh. *He has power. When did he get power?* But that energy felt so good. *Sweet Hecate, it's hard to stop.*

She felt the walls of the house pressing down on her, unraveling his hold on her. Like an invisible shell the magic she had put into the wards came flooding back to shield her from harm.

"No," she whispered. "No, no. I have a lover. I told you that."

"But I want to devour you," he whispered back, his words the merest movement of his lips. Holly could hear him fine, though. He was in her head, uninvited. Groping on the counter behind her, she picked up a knife, bringing it around slowly until she pricked his chin. "I'm not part of your gourmet menu."

Mac snatched air in a quick, surprised breath. With glacial slowness he released her. "I used to be better at self-denial."

"What's happened to you?"

"My id got an upgrade." Then he grabbed for her knife hand faster than she could lash out. Hot before, now his touch was clammy as his fingers closed around her wrist. Holly tried to wrench free, but his grip was as strong as a vampire's. Feeling drained from her fingers, and the knife dropped from her hand, spinning under the table.

"Mac, don't do this! I don't want to have to hurt you!" Trapped against the counter, she stayed still as a hunted rabbit, but coiled her power inside, ready.

"You wouldn't."

"I would," she replied hoarsely, fear knotting her throat. "I don't want to, but I'll get the job done. I'm not as nice as you think."

"I'm not as bad as you think, either."

"Prove it."

For a long time Mac held his eyes closed, mastering himself. Holly's skin grew cold as the heat between them soured into a chill, damp terror. Finally he opened his eyes and released Holly's wrist. "There, you see?"

She wormed out from beneath him, edging down the side of the counter. His eyes were still wide and dark with need. She could see carnal desire trumping reason even as he spoke.

"Holly, admit you want me. We want each other. I can

taste it." His lips curled back from his teeth as he leaned closer again.

She raised her hand to hold him back. "Perhaps," she said, "but I'm invoking my right to be coy."

"But I need you." His nostrils flared, an ember of temper flaring somewhere beneath layers of charm.

Goddess, I hate bad dates. The air in the house was growing heavy, the many amulets hidden in Holly's clothes humming against her skin, releasing their charge. Memories were flooding back: Mac sick, the ambulance, the hospital, the blonde in the red hoodie. *She blocked my memories. There was nothing wrong with my magic at all!*

"That demon got to you, didn't she? What did you call her? Jenny?"

"Geneva." His mouth twisted as he said it, as if the name were a delightful wound. "You'll come to know her when it's time. She wants me to take you to her, Holly. She made me strong to do her bidding. And through me she's tasted you. You'll bow to her when she calls. I did. I couldn't help myself."

Holly's heart seemed to judder with shock. *He's Turned. This Geneva made him into a demon. I've failed him so badly.* "So was that what the little shindig in the graveyard was all about? A retrieval team?"

"I tried force. Now I've tried persuasion."

"Try making yourself go away."

"You may be hard to catch, Holly, but I've kissed you."

"So? Do I need shots?"

Mac squeezed his eyes shut. "There's no vaccine against the Dark Larceny."

"What?" Fear and revulsion lurched in her gut.

"You'll forgive me," he said, casting a glance from under his long lashes. "Eventually."

Holly narrowed her eyes. "Not today, sweetheart." She jerked her hand, snapping the reservoir of her power into play. A searing burn ran up her spine as the magic surged through her body. She staggered, grabbing the counter.

Stay with it. The pain will pass.

The kitchen door flew open, slamming against the wall.

A shudder rattled the dishes in the cupboards and toppled a magazine from the table to the floor. Rain smell began to sweep away the odor of onions and cheese.

The atmosphere of the house began to concentrate around Mac, growing thicker, shimmering like oil. Pushing his hands through the thick, resistant air, he gaped wildly around him. "What's happening?"

Holly blinked hard, clearing her pain-blurred vision. "You're leaving. It's an old hex against unwanted suitors. The house still has it in its bag of tricks."

Mac looked stunned. "Your *suitor*? Who has *suitors* these days?"

Holly gave a lean smile. "You asked if I was available. You qualified for the free ride."

The air around Mac turned hard as glass, an invisible shield that pushed him toward the door. Arms flailing, he glided across the kitchen tile, his stockinged feet offering little resistance. He groped for purchase, grabbing at the handle of the fridge door, the cupboards, tipping over one of the chairs.

"What's happening to me?" he cried.

"Bye." Holly waved.

Inexorably Mac slid toward the open door. A whirlwind churned at the back entry, scattering a stack of old newspapers. Mac clutched at the door frame, arms and legs stiff with resistance. "Holly, help me! *How do I stop what she's done to me?*"

Pain. Desperation. Fear. In those words she had heard Mac the man. Shocked, she took a step forward. His cry rang with confusion, the shreds of a soul clinging to life. He'd said it. *I'm not as bad as you think.* Some part of him had not yet been devoured. *But what can I do?* It would take more than her pity to save him from Geneva.

He had stopped himself once, but that restraint had lasted mere seconds. If she let him back in the house, he was going to kill her, or worse.

The moment she realized it, the house's power peeled him away without mercy, tossing him over the side of the back deck.

The door slammed.

The locks turned.

The bolt shot tight.

A ragged scream. The garden would have its fun next. It wouldn't kill a demon, but it would make him darned reluctant to return.

Holly rushed to peer out the window. The backyard was clogged with shadows, the heavy rain bringing on an early dusk. Still, she could see it was empty. No Mac. *Where did he go? Did he get away already? Is it the kiss that starts the Dark Larceny off and running?*

The kitchen seemed suddenly gloomy and strange, as if the shadows had seeped in around her. *What's going to happen to me now?*

She flipped on the light, blinking as her eyes adjusted. *I need help. We both need help.*

Alessandro. She grabbed the phone and dialed his house, praying the early darkness meant he was up by now. It rang once. Twice.

"Hello? Caravelli residence."

The voice was sultry as a dirty martini, and clearly female. It struck Holly like a two-by-four to the gut.

Holly gaped at the phone. *What the hell?*

This was the hour when vampires were getting out of bed.

Whom was Alessandro entertaining?

Chapter 23

"Give me that." Alessandro stormed into the room and wrenched the phone out of Omara's grip, not caring that she was his queen. "That's Holly's voice."

He had heard it from the next room. At the other end of the phone line. Vampire hearing, yes, but it was the sound that mattered most to his cold, dead heart. He would hear it if she called his name from the other side of the continent.

Omara laughed, letting go of the handset one second before it succumbed to their tug-of-war. "I think your little witch hung up. What, could she be jealous?"

Alessandro put the phone to his ear, but there was only a dial tone. He slammed the handset down, imagining Holly in her kitchen, staring at her own phone and thinking the worst of him.

After his visit to Sinsation, he had thought he and Holly had a measure of hope on their side. Now he could see there was a dark force working against even the smallest spark of sanity, and her name was Omara. An anger close to nausea rolled through his gut. "Why did you do that?"

"Do what? The phone rang; I picked it up. I was merely being courteous."

He flipped clammy hair out of his eyes. He had been drying off from the shower, and now wore only a pair of sweatpants. "You don't *merely* do anything. You do nothing without cause."

Omara stared up from where she lay between his bedsheets, mischief in her honey-colored eyes. She propped her head up, supporting herself on one elbow. "You know, you're a grouch first thing. Very entertaining."

Alessandro rubbed his face, wishing he could think faster. He conceded the point about his mood. A tangle of dark thoughts dragged at him, and his back hurt from sleeping on the couch. Immortality didn't preclude the need for a decent mattress. "I'll call her back."

"First I need to go back to the hotel." Omara sat up, the teasing over. "It's time to convene a council of the local leaders—the packs, the fey courts, the crows, whoever can be counted on to stand with us. Moving against the demon now may expose my vulnerabilities, but we cannot wait any longer to form a plan of action."

"Are you sure?"

"I cannot put my safety before the safety of an entire city. Even I am not that selfish."

The words were bold, but she looked small and vulnerable alone in his king-sized bed. She was drowning in one of his T-shirts, her slight figure lost beneath folds of gray cotton. Last night she had come to Alessandro for safety, slept under his roof—a vampire had no choice but to sleep in the daytime—but she had slept alone.

They had not felt the pull of the Desire. As he stood there looking at Omara now, he admired her courage, but the urge to touch her remained utterly dead. *She saved me from a life of complete loneliness. She gave me a place in society when I lost my clan. She made me her champion. I owe it to her to fight at her side.*

But sex—he wasn't so naive as to believe it ever had been love—wasn't part of the bargain anymore. The queen held his fealty, but he loved Holly. The centuries-old on and off Desire between the queen and her champion was finished. Alessandro felt a door shutting on a part of his long life. He felt no real sense of regret, just an urge to move forward.

Which meant resolving a host of problems. The first was

to get a half-naked vampire queen out of his bed. "Is it safe to go back to the hotel?"

"I don't know, but I need fresh clothes. I wasn't thinking about my wardrobe when I left."

Last night she had caught a cab to Alessandro's house, made herself at home, and waited for him to return from Sinsation. She had a key and the alarm codes to the house of every important member of her court. By vampire law they had to offer her sanctuary from the debilitating sun.

Omara went on. "The only thing I did was phone my security team to say I would not be back last night."

"Do they know where you are?"

"No. I don't trust them. Rather, I don't trust them to be stronger than Geneva." Omara's eyes grew dark. "She was waiting in the lobby, idling by the hotel doors. How did she know where I was?"

"The news of your arrival in town is hardly a secret. If I'm right, Geneva has been walking the streets for at least two days. Finding your location would have been simple."

"To what end? To challenge me now that I'm at a disadvantage? Does she know I no longer have *The Book of Lies*?" Omara pulled the covers closer, as if she meant to burrow under them. "She must. Whoever called her may well have used the spells on its pages."

"You are sure she didn't see you?"

The question seemed to steady Omara. "The moment I spotted her I went back into the elevator and left through the underground parking garage. I don't think she saw me."

Alessandro sat on the edge of the bed. "All right. Geneva is your enemy. You defeated her in a battle in Fairview in the 1880s. I wasn't there. Before we confront her, what else do I need to know about what happened?"

Omara hugged her knees, her cinnamon skin dark against the white sheets. "Our conflict was an old one. It began as a battle for hunting territory, but it escalated into a feud. Geneva loves destruction, the waste and evil of it. I finally trapped her here, at the edge of the ocean. She had run out of places to hide, but she made the town pay for her defeat in blood and fire."

"But you won. The victory assured your status as queen."

Omara nodded. "I stole *The Book of Lies* from Geneva and used it to shut her in the Castle. I believe that, more than anything, is the reason she would have her revenge. She wants to punish me in the same town where I wronged her. You know demons. They adore symbolism. She'll re-create the battle, but she'll win it this time."

They were back on well-trodden ground. "Which is why you want Holly's help, even if it might kill her."

Omara held his gaze for a long moment, and finally nodded. "I've been trying to think of another solution, but I can't. You see, she closed down the Flanders house, and from your description I'm sure that was a partial portal. Your Holly has the same natural abilities as her ancestor, even if she's not got full use of her powers."

My Holly. "But you don't have the book anymore."

"Someone is opening portals. I think we'll find the book right here in town and in the hands of your summoner."

"You overlook an important angle." Alessandro pointed to the phone. "I don't know if Holly's going to be willing to help now that she thinks you were in my bed."

"But I was." Omara shrugged. "Which is significant only if she expects exclusive rights to your affections. Have you finally had a taste of her?"

"No."

"Is that so?" She ran a finger down his chin. "You smelled of her last night."

"We were together."

Omara snatched her hand away and sat up straighter. Alessandro sensed the first breath of a storm. "Together in the fleshly sense?"

He was too tired to lie. "Yes."

"Have you had her before?"

"No."

Her brows drew together. "You slept with her but you did not bite her?"

"Yes."

"That's impossible!"

Alessandro said nothing. It was impossible, and yet it had happened.

She leaned forward, the outline of her breasts briefly visible beneath the borrowed T-shirt. "Have you had anyone to eat since?"

"No."

Omara seemed to collapse, turning her face away. She ran a hand through her long dark hair and muttered something in a language he did not know.

"What of it?" he asked.

She pulled a pillow into her lap, hugging it. "Even I thought it was nothing but a legend."

"What?"

She lifted her head. The fine muscles around her eyes were tight with hurt and anger. "She's Chosen you!"

"What?" He stood up, taking a step back from the bed. "No, she didn't!"

"That's the only way that could have happened!"

Alessandro felt the thump of his heart. A long moment of surprise left him almost disembodied with shock. "Not possible."

"How else could you have a woman without taking her blood?"

"No."

A ruddy flush of emotion blotched her cheeks. "We're not wired any other way."

He felt as if he were standing beside his own body, looking on. "Give me some credit for self-control."

"Idiot!" She slammed the pillow aside. "See what is in front of you!"

"Fables are for fledglings." Alessandro slumped against the wall, his studied ease hiding the tremors racing through him. But what if it was possible? Something that could happen in the future? What then?

"Humans thought vampires were myths. That didn't make us vanish."

"I have lived for six centuries. I would know if I were released from this curse."

Eyes narrowing, Omara raised her chin and sniffed the

air. "Well, you smell the same; I'll give you that. You don't feel any different? Maybe it just takes time to take effect."

"No. And I nearly took her blood afterward. I was ravenous. The fact that I did not was an aberration. An act of willpower. Nothing more."

Omara considered, her color slowly returning to normal. "What if she did Choose you? Why you? *Why you?* And a witch? With you at her side, her powers could draw on your immortality. She would live forever. With access to her magic you could rule us all." Omara shook her head. "And you've never even wanted to be king."

Alessandro gave a short laugh. "I'm just a musician from Florence."

"Yeah, you're such a *regular guy.*" She said the words with venom. "The irony is, that's probably why she loves you. After all this time you act as if you're still half-human."

Alessandro winced, any glimmer of joy dying beneath her rage. "Let's see if Holly still likes me after finding you at my number. I might be *un*-Chosen."

"Don't joke about it."

He swore, suddenly furious. "It never happened. It's just a legend. Honestly, I got lucky."

Omara raised her hands in surrender. "*She* got lucky. You left her free from your control, more than I would have done. If that's all it was, then so be it. I will say no more."

"*That's all it was.* Holly did not Choose me. No miracle could persevere in this toxic world."

Omara threw off the covers and swung her legs over the side of the bed. Alessandro's bed was high, and her bare feet did not quite touch the carpet. Reaching up, she took his hand.

"So, if we are not talking about your salvation, what are we talking about?" She gave an expressive head tilt. "Oh, yes, you betrayed me in the bed of another, and you didn't justify the act by feeding. Should I resent that?"

Alessandro relaxed as the tension in the room shifted. This version of the queen's jealousy was predictable. "You wanted to secure her aid. In fact, I seem to remember you recommending seduction."

She bent her head and kissed his palm. Her lips were soft, the dart of her tongue warm and wet as blood. "I'll hate you later, once I know that Geneva is gone, and that we'll all live long enough to make hating worthwhile. Maybe you'll convince me to love you again."

"You know that I will always serve you." *In all ways except one.*

"Good boy." She gave a slow smile. "In the meantime, find out what the little witch wanted. We need her."

The little witch wanted to kill—perhaps herself, perhaps Alessandro. Definitely whoever had answered the phone.

It might mean nothing. Be mature.

Oh, like hell. He left me without a word and wound up in bed with someone else. Someone he could bite. Someone who would willingly give him what he needed.

What did you expect? She had practically begged Alessandro to let them be together just that once. He'd kept his part of the bargain, and he'd done so without harming her. What more could she ask? In the meantime she had a life to save: hers. That had to take top priority, even if she was breaking to pieces with loss.

Furious, Holly rummaged through the living room, pulling reference books off the shelves. One by one, she read the chapter titles and tossed them aside. Grandma had loaned her a couple of books on demonology, but she *knew* there were others in the house. However, she couldn't find any of the volumes she remembered. She'd gone through her collection before, right after her visit from Sweetie, with equally disappointing results.

Before that, the last time she'd looked for them was . . . well, she never had. They were there when she was a kid, old and musty and full of woodcuts of ugly demon faces. All her life they had been part of her landscape. Now they were gone. She stormed into the den to repeat the shelf-tossing process. Kibs scampered out of her way, wriggling to safety under the couch.

She gave up. She'd already phoned Grandma, but Grandma was out, probably taking a break from demon lore.

She left a message. *Crap.* She couldn't sit still. What else could she try? Then a random memory bobbed to the surface.

Alessandro had said Perry Baker was a competent sorcerer. It was a long shot, but he might know something about antidemon first aid, or know someone local who did. She dug out his office number and dialed. It wasn't during his office hours, but it was worth a try.

"Perry Baker." His voice had the distant quality of someone on a speakerphone. She could hear the tapping of a keyboard. *Multitasking.*

"It's Holly Carver. Do you know much about demons?"

There was a static-filled pause as he picked up the handset. "Come again?"

"I'm in your Monday-night class."

"I know, I know." She heard the rush of his breath against the mouthpiece. "About the demons?"

"Soul suckers. I need info. Fast. I had one over for lunch. He tried to make me an after-dinner mint."

"No shit?" Papers rattled, the sound of hasty shuffling. "Okay, um, are you able to come down to my office?"

"Sure. When?"

"Now. Right away. I'll wait. Just get here."

Perry Baker's office was upstairs in the same building where he taught. It was easy to find. It was the only door that campus security had stenciled with a warning sign emblazoned with a wolf. The door was ajar.

Perry sat at a desk heaped with papers, his face lit by a monitor screen. Food cartons from Wily Wolf Specialty Deli filled the garbage can, while a dozen high-caffeine pop cans lined the windowsill in a carefully constructed tower. A bright yellow pennant was thumbtacked to the wall behind him, cheerfully proclaiming Fairview University and Community College's alternative slogan, "FUCC U!"

"Hey," Perry said, standing. "I'm glad you were able to come so fast."

"Thanks for seeing me."

With a wave of his hand he directed her to a ratty visitor's chair. "Sorry," he said. "First-time profs get all the hand-me-downs."

Holly sat, feeling the chair sag under her. The tiny office was hot from the numerous CPUs in operation, and she began to unzip her coat. Relief at finally having someone to talk to warred with a general sense of confusion. "I'm not sure where to begin. There's so much going on, and what happened this afternoon is just part of it."

Perry sat and leaned forward on the desk, playing with a pen. His bare forearms were corded with muscle—lean, not skinny. He studied her, his dark blue eyes serious behind his glasses. "My dad's, um, pack leader. I've probably heard part of this already."

Holly fumbled for a thought, any coherent idea to launch with. "I have this cop friend. I think he infected me with demon cooties."

Perry set the pen down. "Yeah? How did that happen?"

"I think the changelings called up a demon."

Perry sat forward again. "*They* did it?"

"In the graveyard. I went there today and found the remains of a ritual." Holly fished in her coat pocket. "I found this."

She put the metal object she'd found on the desk. Perry picked it up. "Wow. I've never seen a real one of these. It's an Orpheus token."

"What's it for?"

"The tokens are a vampire thing, but the myth is universal. My people revere Orpheus for his power to calm the wild beasts. There's an obvious appeal there for were-beasts." He met her eyes for a moment, as if monitoring her reaction. "Vampires focus on the other part of his story. Orpheus brought the shade of his wife, Eurydice, out of the halls of death. They believe true love can free a vampire from the need to live on blood. They call it the myth of the Chosen. Some believe they can even have children."

Holly's skin tingled. She knew stranger things were possible. *I love him, but he left my bed for someone else. That's not true love.*

Perry went on. "As for these tokens, vampires sometimes

leave them with their kills. It's a good-luck charm to guide
the soul of their victim into death. Belonged to one of the
changelings, maybe?"

"Lovely. I wonder if the tokens were part of the ritual because they represented a body count."

"Maybe. I've heard rumors that the police found these
with the dead women on campus."

Holly thought of the night she had gone over all this with
Alessandro and Mac—the night Mac had fallen ill. "Blood
is sometimes used as part of a summoning."

"Tricky stuff. I wouldn't think anyone but a trained sorcerer could pull it off. You'd need a proper spell."

She remembered the figure with the book. Then she remembered that Perry was a sorcerer himself. *Did I come to
exactly the wrong person?* Fear crawled over her arms.
"Someone helped them. Who likes the changelings or hates
the vampires enough to do that?"

Perry watched her, as if he could sense her anxiety. "Nobody likes changelings."

"Then who hates vampires enough to call up a demon?"

Perry sighed. "The only people I can think of are all
human. No one else would be that stupid. Demons . . . you
just don't mess with them."

"Macmillan?" Holly said aloud, but even as she spoke,
another dreadful idea was forming. One she wasn't ready to
accept.

"Who's Macmillan?"

"The cop with the demon cooties."

Perry frowned. "What about those cooties? What exactly
happened? You don't catch demon germs from casual contact, you know."

Holly hesitated, realizing she'd been talking around the
problem out of fear. "Mac kissed me. I think he's been
Turned into a demon. He said something about the Dark
Larceny."

Turning pale, Perry picked up the phone with a convul-
sive grab.

The sudden motion made Holly start. "Who are you
calling?"

"The Dark Larceny? I don't mean to frighten you, but this is serious. There's only one person I can think of who's got the books and stuff to deal with that."

"Who?"

"Hey, Alessandro. It's Perry. Yeah, I've got your friend Holly in my office. Do you know where we can find Queen Omara?"

Chapter 24

Dances with Vampires Club Goth-a-Go-Go didn't sound up Holly's alley, but neither did a visit to the Queen of the Damned. Both were lurching like big-screen zombies on Holly's personal horizon.

The queen had gone underground, literally, beneath the club. DwV was just off campus, in one of the ancient hotels on Johnson Street. The top stories were all fancy brickwork and bay windows. By contrast, the main floor was a slice of hell in bloody neon and strobe lighting. Flashes of light smeared the darkness in time to a bone-jarring beat, leakage from the sensory assault within.

Thudda, thudda, thudda. Greatest hits of the Cro-Magnon era.

Icy wind blew up from the harbor a block away. A line of would-be patrons huddled against the ancient brick of the building, cold and miserable in their fishnet and muscle shirts.

Alessandro was there, waiting for Perry and Holly. She lagged behind as they approached, letting Perry move ahead. Alessandro waited, cutting her an anxious glance. "You phoned me," he said.

"Yeah, I did."

He stood in front of her, blocking her way. "The queen is in hiding. She stayed at my place last night."

"Is that who answered?" Holly let a drop of hurt seep into her words.

"She slept there. That's all that happened."

"Does that matter?"

"It does to me." He took her hand. "Believe me."

"Why did you leave?"

"I had to. Like I had to leave the Flanders house." He lifted her hand to his lips.

Holly shivered, cold and attraction creeping over her. "Perry told you what happened with Mac?"

Alessandro gave a single nod, his eyes flaring as they caught the light. His mouth was a hard line. She suddenly realized he'd said nothing about the fact that Mac had kissed her. He had as much right to be jealous as she did.

She pulled her hand away, feeling small and confused.

"We'll figure out what he's done. Don't worry. It might be nothing." He turned, leading them toward the door. The guardians at the gate, a pair of bouncers the size of SUVs, stopped them as they approached.

"Back of the line," one said. A bullet-headed hulk, he was sporting the latest in all-over tattoos. He looked like the victim of a vicious wallpapering accident.

Perry inclined his head, all charm. "This young lady has business with the queen."

"She said no visitors."

"We have an appointment."

Wallpaper Boy was unimpressed. "Yeah, pizza delivery, right? Or was that take-out geek cuisine? Get lost, asshole."

Perry opened his mouth to argue, but Alessandro moved forward. "You have shown how faithfully you serve our mistress, human. Now stand aside."

Alessandro's voice held a haughty tone Holly had never heard him use before. Once again his eyes flared amber in the weird, epileptic light. The bouncer seemed to grow soft and squishy, all the aggression leaving his muscles. Holly and Perry exchanged a glance as Wallpaper Boy shuffled aside, his face slack and vacant. Alessandro had ripped away the bouncer's will.

As vampires went, Alessandro had always kept his presence low-key. Holly knew he had power, but up to that moment she'd had no idea how much. *Not even a sorcerer could do that without using some sort of tool. He did it with just a look.* Her hands grew sticky with nervous sweat. *This is going to be an interesting night.*

As if on cue, Alessandro turned to Perry, his expression contrite. "I thank you sincerely for your help, but it's best you go now."

Perry stepped back. "Yeah, okay. I getcha."

"What?" said Holly, her nerves spiking. "Aren't you coming?"

Perry thrust his hands into his jacket pockets, bouncing a little to keep warm. "Me wolf. Them vamps. It's a bad time. Too much tension."

She looked back to Alessandro. He wore an unhappy frown. "I don't want to risk an incident."

Perry held his hand to his head, mimicking a phone. "Call me later." He turned and began jogging away from the club, back in the direction of the university.

"Wait a minute!" Holly hugged herself. "If he's not safe, then what am I?"

"Under the protection of the queen. Under *my* protection." Alessandro cupped her face in his hands. "Trust me. You are safe tonight."

Holly put her hand over his, willing herself to be calm. "I trust you."

He led them through the heavy wooden doors of the dance club. The sound hit Holly like a physical force, and she saw Alessandro cover his ears. It had to be sheer hell for those with superhearing.

The dance floor was packed solid with bodies vibrating with sound and whatever chemicals they had ingested. Holly elbowed her way through, struggling to stay in Alessandro's wake. She kept her eyes focused on his mane of pale hair, fighting the nausea-inducing flicker of the lights. Reaching back, he grabbed her hand. At his touch a thrill of memories from the night before fluttered through her nerves.

At the back of the main dance area was a service door painted with a yellow STAFF ONLY warning. Two more bouncers stood before it, arms folded across overdeveloped pectorals. Human? Vampire? The lighting was so bad, Holly couldn't tell. Despite the dark, both had eyes hidden by wraparound shades, which must have reduced their vision to an oceanic murk.

Vampire. Alessandro stopped before them, raising his left fist to display one of the many pewter rings he wore. The security men nodded and one opened the door. *Who knew vamps had secret decoder rings?*

They were halfway down the stairs when Holly's hearing started to return, though she could still feel the vibration of the music through the metal handrail. The air was dank, as if the sea were an inch from the concrete walls. At the bottom Alessandro waited until she reached his side.

"When we are in the presence of the queen, do not speak unless she addresses you," he said. There was grim tension in his voice, as if he were waiting in the chair for a root canal. "This is not a formal court, but there will be other vampires present."

"Can I raise my hand for attention if someone tries to bite me?" Holly asked, trying for humor.

Alessandro looked at her with heat in his eyes, possessive and urgent. "I will not allow that to happen."

That old-time caveman philosophy had never sounded so good. "Promise?"

He laid his hand over his heart and smiled faintly. "I don't share well."

More bouncers waited outside a cheap bead curtain that separated the basement storage from the area Omara was using. They stood aside as Alessandro approached. Holly followed him past the guards, listening to the beads clack and swish behind them. They had come through three layers of security, and she was growing fretful about getting back out.

Two steps led down to a large semifinished room, obviously chosen for safety more than style. It was the last place anyone would expect to find a queen. The walls were bare concrete, the ceiling a network of pipes and beams. A balding indoor-outdoor carpet in orange paisley covered the floor. Rather than overhead lighting, candles ringed the room, stuck in tin cans and jars. The only concession to comfort was a collection of lumpy, overstuffed chairs and couches ringing the room. It was, in a word, awful.

And scary. Vampires were everywhere: sitting, standing, slouching against the unfinished walls. A quick count tallied at least thirty, all young-looking, all dressed for dancing at the club upstairs. The room hummed with a vibe both melancholy and wired, manic and depressive all at once—the essence of vamp. A few heads turned as they entered, eyes flaring with a catlike glow. Feeling suddenly tender and juicy, Holly wished she knew an invisibility spell.

At the head of the carpet, a female vampire rose from a faux-leather recliner. *So this is Queen Omara.* Holly tried to guess the queen's age or even her ancestry, but failed.

"My queen." Alessandro dropped to one knee, bowing his head. "I have brought our guest."

Conversation ceased, the other vampires turning their pale faces to watch. The queen's glance flickered over Holly like a physical pressure. Omara wore a long, pleated tunic of gold-painted silk, her feet bare except for intricate henna tracery. As Alessandro rose, the top of her head barely reached his shoulder. Her lips parted as she looked up into his face, and Holly saw the dainty tips of her fangs.

The queen turned to Holly. Lifting one hennaed forefinger, she placed it between Holly's eyes. "Kneel when I approach you, human. I am Omara, Queen of Night Predators."

Her will suspended, Holly sank to the floor.

"Greetings, little witch," she said, leaving the finger between Holly's eyes. "I wonder, shall I be your friend or your foe? Your friend, I hope."

Holly tried to speak, but her tongue was suddenly too dry.

"Forgive the accommodations, but a place so very hidden allows us to make our plans undisturbed. You catch us at an unfortunate time." Omara withdrew her finger. "I need your help. Together, perhaps we can defeat this demon."

Omara bent over until their noses nearly touched. "If I help you, will you help me?"

Alessandro stiffened, but the queen raised a hand to silence him. The room seemed empty, the other vampires still as paintings. Holly could hear the hiss as one of the cheap candles flared and sputtered, filling the air with a whiff of oily smoke.

Holly sucked in a reluctant breath. "I know what happened to Elaine Carver. I know she died in your fight against Geneva. I'd still rather go down fighting than have her do to me what she did to Mac. I think we can do business."

She felt the brush of Alessandro's fingers in her hair. She glanced up to see the cool look Omara gave him. The queen was possessive, but of what? Alessandro's affections? Or did she want a pet witch all to herself?

Alessandro's hand stayed on her head, marking his claim while she remained on her knees. She was grateful for his protection, but the whole subservience-and-domination thing was wearing thin. Her knees hurt from the hard floor.

Ignoring Alessandro, Omara brushed the hair from Holly's forehead. It was more than a physical touch. She could feel the queen's power inside her mind, flickering like the brush of an insect's wings.

"Interesting," said Omara. "Still, it must be done."

"What?" Alessandro asked.

Omara studied Holly, her expression grave. "Geneva, through her servant, has infected you with her touch. There is only one way to combat the Dark Larceny. Fight fire with fire."

That didn't sound good. "What do you mean?"

"You cannot eliminate the infection, but you can counter it with something equally strong."

"How?"

"A vampire must claim you. Mark you."

There was a babble of comment in the room.

"No!" cried Alessandro, silencing every other voice. "I will not permit it."

Holly's stomach clenched from her tailbone clear to her throat. Venom could addict, but a vampire's mark was stronger. It made the victim a vampire's slave. *So not going there.*

She cleared her throat awkwardly. "Aren't there antipossession spells?"

Omara gave a slight shake of her head. "No, my little witch. There is no one who knows more demon magic than I, and this is my solution."

"There has to be another way," Alessandro growled.

"The poison already eats at your soul, little witch. Do you really want to risk the wait? I can sense that your powers are already compromised. The natural immunities of a witch are present, but they cannot act at full strength."

"What are you saying?" Holly breathed, her veins turning to lead. Kneeling made her feel small, like a child. Helpless. That was probably the point.

"A mortal would already be feeling the effects. I would say that, at most, you have a day or two of resistance left. No more. Then you will become hungry, like your policeman friend."

"No!" Holly got to her feet, staggering in her haste.

Alessandro caught her. "This is wrong! There must be other ways."

"Would you lose her to the demons, Caravelli?" Omara snapped. "She would have no choice then but to work against us."

"But if we mark her, she loses her freedom of will."

Holly turned in his arms, searching out his eyes. The spectators whispered, their words sibilant, like the last dry, dead leaves of November. She tried to push the heat of their interest from her mind. This wasn't a moment to be shy.

"Would I have more freedom if you took me?" she asked. "More than the Dark Larceny?"

"Yes," said Omara. "And you could still fight the demons."

"I won't do it," said Alessandro.

Omara waved a hand. "Then I will mark her with my own bite. That or she is executed. I can't let Geneva have a Carver witch as her weapon."

Alessandro grabbed Holly's arm. "She is mine!"

"Wait a minute!" The hair rose on Holly's nape. "Wait an effing minute! I'm right here! I get a vote. No executions. No biting, either."

Omara's eyes went hard as agate. "It's your choice, little witch. Let us cure you, or die. We can save your personality, your soul. A demon's power destroys both."

Holly's overriding instinct was to flee, but Alessandro's grip shackled her. A wise precaution. Running in a roomful of predators was less than smart.

"I'm going now," she said. "I feel fine. Mac was sick. I'm not."

Omara shook her head. "It is already working in you. I can smell it."

"Then I want a cure. One with no puncture wounds."

"There is no cure." Omara reached for her.

Pure panic struck. Every ounce of magic in Holly's body exploded outward. White phosphorescence streaked through the room, popping like old-fashioned flashbulbs. Howls of outrage rose where shadows used to be, blinded vampires clawing at their eyes. Holly screamed, pain rending her flesh. She thought she smelled burning, but her senses reeled, skewed, a juddering nonsense of taste and smell.

Her lashing power fizzled, useless. There was light, but no force behind it.

This isn't right.

Her magic was completely scrambled.

Did the demon poison do this?

Sudden dizziness overtook Holly. She dropped to her hands and knees hard. For a moment she was immobile. Crawling away seemed a good option, but her limbs would not obey. An itching, creeping sensation trickled over her, as if her skin were unzipping in a hundred places.

Alessandro bent over her, his image wavering. He touched her cheek, and his hand seemed like ice. "It's already started," he said. "I have to do something. I'm the lesser evil, I hope. I will give you what freedom I can."

Before Holly could react, Alessandro's arm slid behind her waist, lifting Holly to a sitting position. She could smell the leather of his coat, a rich smell edged with the faint bitterness of tobacco and blood.

The whispers of the spectators knitted into words. *He's doing it. He's going to take the witch.*

She fumbled for her magic, wanting some last line of protection, but it crumbled, spent and dry.

"I've dreamed of this," he said. He ran his fingers over the curve of her ear with gentle possessiveness. The touch, barely felt, made her belly tighten. He was radiating need like a fire gave off warmth, his ache setting hers ablaze.

Ah! How silly she is. The vampires crowded close, shutting off what fresh air there was in the dank basement. *Look, she's still fighting back. Like that will help anything.*

"This is way too public." She put her hands against his chest, but she had no strength. *I'm helpless.* A new panic, one that she had never felt before, began to rise like cold, foul water. *I'm afraid of him. Really afraid.*

"Hush, don't talk," he replied.

"No!"

Lips met lips in a hungry crush. His sharp teeth scraped her tongue in wicked foreplay. *He's not being careful now.* He had been holding back before, always putting her safety before his pleasure. That was over, his conscience salved. *Now he is out for blood.*

Holly could feel the hungry eyes of the other vampires roving over them, every sigh rippling the air over her flesh. Tremors ran through his fingers as he stroked her shoulders, each pass trailing lightly down the backs of her arms. Holly squirmed, terrified.

"Hush," he said, catching her gaze with his eldritch golden eyes. "You said you trusted me. Believe me, Holly; I'm only doing this to save you."

Of course he is, like a spider helps its catch. . . . But her misgivings fell away like melting cobwebs. A pleasant calm stole over Holly, making her forget her last thought. She slid her hands beneath the cool leather of his coat. Silk greeted her fingers as she ran her hands over the sleek tailoring of his shirt. Now the surveilling eyes seemed to heighten the moment, as if she were experiencing arousal and watching it all at once.

He has hypnotized me. He had done it so lightly.

But the fear was gone. He already had possession of her mind.

One of the spectators reached out, touching her cheek. The hand was cold as the grave, the touch of an Undead who had not taken blood for too long.

Alessandro batted the questing hand away. He cradled her where she sat, kissing her brow, running his lips down the edge of her jaw. Holly shuddered.

And then she felt teeth breaking through flesh—bright, tearing pain.

No! Panic shot through her, sharp as an electric shock. Her brain sent flight messages to her limbs, but they were numb, heavy and immobile.

Venom. It gave pleasure, but it also bestowed a mild paralysis.

A collective sigh crept around the room, the vampires slinking closer, standing on tiptoe to see. Holly's pulse hammered, trapped in the universal fear of animals about to become food. Breath, the shreds of a scream, came out in a horrified rasp. *No, no, no!*

Her scalp crawled, the ancient defense of furry creatures trying to make themselves bigger. Alessandro's tongue tenderly touched the wound at her throat, the reverent intimacy contradicting the predatory act. His lips closed around the hot, welling blood, a kiss fiercer and deeper than any yet.

And then she fell into the moment.

With a will of its own her body surged into the caress. Despite all, she burned with a sweet, smoky pain. Her skin stung from everything that touched it: air, light, the breath-soft silk of his shirt. Like something overfull, her flesh strained against its bounds. The very heat in her veins was an itch only the vampire's kiss could relieve.

He was drinking Holly's life, and her libido was begging him to take more. Some of it was the effects of the poison from those delicate fangs; some of it was pure Alessandro. Her hands moved of their own volition, sliding over the leather of his coat, the roughness of his jeans. His muscles were coiled hard and urgent, lifting her into the painful embrace. Cradled against him, she could feel his rod-hard arousal. Her own mouth watered with sexual hunger, her hips yearning to thrust into his.

And then the mark took Holly. Waves of pleasure surged from her core outward, following the branches of her nerves in rippling arousal. She began to pant, her temperature spiking upward. Sweat slicked her skin, making her clothes slippery against her.

She felt her body arch against him as he bit down one more degree. The waves became a crashing flood of need. A hoarse cry of surrender tore from her throat. Her climax was brutal and thorough, sharp as steel.

He swallowed once, twice more and then pulled his mouth away.

Holly felt the fangs leave her flesh empty. Dismay staggered her.

I want more.

Chapter 25

No need for invitation barred Alessandro from Holly's home. He had been there before, and now he was her master. Not even the magic of the house was a barrier. Magic was shaped and given power with will, and he had drunk down Holly's will with her blood.

Like all those bitten for the first time, Holly had collapsed moments after he had finished. She would sleep it off and wake up begging for more. It would be easy to convince her to give her aid to the queen.

He carried Holly into the house, using the key he found in her backpack to unlock the door.

Monster. Murderer. His bite possessed his victim. There was nothing Holly could do but serve his every wish. He hadn't asked for this kind of mastery. He didn't want it. It was vile.

But it was his.

The bedroom was dark. The last time he had been there she had lit a candle with a spell. The memory would have made him sad, but his soul was already gray with grief.

He laid her on the bed, her small form curling onto her side. Then he reached over, clicking on the bedside lamp to comfort her should she wake. The tip of a tail flashed in his vision as Holly's cat crept from the room, its body hunkered close to the floor.

The cat knew something was amiss.

Holly trusted me to keep her safe. I failed. In the end I betrayed her trust.

The price of failure was staggering for him as well as her. If there was such a thing as the Chosen, there was no way she could Choose him now. Only those with free will could save a vampire with their love. He had sacrificed that chance for liberty from the blood hunger.

But I had to save her. I couldn't let her fall to Geneva's evil.

Holly stirred in her sleep. Strands of her hair were scattered over the counterpane, framing her profile like a dark sun. Alessandro sat on the bed, smoothing stray locks into place. His hands wound into the softness, feeling the precious warmth of her skin.

He would make it up to her as best he could. Holly's days would be an idyll of pleasure. Everything he had was hers to enjoy, and he had much. Wealth. Property. Knowledge gleaned from centuries of experience and experimentation. But sooner or later the venom addiction would take her over. Now that he had tasted her, he would not have the strength to deny her. No vampire could resist their human lover's blood forever.

I will have to leave her. Once the demon is gone, I must go, too. The thought washed over him, a fresh agony. *Omara knew just how to punish me for having someone else in my heart. She makes me destroy the woman I love, or else abandon her forever.* But wasn't his bite the antidote for the Dark Larceny? What else could he have done?

Did I accept this as the only solution because it indulged my own gluttony?

No. I spared her when we made love. I have the strength. I did it to save her.

His thoughts swung back and forth, persistent as a clock's pendulum. He did not know the truth, or whether it was all just different views of reality. He was death and a cure both. *What have I done?*

Bending over Holly, he inhaled the scent of her skin, sweet as wild honey. He had tasted the demon in her blood tonight, faint but present. Omara was right: Macmillan's kiss had been eroding her already.

But now the scent of the demon had faded, the mark of Alessandro's venom taking ascendancy. *She is wholly mine now.* A rush of appetite flooded through him, filling his mouth with saliva. He touched the soft, soft curve of her cheek with his lips. *My own.*

An ache of regret and loss caught under his ribs, all the worse because he knew it changed nothing. *I love her. There has to be a way out of this. If I have to I will walk away, but please, please let there be another way.*

Holly came to life, turning beneath him. Blinking sleepily, she wound her arms around his neck. "You're here."

"Of course." Guilt crowded behind the words, the first he had spoken since taking her.

"I'm glad. Don't ever leave." She pulled him down, taking his mouth for a long, breathless moment. "I want us to lie here forever."

That's the venom talking. Alessandro forced a smile. "I'm a terrible conversationalist once the sun comes up."

"I didn't mean we'd be swapping gossip."

Oh, Holly, he thought sadly.

He let her pull him down beside her, his weight jostling the big bed. Holly straddled him, grabbing the waistband of his jeans. "You drove last night. This time I get the car keys, and you enjoy the ride."

Despite himself, Alessandro felt his muscles go slack with pure male delight. *Oh, yes.*

Then sanity bobbed to the surface. She was riding high on the dregs of his last bite. Maybe part of her enthusiasm was real, but part was also chemical.

"Are you sure this is—"

She put her mouth to his ear, the silky curve of her shoulder brushing his chin. "Stop fretting. What does it matter? What can you do that hasn't already been done?"

With a single motion she stripped off her shirt, tossing it over the side of the bed. A black satin bra scalloped the edges of her full breasts, the lace edging cut low enough to show her nipples jutting hard against the net.

How could he resist? His body's response was instant and emphatic, man and vampire on full alert. The blood beneath that fine white skin was so rich with power. A witch tasted heavy and thick, tingling with magic like fine champagne.

He wanted it. And he wanted those breasts in his hands, those legs wrapped around his waist. His fingers hooked under one thin black bra strap and slid it over her shoulder, pressing his lips where it had dented the flesh beneath. As she shifted against him, his tongue found the hollow above her collarbone.

Then air separated them. Her hands had been busy with his jeans, releasing his hot and aching member from imprisoning cloth. Holly's fingers were clever enough, but at the touch of her hot, wet mouth—sucking, licking, teasing him to readiness—his heart thumped suddenly to life. A rush of heat filled him, the energy from the blood he had already consumed sparking a mounting spiral of need.

He shouldn't let her do this. Not twice in one night.

But their clothes went away all the same.

Then Holly was under him.

He filled himself with the taste of her breasts, suckling with a skill that already had her writhing under him. A touch to the dark curls between her legs found her swollen and wet. He slid experimental fingers inside, seeking just the right spot to caress.

Holly moaned. The sound speared him, making him even harder. Working as slowly as he could, he drew out her pleasure with the patience of a craftsman. She dug her heels into the sheets, her neck straining as he stroked and circled her inside and out. Then, with a kiss to her most intimate place, he brought Holly to a hot, slippery, helpless climax.

It pleased Alessandro that he could do that without his bite. Some human skills were well worth preserving.

But that was just the starter course. He allowed a moment for the appetite to recover.

He cuddled her, stroking, coaxing her limbs back to life and kindling new fires of sexual hunger. She slid her leg over his body, the flesh of her thigh petal-smooth. She settled over his erection with ease, gently, slowly, drawing him tight inside the blessed warmth of her body. They rocked gently, building energy with steady, relentless friction.

Now his hungers began to demand their due. Holly arched her back, the light painting the architecture of her body in golden relief, the globes of her breasts moving in rhythm with their bodies. She was making little noises, leaning forward now, shifting to get just the right angle, stroking longer and harder.

The visuals were dazzling.

Her mouth fell open, eyes closed with concentration. He could see the mounting tension, beautiful and wild, taking shape in her features. She found release with a cry.

The leash of his own needs slipped, but he relentlessly caught it, holding on. A rush of wetness cascaded inside her, the convulsions caressing him. She found his mouth, her lips against his in a communion of sex and bliss. A torrent of energy, feminine and witchy, tingled over his skin in beguiling waves.

Ah, there were limits to even his control. He rolled her to her back, bracing himself for maximum thrust. His mouth ached with the need to taste her.

First he had to bury himself inside again and again. Her breasts shuddered with each driving plunge. He was past mere pleasure. His hunger fought loose, male need driving out all thought but taking her for his own. She panted under him, pushed again to the brink of madness, the scent of her arousal only lashing him on. He heard a feral noise that must have been him, and then a final paroxysm shattered his body.

He felt his seed spill as a sharp, choking hunger tore him from within. Suddenly it was impossible to draw breath. Orgasm became a sharp new desire as human impulse fell away, senseless and satiated.

All that was left was the vampire. The beast.

That did not mean he was not tender. He slid down, cupping one arm under her shoulders. He kissed her, kissed the place where he had already plundered her life, licked the wounds open with the savoring caress of a connoisseur.

She arched her throat, giving him access as he bit down.

He shuddered, hardening again as her life flooded into him, sliding down his throat with all the potency of strong liquor. A storm of pleasure took him, leaving him gasping, heavy and drugged with pleasure.

He throbbed, all of him, aching for more, his stamina barely tapped. There were good things about being a vampire.

The night was young, and the banquet had just begun.

When Holly woke it was to an afternoon light. The question was, which afternoon?

She was spooned against Alessandro, one of his arms a heavy weight across her side. She expected to feel pain, but did not.

What she did feel was the mix of their powers woven like a cord between them, twining through their sex, through their blood. Her magic had somehow blended with his vampire energy, fused in a crucible of lust. Above that, his venom sang in her veins, a barely banked wash of heady desire. *Venom. I'm trapped. Oh, Goddess.*

But, strangely, she wasn't afraid. *Is that the venom lulling me? Or do I really have nothing to fear?* Holly had never felt so thoroughly sated. She wriggled under the weight of Alessandro's arm, turning so she could face him. He was in the deep, deep rest of the Undead, pale but peaceful, his hair a tangled mass on the pillow.

Strange clarity pushed away the fog of sleep and sex. She had lost blood, but she felt strong. She knew she was under his influence, but she felt oddly free. *What's happened to me?*

Was it just the outstanding sex? They said it was the bite that trapped a person, ruined them for human lovers, but she was willing to vote for vampire endurance. After that kind of lovemaking, how could anything else compete? She subsided onto her back, snuggling beneath Alessandro's arm. Energy hummed between them, mildly erotic.

Goddess, she was relaxed.

At times, when she was deep in meditation, she could see

the webwork of the house's magic. She could see it now, shining ribbons of power bright in her mind's eye. It flowed like a tangle of roots, branching and branching again, a myriad of tiny golden threads of energy. Holly let her mind float along and through them, aimless, drifting. Comfortable.

There was an unexpected lurch of disconnection, so sudden there was no time to struggle. While Holly's body stayed behind, her soul slid into the darkness like the slow drip of molasses out of a cold bottle.

What's going on? Hello?

For a moment it felt as if she floated backward out of her skull, rising higher and higher into an airless void. The house, the bed faded from sight, melting into a swirling gray soup with no horizon. Holly's stomach rolled, reminding her of late-night drinking sessions and bad seafood. *Should I be panicking?*

Holly's eyes snapped open. She was standing upstairs on the same floor as the nursery, but was down the hall near the back bedrooms.

How did I get here? Wait a minute. . . .

The doors to the rooms were open, early evening sunshine slanting at a low angle through the dust motes. *But it was afternoon a moment ago.*

A hamper stood in the hall, overflowing with laundry awaiting attention. Strains of teenybopper radio sugared the air. Automatically Holly picked up one of the shirts that had missed the hamper. Familiar pink-and-white cotton draped over her hand, limp with too many wearings. Years and years ago it had been her favorite.

Fear flooded her mouth with a metallic tang. Those rooms had been shut up since she was a child. That shirt had fallen apart and been cut up for rags. *I'm in the past.*

This early summer evening, with the sun just like that, was one of the last things she remembered before the hole in her memory. Her hands began to shake. She stuffed the shirt in the hamper and crept into her old room. The sight of the baby-aspirin pink walls set the hair on her neck crawling with apprehension.

I was here right before the terrible thing happened.

It all looked so mundane. Magazines and more clothes littered the shaggy throw rug. Unicorn posters were taped to the closet doors. A math workbook was open on the faux–French provincial desk, the pages held open by a plush bear. Holly remembered, with a pang for her lost younger self, wishing Teddy knew how to do fractions. Problems had been simpler then.

She found the source of the saccharine pop music—her old clock radio—and switched it off.

"Holly? Hol?"

Her hand froze on the radio button, her whole body clammy with dread.

"Holly? C'mere."

She tried to swallow, but the frantic beating of her heart interfered. "Ashe?" she said, but the reply was no louder than a whisper.

This night, the one about to start. She had forgotten it, forced it away, buried it, but it was still there, etched deep inside like the serial number of her soul. Turning toward the door, she followed the sound of her sister's voice.

"Ashe?" she said again, stronger this time. The sight line through her sister's doorway was blocked by a blue dresser piled with feminine detritus. There were posters of heavy-metal bands on her ceiling—men writhing in explosions of artistically lit sweat.

"I need your help," Ashe said in her pseudo-adult voice, the words confident and clipped.

"It'll cost you ten bucks." Holly's words came out automatically. It was what she had said the first time this scene had unrolled.

"Holllleeeee," Ashe wheedled, a momentary lapse into the little girl she had been a summer or two past. "Please. I'll give you five."

"What do you want?" Holly rounded the corner of the dresser. Part of her already knew what Ashe would ask, but the details floated just outside her conscious grasp.

Whatever it was, it was something to do with big-M magic.

Ashe was kneeling on the floor, facing Holly. She had spread out a white cloth on the hardwood, as if setting out a picnic. Pretty china candlesticks sat in the center, their white tapers already lit. Feathers. Salt. Their mother's hairbrush. One of their father's ties. A dish of incense that smelled like the sweet, stale crumbs from the bottom of a chocolate box. She was planning a ritual. Ashe Carver was a talented worker of magic.

She looked up, not seeming to notice Holly's grown-up body. At this moment in time Ashe was sixteen; Holly was eight.

Girl-slim and long-legged, Ashe wore a sundress and mauve plastic sandals. Her hair was blonder than Holly's, ironed straight, with wispy bangs. She had too much makeup around her huge green eyes, a sure sign she was meeting her boyfriend later.

"I need to go out, Hol," she said, smoothing a corner of the cloth. "I just have to. Glen's got tickets to Blue Murder."

Did something so small, so petty, cause everything that came after?

Holly's reply came, sulky and petulant. "You can't leave. You're supposed to stay here with me until Mom and Dad get home." Grandma, she remembered, had been visiting family in Halifax.

"This is more important." Ashe flicked some of the incense smoke around the room with a feather. "You're a big girl. You can manage."

Holly felt a glob of nausea working its way up her throat. *No, no, don't do this.* The next line in the script left her tongue. "They'll kill you."

Ashe gave Holly a look of green-eyed contempt. "Not if they don't find out. I just need to delay them until the concert's over."

"They'll be home long before that. You'll be toast," Holly said with gory, kid-sister satisfaction.

"Not if they have a flat tire."

She turned and picked up a white shoe box. Blithely she pulled off the lid. "Remember these?"

Sweet Hecate. Holly remembered everything.

A wave of heat seared through her, followed instantly by cold sweat. Holly scrambled out of Ashe's room and down the hall to the bathroom. Barely making it, she threw up in the old pedestal sink. She vomited over and over until her ribs ached with it and nothing came up but scalding bile.

Last time Ashe had opened the box, Holly's soul was innocent. She had known no terrors. Now she saw it all with adult eyes. After a long moment she washed out her mouth, her skin taut with drying perspiration. Outside the open window, a robin chirruped in the apple tree.

Ashe stood in the doorway. "Are you okay?" Her face held a mix of concern, both for her sister and for the disruption of her plans. "You got the flu?"

Holly dried her face with a towel that smelled like kids' toothpaste. "You're making a terrible mistake."

Ashe's eyebrows drew together. "You're afraid. What for? We do this stuff all the time."

"I know what's going to happen."

Ashe fixed Holly with dizzying peridot eyes, their depths full of youth's desire for freedom and rebellion. As a girl Holly had adored her. Ashe was older, sophisticated, wise in the ways of the adult world.

"You're going to help me make that car trouble happen," she said. "The spell takes two. I need you. I'll be in your debt."

Holly met her fiery gaze for a long, difficult moment. "Damn you. I'm not going to let you seduce me for five bucks. Not last time. Not this time."

"What are you talking about?" Her lip curled in contempt and just a twinge of fear.

Holly flung herself out of the bathroom and stormed back down the hall. In Ashe's room the shoe box sat on the floor, open on the edge of the ritual cloth. It was filled with plastic animals, junk jewelry, and toy cars. Kid stuff. Ashe had taken the box from Holly's closet.

Ashe came up behind Holly. Just as Ashe had years before, she pulled out a miniature blue sedan, perfect in every die-cast detail. It looked just like their parents' car. "What's going to happen? What do you see?" Ashe asked, her manner now more that of an equal than a big sister.

Holly turned her eyes from the blue toy car, the sight of it filling her with fresh nausea. "You're going to perform the ritual, but I'm going to refuse to help, even though you offer me five dollars. You'll go out with Glen and see the concert."

"So what's bad about that?" She turned the car over in her hand.

Holly's answer was cold and perfectly level. It was that or hysteria. "You're doing two-person magic by yourself. The spell won't go as expected. The car will go off the road by the golf course and over the railing. Mom and Dad will burn to death on the beach, just feet from the ocean."

Ashe said nothing, but twin tears slid with slow delicacy over her cheeks. "So I killed them."

"If I had helped, maybe it would have worked right. Maybe they would have lived."

Ashe looked at the car with the same horror Holly felt, and set it gingerly in the white box. Finally she said what Holly had needed her to say all these years: "It was my ritual. My magic. You were wiser, even though you were just a kid. It wasn't your fault."

Holly thought of what misery lay in Ashe's future, and in her own, and began to quake with tears. She had never wanted to face this. She felt so angry, and hurt, and guilty.

And *there* was the answer to so much. She had buried both the memory and the larger part of her magic from view, punishing herself with pain whenever she tried to use it.

"Stop hurting yourself. It was up to me to look out for you, not the other way around." Ashe put her hands on Holly's shoulders, one of her favorite gestures. Ashe suddenly looked small and very young, not at all the omnipotent goddess Holly's child-self had perceived. Tears washed over her huge green eyes.

Holly put a hand over hers, feeling warmth toward her sister for the first time since she was a child. "How can I change the past?"

Ashe shook her head. "You can't, Holly. You just have to

go on and fight. Forgive yourself for refusing to help me do something that was wrong."

Holly squeezed her sister's fingers. "What about you?"

"Me?" That intense gaze searched Holly's face. "I'm only your memory. The real Ashe has to find her own way here."

Holly wanted to embrace her, but the world went dark.

Her first thought was that she had fainted, but then she saw a field of stars on all sides. Ashe, or Holly's memory of her, was gone.

Chapter 26

Holly awoke and leaped out of bed in one ungainly maneuver. She staggered, grabbed her robe, and looked around. Alessandro was gone, the sheets on the bed a tangled mass.

Where is he? Violent need smashed through her until her conscious mind overrode the venom. *No, no, calm, calm, calm.*

She shivered as she put on the robe, cool air caressing her sweat-dampened skin. Switching on the bedside lamp, she listened. Splashing came from the bathroom down the hall, the sound of the shower. Alessandro was up, but he hadn't left.

He wouldn't do that. Her nerves jittered. *Would he?*

Holly glanced at the bedside clock. It was eight at night. *I slept through the day, just like a vampire.* She was sore, aching, hungry, and bewildered. It felt as though Alessandro were a million miles away. She needed him by her side.

That's ridiculous. He's right down the hall. She sat down on the edge of the bed, fumbling on the floor for her slippers. She found one of his socks instead. *Goddess, what a night.*

A dozen thoughts clamored for attention, some making her body heat, others freezing her with misgivings. One stood out, different from the rest. The vision of Ashe was still with her, lost memories in place. Unblocked power rushed like fresh air through her system. Mixed with power, sex—especially sex like she'd just had—possessed magic of its own. That last bout of lovemaking had opened a door inside her, and the space and freedom of her magic suddenly belonged to her once more.

Experimentally she flicked all the candles in the room alight, then extinguished them. On. Off. On. Off. She could do that before, but now it came easily, like breathing. *This is what it felt like when I was little. Before all that happened. Back when I wasn't afraid of my magic.*

So much had been lost because of that single spell. Holly had mourned her parents, grieved for them for years, but their deaths had been only part of the tragedy. She'd lost Ashe, too. Their relationship had never been the same.

And she'd grown afraid of her own power. If a spell could kill her parents, what other tragedies could magic cause? She was afraid of herself, and felt guilty because she hadn't known what to do to stop Ashe. With a child's sense of absolute justice, she had crippled her power to keep herself and everyone around her safe. She had even erased the memory of the spell and the months surrounding it.

That tragedy was finally drawing to a close. Holly touched her neck, shivering at the brush of her fingertips on Alessandro's bite. *Just in time to make room for my future as a venom slave.*

I can't live like this. Half of magic depended on the practitioner's clarity of will. She couldn't regain her memories and her magic just to lose them again. *I have to fight the mark, grab what I can of my life and hold on.* Holly went downstairs to take a shower. Routine, *her* routine, untouched by another's will, was suddenly vital.

When she returned to the bedroom Alessandro was there, half-dressed. The bed lay rumpled and inviting behind him. Holly stopped in the doorway, her arms hugging her robe around her. The sight of him spiked her to the floor.

Need, desire, attraction, belonging. They were all good emotions—but not in this insane intensity. All Holly wanted to do was to pick up where they'd left off the night before, naked and writhing. A tiny whimper escaped her as she forced herself to stay put. *I want him. I want him, Iwanthim.*

He stopped what he was doing, his shirt in one hand. He studied her, amber eyes filled with concern. "How are you feeling?"

How can he even ask? Holly looked at the floor, not sure where to start. "If you don't cover up, I won't speak for my self-control."

There was a soft rustle of silk. When she looked up he had the shirt on but the buttons were undone, leaving a stripe of chest exposed. *Not helpful.* She rubbed a hand over her face. "You're really good, you know. Sex Hall of Fame material. Whatever you did unblocked my magic."

His brows drew together. "I don't understand."

She told him about the dream.

"So that means your magic won't be painful anymore?" he asked.

"An interesting trade-off, isn't it?"

He drew closer, his fingers brushing the place on her neck where he had marked her. She flinched, more from his touch than from the wound. It was electric. Power still coursed between them, a continuous circuit pulling them together.

"Did I cause you pain?" he murmured, kissing her lips lightly. The lamplight turned his hair a silvery gold, bright against the dark fabric of his shirt.

"Some. The first time, yes. Fangs versus flesh." She closed the few inches between them, resting her hand against the bare skin of his chest. He was warm, full of her life. Desire dampened her sex. "Am I always going to want you so much?"

"Yes," he said, one hand stroking her hair. "I'm sorry." He said it with ineffable melancholy.

Holly gave an uncomfortable laugh. She couldn't stop stroking his smooth, strong muscles. Petting him. Reveling in his presence. "Isn't having a love slave supposed to be a good thing?"

The bedroom light was dim, the corners of the room in shadow. Holly felt as though her whole world were in that circle of lamplight, what fell outside it lost in the realms of myth. Alessandro pulled Holly to him, resting her head on his shoulder. It felt wonderful. Safe. Connected. Cherished.

His voice was deep, resonating in his chest. "A large part of me rejoices at binding you to me, but there is a cost. You're dear to me. I love you. I don't want to hurt you, ever, and I'm afraid I have."

Now that he had said the words, Holly could feel his control. It was part of that circuit, that binding of their energies that tied them together. The effect was an ultimate veto on her every thought or action. She walked and talked only because he let her. He hadn't compelled her yet, but that could change in a blink.

"Give me back my will."

"I would if I could. I don't know how."

Suddenly what had happened was cold and real. With the mark came an imperative to touch him. To pleasure him. To feed him. To ultimately be consumed by him until there was nothing left. *This is how vampires survive.*

A solemn feeling came over her, stilling every function of her body. She couldn't quite encompass the realization of what had happened. *I can't do this. I can't be this way.*

"I did it to save you."

Her gaze dragged up to Alessandro's face. "You're a predator."

"Maybe, but I lost something, too. You could have Chosen me. If I'd won your heart, you could have freed me from the blood hunger. I had *hoped*"—he said the word strangely, as if it were unfamiliar—"that we had a different future. One my curse couldn't touch."

His words wrenched her heart. "You never told me any of this."

He blinked, obviously fighting his own wash of emotion. "How could I? Not without blackmailing you. Not without admitting it to myself. Not without risking that you *didn't* love me, even when I adored you."

Holly's mouth was parched. She hurt for him. She hurt for herself. "I did love you."

"But not anymore." The words were barely there. "It doesn't matter; the Chosen is only a legend."

"I can't tell what's real anymore." Her eyes stung, but she was past tears. A heavy weight hung in her chest, dragging on her every breath. Through the circuit of their energy she knew Alessandro felt it, too.

They wanted to be together, but not like this.

Like an alien invader, the phone rang. It took a moment for Holly to register what the sound meant. At the same time Alessandro's cell phone pinged Beethoven's Fifth. They released each other, at once reluctant and relieved. They stood, holding hands, not quite ready to break the contact of skin to skin.

"I'll get the one in the office," Holly said.

"No, don't go," he said, the casual phrase of someone reluctant to release his lover.

And then it happened. The sound of the phones drifted away, meaningless. Holly snuggled back onto his chest, only dimly remembering there was something she had meant to do.

Alessandro's eyes grew wide. Holly saw the horror, but didn't understand it at first.

"What?" she asked.

His face twisted with self-loathing. "You were going to answer the phone. Go do it." His voice charred her with its bitter regret.

Sweet Hecate. She felt herself turn, helpless as a doll. Helpless as Mac being tossed into the garden. Holly stumbled to the den, disbelief numbing her limbs.

Kibs was sitting on the desk, staring at the phone. With a wave of guilt she wondered when she'd last filled his food bowl. He butted her hand as she picked up the receiver.

"Hey, kid," said Grandma. "I've got some info for you."

"Good. I could use answers about now." Holly sank down on the desk chair, sick with shock. *What the hell just happened there? Was that a demonstration of his vampire power?* It was far, far stronger than she would have guessed. *I am in such trouble.*

It made it hard to focus on her grandmother's voice. She

wanted to say something, to beg for help, but the words just wouldn't come. Was it some magical compulsion, or just plain shame?

"I was consulting with colleagues about your demon problem. Some scuttlebutt came up that I thought you'd want to hear," Grandma began. Holly heard the flip of a page, as if her grandmother were consulting notes. "The best book on demon wrangling is something called *The Book of Lies*. Word has it that it was sold privately about a month ago. Dirty sale. Stolen from the vamp queen. Very hush-hush, go-betweens, the lot."

That was just interesting enough to snap Holly's mind back on track.

"Stolen from Omara?" She kept her voice low. *So that's the book they were looking for!* "Do they know who bought it?"

"Someone local with a lot of money. Seller was a vampire."

Inside job? She scratched Kibs's spine and was rewarded with a tail up her nose. "So you think this local buyer opened the portal with the book?"

"Yup. If you can get your hands on it, you're well on your way to getting rid of your demon friend. It also has a ton of spells for weakening hellspawn and making them easier to manage."

"Apparently the hellspawn's name is Geneva."

"That's the same one Elaine fought." Grandma's voice was hoarse with worry. "Look, we need more information before we tackle her. She's a nasty piece of work."

"What if things come to a head sooner?"

"Pray that doesn't happen. With or without the book, the only real tool you have is pure energy. If you can back the demon into a portal, use raw energy like a water cannon. They can't digest your power in that form. The two sources I found recommend Aurelia's matrix or the Caer Gwydion reduction spells to augment your control. That'll hold your demon, but it's going to take a lot of strength. For you, it's going to hurt like blazes."

"Okay." *Maybe. Maybe not.* With her power unblocked, she just might skip the agony part.

"The trick is closing the portal. When a working portal shuts, normally it just closes to a trickle on its own. If you slam it shut, it releases a blast of magic that'll kill you. That was the mistake Elaine made. *Don't do that.*"

"So get the demon on the other side and hold it there till the hole closes on its own."

"Bingo. But. Be. Careful." It was the closest to fussing that Grandma would ever get, but Holly heard the unspoken fear in her voice.

Holly thought about her dream. Grandma needed to know all about it, but Holly didn't have the strength to discuss it. *Not now.* She took a deep breath. "Will raw energy kill the demon?"

"Enough will. Witches can't pull that much, though. We just don't have the juice."

Damn. "I left you a message about the Dark Larceny. That cop friend of mine . . ."

"If he's already started to Turn, it's doubtful you can pull him back. Too bad, I know."

Holly looked outside again. The lonely streets were desolately beautiful until the image drowned in tears. "He kissed me." The words were wistful, more a tribute than anything else. *Poor Mac.*

"Ah, he's a baby demon. No worries."

"I think his mistress gave him extra power. He's not so much a baby as her proxy."

Grandma paused a heartbeat, tension surging down the phone line like something solid. "That might screw up your magic for a bit, but you should get over it. Get the demon on the other side of the portal however you can, and it won't matter. She can't reach you from there."

Holly froze, the world shifting as Grandma's words hit home. "Someone said a vampire bite was the best antidote. Doesn't that work?"

Grandma laughed, but not with mirth. "Oh, yeah, it'll work, but there're better ways. That's like treating Ebola with bubonic plague. Why the hell would you do that?"

Chapter 27

While Holly and Alessandro had slept, Geneva had dared the nonhumans to do battle with her on campus that night. She had done it the traditional way, with a written challenge and the gift of a silver knife. The bloodied silver blade meant it was a fight to the death.

It was cold, the skies clear and starry. The south campus—farthest from the coffee shops and movies—was all but deserted, as if the humans sensed coming danger and huddled indoors. It was only eleven o'clock, but the windows of the nearby residences were mostly dark. Vampires, werebeasts, and other creatures hid in the shadows, waiting.

Omara and the other leaders of pack and clan conceded that the demon's choice of location was logical. Fairview U was dead center of the successful portals. For whatever reason this was where Geneva's magic worked best. Nor was the challenge itself a surprise, though it had come sooner than expected. Fresh from the Castle, Geneva should still have been weak.

That raised questions.

They were nervous. Not sure what to expect. Worried about keeping the humans safe. Worried about humans seeing what they shouldn't.

How Geneva would wage her war was unknown, but nobody thought she'd do it alone.

Accordingly, Queen Omara summoned her champion to join her on the campus at once.

Alessandro found Omara striding across the dew-laden lawns. With cold, fixed purpose, he descended like an evil storm.

Grabbing her arm, he dragged her away from her two guardsmen. With a regal flick she waved them away as they hastened to intervene. Her expression was unconcerned. As Alessandro released her, she smoothed her hair into place and slipped her hands into the pockets of her long, fur-trimmed coat. Queens did not show fear.

Alessandro ached to change that. "Malevolent bitch!" he snarled. "You knew. You *knew* there were other ways to save Holly."

Omara's response showed only in the sharp line of her mouth, the widening of her eyes. The queen was still, but her stance was a haiku of future violence.

Alessandro wasn't sure he cared anymore.

"I had to be sure that we were in control of your witch's magic," she said with utter calm. "The risk that she would Turn before we could help her was too great."

"Not if you had *wanted* to save her. Then your reasoning would be quite different."

"You malign me."

"I know you."

"You took what you craved."

"I could have controlled myself."

"I wonder. I wager you ache to savor her blood even now."

There was no good reply to that. Alessandro glanced away from Omara. *If I love Holly, I must face the hell of leaving her. Anything less will be her destruction.* Sick anger seared him like poison. Omara would have been kinder to kill him.

He still reeled from the look on Holly's face when she relayed what her grandmother had said. She had gone specter-white with shock. Oh, Holly was strong. There were no tears, no wild exclamations, but her eyes had been full of hollow disbelief that their lives had been shattered for nothing, because vampires played cruel games.

That moment changed everything. Something inside his soul had slammed shut with a sepulchral clang. Now he turned back to Omara, decisions made, past loyalties sealed behind that door.

"You grow reckless with my goodwill, my champion." Omara's upper lip curled, showing fang. "Your affairs of the heart are not my concern."

Alessandro nearly laughed. The irony of it all sickened him. "Goodwill? You destroyed the one bit of peace that I had found. Whether it was for jealousy or convenience doesn't matter."

A moment passed as the truth hung in the air, noxious and thick enough to choke. He was calmer now that he had said it. The real question was what he did next.

"I have always served the good of our people."

"Public concern does not excuse private cruelty."

She opened her mouth, then closed it again, a mix of affront and surprise on her face. Alessandro did not flinch.

"There are more important things." Omara brushed away a strand of hair. She had been so still, the gesture seemed monumental. "Geneva didn't neglect the niceties. She couriered each of the nonhuman leaders a knife."

"Impressive. At least she has style."

Omara waited while the wind stirred their hair, his bright, hers dark. "Is that all you have to say?"

The moment had come, the fork in the road. He took it. "What is there to say? I will fight this night, but only because the demon threatens us all. I will not fight for *you*. I've been your knight, but you betrayed all the loyalty I've given you. All my trust. You do not deserve my fealty."

Omara's eyes flared a pale gold. "You are my retainer."

"And you repaid my services so well."

"I'm sorry. That was my blunder." Omara met his eyes, but her boldness had faded.

Alessandro read the expression. "What happened?"

"Clan Albion did not answer my summons. The entire clan has disappeared from Fairview, down to the last fledgling."

Pierce's clan. "Treason."

Omara gave a helpless gesture. "You win. I should have listened to you. You guessed they had a hand in it."

The queen had effectively steered him away from venting his anger. He knew it, but Alessandro still considered what she had just told him. Albion had the best fighters.

She put her hand on his, wordless. All she had to say was in her touch. *Come back to me.*

Alessandro's breath caught. "No," he said, ending her unspoken plea.

"You will fight for me this night?" she asked. The question was bald, querulous, perhaps the only words he had ever heard that came straight from her heart.

"Yes."

After, if there was an after, he would walk away from Omara's service and any place in the society of his kind. There were things worse than loneliness. Chief among them was dishonorable servitude.

One bitch queen at a time.

Focus on Geneva and whoever brought the soul-sucking road show to Fairview. Once this is over, you can find some way of grinding Omara's bones to dust.

Besides, the vampire diva of evil was already occupied.

Holly could see Alessandro and Omara as distant shadows, their gestures backlit by the haze of the lampposts that dotted the paths across the campus lawn. She didn't need to hear their words to understand that their long relationship was tearing apart. Their hands sketched the pain in understated slashes as they spoke.

Holly turned away, feeling like a voyeur.

A whiff of leather and pine hung on the breeze, an odor of wild and ancient places. Werebeasts. The packs and prides had begun to arrive, roaming the pathways in groups of two and three. The appointed time for battle was drawing near.

Down to work. Holly narrowed her focus, shutting out the

scene around her. The murder victims had mostly been students. All the recent portals had happened at or near the university: the Flanders house, the faculty club, Sinsation, the cemetery, and even her own house weren't that far distant. That meant something local facilitated the magic, something that touched all those places. *A natural power source?* That could be bodies of water. Fissures in the earth. *Ley lines.*

She knelt in the grass, pushing her hands into the dense, damp lawn. She scanned the earth lightly, the same way she had in the graveyard. With her power unblocked it was too easy, almost laughable. Holly sank into the scan, deepening it, digging in.

Holly saw them. Thick, gold streams of magnetic power streaked under the earth, brush strokes of brilliant energy throbbing with the force of the earth's core. Holly inhaled in wonder. She had never been able to see ley lines before. They ran too deep for most witches to get a visual. She didn't just have power; she had a *lot* of power. *And there's no pain!*

Holly followed the streams with her mind. They branched and trailed in every direction, but flowed more or less toward the east, under the university and then south to the cemetery. She let the largest line take her, pushing her mind along like a tiny craft in a race to the sea.

The earth sped by, the current of the ley line covering city blocks as quickly as a car. It was less than a minute before turbulence came. Electricity raced through Holly, a physical feeling, even though it was only her thoughts that it touched. And then the power began to whirl.

There was another line flowing from north to south. A mightier line, dark as old rum, pounded past her. It was chill and wild, bleak as the forsaken lands of ice. The two flows collided, smashing with a force that made the etheric atmosphere shake and shudder. Power zinged in ripples of lightning, circling outward from the whirlpool of magic. It was hair-raising, beautiful, terrible. She let her mind float upward, pinpointing the location of the storm.

It was right under the Flanders house. *Well, that explains a thing or two.*

What a choice location for a witch's house! Even without an added dash of demon, the spell that gave the house its sentience would have gained power from the maelstrom of power under its foundations. No wonder it had been so hard to defeat.

With this network of power under the area, it was obvious why the summoning rituals had worked. Power permeated the campus air like fog. Geneva could harness it easily. She had chosen an arsenal for her battleground.

But I can use that weapon, too. Holly withdrew her mind, slowly returning to herself. She staggered a little, then slowly sank to the wet grass, putting her head between her knees.

"Are you all right?"

The blackness of the night compounded her dizziness. She blinked her vision clear to see Perry dressed in a plaid shirt and jeans. His forehead was creased with concern.

"Yeah, I'm okay. I was just doing some magical scouting. I came back a little fast."

She needed practice with her newfound powers, but there was no time. She was taking her driver's test during the Grand Prix. *Sink or swim, honey.* She let Perry pull her to her feet.

Behind Perry stood a tall, dark-haired young man with sharp cheekbones and wary eyes. *A strange expression for one so obviously strong,* she thought. His whole body spoke of fleet physical strength.

"This is Lore," said Perry. "He came from the other side of the portal, along with the rest of his pack. He's their alpha."

"Pack?" Holly dusted the grass off her damp rump. The clammy cloth made her shiver.

"We are hellhounds." Lore said it like a dare, as if he expected her to slap him.

"They're fighting with us in return for amnesty. They want to live in Fairview," Perry explained. He looked shell-shocked. "I had no idea what sort of a hell . . . I mean . . . I knew about the demons, but . . ."

Lore gave a single, solemn nod that might have been

meant as a greeting. "If you are to fight Geneva, you need to hear this. The portals enter a place called the Castle." He spoke slowly, with the precise measure of someone coping in a foreign language. On the other hand, he didn't seem to have an accent. *Maybe he just doesn't talk much.*

"The demon prison," Holly replied, wondering what the hellhounds had been on the other side of the portal. Then she thought of the picture in Grandma's book. Lore did look like he'd fit right into a Gothic decorating scheme.

"It is more than that. There are many who live there, creatures of all kinds. It is a huge, winding place without end. There are no doors or windows. No one has ever walked the length of one wall and returned to tell his tale."

"More than just demons live there?" Holly said, confused.

"There are many prisoners. Many peoples. All are forgotten there."

Holly was speechless. *How did that happen?* she wondered.

He went on. "Your summoner has made many tries to free this demon. Whenever a doorway opened, as many as could escaped. Many changelings. The hounds. Then at last the demon herself."

Perry interrupted, speaking about twice as fast. "It sounds like a few changelings from our side of things were involved at first, then invited their friends from the Castle to come on over and form an army. They're crossing back and forth, using the Castle as their barracks. They've got a spell book they're using like a passkey."

An army. That explains what I saw at the cemetery, Holly thought.

Lore continued. "We lived quietly for years, and the Castle guards forgot our corner of the prison. If Geneva or her soldiers attract their notice, they will remember that part of the Castle. They will punish any they find still living there."

"Will the guards cross the portal to our side?" Holly asked.

"Yes. The guardsmen are to be feared." Lore clenched one fist, the gesture expressing far more than his simple words. "I regret that there is no way to keep the door open and let those who deserve it go free."

Holly studied Lore, taking in his rough clothes, the constant vigilance of his gaze. *An escaped prisoner. A refugee.* How many others like him were still in the Castle?

Her thoughts took a sharp turn. Alessandro crossed the lawn toward them, his long, worn leather coat flaring behind him. In addition to his usual weapons, a studded baldric crossed his chest, supporting a silver-edged broadsword. The champion's badge of office, the huge weapon was forged to kill immortals. Beheading with a silver blade was forever.

He stopped before Holly, cupping her face and kissing her. The power between them flared, making her knees go soft. The demon could wait. She wanted, *needed* to have him in her arms. There had to be couches in the student lounge. An empty dorm room. A study carrel.

Perry and Lore shuffled, the embarrassed-guy noises bringing the embrace to an end. Alessandro released her, raising his head to sniff the wind. A paper coffee cup skittered down the path, chased by the rising breeze.

"The fey have arrived."

"I thought they were neutral," said Perry.

"They won't fight, but they've agreed to keep the humans out of it. They've made their base to the north," said Alessandro. He turned to Lore. "Hounds patrol the perimeter. Keep any humans who get past the fey clear of the action. Frighten them if you have to. Wolves fight with the vampires. Omara's forces cover the south. She leads them herself."

"If she leads the vampires, what are you doing?" Perry asked.

"I guard Holly. She is our chief weapon of magic. Call my cell the moment you have any knowledge of where Geneva has shown herself."

"I found the energy web of this place," Holly put in. "We may gain some advantage if I watch for disturbances. There'll be a power spike before a portal appears. If we catch it soon enough, we can be waiting."

"How do we know she'll open one?" asked Alessandro.

"Lore says she's been stashing her army inside the Castle."

Alessandro looked at the hellhound with interest. "Inside the Castle? No wonder we could never find the changelings."

Perry slapped Lore's shoulder. "Let's go." They turned and ran north.

Alessandro drew near Holly, so close their sleeves nearly brushed. She could feel the tension in the air, as if she could touch the combined dread and excitement of every creature in the area. It reminded her of a stadium before the big game.

"How did it go with Omara?" Holly asked.

"I'm no longer her servant. I'm through tangling myself in her lies." He shifted, settling his baldric more comfortably. "We should get you somewhere safe while you look for . . . whatever it is you need to see."

"I don't need safe. I need to be in the thick of the energy."

"Where, then?"

"We have to go back to the Flanders house."

Alessandro did not look impressed.

Chapter 28

The Flanders house was no longer dead.

Holly stood at the gate as she had days before, her hand on the gatepost, Alessandro's coat brushing against her side. The house glowered from under its gables, its porch wrapped around like folded arms. That was the same.

But not everything was. A streamer of crime-scene tape dangled from the pear tree. The lawn was churned to mud where dozens of heavy boots had tromped to and fro. And her fantasies about Alessandro had become real. *Be careful what you wish for.*

Venom prickled through her veins, a low, constant urge. She was hungry for his touch. Famished. Being near him was barely enough to control the ache. Sheer stubbornness was the only thing forcing Holly to concentrate. That and wariness of the house.

There were no whispers, no voices, but she could feel its dislike. No, it was no longer dead. Something—someone—had revived it.

The flare of orange light from the upstairs windows was the first clue.

The terrified scream and sound of splintering wood was the next.

Alessandro bounded over the gate, drawing his sword as he ran. Holly followed on his heels, leaping up the porch steps in two bounds.

"Door's locked!" said Alessandro.

"Stand back," Holly said.

Now that she knew energy lay beneath the house, it was easy to tap into it with her newly unblocked power. Just a drop. Just a quick snatch and twist with the spell, and . . . the door blew off its hinges, startling Alessandro into a quick flight backward.

Okay, save that one for special occasions.

He threw her a wide-eyed look as he sprang through the smoking hole in the wall. Holly followed a fraction slower, opening her senses, scanning the house's consciousness. The blast had hurt it, driving its sense of self deep into the foundations. When it recovered, its fury would be profound.

A faint voice drifted into her mind, the barest rustle from the stony, crumbling foundations. *You again?*

You don't have the strength of a demon helping you this time, Demolition Sale.

No, the house replied. It sounded morose. *This one doesn't share power.*

This one? Holly wondered with alarm.

Alessandro was already mounting the stairs, sword in hand. The orange light from above was swelling, the glow painting a stark shadow of the staircase on the wall. There, the light was yet brighter, sliding off the length of Alessandro's blade and turning his hair to a corona of gold.

She remembered all too strongly the last time they had gone up these steps. They had found Ben's backpack just there. Over there was the room where the black slime had nearly killed her. The drop cloth still sat on the landing, except now every crease and fold was picked out in that oily orange glow.

The light came from one of the small back bedrooms, pulsing like a satanic disco. On the floor lay the remains of something that looked like melting tomato aspic.

"Oh, Goddess," Holly gasped, covering her nose. The smell made her tear up. "Was that what screamed?"

"A changeling," Alessandro muttered, lifting his sword and moving down the hall in a smooth, deadly glide. "Have I ever mentioned how much I hate this house?"

Nausea sucked at Holly's gut as she stepped around the mess.

The bedroom doorway was narrow. Alessandro's bulk filled it, blocking Holly's view. He slipped sideways to get sword and shoulders past the jamb. Holly followed. She had just enough time to see that the light came from the corner of the room before brightness blinded her, shrouding the features of the man standing in front of the light. The man opening the portal.

Like Alessandro, he carried a broadsword.

"Holly, get back!"

Pure instinct made her drop and roll out of the way as the man swung his sword in a scything arc. Holly smacked into the corner of the door, bouncing the tender part of her elbow off the door's sharp edge. Frantic tingling numbed her hand, leaving her to make a three-limbed crawl for the safety of the hallway.

A clash of steel raised the hair on Holly's arms. That was the sound of invasion, of brute strength conquering without cause or pity. It was the sound of final death.

She scrambled into an empty bedroom.

The floor vibrated with the weight of the opponents as they pounced and slid on the gritty hardwood. Holly crouched, peering around the door frame of her bedroom toward the fight. She heard a whistling slice and a thunk as one of the swords crashed into the woodwork, splintering it to pieces. *That's what we heard from outside.*

She could see them, or a sliver of them, as they moved back and forth in front of the bedroom doorway. This was a two-handed, slashing fight. No points for elegance. Brute male force. Bunching muscles. Snarling teeth.

The other man was as big as Alessandro, bare-armed and tattooed with intricate blue spirals. Black hair hung to his hips in one long braid, swinging like a serpent as he moved. He wore a bronze breastplate over rags of scarlet silk, his skin haggard and his eyes pits of madness. He was shouting in a language she didn't know. *Who is this guy? What's he saying?*

The swords connected again with a crash and a hiss of scraping metal. Reflexively Holly fell back, covering her ears against the noise. She had been able to fight during the skirmish in the cemetery, but this was far trickier. *How do I get a clear shot? They're too close together.*

Holly nearly had her chance when their attacker stumbled backward out of the bedroom, one massive hand clutching what looked like a huge tome. But as he slammed into the wall, Alessandro was on him, sword raised for a killing stroke.

Alessandro was a beat too late.

His opponent rebounded into a somersault, landing outside the path of the blade. As soon as his feet touched the floor, he sprang into a run, charging for the stairs. Holly ducked out of the way, feeling the rush of air as he raced past.

Alessandro slid to a halt beside her. "I have to catch him. He said he's a Castle guardsman."

"Is that what he was saying?"

"Yes, and he has the book."

"*The Book of Lies*?"

Alessandro looked startled that she knew the name of it. "Yes. Call Perry; he's minutes away. Get him to escort you to Omara."

"No!" The venom in her system erupted, making her frantic that he was leaving her side. "Don't do this! Don't go!" She covered her face with her hands, mortified.

He said nothing.

"I'm sorry." She looked up. "Venom talking. Of course you have to."

He looked crushed, but at the same time impatient. "Go outside and wait. Stay out of sight. You've got your magic. You'll be safe, but stay out of there." He pointed to the bedroom. "Get away from the portal."

With that Alessandro rushed toward the stairway. Holly

caught her breath as he leaped, spread his arms, and sailed over the banister rail, his long coat floating out behind him. He hung in midair for the barest second. Then he was gone, swooping down the stairwell.

Emotions muddy with frustration, Holly stared at the spot where Alessandro had hovered a moment before plunging after his quarry. They had found the book. That was great, but now she was alone.

She could feel the venom itching along her nerves with doubled intensity. It was so much easier to cope with when Alessandro was nearby. She took a deep breath and let it out slowly, doing her best to pretend the gnawing sensation was happening to somebody else.

Her call to Perry went to voice mail. She left a message. The cell reception was bad, probably the fault of the portal.

Alessandro had said to leave the house. He had ordered her to go. Her feet turned, driven by his command—but being told not to do something was the biggest incentive to do it. Automatically she looked at the forbidden bedroom. *I want to see the portal.*

Now that the guardsman had gone, there was only a trickle of orange light. The spell had not been complete, and now it was collapsing. Watching that might teach her something useful, like how to close a portal herself.

But Alessandro's command had been clear, and she bore his mark. Her feet began to take her toward the stairs. The compulsion felt like a sticky web dragging her forward.

Get off me!

She tried to yank herself free of the clinging energy, but it stuck fast, winding her tighter in its hold. Anger, frantic and hot, shredded her focus, miring her deeper in the web.

Get. Off. Me. She was caught tighter than ever.

So she froze, giving the trap no more energy. She panted, short, sharp gulps, stilling her wheeling brain. *I can't be like this. I can't. I can't.*

Rage. Despair. It was all useless. Instead she found the ghost of her will, the flickering shadow the mark had left behind. *I'm strong enough. Of course I am. I rode the ley lines. I blew off the door.*

Disobedience was harder.

Never mind. With the pool of energy under this house, I can still use my magic.

Forming the image of a knife in her mind, she reached down beneath the house, accessing the wild earth energy. It roiled under her touch, brazen with vitality. It was the stuff of nature, the soul of the ground beneath her. Riotous. Feral. Untamed. *Free.*

She poured power into her will, shaping it, refining it. She imagined the silver-bladed knife on her dresser at home, one she had reclaimed from the box under her bed. She was through hiding her tools, through bowing to the will of other people, even those she loved.

> *Let the winds of the East give me wings.*
> *Let the fires of the South give me passion.*
> *Let the seas of the West give me life.*
> *Let the stones of the North give me strength.*
> *Goddess and God, let this prayer set me free.*

The short, sharp blade was bright as starlight. The pleasure of its familiar form, worn to the shape of her hand, restored a sense of balance to her mind.

She knew this knife. She knew how to use it. It was hers.

A new equilibrium hushed the clamor of the venom. Stilled the cloying pull of the mark.

The knife was straight.

Graceful.

Honed sharp and true.

In her mind Holly took it in her hand and used that knife, her will, to cut herself free. The web of the mark fell limply into nothing, dissolving to pale light before it smeared to a wisp.

Oh, Goddess. Stomach unwinding, shoulders easing, Holly drew her first deep breath since Mac had shown up on her porch. Tears surprised her aching eyelids, and she trembled with grief and release. Now she could move where she wanted to go. Her will was her own.

Not even a powerful witch was supposed to be able to

break the spell of venom. She's been given a rare gift. She slumped against the wall, trembling with relief. *Thank you.*

Time to act. Slowly Holly entered the bedroom, trying to look everywhere at once. All that was left of the portal was a swirling, pumpkin-hued glob about the size of a manhole cover. It drooled ectoplasm down the wall with the enthusiasm of a Newfoundland dog. The room smelled like burned toast.

She heard the scrape of a shoe behind her.

Holly whirled, searching the shadows. In the back of her mind the house chuckled. Nerves and irritation jittered down Holly's spine. Cursing the failing light, she let her gaze flit from corner to corner.

"Hello, Holly."

The words, the voice, were too familiar. She spun around, terror jamming in her chest. She'd heard those words too often, whispered sweetly in the dark.

Ben stood in the doorway, with a gun.

Her throat closed until she could barely breathe out her words. "What in Hades are you doing here?"

"Keeping very quiet and hoping the monsters won't find me. But look, you're here."

"Talk." Her patience ripped like wet paper. "Because I'll blow your face off if you don't."

Ben looked at her stubbornly. "I have a gun. Silver bullets."

Holly raised her hand, wiggling her fingers. "I've already got my weapon out."

"Witch." His mouth curled in disgust.

"Why are you here, Ben? This place nearly killed you."

"I'm here because the guardsmen turned on me. Took my book. It's not fair. I paid a lot of money for it."

"The Book of Lies? You bought it?" Holly's voice rose with incredulity. Of course, his family had that kind of money.

"Yeah, and the guards have been after it—and me—since the demon came through." He looked at the gun in his hand. "I was going to force the guardsman to give it back, but I . . ."

He didn't have to finish. Holly knew Ben had never been physically brave. He would never have confronted the guard.

He sighed. "I tried to hide here. The house knows me. I've bargained with it before."

"Bargained? What would you have that the house wants?"

Ben said nothing, letting the gun drift to his side. His expression was odd, pinched.

Then she knew. Ben was one of the fraternity sponsors who bought the Flanders house from Raglan. *The house needs lives.*

"The fraternity? You led them to this place? You ... Why the ..." Holly choked, suddenly at a loss for air. *"Why?"* She stopped, breathing hard. "What are you doing, Ben?"

"What I have to."

"But *why*?" Holly's mind raced, clicking facts into place. The ooze, against all odds, hadn't hurt him. Her books on demonology were missing. "How long have you been at this?"

"Years. I did some reading. I mean real reading, real research. There are plenty of prohuman groups willing to lend a hand if they think you're looking for an answer to the supernatural problem. People with money and connections."

Fear and suspicion had drawn ugly lines around his mouth, but she'd never noticed them before. *He fooled me all along. He's a consummate actor.*

He returned her gaze, shaking his head as if she were a slow student. "Don't you get it? The Castle was the answer. Humanity had the same problem long ago and built a prison to take care of the *others*. It was already there, with guardsmen in place to keep the monsters inside. If I summoned something through a portal to earth, the guardsmen would come to get it back. Along the way they'd take everything nonhuman back with them into their prison. Nothing but humans would be left behind. Simple as calling for a garbage pickup."

"But I *don't* get it," Holly said, bewildered.

Impatient, Ben slapped the flat of his hand on the door

frame. "How could the humans clean up Fairview? We don't have the power to do it ourselves. We've lost. *Someone* had to arrange a way to get help, so I did."

"There were murders," Holly retorted. "Blood rituals. Human girls were killed."

"Price of doing business. The changelings were happy to help with that part." Ben looked away. "Though I should have done it myself. One or two of those creatures were manageable, but they called their friends. That's when things started to get out of hand."

"What do you mean?"

"The changelings have a taste for murder. An addiction. They should never have come out of the Castle."

"And you *worked* with them? *You?*"

Ben started forward, but Holly used a small push of magic to knock him back. His eyes grew wide, as if he'd just truly realized that she might be dangerous.

The gun came up again, but she didn't care anymore. "What the hell were you thinking?"

He lifted his head, as if telling himself to be brave. "They were eager, more than happy to help call up a demon. Best of all, I knew that once we did the summoning, I just had to sit back and wait for the guardsmen to mop them up along with the rest of the spooks."

He gave an ugly curl of his lip. "And the changelings did it all for a handful of those tokens. Like they're so precious. I bought them online for a song." He snorted. "Or maybe it was just the chance to murder humans again that brought the ugly bastards running."

Holly gulped air, sick and appalled. "Do you know what you've done? The demon is already taking souls!" She gave him another little push. "You screwed up. The demon is loose. It's all spiraling out of control, and that was the first guardsman I've seen. Where's the cavalry, Ben? When are they going to save you?"

Ben raised his hands, gun and all, but it wasn't a gesture of surrender. He was trying to placate her. "I didn't know. I didn't realize. The guardsmen . . . there are too few. They haven't come like I thought they would. I thought it was going to be a lot less . . . complicated."

"Like you thought you and I would be?"

Ben's expression grew condescending. "I'm sorry. I truly am. You'd said once that your magic didn't really work. I thought that meant you were as good as human."

"And then at the Flanders house you saw what I could do." Holly didn't really need confirmation. This part she had guessed already.

"I saw you were one of them. There was no way I could save you after that. Not when it was clear you'd never use your magic for our side."

"*Save* me?" She shot a bolt of energy that smacked inches from his foot. "I was trying to save you from the house you'd apparently already fed Bill Gamble, your *best friend.* What were you doing there, anyway?"

Ben stared at the floor, where a wisp of smoke curled from a charred spot on the wood. "The idiots murdered that girl right inside the house, left her lying there for anyone to find. My prints were all over the place. I needed to be sure I was counted as just another victim."

"Just another victim. So you hid in the slime. The house wouldn't hurt you because you were feeding it. No wonder you wouldn't go to the hospital. A thorough checkup would have shown that you'd never been attacked. Well, you were right. Your ruse fooled everybody. We never guessed you were the killer."

Ben looked affronted. "Oh, I just resourced the operation. I was the organizer. I never killed anyone. I certainly never got involved in the magic."

"What about the look-away spells? They were all over the house."

"I hired the guy who sold me the book. He'd do anything for a dollar. He does all the spell casting I need."

Holly struggled for words, overwhelmed. "Goddess, I hate you."

A shudder ran through the house, the sideways shuffle of an earthquake. Ben raised a hand, pointing at the wall behind Holly. His eyes went round. "The portal is opening up again."

Holly stepped sideways, needing to look behind her but reluctant to turn her back on Ben. He was correct. The portal was swirling wider, new light brightening the room with the garish orange of a jack-o'-lantern. She touched the portal with her power, barely a brush.

It gave enough information to swamp her with terror. "It never completely closed. Something on the inside is giving the door a shove." Would that be the changeling army?

Holly snapped her thoughts into line, refusing to drown in the panic that lapped at her senses. "We're getting out of here."

Fixated on Ben, she had stopped monitoring the house. Now she probed it with her thoughts. It was still weak from her assault on the front door, but the portal was using the house like a straw, sucking ley-line power from beneath the foundations. Some of that power was bleeding off into the structure. Waking it up. Things were about to turn nasty.

"Stairs!" she yelled, diving for the door.

Holly moved so fast, her feet barely found purchase. She flew into the hallway, half-blind with the need to flee. When Ben grabbed her from behind, the sudden jerk flung her into the wall.

"What is that? Holly, what is that?"

Holly clutched her head, wishing it would stop ringing. "What? We don't have time—"

"That!"

She squinted. A large, ballooning shape of white poofed over the upstairs landing like a giant jellyfish. For a moment surprise overcame her urge to run. "I think it's the drop cloth."

"Why is it doing that?"

"On a wild guess, I'd say it was possessed."

"Oh, shit!"

"It'll probably smother us if we try to escape." She squeezed Ben's arm and gave him a sweet smile. "Would you like me to take care of that for you? Somewhere in between saving your ungrateful ass again and figuring out how to save Fairview from being eaten alive?"

"Just do something. *Please!*"

"Then give me the gun."

After a moment's pause, he did.

Holly shoved Ben aside, her attention fully on the drop cloth. How the blazes was she going to manage this?

Blazes.

Well, I signed the burn order, didn't I?

It was just like lighting a huge candle, a trick she had done a hundred times with the snap of her fingers. The drop cloth had been the first to go. Then the stairway carpet. Stray newspapers. With all the paints and solvents Raglan had left inside, the rest was a foregone conclusion.

Holly worked most of her magic from the blasted front lawn, where the house couldn't reach her. Power flowed, liquid and graceful. The hardest part was shutting off her mind to the house's screams. Mad and evil though it was, it was still conscious.

Sadly, fire was the only sure way to disrupt the half-opened portal. Fire disturbed the flow of energy. It also had the potential to attract a lot of attention. Holly conjured a glamour to hide the fact that a house was burning in plain view. At the same time she set wards to keep the blaze contained. The only evidence of the fire was a faint smoky smell she couldn't seem to banish. The neighbors would wake up to a vacant lot and a pile of ash.

Ben stood quietly by, as if he had lost the will to move. He just stared. Then she realized he was staring at something specific down the street, his face washing an interesting shade of white.

Holly turned. *Werewolves.*

They poured down the street in a silent, furry river, shadows punctuated by the flare of hunters' eyes. Muscled haunches worked as they ran, their flowing lope eating ground with the speed of nightmares. The wolves were big but lean, their legs almost delicate. Their thick coats were mostly gray, but there were black wolves and tawny ones, chocolate brown and white. All were red-tongued and brush-tailed; all had fierce ivory teeth. When they reached Holly and Ben they stopped of one accord, eerie and noiseless. Only the huffing of their breath made them seem more than a dream.

One came to Holly, its nails clicking on the pavement. A gray one. Male. Not the largest, but clearly the one in command. It sat, ears forward.

"We have a prisoner," said Holly.

With a lupine grin, Perry scanned Ben's face with feral yellow eyes.

Chapter 29

Running with wolves exceeded Holly's fitness plan. It was like sprinting for the bus, except it went on forever. She just couldn't keep up.

After a few frustrating blocks and a doggy huddle, the pack split into three. The largest group ran ahead. One group escorted Ben in the opposite direction, to be placed, she presumed, in a metaphorical and perhaps literal doghouse. Perry and a handful of others stayed with Holly, slowing their pace to a brisk trot as they went to rendezvous with Queen Omara.

Their journey took them back to the main part of the campus. It seemed unreal. Holly had just been up there taking classes, but she'd never been to this part of the grounds. She did her best to orient herself, recognizing the Arts Building behind her and the main lawns rimmed by the dormitories straight ahead. Their destination was a small playing field at the south end of the lawns. There Queen Omara had made her headquarters.

Long before they reached it, though, they had to stop. The wolves and hounds had formed a security cordon, marking a wide perimeter. Holly and her escort were thoroughly sniffed before they were allowed to cross. The pause was fine with Holly, who bent over, hands on knees, to catch her breath and nurse the stitch in her side. Perry butted his nose against her.

"Just a minute." Holly gasped, straightening. "Iron endurance isn't one of my superpowers."

Perry bumped her again, making a doggy whine. Holly switched her attention from her aching lungs to the world around her. She began plodding forward. Now she could see the pale-faced Undead pacing near the goalposts, making the scene look like some avant-garde sportscast with no color and less dialogue.

The creepiness quotient was in hyperdrive. The vamps seemed to be already in battle mode, moving with the sliding grace of predators, forming into shadowy clots to talk, point, and shake their heads. *What are they doing?* They all seemed to be facing north, watching for something.

Holly turned, and it was then that she saw that the enemy had arrived. The changeling army, complete with their packs of ghouls, emerged from between the dormitory buildings, a rolling wave of grotesquerie.

Not possible! She had kept her senses open to the ley lines. She hadn't felt any portals besides the one in the house.

But here they were.

Perry tensed, his tail going bushy. He began running for the bleachers, barking at Holly to follow. She froze for a split second, adrenaline overloading her nerves. *Oh, no, oh, no, no, no!* Then she sprang after him, legs pumping. The ground seemed suddenly alive with hazards, the grass bunching up to catch her feet. She had never run so fast.

The changelings came faster. They came in force, nearly beating Holly to the safety of the front lines. The wolves and hellhounds swarmed them, but numbers were against the werebeasts. For every changeling there seemed to be at least three ghouls.

Holly's eyes searched the field ahead. There was no sign of Alessandro, but she spotted Omara. The queen had thrown aside her coat, and the bright green silk of her long shift caught the cloud-mottled moonlight. Omara was on her cell phone, yelling into it. It sounded as though she were calling for reinforcements.

Perry and Holly reached the battle area, three of the changelings hard on their heels. Wheeling, Holly fired Ben's gun until it was empty, then threw it aside. She scrambled up the bleachers, praying the height would buy her safety long enough to figure out how to use her powers effectively. She couldn't just blast into the crowd without taking out friend as well as foe.

The battle had begun. Where was Alessandro?

Merda.

The guardsman ran from the Flanders house with the speed and cunning of a fox. A hundred yards beyond the house he had given Alessandro the slip, demonstrating an uncanny ability to hide where there was no real cover. Evidently the Castle guard had been granted extraordinary powers of their own.

Alessandro flew to the top of a bus shelter, his boots landing lightly on its metal framework. He scanned the south campus, searching for the gleam of the guardsman's metal breastplate. From his vantage point the lawn looked like dark water, the ring of campus lights a glittering shore. He listened, hearing distant music, the wind in the trees, but no sound of running feet. He could smell werebeasts and, from farther off, the scent of movie-house popcorn. Nothing out of the ordinary.

Which was magic in itself. The fey were at work. If he relaxed the focus of his eyes, he could see the faint blue glow that showed that a building had been magically sealed. Humans would find excuses not to leave—they would sleep longer, have another latte, or find their conversation too compelling to abandon. The north campus was covered, and the blue glow crept toward the first of the dormitories. The fey were working south.

As he looked toward the dorms, he saw what he had been looking for—the momentary flash of a tattooed sword arm flickering in and out of the shadows. Alessandro leaped into the air with an audible whoosh.

He landed in a crouch and ran hard. The dormitories had irregular walls, deep entrances, a thousand places an enemy could hide. Garbage rustled in the wind, faking the sound of a footfall, the whisper of a drawn sword.

There!

Alessandro had his blade in hand, ready. The guardsman wheeled from the shadows, the whole weight of his motion in the stroke. Their blades crashed in a two-handed parry, the shock vibrating clear to Alessandro's spine.

Where is the book? The guardsman must have set it down somewhere to free his hands for the fight. He set the thought aside. Danger gave the moment clarity, a still calm that cleared his senses of extraneous detail. The guardsman thrust; Alessandro melted out of reach, turning and driving back in with a blow of his own. His blade slid off the breastplate, skimming the man's bare arm. He smelled the spurt of blood, the sharp scent honing the moment.

Injury upped the ante. The guardsman fought back, thundering a rain of blows against Alessandro's defenses. Alessandro was forced to retreat a few steps, surprised at the guard's enormous strength. He ducked under humming metal, trying to get inside the man's defenses, but every time he was blocked.

The guardsman swung again, a furious blow that drove Alessandro even farther back. Dodging behind a bicycle rack, the guardsman snatched up *The Book of Lies* and whirled away, bolting across the lawn.

Alessandro sped after him. As the guardsman angled close to one of the dorms, four changelings converged out of nowhere, pouncing on the guard. They fell into a snarl of bodies, the guardsman shaking them off like a hound shedding water, breaking the neck of one—but he had to use both hands for that.

He dropped the book.

Alessandro was right there, cleaving a changeling in two, but another crept behind him, waiting till Alessandro raised his arms to slide a silver knife between his ribs.

Pain arched clear to the roof of his mouth, the silver flying inside him like acid, vibrating on every nerve. His vision went black. He dropped his sword, fell to his knees with a violent curse.

Breath failed Alessandro as he groped for the hilt of the knife. It slid from his flesh in a gush of blood, leaving him sick and sweating. He retched into the grass, lungs flailing for air. A fraction higher and the blade would have pierced his heart.

The two surviving changelings scuttled across the lawn with the book, the guardsman in pursuit. The skirmish was over in a matter of a minute.

Alessandro picked himself up. He felt like cracked glass, fissures of white-hot nerves spidering out from where the knife had thrust. Blood coursed from the wound, taking his strength with it. If he got help he would recover, but the blade had been silver. Healing would be slow.

"Score one for the bad guys." Macmillan sauntered into Alessandro's field of vision, materializing from thin air. Alessandro lunged at Macmillan, but the demon cop danced away, his laugh taunting. "Hey, you might be fast, but I'm barely even here."

Alessandro held the wound in his side, feeling wetness ooze between his fingers. "What do you want?"

Macmillan waved a hand. He looked oddly transparent, even in the darkness. "Nothing that tattooed goof hasn't already accomplished. We have the book. The queen's champion is wounded and stalled outside enemy lines. I'm pretty much done for the night. After years of mopping up after criminals, it's kind of nice being on the winning side for a change. Basically I'm just here to gloat."

"You haven't won yet."

"Oh, suck it up, vampire. There's no way you're pulling a victory out of this mess." The detective turned his back, apparently intending to simply walk away.

"Is that it? Has Geneva eaten your entire soul?"

"What? You want us to have a buddy moment and save the day?" Macmillan looked back, the horror in his eyes belying his light words. "The worst part of this, Caravelli, is that with every passing minute I lose a piece of what made me human. There's nothing left but the impulse to feed.

Thank whoever you pray to that vampires don't smell like food."

Macmillan held up his hands, showing their translucence against the dormitory lights. "You see, I haven't eaten in a few hours. I can't last that long. She tells me it gets easier the longer you're a demon, but right now . . . God, I hate this part."

Alessandro stared at Macmillan, forgetting his own pain in a wash of revulsion. He'd seen this before, but it never got any more pleasant to look at.

The detective's hands were knotted with dark veins, the ropy, engorged ridges so thick and black they seemed the very absence of light. They seemed to flow with darkness, bubbling and pulsing until the flesh between vanished.

Now wholly shadows, Macmillan's fingers crumbled into blackness like a dry, rotted leaf succumbing to the wind. He was powdering into a mist, powerless, a shade, a nothing. His hands, his feet, and his arms fell away, nothing left but a blot against the empty night air. Then, mercifully, he was gone.

Gone somewhere to envelop an unsuspecting victim and drain his life. How many would it take before he could resume his own form again? Or that of some creeping or scurrying beast?

Alessandro felt sick. A mere handful of days before, Macmillan had been a good man doing honorable work. This was what it meant when a demon infected your soul.

But whether he meant to or not, Macmillan had given him a warning: *The queen's champion is wounded and stalled outside enemy lines.* Alessandro was the wounded champion. The enemy wasn't there yet, but he'd better hurry to avoid getting caught on the wrong side of the battle.

Alessandro started off at a slow jog, as fast as his wound would allow. When he got near the Arts Building, he leaped to a low balcony, then to the third-floor roof. The exertion tore at his side, but the improved view was worth it. Macmillan's tip had been good.

But Alessandro was too late.

In the parking lot behind the dormitories, a series of yellow school buses were disgorging ghouls and changelings. Buses? It was clever. There was no hint of magic to tip their hand, and no one would ever expect the enemy to arrive in something so mundane. Of course, this was just the advance guard. They would have to use a portal for an army large enough to take the whole town. *But this is enough to keep us distracted while they get down to business.*

At the far end, closest to the playing field, he saw a handful of changelings setting up a ritual circle. And there . . . Alessandro flew forward, eyes wide in shock. He gripped the balcony rail to stop himself, the tails of his coat flowing around his legs. *Merda!*

The figure standing to one side was John Pierce— *Pierce!*—holding what had to be *The Book of Lies. Of course. He knows enough sorcery to use it. He's depraved enough to do it.* Pierce would open a portal to let Geneva's army through. An entire battleground separated Alessandro from Pierce. And, for that matter, from the queen. He looked around, desperate for a solution.

So much was happening. At the edge of the campus he saw the flashing lights of police vehicles. Now the humans were aware something was going on, but hellhounds and the fey were holding them back—the hounds with sheer ferocity. The fey were raising a fog, blanketing the campus north of the battlefield. Soon visibility would be next to nothing. *At least one thing's going right.*

Then his eye caught something farther off, where the land rose behind the playing field. More vehicles, this time pulling into the southernmost lot. Even to vampire sight it was too far away to make out the faces of the figures leaving the vehicles, but the luxury six-seat SUVs were impossible to miss. No one else in Fairview drove anything like that. Clan Albion had come for the show, and they were arriving from the south.

They weren't going to be cheering for Omara.

The queen was caught between enemies.

Then Alessandro saw a figure climbing up the bleachers. He turned cold, as if his final death had crept into his bones unannounced. *Holly.* She was trapped right along with his queen.

From the safety of the bleachers, Holly searched under the earth for stores of energy. There were ley lines down there, but the raging battle made it hard to concentrate. It was as if her magic seized up along with the cold, hard knot that used to be her stomach.

There. She found the main line beneath the playing field, ripe with a thick, golden energy. Though not turbulent like the ones under the Flanders property, it was still wild. Not all that easy to handle. She'd have to be careful.

Suddenly something whistled by Holly's arm, and she leaped into the air with sheer surprise. A changeling hunched in the shadow of the bleachers, its maw tight with concentration as it aimed what looked like a small crossbow. She summoned a quick bolt of energy, so fast it was more of a flash than a strike. It was enough to make the thing drop its weapon, but three ghouls raced from behind it, bounding up the bleachers toward her. They were moving too fast for more than a sputter of power.

"Perry!" Holly cried as she scampered the length of the bleacher seats, hearing the old wood creak and moan. At the end, she grabbed the handrail and started toward the ground, half climbing, half tumbling as she went. When she hit the grass she bolted, the ghouls hot on her tail.

Unfortunately, where Holly could run faster, so could they. She turned again, heading south. Here the lawn sloped up a sharp incline, and she grabbed at branches and tufts of grass to gain momentum. Cursing, she heard the ghouls closing in, making the sickening yip they gave when scenting prey.

Perry sprang from the shadows in an arcing, elegant bound. The wolf snarled, making Holly's every nerve recoil. Perry landed on the ghouls in a fury of fangs. The ghouls' yipping stopped in a sudden, profound silence. The wolf had ripped the throats from all three of the lethal monsters in record time.

Job done, Perry chased after the changeling with the

crossbow. Holly's mind stalled. She would never regard Perry's sweet, scholarly smile quite the same way again.

She ran the rest of the way up the hill and flung herself on the damp grass, trying to stay flat and out of sight as she surveyed the scene of the battle. Up here she was as high as the uppermost bleachers, but now she was facing the action. There was Omara, over there the tight S-curve that was her line of defenders. The vampires seemed to be using any and all weapons, firearms, blades, and magic included. Through the tiny queen's generalship they were holding their own, and the mob of changelings and ghouls had thinned out.

Then she saw Alessandro, and her heart seemed to shatter. He was on the far side of the battle lines, the enemy side, running straight into the melee. His coat flowed behind him, his sword mowing through the throng like a clever scythe. Ghouls jumped him from behind, but he swung, backhanding them into the air. Three flew up, landing in ragged heaps, but at least a dozen were closing in behind them.

And he was wounded. She could see it in his movements. That, more than anything, galvanized her. *I have to help him. I have to help all of them.* Now she understood Elaine Carver, dying to keep Fairview safe. She did it because she was the only one who could.

A tug twinged in the energy field. Holly turned left, looking with her eyes and with her mind. She saw the figure with the book, the changelings, the ad hoc ritual circle in the parking lot. *They're opening a portal.* It was time to do her job.

Holly scrambled to her feet. Perry thundered up with a deep woof, his ears going back.

"What?" Holly looked where Perry's gaze was fixed.

There was a line of sullen-looking vamps walking up the hill behind her. They came side by side, black coats flying, like the title shot of a trendy TV show. *Oh, crap, it's the designer vamps.*

Nothing about them said *good guys. Why does everything have to be so bloody complicated?* "Get behind me," she said to Perry.

The wolf looked at her in disbelief.

"I mean it."

He made a doggy protest. One tall vamp in the middle smiled, showing the full length of his fangs. He ran his tongue over his teeth, the meaning clear. Holly moved beyond being afraid and on to fed up. *Oh, spare me the foreplay.*

She needed a few practice shots. Here was a row of perfectly good targets.

She let her consciousness sink into the earth and felt the hum of power through her toes, then creeping up her thighs in an erotic column of power. The sensation was like standing in a bathtub of champagne, golden bubbles of energy exploding under her skin. It felt good, and right, and deadly. Shifting her weight, Holly felt the thrum of potential reach her belly.

A laugh welled up from wherever inappropriate jokes were born. "Hey, boys!"

A dozen pairs of vampire eyes glinted evilly in the darkness—at least, those not wearing shades despite the pitch-black night. *I bet they practice that glint in front of the mirror.*

She raised her hands, wiggling her fingers. "Wanna play?"

From their expressions, she didn't scare them one little bit. They were halfway up the hillside before she released her first bolt.

It hung in the air, a scrap of sun in the night, incandescence where the moment before, a vampire had stood. The vamp twisted in the air, landed with a splat, and exploded in a shower of grave dust.

Cool.

Perry howled with triumph. Holly aimed again, feeling the pressure of all that glorious energy against her diaphragm. Her will—*my free will!*—harnessed the shot, making the aim true and fierce.

Best of all, it was easy. She could fight without pain, without being drained. She fired again and again. The shadows around the bleachers faded to white, the light washing the stars from sight. Each shot exploded a vampire.

They ran. The prey had suddenly become the hunter. Perry chased them down the hill, calling his wolves to the chase.

Now, the ritual and Alessandro.

Descending the hill, Holly moved slowly, using an odd crab walk to keep her footing on the steep slope. She could smell churned earth and crushed grass, blood and rent flesh. Sweat slicked her skin, turning icy in the rising breeze. The stink of death made her mouth water in a bad way.

The battle was changing shape, neat battle lines collapsing into a brawl. To every side there was yipping and yelling. Metal crashed on metal. Spells cracked the air with the snap of bullwhips. Holly stopped to fire a blast once, twice. Cries of anger came as the flash blinded the nocturnal creatures. As they covered their eyes she streaked past, brushing sleeve on sleeve with a particularly ugly changeling.

She spotted Omara's green shift. The gold decoration on the queen's garb flashed as she threw a ghoul to the earth, crushing its throat with a twist of her dainty hands. *Good to be on her side.*

Holly felt a hand clutch the back of her jacket. Then claws were at her sleeves, her ankles, her belt. The night had grown talons. Teeth wrenched the flesh of her calf. *Ghouls.*

Holly kicked out but lost her balance as a dozen bony arms grabbed for her limbs. Ghoul claws raked down her face, scraping but not yet tearing the flesh. Holly's leg throbbed, her shoe hot with blood. Fangs sank into her shoulder, and Holly lost her temper. Screaming in pain and fury, she elbowed the thing in the face, at the same time letting fly a firestorm of white heat. Steam shot upward from the ghoul, the blast too hot for mere smoke, leaving nothing but a carbonized twist of flesh. Kicking the charred creature away, Holly watched it shatter on the grass to flakes of black ick.

The other ghouls gibbered in terror, dropping to all fours to run. Holly took three or four steps toward them. It was enough to send them bolting.

The bites from the ghouls' visclike jaws knifed through her leg and arm, bringing nausea in their wake. Holly's journey shrank to putting one foot before the other. She stumbled the last yards to where the vampires were bunched in a tight, defensive circle. No creature bothered her for those excruciating steps. Apparently the ability to barbecue at will had earned her some street cred.

Then Alessandro shouldered through the wall of vamps, looking around wildly until he saw her. He was a mess, his hair straggling in a shredded aureole, his coat torn and covered with muck and blood. He was taking her into his arms, and then pulling her to safety behind the front ranks of the vampire warriors. He felt so good, so strong, that Holly melted against him. At the moment nothing mattered but the fact that they were both still standing.

"You're hurt," she mumbled into the collar of his filthy coat.

"So are you. Don't worry about me. I'll heal." From the way he held himself, she wasn't sure about that. She gave him the best of her kisses, her hands clinging to his sleeves.

"You're free of my mark," he said, sounding awestruck. "How?"

But she could afford no more time. "I have to stop the ritual."

He dug his fingers into the snarled mass of her hair, tipping up her face so that his golden eyes could hold her gaze. His look was possessive, full of battle fire. "Whatever you need. I'll get you there."

Her knees wobbled as Alessandro opened his mouth to say more. She grabbed for him just as he stumbled, trying to steady himself. The ground was shaking, rolling with sickening heaves. *We're too late.*

With one last jolt the tremor stopped. Holly panted, still as a mouse within the circle of Alessandro's arm. Seconds passed. Then, as if invisible hands parted the sea of warring bodies, the combatants drew back from the goalposts dead ahead. All fighting ceased, every vampire, ghoul, and changeling stopping to stare at the aurora borealis flickering between the two uprights. Sickly green, the pale sheen spiraled in a roiling flutter that brought bile up the throat. A portal.

At least it's a change from orange.

Omara came up beside them, her face set in a fierce mask. "I beg you, Holly Carver, stand with us now. If I have wronged you, do not hold it against my people. Help me save them."

Brighter light rippled around the green whirlpool. A howl went up from the changelings, part jubilation, part terror. The vampires, to a fang, were silent and still. The ghouls just ran. Contrary to all expectations, they were the smart ones.

Two hands parted the swirl of green like a curtain and a figure stepped through. To no one's surprise, it was Geneva. She wore full battle uniform: boots, camouflage, and a bandanna around her long golden hair.

What did catch Holly off guard was Mac appearing at her elbow, wiping his lips with the back of his hand. He smiled at her. It was like a cold, glutinous slug sliding down her spine.

Geneva came forward, Mac a pace or two behind. Swiftly Omara put herself between her court and the advancing demon. The queen was filthy, her torn silks trailing shreds like pennants as she moved, but her spine was arrow-straight. She stopped when there were only about eight feet between them. Only the tightness in Omara's jaw showed her fear.

"Here we are again," Geneva said simply. She was taller by a head.

"And here you lose again," Omara said, loudly enough for all to hear.

Holly started to spool the golden energy inside her. *Okay, power as water cannon—hold it till the portal closes. How hard can that be?*

"You have the witch, but I have the book." Geneva smiled. "And I have to say you are all looking . . . well, a bit grubby. Softened up by my advance troops."

The posturing was lost on Holly. Behind the goalposts, small orange portals were sprouting up all over the campus lawn with audible pops. Out of each miniportal stepped a guardsman, dozens and dozens of them, gigantic swords in hand. *Ben's cavalry, come to take us all to prison. They just waited until the gang was all here, nice and convenient.*

Geneva finally noticed no one was paying attention to her. She slowly turned her head, looking over her shoulder. "Oh."

The guardsmen charged the watching crowd, a chilling battle cry thundering from their massive chests. The supernatural armies moved as one, enemies suddenly united against this new emergency. Holly saw Perry and his wolves, and her stomach jumped with fear for their safety.

Distracted, no one saw Geneva lunge for Holly. "Now you're mine!"

Holly felt cold, cold energy streak up her arm, as if the demon were drawing life away by mere touch. "Back off!"

She threw a blast of power, twisting away as Geneva staggered. Mac caught the demon as she fell. Holly fell back, her flesh dead white where the demon's touch had been. Golden power flooded her limbs, healing the wound, healing the throbbing ghoul bites, but there was nothing left to defend herself.

Alessandro rushed in, fangs bared and sword raised high for a sweeping blow.

Oh, Goddess, thought Holly, seeing the wound in his side. *He's bleeding!*

Mac lunged to block him, but too late. The blade arced in a moonlit crescent of deadly grace, Alessandro's charge lending force to the stroke. The slice went from Geneva's shoulder to her opposite hip in what should have been a catastrophic wound. Instead she flickered for an instant, letting the sword pass through thin air. The sudden absence of resistance made Alessandro stagger with the impetus, driving him close to the portal.

Wheeling, he dropped the blade and crouched, changing tactics. He flexed his hands like claws, ready to spring. With a sound like rushing flames, Geneva hissed with rage.

Holly shook herself, feeling her magic click back on track. Alessandro was on his feet again, too. He sprang forward, but Mac jumped to meet him, wrestling Alessandro with a strength he had never before possessed.

The portal flickered, throwing lurid green waves of light over the scene. Glancing up, Holly could see it was growing, like a tear in the sky unraveling as she watched. Soon they would be able to get a good look at what lay on the other side.

Including, apparently, the main changeling army. They started swarming out of the rift like an infestation of ants. *Oh, Goddess, there're hundreds of them. Not even the guardsmen could stop all these!*

From where she stood next to the portal, Geneva grinned. The shifting green light made the spots on her camo gear shift and swirl. "Just wait."

The words were clear inside Holly's head, as if the demon were standing next to her. *I think I liked her better as a mouse.*

Geneva's eyes shone. "I'm already inside you. The vampires have you now, but when they're gone, the taste of your soul will be mine."

"Will you people stop trying to eat me?" Holly yelled. "It's pissing me off!" Earth power flowed into her, rising like sweet wine to her head. Wild with primal anger, she took in more and more. The earth yielded it up willingly, lovingly. *"I can't take one more goddess-damned thing trying to chew on me!"*

The blast blew Geneva backward through the rift with a satisfying *ka-foom*. The emerging changeling army just happened to be in the way, bugs smashed on the windshield.

Holly tried to broaden the focus of her stream of power, leaving the demon nowhere to move. The flow juddered, sucking more energy, wobbling like a car with a flat tire. Holly panted, desperate for a means of control. What was it Grandma had suggested? Aurelia's matrix? The Caer Gwydion reduction? Holly could barely think. *I have to do this. I have to hang on.*

Holly's perceptions expanded, gorged on power. Every detail was clear, movements graceful as a film in slow motion. Mac slipped Alessandro's grip and ran toward Geneva. Alessandro fell to one knee, grabbing his sword and sweeping it up to cleave a changeling in two.

Holly could still see Geneva undulating in the blast of power, a rag in the wind.

Mac skidded to a halt next to the rift, the whirling light of the portal painting his features like a ritual mask. Geneva reached toward him, her hair blown wild, hiding her face.

Mac's eyes sought Holly's like a drowning sailor sought a floating plank of wood. He found her gaze and clung fast. His expression was pained, mad, exhilarated, horrified—but Holly was slipping away, gulping down the rush of magic, letting it burst from her in an improvised weapon. She felt as if she were turning inside out.

Geneva began to resist, slamming back against Holly's force.

Thud.

Holly jerked, her feet sliding on the grass. *Oh, crap.*

Thud.

Tears sprang to her eyes, sharp pangs of tension fingering the space between her shoulder blades. She could feel her heart pounding, the urgent rhythm matching the pulse in the energy flow.

Thud.

Holly stumbled, her concentration broken. The flow sputtered. Panic grabbed her. *No, no, no!* She opened the stream full throttle, a desperate negation of terror. Energy reamed through her, hollowing her core. She gave herself up to it completely, surrendering herself the way Elaine Carver had done. *I'm going to die.*

It was hard to tell what was happening. Holly could feel the portal spinning wider and wider, but Geneva no longer struggled beneath her magic.

This is weird.

Holly wasn't even sure whether she was touching the ground. She rode the pressure of the golden fire, her eyes wide-open, seeing but not seeing the physical world. She floated in a geyser of light. The flow blasted away the Dark Larceny, whatever traces remained of Alessandro's vampire mark, anything that was not truly hers. In fact, there wasn't much left at all. Her body was the thinnest shell, everything within and without filled with energy from deep in the primordial earth.

She probed the portal. The tear in reality was out of control—but if Holly slammed it shut the blast would kill her. No point in repeating Elaine's mistake.

Lore had given her an idea. Not all denizens of the Castle should stay there. Others should. Why not have a door and keep the key? Let the portal stay open, but create a means to control it?

Arts and crafts were never her thing, but Holly set to work. She cauterized the rift, burning the wound in the ether until it scarred over, folding the universe over and over until the tear in its fabric was reshaped and made useful. Holly worked quickly, but the golden light gushed forth faster than she could direct it. The effect was like swallowing water while she was swimming—except this hit her like one too many drinks. The earth was giving her undiluted power, and it was strong stuff.

The golden hum of Holly's magic amplified, the volume creeping up the way a teenager cranked up her headphones. Her perception went wild, everything she was doing suddenly lost in a firestorm of bliss. She threw her head back, feeling the tingle of energy on her throat, down her breasts. This was the kind of magic that made a witch immortal, renewed in the crucible of her own power. She was pumped, jazzed, stoked on the sheer strength of it.

Until she lost control and it all exploded like a Roman candle.

Chapter 30

Alessandro stared at the empty air where the portal had been. Geneva was gone. So were the guardsmen, the changelings, and Macmillan.

And so was Holly. A long moment of disconnection passed. *This can't be real.* "What the hell just happened?" he asked Omara.

"Your little witch defeated the demon and closed the portal," Omara replied, her voice softened with amazement. "I would not have believed it, but she was stronger than her ancestor. In the end there was no need for *The Book of Lies.*"

Alessandro was barely listening. Panic and loss finally caught up. He couldn't sense Holly anywhere. He clutched his side, as if the changeling's knife wound were the same as the one draining his heart. "But where did she go?"

"I don't know. Where did any of them go?" The queen sounded exhausted. She looked around, her shoulders uncharacteristically slumped. "Where did the book go? I want it back."

Alessandro's eyes automatically sought out the wolves. Perry was there, patches of fur torn from his coat, but he was safe. Others of his pack lay still and cold on the grass, returned to their human form in death. A strange hush permeated the field.

His own loss dulled the scene. It felt like a newscast, something happening to someone else far away. *So tired. I wish I could just lie down.*

The eerie silence made the rumble of a high-end ignition in the nearest parking lot all the more audible. A dozen heads turned in that direction.

"It's Pierce," said Alessandro. He knew the purr of that expensive motor.

"Pierce?" Omara looked at him, her eyes wide.

Tires squealed as the car sped toward the lot entrance. *She doesn't know. Unbelievable.* "He opened the portal. He had the book. I would lay good money he was your thief. If he shared your bed, he had access to your home."

Omara recoiled, that blow the hardest of the night. *"John!"*

Hands fisted, clenched tight to her breast, she spun in a circle, a gesture of agony and rage. The rags of her dress swirled in her wake, exclamations of all the bitter hurt Alessandro knew she throttled inside.

"Traitor," she said, quietly this time. "Traitor. I protected him. I refused to hear ill of him!"

Pierce turned onto the exit road, the big motor thrumming its acceleration. There were others watching the scene, hounds and vampires, weary but game for one more kill.

"Get him," she cried. *"Bring him down!"* She exploded into the air, silks trailing like broken feathers. Hounds, wolves, vampires boiled after her, a dark, angry river of retribution.

Alessandro stayed where he was. He was hurt. There was no way he could catch up to that car. Neither could Omara. She landed a little way off, crumpling to the grass, spent. The hounds and wolves streamed past her. This hunt didn't need a leader. They had caught the scent of blind vengeance and could follow it well enough on their own.

Someone would pay for their losses that night. Pierce would do.

Alessandro flew to where the queen huddled, her head in her hands. Her shoulders were shaking, but he had no urge to comfort her. In so many ways she had caused it all.

She pressed the heels of her hands against her eyes, stopping the tears by force. Queens didn't cry. "Why?"

Because you toyed with him when he wasn't strong enough to fight back. Because you showed him his weakness and then rubbed his face in it. Because when he thought all was lost, you gave him a treat and started the game over. I know, because for centuries that was me—except I never gave in.

But Alessandro said nothing. If he tried to answer her question, he wouldn't know where to begin, and he was too tired. Instead he told her what she wanted to hear. "Don't worry; they'll get him."

Omara sniffed. Her face was dry, only the brightness in her eyes betraying emotion. "We have to clean up and get out of here. The fey can't hold the humans off forever."

Alessandro helped her to her feet. "Your throne is safe. Do what you must. I have to find Holly."

The queen opened her mouth to reply, but her cell rang. She flipped it open. "Omara."

Alessandro watched as new interest filled her eyes. "What is it?"

She closed the phone, gave him a look that was at once hard and yet full of pity. "That was the hellhound Lore. There's hope. We may have a clue to what became of your witch."

As the fey relaxed their cordon, police swarmed to the area, responding to reports of lights and noise. Cop cars flashed like blue and red beacons. Their search would find nothing, but, for Alessandro and Omara, avoiding the roadblocks made progress frustratingly slow.

Eventually they parked at the mouth of a narrow, grimy alley that ran behind the abandoned Empire Hotel. It was downtown, close to the university and not far from Alessandro's apartment. Much of the paranormal community lived and worked in the area, earning the neighborhood the reputation of a ghetto in the making.

The alley had wrought-iron gates, but the padlock was broken. A few feet inside the entry Lore was waiting, leaning against the brick wall. Impassive, he gave Omara a polite nod of greeting. Hellhounds did not bow.

The narrow passage looked as old as Fairview, paved with sagging blocks of cedar. Tiny windows punched through the blackened brick walls, but none were lit. The back door of a Chinese restaurant stood open far down the passageway. Alessandro could smell it, heavy with the stench of human food. Lore beckoned, leading them into the alley.

"The witch made this."

The hellhound stopped before an arched wooden door that was reinforced with black iron straps. The center of the arch was perhaps nine feet high, thick planks of weathered oak arranged vertically. A heavy bolt secured it from the outside. It looked like something out of a children's illustrated fairy tale.

"She made a doorway to the Castle." Lore's voice was full of reverence. "She made freedom possible."

Alessandro closed his eyes, his wound pulsing with new pain as his heart pounded with love and fear. *What did it cost her to do this? What happened to her?*

"What's the door doing here in the alley? How do you know it leads to the Castle?" Omara asked.

Lore gestured to two of his men, who were waiting farther down the alley. "My hounds were chasing the ghouls. They saw a terrible flash of light over this alleyway and felt the rush of power in the air. The hounds came here, with the fey, to investigate and to keep the humans from walking into danger. All they found was this door. The fey knew it for what it was. They said spells like this settle where they please. The door found this place to its liking."

Lore touched the wood. "I can feel the Castle behind it. It calls like old, bad dreams." He dropped his hand, stepping away as if repulsed. "I have nightmares enough."

"We thank you for your aid," Omara said after a long moment. "You have done more than enough. Go tend to your wounded."

Lore nodded and left, the other hounds at his heels.

Alessandro crossed to the door, putting one hand flat

against the wood. Loss of blood slowed his limbs, adding weight to every step he took, but he ignored the weakness. He had kept going so far. He could go on a while longer.

Omara watched, saying nothing.

He slid his hand down the wood, feeling its roughness. A long existence had inured him to fear, yet the Castle, as Lore had put it, was like old, bad dreams. It was a hell built for the vampires and the wolves, the dragons, the demons, and the fey, made for their eternal imprisonment. Made to keep his kind trapped forever. The guardsmen were mad and merciless. Holly had made a door, but who was to say that it would work from the inside?

Holly had disappeared. Logic said she was in the Castle, perhaps lost or hurt or worse. He touched the cold iron strapping, the metal dented as if from a blacksmith's hammer. Anxiety pounded like a full-body migraine. Alessandro drew the bolt. It slid without resistance.

Omara broke her silence. "I forbid it!" she snapped. "You need to rest. You'll bleed into insensibility and lie there like a great idiot until a guardsman trips over you."

The door swung out on massive hinges that gave a sighing groan.

"Alessandro!" Omara cried, her voice sliding from command to entreaty.

"I'm sure you'd be happy enough to see me if you were the one trapped inside."

He walked into hell.

When Holly awoke she was sprawled on a cold floor of stone. The chill went bone-deep, the air around her clinging with damp. The light was faint, but enough for her to see that the wall in front of her eyes was stone, too. *Where am I?*

She jumped to her feet, then fell against the wall, dizzy. She'd moved too fast. She felt sick, spent. Almost hungover. But she was unhurt and alone. For the first time in days no one was trying to bite her. Sluggishly, memory flowed back.

Sweet Hecate, I'm inside the Castle. Holly looked around. She'd tried to make the portal into a doorway, but there was no doorway in sight. *I could have been thrown. Someone could have brought me here. It might not have worked at all, and I'm trapped.*

Holly looked beyond the presence or absence of a door. What she saw wasn't reassuring. The picture in Grandma's book was pretty accurate. The Castle was a wilderness of gray stone. Torches set into the walls threw smears of smoky light, but the glow died within feet of the flames.

Every few hundred feet, passageways intersected the hall where she stood, regular and endless. Holly walked to the nearest corner, cautiously peering around its edge. The new passageway looked much like the last, its ceiling hidden in a fog of shifting shadow.

Movement. A few hundred feet away two guardsmen herded a cluster of changelings, swords and whips at the ready. Prisoners from the battle? They crossed the hallway, following yet another passage deep into the Castle's maze. Holly pulled back, afraid she would be seen.

She turned the other way and nearly walked straight into the guardsman with the braid—the same one she had seen in the Flanders house. He had a thing on a chain that was probably a wolf, but looked as big as a bear.

The wolf looked as crazed and brutal as the man.

"Hi," she said stupidly. She reached for magic, but there was nothing there.

Holly spun and took off down the nearest side corridor, lungs burning as she gulped the musty, damp air. She heard the rattle of a chain, and the guardsman released the wolf, shouting something in a tongue she didn't know. The wolf lolloped after, his juggernaut form crashing into corners whenever his bulk refused to turn quickly. The Castle, solid stone, didn't even quiver.

The only thing in Holly's favor was a head start. Using one hand as a brace, she swung around a corner, then raced off in a new direction. She was utterly lost. The wolf's panting echoed behind her, gusting as if there were fifty beasts hurtling along the corridors. Claws scraped as he moved, the · sound like the drag of chalk on slate.

Cold stone smacked against Holly's sneakers, hard even

through the cushioned soles. If she could find a room, some doorway too small for the wolf to pass through, she would be safe.

Before her she could see the foot of a stairway. The light barely touched it, showing only a few horizontal edges highlighted against the prevailing murk. She hurtled up the stairs, using hands as well as feet.

Her fingers slipped on slime—some mold that grew in the dark, or else the trail of something she did not care to meet. Shuddering, she pulled her hands away and tried to ignore the slick sensation beneath her running feet.

The stairway was steep, going up and up an irregular slope. At the top of the stairs she froze, counting on the darkness to hide her. Slowly, careful of the long drop at her feet, she turned and looked down, her stomach cold.

The wolf was nosing the bottom step as if it wasn't sure it wanted to make the effort to climb. From Holly's vantage point he was a shapeless mass of dark brown fur, his head a matted wedge. He put one massive paw on the bottom step, and she could hear the clack of the scythe-sharp claws over his wet, slurping snuffle.

Surely a wolf could smell my trail? Maybe it was a wolf with a sinus disorder. Maybe it was senile. Silence might save her, make it forget she was there.

She barely dared to breathe. Behind her, in the unseen tunnel, she could hear the distant moaning of wind. Grit and dust sifted over her toes, blown by an errant gust of air.

Holly's gaze stayed locked on the wolf. He lifted his head, looking from side to side and making a doggy whine of boredom. She dared let a tendril of hope unfurl in her breast.

Then some *thing* crawled over Holly's foot. Instinctively she flicked it away. The infinitesimal scritch of the creature's carapace hitting the stone floor was enough. Ears pricked. The wolf's eyes, crimson as sin, looked up into hers. *Hecate!*

Spinning, Holly resumed her flight, shadows and puddles of torchlight mottling the long hall. The passageway angled,

breaking her line of sight. There were rooms branching off
the passage, and she was running out of strength.

Holly ducked into a large room on her left, curling into
the darkest corner. Here the movement of air gave the impression of a high ceiling. It almost smelled fresh.

Then it smelled like wolf. Two eyes like red coals peered
through the door.

"Viktor!" bellowed healthy male lungs. The echo
bounced through the stone halls.

The wolf whined, backing away.

"Viktor!"

The wolf barked, a deep, hair-raising woof. With a scrab-
ble of nails on stone, the thing lolloped away to answer its
master's voice.

Holly slid up the wall, trembling. Something brushed her
cheek and she jumped, barely stifling a squeak. She slapped
at it, finally realizing it was only cloth. Her foot sank into
something soft, and she bent to touch it. Carpet.

This was no prisoner's cell.

Alessandro prowled the stone corridors, sword drawn. He
was growing weaker, blackness edging his vision. Omara
was right: He was pushing his endurance to a foolish degree,
but he could feel Holly's presence now. The blood bond between them had been erased by the sheer volume of power
she had channeled, but a connection remained. He knew
where she was as surely as the ocean felt the pull of the
moon.

However, knowing where she was and getting there were
two different things. The Castle was a maze filled with un-
pleasant surprises, some of them large and furry.

Others told dire stories. He found *The Book of Lies*, the
cover bloodied and torn, lying abandoned in one passageway. If Pierce drove away from the campus, how did the
book get here? Who had taken it? There was no way to
know. Alessandro picked it up. It could well be their ticket
out of the Castle.

And then, an hour into his search, he discovered a

woman's body, facedown. From the camouflage pattern on the outfit and the long fair hair, he knew it was Geneva.

He crept up on her slowly, unwilling to make any assumptions. There was no heartbeat, no respiration, but then demons were smoke and energy. They didn't need to breathe.

He drew close enough to nudge her gently with the tip of his sword.

Nothing. He placed his sword down close at hand and knelt by her, feeling a strange familiarity with the scene. Her human form was young and pretty. The long hair fell around her like a wreath of silk, glimmering in the torchlight. Tentatively he put his fingers against the skin of her neck.

She was cold, as cold as his own bloodless hands, and she smelled all wrong. Startled, he rolled her to her back. The corpse fell with the limpness of the recently dead. He stared.

Shock numbed his face. *She is human!*

She had been restored to her original living state. The powerful collision between the portal and Holly's earth magic had purified even Geneva.

For what good it had done her. A changeling's bite crimsoned her throat. She had probably been killed before she even had a chance to realize what had happened to her.

Blond and pretty, Geneva was the last of the Fairview murders, felled by the very creatures that had murdered to summon her. She even had an Orpheus token in one hand.

Chapter 31

Groping, Holly felt around the entranceway to the chamber. There was a door. She pushed it shut and, hoping for the best, tried her candle-lighting spell. Magic felt different here, awkward, as if she were trying to write with her other hand. It took a few tries, but finally it worked.

A dozen black pillar candles sprang to life, lighting the chamber. Holly gaped. Tapestries hung on the walls, abstract birds and animals glittering with silver thread. The room was huge, the ceilings high and draped with swaths of silk. There were couches and chairs and a canopied bed in the corner, piled high with cushions of black velvet and gold braid. A violin case rested on a bookcase decorated in gold leaf, and a waterfall ran down one corner of the stone wall, splashing into an enormous marble basin that drained somewhere in the floor.

The whole was covered with a thick layer of dust. Whoever had lived here was long gone. Holly had met Lore and the hellhounds, seen the brutality of the guardsmen and their wolf, and here was another face of the Castle—evidence of a luxurious melancholy, pungent as incense.

First she carefully warded the door. Next she invoked a cleaning spell. Partially she wanted the comfort of a clean room to rest in. Mostly she wanted to find her magical footing in the Castle, and domestic spells were fairly safe to practice with. She'd never used them before, but now that she could cast them pain free, they'd be at the top of her list of favorites.

After she cleaned up, she tried some defensive spells. She wasn't leaving her new haven before she could fire a decent shot. Not with that wolf out there.

The delay was a blessing. It was the first moment Holly had possessed to think—but what moment was it? Thursday? Friday? Night or day? *So much for making my first week of classes.* Her goals of boyfriend, business, and school had shrunk to one imperative—get home alive, with soul and will intact.

In the last few days she'd been infected with the Dark Larceny, was tricked by Omara, and learned the depths of Ben's paranoid betrayal. *But I won. I reclaimed my memory and my magic, kicked Geneva's backside, and neutralized both Mac's kiss and Alessandro's bite. Go, me.*

That wasn't all. *I've fallen in love. Really, really in love.*

Not so smart to pick a vampire. She had known that from the start. He had stolen her will. Marked her. Whatever his motivation, that made her *angry*. She hadn't realized how much until she had space to think about it. Tears ached at the back of Holly's throat.

He had no right. Worse, it's in his nature. He's pushy. Fangs or not, he's one of those I-know-best guys. On the other hand, Alessandro was a big reason she was around to get angry in the first place. He was honorable. He protected her. He had spared her that first night, giving her pleasure, denying himself. He had always loved her as best as he could. How could she do anything but forgive him for trying to keep her safe?

She sat down on the end of the bed, her face in her hands. The last time she saw Alessandro, he was hurt. *Please, Goddess, let him be all right.*

Holly licked her lips, tasting the dust of the chamber on her skin. It tasted bitter, like ashes.

He is coming for me.

As if conjured by her thoughts, Holly could feel Alessandro seeking her, intent on gathering her back under his protection. He was close. He no longer possessed her will, but the connection between them still burned. *Oh, thank the Goddess. If he's coming, that means he is fine.*

Holly didn't like to think she needed rescuing, but she sure wasn't going to object if he arrived with a map showing the exits. She doused the candles, releasing the wards and opening the door a crack. The torches, apparently as eternal as the stones they lit, burned with the same smoky glow as before. Slipping out of the room, she crept toward a junction of three corridors. He was somewhere near there.

But Holly didn't see Alessandro when she paused where the three paths crossed. She heard no sound of footfalls drawing near. And yet he seemed so close. Holly hurried across the junction to the corridor straight ahead, anxious not to be seen. That wolf was still too fresh in her mind.

She found him in the shadows, *The Book of Lies* cradled in his lap. He was slumped at the foot of the wall, sword in hand, bone-pale. Panic thrummed through her.

"Alessandro!" she whispered, kneeling at his side. She picked up his hand. It was heavy and cold. *He came for me. He is bleeding to his final death, and still he came.*

His head turned a fraction, his eyes opening to slits. "There you are," he said, as if she were something he had simply mislaid.

"I found a place. A safe place," she said, warming his hand in hers. "Come on; get up."

With painful slowness, Alessandro shifted the book and gathered himself to move, his boots scraping on the stone. Standing seemed to exhaust him, even with Holly's help. He leaned against the wall, a damp sheen glossing his skin.

Holly put an arm around him, helping him stand, and felt the sticky wetness on his side. Her heart hovered in her throat. "What do you need? Blood?"

He closed his eyes again, leaning his head against the stone. "No. I won't risk biting you. My mark on you is gone. The demon mark is gone. You're free. Leave it that way."

"You think you can take my will again," she said. "It's not going to be that easy."

"Holly, think. I'm not worth your freedom. No one is. Let me go."

"Like hell, Caravelli." Holly bit the inside of her lips, keeping them steady.

He said nothing, just gripped the wall as if that alone would keep him on his feet. His eyes were growing dark, the gold fading bit by bit.

How can I trust him? He used his power to save me, but he still made me his slave.

The answer surprised her. *Because I have my magic. I can make doorways out of more than one kind of prison. I can take a myth and make it real in every way.*

Holly turned in to him, rising on her toes. She pressed her lips against his, grabbing the energy from the stones around her and putting a rush of the Castle's power into the kiss, into the words she spoke. "So I Choose you, Alessandro Caravelli. With free will and sound mind, I want you above all others to be mine."

As she spoke, Holly felt a burst of energy between them, the very heat of her emotion. She was feeding him her love.

His cold lips suddenly flooded with warmth. He pushed away from the wall and folded his arms around her, deepening the kiss into a sensual act of devotion. "You Choose *me*?"

Holly grinned, unable to contain herself. "I wanted you long ago, but I didn't realize you were up for grabs. Otherwise I would have flung you over my shoulder and carted you off to my cave long ago."

"I was afraid of hurting you, and with good reason."

She stroked his face, her thumb tracing the arch of his mouth. "If you're my Chosen one, you can't mark me again."

"I don't need to. I don't need your blood. You'll feed me in other ways." His amber eyes were hot and greedy. "As I will feed you, *cara*."

He was standing straight, but Holly could tell he was far from healed. In her happy estimation, it was going to take a thorough session of lovemaking to set things to rights. She knelt and picked up his sword, passing him the hilt. "In that case, you look like you could use a good meal. You know, I have a rather nice place nearby. Shall I carry you off?"

She bent and retrieved *The Book of Lies.*

"I count on it." He sheathed the blade with a suggestive slither. Then, with unexpected speed, he swept her off her feet and into his arms. "But your love gives me strength. Tonight I am driving."

Holly conjured a fire in the fireplace, using magic to create heat from the power of the Castle itself. Alessandro filled a kettle from the waterfall and hung it over the fire. There were tiny cakes of hard, herb-scented soap, and plenty of towels. As the damp air warmed, they stripped off their filthy clothes and used the marble basin to wash.

First Holly bathed Alessandro's wound. The gash had finally ceased to bleed and closed with a slight push of magical energy. Then it was her turn. The ghoul bites had healed with magic, but she still wanted their slobber off her flesh.

Alessandro pressed Holly to him, his soap-slicked muscles hard against the sensitive flesh of her breasts. Hot and hungry, his mouth found hers, the faint taste of soap strangely exotic as they kissed, man and woman, with no marks but the oldest bonds of nature between them.

Soap swirled away as they used the chill waterfall to rinse. Holly caught his lip with her teeth, tugging. A pleased growl rose in his chest, the vibration tickling her skin. She shivered, part cold, part anticipation, and made him give a low, intimate chuckle. The sound turned Holly liquid inside.

Alessandro dried her face with the softest of the white towels they found, working his way down her arms and back, saving the most erogenous parts for last. It was a possessive ritual, a little rough in his eagerness to claim each toe and elbow with strokes of the thickly woven cloth. Holly closed her eyes, feeling the towel like a tongue on her flesh.

He pushed her down on the old, worn velvet of the seat closest to the fire, her damp skin sticking to the soft fabric as they moved. Alessandro's hair hung down his chest in dark, damp curls, water making glistening rivulets over his skin. So help her, Holly began to salivate. He leaned over to press his lips to the tip of her shoulder. He was warm now, but she still felt gooseflesh rise on her skin, driven by the desire rearing like madness in her blood.

He ran his tongue up her sensitive inner arm, his teeth resting lightly at the crook of her elbow. As he moved to look at her, his eyes flashed the yellow of the hunter poised above his prey.

A new chill took the air from her throat. "I thought I didn't tempt you that way anymore."

He kissed the skin, his fangs just denting the soft flesh. "I am what I am. I will never steal your will again, I do not need to consume your blood, but that does not mean I will never want to taste you. My venom cannot addict you now, but that doesn't mean it's not there for your pleasure."

His mouth fastened onto hers, his tongue demanding new secrets. The faint taste of fennel brought a welter of erotic associations. Her hands ran down his lean flanks, feeling the muscles tighten, feeling the hardening of flesh.

He was recovering nicely.

Holly's power stirred, humming against his, another layer of pleasant arousal. Her skin was beginning to burn with wanting, as if it had suddenly grown too small.

They slipped between the sheets of the bed, the smell of old lavender wafting from the linens. Grateful for the warmth of the covers, she snuggled close, letting him cherish her curves and hollows with slow delectation. She was wet with need, aching and greedy.

"I have waited hundreds of years to hold a woman like this," said Alessandro. "To make love for its own sake, without the struggle to keep myself in check. To make love with only pleasure in mind."

"Do you think you remember how?" she teased, feeling the press of him against her thigh.

"I am old, not senile," he said acidly, but his smile was wanton.

Fingers wandered up her belly to play with the secrets of her navel, dipping in, exploring, toying with her. He traced the areola of her breast, the touch almost more suggestion than contact. Her nipple contracted, every nerve sparking with heavy fire. His lips fastened on the swollen nub, spreading the blaze of need through her belly.

Oh, yes, he knows it all, she thought as he moved his attention to her other breast. His mouth was busy, but so were his fingers, unfolding the petals of her sex and finding her slick and ready, but, damnably, he was in no rush. The pressure grew harder and more evocative, stroking against her swollen, eager folds. Holly reared against him, suddenly past words.

She reached for him, finding what she wanted. She ran her fingernails over his most sensitive places, letting the suggestion of pain salt his obvious pleasure. His ragged intake of breath told her all she needed to know. The sound made her nipples ache for the return of his clever mouth.

Trembling with the need for control, he finally grasped her hands, pinning them above her head. The old mattress swayed as he moved above her, poised for his conquest.

Her power, full and free, reached out and balanced his, strength for strength. His darkness would never overwhelm Holly's brightness; nor would she ever banish his night. No need for either of them to hold back now.

His hands released their iron grip, slowly, patiently sliding down her flesh, tracing the flare of her hips, cupping the mounds of her rich femininity. He kissed her right *there*, the suggestion of his lips and tongue making her part and arch in welcome.

He entered with a deep stroke, filling her, stretching her, holding still for a long moment before either of them could bear to move. Then, unable to wait another second, she thrust her hips again and again, finding the position, the rhythm, drawing him in inch after thick, delicious inch. Discomfort danced with sensuous hunger.

More. Harder.

She undulated beneath him, near bliss. Pulsing in concert with their bodies, their power laced like the clasp of fingers. Holly loosed her hands, digging her fingers into his smooth flesh, fighting for better purchase, more leverage.

Hot, agonizing fullness rose as their bodies met, push

after push. She gasped, driven toward the inevitable crest. Dazzled. Desperate to drive him deeper.

Just as she felt reason falling away, he stopped, holding her quiet with a grip of iron.

"No!" Holly protested. *No, no, don't stop now!*

He placed his mouth low on her belly and licked a long, slow stroke the length of her, ending at her throat, the faintest rasp of fang along her hypersensitive flesh.

"You're mine," he said, and gave her a long, slow kiss. "I Desire you, Holly. I love you."

Then came the final, perfectly aimed thrust.

She imploded in a spasm of pleasure, blind and deaf. A torrent of sensation shredded her, every muscle and nerve torn asunder. He came, hot and full with the power of their union. It was magic of the most ancient, most powerful kind.

Later her memory was made up of fragments of torch-light, old herbs, the stillness of the Castle, and of Alessandro. He was laughing with pure joy.

"I suppose," he said, toying with her hair, "that we really should go."

Holly lifted her head from where it rested on Alessandro's chest. Her limbs felt rubbery with satiation. He was right—they should be getting out of the Castle—but she wasn't sure she could walk. Lying in the warm bed, murmuring about everything and nothing between bouts of passion, was much more pleasant.

"In a minute," she said, fondling the thin line of gold hair that crossed his belly, growing darker as it marched south toward magnificence.

Her heart expanded, full of amazement. His skin was warm, his cheeks flushed with lovemaking. He looked alive. Almost. Incredible but true, he was feeding on pure emotion. *So this is what it means to be Chosen. As long as we love, he can live without taking from another.*

There was no danger of running out of food. Holly could see a steady diet of mutual lust in their future, and that would be a long one. An immortal one. This kind of magic kept a witch young forever. That thought penetrated her happy delirium. *Immortality.* She had power now, more than she had ever dreamed, and much she needed to learn about it. There was more than a lifetime's work ahead.

Even the immediate future looked crowded. Now she had a mate, one who would form the center of her life. There was school. There was the business. She wanted to make things right with Ashe, to bring her back into the family. She wanted to know more about the castle, much more—like whose room was this, anyway?

And they had to find Mac. She had already let her magic wander the Castle in search of the detective, but she couldn't find him. That worried her. Hopefully she would find him in Fairview. If he was human again, as Geneva so briefly became, he was going to need help. No one could go through what he had without consequences.

Holly shifted her cheek against Alessandro's chest. She could hear his heart, faint and slow, but it had a steady beat. Vampires' hearts beat now and then under the influence of extreme emotion, but this sounded content. *An interesting bit of magic, bringing his heart to life.*

Other parts of him were also stirring beneath the sheets. Her own heart sped up, a tingle of excitement curling her lips into a smile.

Then the pounding was outside their bubble of warmth, battering at the door. Before Holly completely sat up, Alessandro was off the bed, into his jeans, sword in hand. They exchanged a look after Holly pulled on her clothes. He nodded slowly, and Holly removed the wards she had placed around the door. Alessandro raised the sword.

The door burst open, magically pushed from the outside. It was Omara, chic in a pin-striped pantsuit and square-heeled pumps.

"I felt that," she said softly. "I tasted it on my tongue like dark wine. I thought you might be Chosen before, but this time it is real." She looked from Holly to the bed to Alessandro's naked chest. Her expression was indescribable, like a child lost in wonder. Like a jealous queen. There was love and loss and something calculating in those eyes. Something hungry.

Despite all her newfound strength, Holly felt a brush of fear.

Omara's gaze found Alessandro's. "When you didn't come out of the Castle, I discovered that I cared too much to leave you here. You were injured." The words seemed to catch in her throat. "Your blood scent made you easy to find."

Alessandro lowered his sword. "I wish I could believe that's really why you came. More to the point, it would reflect poorly on a victorious queen to abandon her best warriors after the battle was won. It might make it hard to get good help."

Omara looked away, finding something interesting in the tapestry beside her. Her profile was perfect, except for a faint quiver of emotion in the lips. "I am not entirely without tender feelings. Don't underestimate me."

"I never do."

Soon the three of them stood outside the arched wooden door in the alley. After the Castle's dusty damp, the sea air had never smelled so good and clean.

Holly admired the door. Both inside and outside the Castle, it seemed to have shifted a few blocks from where Geneva's portal had opened. Unexpected, but not a bad thing. A door in an alley was easier to manage than one hanging in midair on a playing field. *Nice of the universe to catch that design flaw.*

Holly pushed the bolt shut, her other hand resting against the iron strapping. She could feel power rippling beneath the physical surface—not just hers, but the power of the Castle itself. There was also Elaine's magic, and Geneva's. They had all left their traces in the matrix that made up the passage between her world and the Castle.

Omara stood a few steps away, watching Holly. The look was at once critical and grudgingly impressed. "Your permanent portal is very clever, but it can't be left unattended."

"I know," said Holly, not really interested in Omara's input. She slid both hands along the iron until they touched the wood. The magic of the door knew her, leaping like an eager puppy. The current coursed through her body, up one arm and down the other, brushing against her in silent greeting.

Holly drank it in, considering what she needed to do. The door opened on an entire realm of possibility. People who needed saving. Monsters that really should be locked up forever. She had created access to her world. Was she going to take responsibility for who passed through?

Alessandro stood close, there if she needed him, but he said nothing. The choice was hers to make.

Holly turned to Omara. "I will be the gatekeeper. I made it, after all."

The queen inclined her head. "Good. That is as it should be, but know that most whom you find in there cannot leave. This is a prison for a reason, and the guardsmen are jealous of their charges. You cannot decide alone who enters through that door to walk in our world. Now that the Castle is but a step away, its affairs affect all of us, human and nonhuman alike."

Holly nodded, feeling the weight of Omara's gaze on her, then on Alessandro, then on the two of them together. There seemed to be an ocean of distance between them and the fierce, tiny queen who stood utterly alone.

The moment broke, as if Omara, on some level, had given in.

"You have my profound thanks, Holly Carver," she said. "You earned your rest tonight." She turned on her heel, starting toward the gate at the mouth of the alley. "Take her home, my champion. Be happy."

"What are you going to do?" Holly asked. "What happens now that the portal is closed?"

Omara stopped, her honey-gold eyes amused. "As queen, I do not get to go home to a soft bed. I get to tie up loose ends, starting with a search for your missing detective. I want to be sure of him before I lay my head down and rest."

Holly opened her mouth, but Omara raised her hand for silence. "I give you my word: I will call you the moment I find him. As for you, my young witch, you have done enough. You gave everything you had to give. Now let responsibility shift to others."

Omara turned and walked away, the long curtain of her hair swinging as she moved. Holly saw the light of her cell phone as she opened it, calling for a ride.

Holly waited until she was sure the queen was gone. "Alessandro, what did you do with *The Book of Lies*?"

"I hid it under the bed. We can go back and get it later."

"Why'd you do that?"

Alessandro looked up at the thin strip of stars above the alley. "I think it's best if the queen rules, but is held in reasonable check. I'd rather hang on to one or two high cards, at least until I am sure she has forgiven me for leaving her service. Absolute power does not become Omara. She has occasional difficulties with impulse control."

Holly felt the beginnings of a grin. "Are you sure you're not a politician at heart?"

Alessandro held her under his arm, the weight of his touch a promise of forever. "I like peace, order, and good government. Omara is the one who enjoys the excitement of power games."

"I'm sorry she is so alone," said Holly. "If she were happy, she might be easier to take."

Alessandro shrugged. "Someday she will find the right sparring partner. Perhaps a large and well-armored dragon."

Holly yawned. "Mmm." She leaned against his chest.

"We need to get you home." He kissed her cheek.

"What's the rush? The night is young."

"Don't you have school in the morning? Tomorrow is Thursday."

"Oh, Goddess, it's calculus. Can I have another demon instead?"

Read on for a special preview of
Sharon Ashwood's next novel,
coming soon from Signet Eclipse.

*B*ack in the Castle five friggin' minutes and I'm in the mid-dle of an ass-kicking. Mac wiped a sudden sweat from his face. *Same old Club Dread.*

Mac circled his opponent, who mirrored his low, watch-ful crouch. Bran was a huge, bare-armed hulk covered with spiraling blue tattoos. He stank like old leather shut up in an attic trunk for far too long. A black braid swung past the man's hips as he moved, a dark slash against the scarlet and gold silk of his tunic.

Bran was one scary, ugly mother. He was also one of the guards of the Castle prison.

Shadows ate at the ceiling and surrounding passageways, giving the illusion there was no reality beyond the circle of their combat. The solitary sound in the corridor was the shuffling of their feet on the stone floor. Torchlight played along Bran's short sword, reminding Mac the guardian was armed and he wasn't.

Sharp objects mattered, but Mac's pulse roared in his head, drowning out fear with every heartbeat. He felt drunk, high, complete, even relieved. He was ready to pound this grunt and love every minute of it. *Kill or die.* The shredded remainder of his demon side had finally slipped its leash.

Mac lunged. Bran was quick, blocking him, slashing at

Mac's ribs—but Mac was supernaturally fast, dancing aside before the blade could land.

They sprang apart, circling again.

"Nice to see you, too," Mac said with a taunting grin. Without warning, he changed direction, but Bran followed the sudden shift with the poise of a gymnast. Mac licked his lips, his mouth dry from breathing hard. "Interesting tats. Still working the Bronze Age look?"

"Be silent." Bran curled his lip, his white teeth and pale skin making him look more like a vampire than a guardian. "I found you, fugitive. No one escapes twice."

"C'mon, saying that's just tempting fate."

They closed again, grappling and snarling. Bran swept Mac's feet from under him, but they both fell, Mac on top. Mac's vision turned white, then red with bloodlust and rage. With his knee on Bran's throat, Mac smashed the guardian's sword hand into the stone floor. The blade fell loose and spun away.

Bran surged, tossing Mac off. Rolling to his back, Mac brought his feet up just in time to catch Bran in the chest with a satisfying thump. The guardian stumbled, air whooshing from his lungs. Mac flipped to his feet, running two steps to sink a hard, knuckle-bruising shot to Bran's midriff. The man was solid as granite, but no match.

Bran doubled over. Mac grabbed the sword and brought the hilt down with a smack, catching the guardian behind his left ear. Bran dropped like a stone in a facedown sprawl at Mac's feet.

The thud of his fall, like so much dirty laundry, echoed in the cavernous dark. Mac bent, feeling for a pulse. The guardian was still alive but would be out for a good long time.

As he rose, Mac felt the surge of his own blood, the tingle and rush of human life in every limb. Behind it pulsed the demon, gleeful—lustful—at the prospect of even more violence. The weight of the sword was a suggestion, the hilt hard and perfect in his greedy palm. There were so many ways to kill. A quick blade in the spine. The slow agony of a gut wound.

Gritting his teeth, Mac backed away. *I'm still too much a cop to kill a man when he's down. Even this one.* He clutched at that thought, holding it like a talisman that would preserve his slipping humanity.

But in the Castle, every moment was fight or die. Here, he needed his demon side to survive. Staying human would be a losing battle. *I have to get out of here, or lose my soul again.*

A flicker at the edge of his vision made him look up, reflexes poised.

Mac glimpsed a face, all wide eyes and pointed chin. It was a woman, barely more than a girl, with a thick fall of midnight hair long past her waist. Every line of her thin body looked startled.

All was silent but for the sound of Bran's faint, slow breathing. The woman just stared, her mouth pulled down at the corners.

She's afraid. He stepped over Bran and toward the woman. With a birdlike hop she whisked around the corner. After a second's hesitation, Mac sprinted after her. Until he knew whether she was running from simple fear or running to get Bran's friends, he couldn't let her get away.

By the time he got to the corner, she was already out of sight, but he could smell a trace of sweet perfume. He followed it, mapping this new direction in his mind so he could retrace his steps.

She hadn't gone far, only down another turning. There she hovered, her back to Mac, peering anxiously around the far corner. He came up behind her, his movements utterly silent.

He hadn't realized how much noise a human made—breathing, rustling, swallowing—until, as a demon, he'd stopped. He'd had no scent, moved no air when he passed by. Now, partially human again, he could switch the ability on or off. Going stealth mode freaked him out a bit, but it came in handy.

He was close enough now to see the woman clearly. Her dress fell to the floor and was made of a heavy indigo fabric, worn threadbare along the hem. She was small—barely five feet, small-boned, and almost frail. He could have picked her up in one hand. Most of her weight was surely in that thick, straight hair.

Just when he was close enough to notice a strip of dusty lace peeking out from beneath her skirt, her shoulders stiffened. She'd made him. Soundless or not, even demons couldn't hide from that sixth-sense survival instinct that makes a deer run before the cougar breaks cover.

She whipped around to face him, eyes wide with fear, white edging their deep blue centers. With the jerking motion of a cartoon character, she looked around the corner again, then back to him. *Caught between two bad choices.*

"What's there?" Mac asked in a quiet voice, wondering if she spoke English. The Castle didn't have a universal language, unless one counted despair.

"More guardians," she answered, almost whispering.

Not going to warn Bran's friends, then.

"Three of them, heading toward their quarters." Her words lilted. Irish, perhaps? She searched his face, clearly measuring the level of threat he presented. "Who are you?"

"Conall Macmillan, ma'am." Somehow it seemed right to use his best manners, as if the shade of his great-grandmother was cuffing him on the ear. "At your service."

"At my service, now, is it?" There was a flash of irony in her eyes. "And how is it that anyone who defeats a guardian is serving the likes of me? They're made so that we can't do that. We can't beat them, and yet there you were looming over Bran's broken body."

Uncertainty squeezed Mac's chest. He didn't want to hear from a pretty woman how he was not quite normal, much less that he loomed. "I'm just passing through. Maybe the rules don't apply to me."

Her gaze caught his, deadly serious. "No one just passes through here."

"I've done it before."

"You have a key, then." She said it naturally, as if it were no great marvel.

There's a key? Maybe more than one? Mac didn't answer, wondering what else she might reveal.

"Well, then." She was calming down, but still looked like she was expecting a dirty trick. "That would answer why I've never seen you before."

"I hope that means you wouldn't forget me if you had." He sneaked a glance at the neckline of her dress. Her low-cut gown was laced up the front, the tight crisscross of ribbons making the most of her slender shape. She wore a scarf of thin white fabric around her shoulders, the ends tucked modestly down her front and foiling any clear views of cleavage. *Damn.*

She caught the look. "And if I remembered you, would that be on account of your smooth tongue and practiced smile?"

"I have better qualities." *Careful, the last woman you thought was cute turned you into a demon.*

She ignored his comment and looked around the corner instead, this time letting her spine sag with relief. "They're gone."

"Good." The sword, once so important, now felt cumbersome in his hand. He wanted an excuse to touch this woman. It was pure instinct. She was beautiful and achingly young. The fact that she was hiding from the guardians only added a protective urge to the mix. "What's your name?"

"Constance," she said, then added, "Moore," as if it was a piece of information she rarely needed.

"Were the guardians chasing you?" he asked.

"Yes."

"Why?"

"It's a long story."

"I'm a patient man."

"I've heard that one before." She gave him a bold look that almost contradicted her earlier caution. "You men never make it to the climax of a tale."

Mac raised an eyebrow. "You must be one helluva storyteller."

She gave a sly, close-lipped smile that would have shamed the Mona Lisa. Her eyes dared him right up until they shifted away, a nervous tell. "I am."

Mac folded his arms, an awkward process when holding a sword. "Oh yeah?"

She leaned against the stone wall, all fair skin, black hair, and cherry lips. Snow White in a reckless mood. "Indeed."

Despite the taunting jut of her chin, he could see the tremor in her fingers, the quick pant of her breath. His demon side licked up her fear like a cat lapped cream. He reached out with his free hand and cupped her jaw, tilting her face up to him. "What do you know about a key?"

Her eyes narrowed. "I know they exist. This place isn't as airtight as one might think."

He dropped his hand, but didn't move away. "You got one?"

"No." She tried to hold his gaze, but failed. "You can trust my word on that."

"Worried that I might search you?"

"You'd probably like that."

"You think so, eh?"

"You're male, aren't you?" The words were more defeated than bitter, and somehow that made them worse.

"Yeah, but I'm not a ravening beast." *Not the human part, anyway.* "Trust me, undressing a woman is more fun when you're invited."

She laughed, but it wasn't mirthful. "And you're an expert, I suppose."

"Practice makes perfect."

"I'm sure it does." Again, the Mona Lisa smile. There was a history that went with that sweet, self-mocking sadness.

Definitely more temptation than he could handle. He bent and pressed his lips to hers, perhaps to taste that puzzling smile, perhaps to kiss it away. Or maybe just to prove his expertise.

Constance inhaled, a quick, light gasp ended by his capture of her mouth. Her lips were cool and soft, returning his kiss with surprised hesitation. That perfume he had smelled earlier, something flowery and old-fashioned, wafted up from her skin. He felt the tentative brush of her fingers in his hair, light as a moth's wings. Finally her hand settled on his cheek, a girlish, uncertain touch so gentle that it tickled.

She was no practiced flirt, and he'd just called her bluff.

At a twinge from his conscience, he drew back. "I'm sorry. I didn't mean—"

She used both hands to pull his head down, bringing his mouth back to hers.

Okay. Mac wasn't about to argue. Heat surged through him, thick and electric. He drew his hand up her spine, over her ribs, up the side of her breast. Constance murmured in pleasure, rising onto her toes. Her body brushed against his. *Oh, yeah. Unexpected, but oh, yeah.*

He felt the tip of her tongue meet his, a shy inquiry. Constance tasted as sweet and wild as blackberries still hot from the sun. He couldn't drink down her soul as he could have in his demon days, but he could savor it, sad and pure, like her smile.

He already ached in his body, but that taste of her spirit made him ache in his heart. He caught the salty tang of loneliness. *That's just not right.* Was there no one to look after her? A tiny creature like Constance shouldn't be out wandering the halls of the Castle by herself. She was so small, he could nearly span her waist with his hands. The fabric of her dress felt rough, too coarse for such tiny perfection. And there was far, far too much clothing for satisfactory exploration.

Okay, whoa, buddy. In five seconds flat you've gone from sneaking a kiss to planning to get naked with someone you've just met. Get a grip.

Heedless, Mac's fingers slid beneath the flimsy fabric of her scarf, finding soft, cool skin and the gently rounded tops of her breasts. He kept his touch featherlight and was rewarded with a delicate shiver. Tracing his thumb over her collarbone, he caressed the silken flesh of her shoulder. *Nice.*

He deepened the kiss, but kept his beast tightly leashed. Whoever this girl was, she wasn't ready for his demon side. Hell, most of the time neither was he.

So sweet. She knew about a key, a way for Mac to escape.

It was almost a shame. This moment, so full of new promise, almost justified an eternity in the Castle.

And yet . . .

Yeah, okay, Macmillan, what's with the hearts and flowers? This isn't you.

Something was not right.

No shit, Sherlock. Nothing's been right for over a year. Was it the soul-sucking demon shtick or the eternal prison of darkness that tipped you off? As for the girl . . .

Mac winced, suddenly going very still. *Women. There's always something.*

Yeah, Constance was sweet. The teeth, however, were a surprise.

Gently, he pulled away. Her eyes were closed, her lips flushed and slightly parted to reveal tiny, perfect fangs. *A vampire.* But an innocent one that sent off none of the usual vampiric vibes. There was only one way that happened.

Constance had never tasted blood.

Pheromones. That answered why she had fascinated him so completely, sent him head over heels in less time than it took your average speed date.

But it raised still another interesting question.

A really good one.

Am I meant to be her first kiss or her first kill?

EMBRACE THE NIGHT

by Karen Chance

Cassandra Palmer may be the world's chief clairvoyant, but she's still magically bound to a master vampire. Only an ancient book called the *Codex Merlini* possesses the incantation to free Cassie—but harnessing its limitless power could endanger the world...

<u>ALSO AVAILABLE</u>

Claimed By Shadow

Touch the Dark

Midnight's Daughter

Available wherever books are sold or at penguin.com